# Summer Camp Secrets

*by*

Katy Grant

**ALADDIN PAPERBACKS**

New York   London   Toronto   Sydney

ALADDIN PAPERBACKS
An imprint of Simon & Schuster Children's Publishing Division
1230 Avenue of the Americas, New York, NY 10020
Summer Camp Secrets: *Pranked*, Summer Camp Secrets: *Acting Out*,
and Summer Camp Secrets: *Friends ForNever* copyright © 2008 by Katy Grant
These works were previously published individually by Aladdin Paperbacks.
All rights reserved, including the right of reproduction
in whole or in part in any form.
ALADDIN PAPERBACKS and related logo are registered trademarks
of Simon & Schuster, Inc.
Designed by Christopher Grassi
The text of this book was set in Perpetua.
Manufactured in the United States of America
This Aladdin Paperbacks edition May 2009
10 9 8 7 6 5 4 3 2 1
Library of Congress Control Number
*Pranked*: 2007935961
*Acting Out*: 2007935962
*Friends Fornever*: 2007935963

ISBN: 978-1-4169-9105-2

# Summer Camp Secrets

For my father, Bill Arbuckle,
who has always told me I can do anything I want—
you were right

# Acknowledgments

Many, many thanks to Jen Klonsky, who first read the manuscript for this book way back in 2000, and who sent me the heart-stopping e-mail saying she liked this book and would I be interested in writing a trilogy? Even though the deal did not go through back then, Jen never forgot my camp stories.

Thanks also to my agent, Erin Murphy, who signed me when she was just starting out and who kept me on her list during my long fallow period. Like a good agent should, Erin stayed in touch with Jen over the course of six years and through the birth of two babies, and finally in 2006, the two of them made this happen.

And last, but most important, thanks to my editor, Liesa Abrams, who arrived at Aladdin in fall 2006 and hit the ground running. She hasn't slowed down since.

Where would I be without the three of you? Unpublished—that's where.

**CHAPTER** *1*

## Sunday, June 15

This was definitely going to be the worst summer of my life.

I got out of the car and looked at all the people swarming around. It was mostly parents, but there were some other girls too, and even some brothers who looked as thrilled as I was to be here. Everyone was carrying something, and everyone seemed to know what to do and where to go. Except for us.

I just stood there holding my pillow. Then this woman who seemed to be in charge walked up. She had on a green polo shirt with a little pine tree on it. "I'm Eda Thompson, the camp director. Welcome to Pine Haven!"

My mom smiled with relief, and the two of them

started talking. Dad tried to wink at me, but I acted like I had to scratch my knee.

"This is our daughter, Kelly," my mom said.

"Hi, Kelly." The director smiled at me, then checked her clipboard. "Kelly Hedges, right? And you're twelve?"

I said yes, but it came out all croaky. I cleared my throat. "That's right."

She probably thought I didn't look twelve because I'm so vertically challenged. The director walked over to a group of people wearing green polos just like hers and motioned one of them to follow her back to us.

"This is Rachel Hoffstedder, and she's your counselor." Rachel shook hands with Mom and Dad, and then she shook my hand. She looked okay. She had really short dark brown hair, and she seemed friendly. And she was pretty vertically challenged herself. "Rachel will take you to your cabin." Then the director left to say hello to some other unhappy campers.

"Our cabin's that way." Rachel pointed up a steep hill. I could kind of see some cabins at the top of the hill, hidden in a bunch of trees. My dad was trying to wrestle my new metallic blue trunk out of the back of the car. The website had said we needed trunks to keep all our stuff in because there wasn't any place to store luggage.

"Why don't I get this end?" Rachel grabbed one of the trunk handles before my dad made a complete idiot of himself. Mom had my sleeping bag and tennis racket. I didn't have anything to carry but my pillow, which was better than nothing. At least it gave me something to hold on to.

We passed a bunch of other campers and parents going up the hill. I could tell some of them were really nervous. But then a lot of them acted like old friends. Girls kept shrieking at each other and hugging. It was beyond stupid to watch. I tried to relax my face and look casual, but my heart was pounding so hard I could feel the pulse in my throat.

What was I thinking when I agreed to this? Did they hypnotize me? Was it one of those weird parental mind control things? How had my parents ever talked me into spending a month at summer camp?

They started talking about camp back in March. They showed me the brochure and the website, and at that time it looked pretty cool. *Camp Pine Haven for Girls, located in the scenic mountains of North Carolina. A camping tradition since 1921.* Anyway, my best friend, Amanda, was going to be in Hawaii for two weeks, lying on a beach surrounded by a hundred gorgeous surfers. I figured she could miss me for two weeks after she got back from her dream vacation. In March camp seemed like a good idea. But that was March.

We walked up a dirt path and came to this big stone building with a porch. "That's Middler Lodge," said Rachel, and then we turned up another path and climbed a bunch of stone steps that went up yet another hill. There sure were lots of hills. My dad tried desperately not to pant, because Rachel wasn't breathing hard at all. She'd told us she was on the hiking staff, so she probably walked about thirty miles a day or something.

By now we were finally at the top of the hill where all the cabins were. There was a really wide dirt path, and all down one side was a long row of cabins. "This is Middler Line, and we're in Cabin 1A. You guys are in the middle between the Juniors—the little kids—and the Seniors—the oldest girls."

Rachel pushed open the screen door of the first cabin we came to, and she and my dad stumbled in and plopped my trunk on the floor. They each took a big breath.

"How many girls in each cabin again?" asked Mom.

"Eight, with two counselors. This is 1A, Kelly, and that's 1B." She waved to the left side of the cabin.

"You're number one! You're number one!" Dad

chanted. I wanted to hit him with my pillow, but I just looked around at everything.

Rachel laughed at his stupid joke, then spread out her arms. "Well, here it is. Your home away from home."

I'd seen the cabins in pictures on the website, but that didn't really give me an accurate view. I wouldn't be surprised if this cabin was built in 1921. It was all gray wood. The top half of the front and back walls were really just screens. The ceiling had wood beams across it with a couple of bare lightbulbs hanging down from them. But the weirdest thing was that there was graffiti *all* over the walls. Everywhere you looked, you could see where someone had written her name. There wasn't a blank space of wall anywhere. The website had called the cabins "rustic." "Primitive" was more like it.

"You're the first one here, so you get your choice of beds. This is mine, of course." Rachel pointed to a made-up cot against the wall. I had my choice of one set of bunk beds or two single cots next to them. They all looked uncomfortable. "The bottom bunk has extra shelf space. That's always a plus."

"Okay." I dropped my pillow on the bed.

"Let's get your bed made," said Mom. Rachel and my dad stood around looking useless, and I wandered toward the other side of the cabin, which was also full of empty bunks. And then I noticed something.

"Ah, excuse me, but . . . where's the bathroom?"

"They're not in the cabins. They're in another building down the line."

"You're kidding." I crossed my arms and glared at my dad. At home we didn't have to hike to the bathroom.

"Oh, it's not that bad." Dad tried not to smile. "It's like a college dorm. Let's see the rest of camp before your mom and I take off."

Just then another counselor and camper came in. Rachel helped them with all the stuff they were carrying. Then she introduced the counselor in 1B, Andrea Tisdale, who she said was a CA—a Counselor Assistant. I'm sure Mom and Dad were glad I didn't get her, because she was, like, in training or something. She said her activity was tennis. She was a lot taller than Rachel, and her long blond hair was in a ponytail.

As we were leaving, Andrea leaned over to Rachel and kind of whispered, "No sign of the Evil Twins yet, huh?"

Rachel laughed and shook her head. *Evil Twins?* What was that supposed to mean? My heart skipped three beats.

Rachel showed us the bathrooms. They were in

a building that looked kind of like the other cabins, except it was larger and had no screens. One side had a bunch of sinks, and the other side had a bunch of stalls. "This is 'Solitary.' And the showers are over there." She pointed to another building across from the bathrooms.

"Solitary?" I asked. I watched a granddaddy longlegs crawl down the wall of one stall.

Rachel smiled. "Yeah, that's what we call the bathrooms at Pine Haven."

"Why?" I mean, seriously. Why not just call it a bathroom?

"I'm not sure. Maybe because you're supposed to be by yourself but it's a communal toilet, so you're not really, or . . ." She just looked at me and shrugged.

Whatever. I know you're supposed to "rough it" at camp and all, but actually giving up private bathrooms, hair dryers, and air-conditioned houses with no crawly things—hey, this wasn't going to be easy. How long was I stuck here for? Four weeks—twenty-eight days. All right. Twenty-eight and counting.

After that Mom and Dad hung out for a while, looking at the camp. New campers were arriving all the time. I kept wondering about the *Evil Twins*. What was that all about? And were they in *my* cabin? The counselors had laughed about it, but that name didn't sound funny to me. I looked at all the strange faces around me. Who were the evil ones?

Then we heard a loud bell ringing—a real bell that a counselor was ringing by pulling a rope to make it clang.

"Lunchtime, Kelly. I'll see you in the dining hall," said Rachel.

Okay, so now my parents had to leave. My heart was beating about two hundred beats a minute. Dad gave me a bear hug and reminded me to write lots of long letters.

"We'll miss you so much!" said Mom. I could tell she was trying not to cry, which made me want to walk off without even saying good-bye.

"I'll be okay." My voice sounded like somebody else's. I hugged Mom really fast and then walked toward the dining hall without looking back. I could barely see it through the blur, but I blinked enough so that none of the tears rolled out.

Okay. So far, so good. I'd managed to say good-bye without crying. Much.

The dining hall had two screen doors, and I got squished by the crowd, all trying to squeeze through at the same time. Inside was a bunch of green wooden tables. I looked around, not sure what to do. I was still blinking really hard, and my nose tingled.

"Kelly, over here!" I saw Rachel and Andrea at a table in the corner, so I wiggled through the mob. On the table was a little white card folded in half with MIDDLER CABIN 1 printed on both sides. I sighed and sat down. At least I wasn't going to have to eat by myself. Four other girls were already at the table. None of them looked evil, but then sometimes you can't tell by looking.

We had tacos and fruit salad, but I had a hard time swallowing, because there was something like a walnut stuck in my throat. I got to meet Jordan, Molly, and Erin, who were all on Side B. Jordan and Molly came together, and they were obviously best friends. They spent the whole time talking about horses. Molly had dark hair and dark eyes, and she was short and squatty, kind of like a fire hydrant. But she seemed more outgoing than Jordan, who was quiet and pretty. There was something about Erin that seemed really grown-up. The only other Side A person was Melissa, and everything about her was pale— pale skin, pale eyes, even pale hair.

"Is this your first year?" Molly asked me, the second after I took a bite of taco.

I chewed fast. "Yeth." I swallowed and tried not to cough.

"It's our second."

That started a conversation about how long everyone had been coming here. Everyone was really impressed that it was Andrea's seventh summer. It seemed like the longer you'd been coming here, the more status you had.

That meant I had no status. No status and no friends. I looked at all these new faces. Did any of them look like friend material? Probably not Molly and Jordan. They had each other, so they didn't need me. Maybe Erin or Melissa. There were three empty chairs for the girls who still weren't here, and two of those chairs were for the Evil Twins. Just thinking about them made me want to heave up my tacos.

After lunch we went back to the cabin for rest hour.

"Okay, ladies—so we all get to know one another, we wear these the first week," said Rachel. Then she and Andrea passed around name tags made out of little circles of wood with a string to hang them around our necks. Andrea's said TIS, which was short for Tisdale. That's what everyone had called her at lunch.

Rachel hung up two name tags on a nail by the door. One said REB; the other said JENNIFER. The wooden circles swung back and forth on the nail and then stopped. I tried not to look at them. At least they didn't say Darth Vader and Lord Voldemort.

"So, Melissa, which bed do you want?" Rachel asked the pale girl.

"The one by the wall, I guess."

From my bottom bunk, I watched her and Rachel make up one of the single cots. After they finished, Melissa sat on her bed and organized her stuff on the shelves. Any time I glanced at her, she looked away. Whatever.

Rachel sat on her bed listening to her iPod and shuffling through papers on her clipboard. She told us that rest hour was the only time we could listen to our MP3 players. We also had to be quiet, which was no problem.

Who was I going to talk to? I held a book in front of my face so I didn't have to stare at all the graffiti.

I must've been out of my mind coming to a camp where I didn't know one single human being. I knew this was a bad idea when Mom started sewing name tags in all my clothes. "What if nobody there likes me?" I'd asked.

Mom had just stared at me as if I'd said something random, like, *What if everyone there secretly turns out to be an extraterrestrial?*

"Now why wouldn't they like you?" she'd replied.

I wished it was that simple. I wasn't used to making new friends. I've always gone to the same school, and I've known all my friends forever. What if I didn't know how to make new ones? Mom made it sound like making friends was no big deal. But obviously lots of girls here already had friends. What if the new girls paired up, like, *today*, and I was a leftover—like the extra odd number when you count off in twos for teams in PE.

A bell rang, which must've meant the end of rest hour, because Rachel put down her clipboard and pulled her earbuds out. She smiled at Melissa and me. "Time for swim tests," she announced, jumping off her cot. "Everybody does it the first day. Get your suits on, ladies, and let's go to the lake!"

I got up and looked through my trunk for my suit.

When I found it, I turned toward the wall, with my back to Melissa and Rachel.

I hated this part. Why was it that some girls never seemed to mind getting naked in front of other people? They always acted really casual, like it was natural to take off your clothes in front of twenty other people. But they were usually the ones with boobs, so they had something to flaunt.

I just barely got a bra this year. And I almost died when I saw the camp application. It had a question that said, "Has your daughter begun menstruating?" My mom had written "No" in the blank. What if my dad had seen that? Why was it their business, anyway?

After we had our suits on, we all walked out together. Molly and Jordan talked to each other about horses, but the rest of us kept quiet. I was so glad we were in a group. I'd die if I had to walk to the lake alone. Then it was obvious you didn't have friends.

As lakes go, this one was really pretty small. I couldn't believe there wasn't a pool. Was it safe to swim in a lake? The water was green, but not slimy green. It looked just like a mirror, the way it reflected the trees and grass. I could see the wet heads of a few girls bobbing up and down in the water, and a couple of counselors stood on a wooden dock, holding clipboards and shouting directions.

A bunch of girls sat on a large, flat rock by the edge of the lake, waiting their turn, so we all sat down too.

"The water's really cold."

I turned around to see who'd said that. It was Melissa, the pale girl.

"Is it?" It was stupid, but it was all I could think of.

"Yeah, it's freezing. The lake water comes from that little stream over there."

"Ugh. I hate swimming in cold water."

"Me too." She sat there, hugging her knees under her chin.

I stared at the edge of the water and noticed some little squiggly things swimming around. "What are those? There's something alive in there!"

"It's just tadpoles," said Melissa.

"Tadpoles?"

"Yeah. They won't hurt you." Then she didn't say anything else. If she hadn't talked to me first, I sure wouldn't have gone out of my way to get to know her.

But at least now I had someone to talk to. It was better than nothing. Besides, I might need some help to ward off any evil influences.

After the swim tests Melissa and I walked back to the cabin together wrapped in our towels. We were both still shivering, and Melissa's lips were blue. One girl had to be pulled out when she got tired. It was pretty dramatic, and everyone was talking about it. I was so glad something embarrassing like that didn't happen to me.

"So this is your second year?" I asked Melissa.

"Yeah." She shuddered and clutched her towel tighter.

"I guess you know a lot of people then, huh?" Any minute now, Melissa could run into some old friends and hug them, and I'd be all alone again.

"Well, some people are back from last year, but not everyone came back."

"What about the other two Side A girls? Rachel

called them the Evil Twins. Do you know them?" Saying their nickname out loud made me feel like I was calling upon demon spirits.

"Oh, yeah. Reb Callison and Jennifer Lawrence. I can't believe I got into *their* cabin."

"How'd they get that nickname?" My heart was pounding a little, like I'd just asked her to tell me a ghost story.

Melissa bit her bottom lip. "I don't know. Last summer they were sort of . . . wild. You know, during assemblies and stuff."

She watched her flip-flops kick the loose gravel of the road and didn't say anything else. I waited for more information. Did she not want to talk about them?

"Do you wish they weren't in our cabin?" I asked finally.

Melissa looked up. "What I do wish is that Annie Miller was in our cabin. She was supposed to be, till she broke her ankle playing soccer. So now she's going to miss the whole camp session! She was my best friend last summer."

"Wow, that's too bad." Okay, good. It was a relief to know she didn't have a best friend waiting somewhere.

When we got to Middler Line, Melissa stopped in the bathrooms—Solitary, or whatever—and I waited around for a second. Should I wait for her, or would that seem weird? I decided to go to the cabin. I didn't want her to think I was stalking her. But after I left, I wondered if she'd wonder why I didn't wait for her. Maybe I should've just pretended to go to the bathroom too, and timed it so we left together.

When I got to the cabin, there was someone new inside. She was tall and skinny, with bushy, reddish brown hair. Whoever this was, she must be one of the twins. I tried not to make eye contact.

"Hi. Are you in the bottom bunk?"

"Yeah." I wished Melissa would come back from the bathroom. I didn't want to face this twin alone.

But this new girl was busy looking over her choice of beds: the top bunk or the other single between Melissa's and the bunk beds. While she was distracted with that, I rummaged through my trunk for some clothes.

"I'm Jennifer."

"I'm Kelly."

"Is this your first year?"

"Yeah."

"It's my second." See, that whole status thing again. "Do you know if Rebecca Callison is here yet?"

"I'm not sure. A girl named Melissa has that bed."

Her eyes grew two sizes. "Melissa? You mean Melissa Bledsoe?"

"I think so. Blond hair, skinny, kind of quiet . . ."

"Yeah, that's her." Jennifer shook her head and looked at the two empty bunks. I draped my beach towel over me and pulled on jeans and a T-shirt.

"Well, I guess I should take the top bunk. Reb will want the single." She started moving her things. I noticed she had braces, and her eyes were covered by long, shaggy bangs. She honestly didn't seem evil. So far, at least.

When Melissa walked in, she and Jennifer just kind of looked at each other.

Wow, don't everybody talk at once.

"Um, Melissa? Do you want to switch with me? I don't like the top bunk—you know, it's hard to climb up and everything. Do you want it?"

Melissa looked at her, then looked away. I just sat on my bottom bunk and kept quiet. If she asked me to switch, what should I say? I didn't want to switch either.

"You could take that one," Melissa said, meaning the other single cot next to hers.

"Reb will want that one. See, I was thinking, if you'd switch, you two guys"—she turned and nodded at me—"could have the bunk beds and Reb and I could have these singles. Do you mind switching?"

Melissa stared at her bed. "Um, I've already put sheets on."

Just then Rachel walked in and gave Jennifer a big hug.

"So, Jennifer," said Rachel with a smile, "you can have the top bunk or that single one there. What's it gonna be? I'll help you make your bed."

Jennifer looked at Melissa. "So are we going to switch?"

"Uh, no thanks." Melissa looked away and arranged some stuff on her shelf.

Jennifer glared at her. "The top one." Then she and Rachel made up the top bunk, and I sat underneath on my bunk and watched. OMG. I had no idea picking a bed was such an enormous deal. What was up with the two of them? It was a good thing Rachel had walked in.

When her bed was made, Jennifer stood in front of the little mirror nailed to the wall and clenched her teeth together, looking at her braces. Except for the whole bed thing, she seemed pretty normal. So what was evil about her? And what about her missing twin?

"I've only had these two months. Do they look weird?" Jennifer asked the mirror. I wasn't sure who she was talking to. She looked at me.

"Uh, no," I said.

She turned back to the mirror. "Well, I hate them."

Just then a counselor yelled outside the screen window, "Reb Callison! Get out here!"

Jennifer ran out the door. "Alex!" The two of them hugged and screamed. I heard Jennifer tell her Reb wasn't here yet. Then a couple of other girls walked up, and *they* asked about Reb too.

Rachel saw me watching them through the screen and smiled. "Reb's fan club."

I nodded and acted like I had to get something from my trunk. This other girl had a fan club? Great. But what happened to anyone who wasn't a member? I had a sick feeling deep in my stomach. Jennifer wasn't the twin to worry about. It was the other one.

Finally the bell rang for dinner. Without that bell, we'd never know what to do. I was so glad I knew where our table was. Counselors went back and forth to the kitchen with dishes of food and pitchers of this drink everyone called "bug juice."

The last girl from Side B was here—Brittany. She smiled all the time. That was a good sign, so I put her on the potential friend list. Was anyone else doing this too—looking around, checking out possible friends? I felt kind of pathetic. Nobody else looked lonely. But then, I probably didn't either. Little did they know.

Now our table had only one empty chair. Tis passed around plates of chicken, green beans, and mashed potatoes. Rachel tried to get everybody talking. She was telling us about the hikes we could go on.

"Thursday we're going to Angelhair Falls. And there's rock climbing and . . ." All of a sudden, the dining hall's screen doors smacked against the wall so hard that everyone stopped and stared. In the doorway a girl stood looking around at everyone. She was kind of smiling, like she was glad she'd gotten everyone's attention. All I could think was, if that'd happened to me, I'd be having one of the most embarrassing moments of my life right now. But she wasn't the least bit embarrassed.

"Reb! Reb! Over here!" screamed Jennifer.

Wow. So this was Rebecca Callison, the missing Evil Twin.

# CHAPTER 4

At first I had the impression that everyone in the dining hall stopped and called out in perfect unison, "Reb is here!" like in those musicals, when everyone is acting semi-normal, and then all of a sudden they start singing a song together. I know it wasn't quite like that, but it did kind of seem that way.

Several people called out her name, and it took her a while to get to our table, because girls kept stopping her and hugging her. Fan club members, obviously. I chewed a bite of green beans, but I couldn't stop watching her move across the dining hall.

I thought Jennifer was going to jump up on the table and start tap dancing, she was so relieved. "Well, it's about time!" She and Reb shrieked and hugged. Were they old war buddies who'd saved each other's lives or something? Finally Reb sat down at our table, all flushed and excited.

Right away I could tell she was a tomboy. She had on a "Got Game?" T-shirt, and her blond hair was really short, like she couldn't be bothered by a brush. She was only a little taller than me, and she was just as flat-chested. She ran her hands through her hair, then looked at all of us and smiled.

"That was quite an entrance, Rebecca," said Rachel, kind of teasing.

"Glad you liked it, Hoffstedder," she answered in the exact same tone. "And if you call me Rebecca again, I'll be forced to flush your hiking boots down the toilet. With you in them. Hey, Tis. Are you our counselor too?"

"Rachel's your counselor, thank God. I'm on Side B. I came this close to drowning myself in the lake"—Tis held up her fingers to show how close—"when I found out the Evil Twins were in the same cabin with me."

"Ah, that's so sweet!" said Reb. "Are we your worst nightmare?"

Rachel and Tis both laughed. "Absolutely."

Tis gave Reb her plate, and Rachel introduced her to all the new campers. She seemed friendly. She asked us all where we were from. It was weird. Rachel had kind of been in charge of the conversation before, but now Reb took over that spot, because she was the one asking everyone questions. She talked to everyone at the table. Well, except Melissa. But then Melissa wasn't exactly the chatty type.

Reb looked right at me and said, "You're on Side A with us? Cool." I felt a rush of warmth at the compliment.

"I figured I'd be the last one in the cabin to get here. You better have saved me a good bunk," she said to Jennifer.

"Yes, Your Highness. You know I did."

After dinner it was just after sunset, and everything was all shadowy and dim, but I watched Reb walking along with her elbow propped on Jennifer's shoulder. Girls were still coming up to her to say hi. She was laughing and talking, and I couldn't stop watching her. Now that I saw her, I got it. The fan club, all the people coming by—it all made sense. There was just something about her—like a magnet. People watched her and followed her and listened to everything she said. It was like we were all waiting for her to show us what to do.

When the other girls walked away, I heard her say to Jennifer, "Oh my God, this is the worst. I can't believe *she's* in our cabin!" Then they started whispering, so I couldn't hear anything else.

My heart pounded. Did she mean me? Did I have bad breath, body odor, a booger on the end of my nose?

Wait a second. She'd just met me. She couldn't mean me. But then who? I had a feeling she probably meant Melissa. But why? I looked around for Melissa, but I didn't see her in the crowd. I'd been too busy watching Reb and Jennifer.

After dinner we went to evening program and played a bunch of "get acquainted" games in the lodge, and then it was time for bed. Everyone crowded into Solitary to brush their teeth and go to the bathroom. A lot of girls were already in pajama pants and T-shirts. Camp seemed like it was going to be one long sleepover.

Back in the cabin, Jennifer groaned about climbing up to the top bunk. "I hope I don't get on your nerves too bad, climbing up all the time," she said to me.

"Don't worry about it," I told her. I was just glad I got to keep my bottom bunk.

Reb picked up Rachel's clipboard. "Do any of you sleepwalk, snore, wet the bed, or have night terrors? Let me know so I can stuff your mouths with socks, strap you down, and put rubber sheets on your mattress." She stood there looking serious until Rachel walked up behind her and snatched the clipboard away.

"Melissa, any issues we should know about?" asked Reb with her arms crossed. She sounded like a teacher getting onto a student about something.

Melissa let out a nervous little laugh. She looked even paler than usual.

"Get in bed, sweet pea," said Rachel.

Reb just ignored her. "Kelly, I want to formally welcome you to Camp Pine Haven. Let me know if I can do anything to make your stay more pleasant. Camp is truly a swell learning experience for us all."

I couldn't help smiling. "Thanks." I knew she was just showing off, but I was glad she welcomed me. And she remembered my name.

Rachel picked up Reb's pillow off her newly made bed and smacked her with it. "I'm having a night terror. I need to stuff a sock in Reb's mouth so it'll stop."

"Ouch! Camper abuse! Tisdale, help me! Rachel's killing me over here!"

Rachel rolled her eyes. "Reb, give me a break. It's only the first night."

Outside someone yelled, "Lights out!" so Rachel turned off the lights.

What a long day. Had it been only this morning when my parents dropped me off? I turned my face into my pillow, and my sheets still smelled like home. All of a sudden that walnut popped back into my throat. Last night my cat, Cheshire, had slept at the foot of my bed like he always did. Now it felt weird to move my feet around without feeling his warm weight.

Cheshire was probably sleeping in my empty bed right now. And here I was, in this strange bed, hundreds of miles from home, surrounded by two counselors and seven strange girls—two of them potentially evil.

I'd never felt so lonely in my whole life.

CHAPTER 5

# Wednesday, June 18

"Which activity do you want to go to?" I asked Melissa.

"I don't care. Which activity would *you* like to go to?"

I looked at the list of choices on the paper stapled to the wall by the cabin door. "Well, I could do tennis or canoeing. I wouldn't mind crafts, either. Do you have a preference?"

"Not really. Why don't you pick?" said Melissa.

"How about canoeing?" I asked.

"Well, okay. But I'm not very good at it."

"Then would you rather play tennis or go to crafts?"

"No. Canoeing's fine. Tennis is fine. Or crafts. I really don't care."

I nodded, trying hard not to grab Melissa around the neck and choke her. Melissa was nice—actually too nice. I just wanted her to grow a backbone and pick an activity for a change. But she always let me choose.

Everyone in our cabin had turned out to be okay. Rachel tried really hard to make sure we were all getting used to camp. "Everyone having a good time?" she kept asking. But Tis was hardly ever in our cabin. She mostly hung out with all the other CAs.

Molly and Jordan were best friends. Molly, the one who looked like a fire hydrant, was outgoing and friendly. On the second day she'd held up three books and said, "I've got all these to read this summer. I can't wait!" The weird thing was, they were all about the Titanic, which she was totally obsessed with. Jordan, the pretty one, always seemed stressed about something. She worried about being able to do a jump on her horse this summer.

Erin was serious. She wasn't unfriendly; she just seemed older than the rest of us, like she'd seen and done all this before. Brittany, who was always all smiles, had immediately made friends with a lot of people, even from other cabins.

Then there were the Evil Twins. Every chance I got, I watched them. I still hadn't figured out where their nickname came from. But if anything, they seemed more fun-loving than evil. They were always joking around. I'd thought they were going to be snobs, but they weren't like that at all.

When we had to go to activities for the first time, I watched to see where everyone was going. I wanted to follow Reb and Jennifer, but I lost them in the crowd on the first morning. Melissa was following me and asked if I wanted to go to riflery. Since then we'd kind of been hanging out. It was better than being alone.

On the way to the lake Melissa and I didn't say much. I tried to make conversation at first, but after a while, I got tired of doing all the work. It was a relief to get to the lake and have something to do. Michelle Burns, one of the canoeing counselors, demonstrated a few strokes to all of us standing around the lake edge, and then she let us get into the canoes and try them out. Melissa and I paddled around, but we kept going in circles.

"Use the J stroke!" yelled Michelle. She'd told us that stroke would help us go straight, and the girl in the stern was supposed to do it. That was Melissa.

"I don't think I'm doing this right," she said. Obviously not. I watched a couple of other girls, Chris and Maggie, moving straight as an arrow across the lake. They smiled as they passed us.

"Here, like this." I showed Melissa. "Remember how

Michelle said to turn the paddle so it's like you're writing a *J* in the water?"

"Okay."

But she still couldn't get it right.

"Maybe we should switch places," I suggested.

"Okay. If you think so." Melissa stood up, but that just made the canoe wobble, which made her grab the sides, which made her drop her paddle in the water. She sat down really quickly and leaned over the side to grab her paddle, but that made the canoe tilt over, and she came very close to falling headfirst into the lake.

"Hang on a second. I think I can reach it." With my paddle, I managed to steer us over to where her paddle was floating, and I leaned out and grabbed it. "Here ya go."

"Thanks. I'm sorry I'm so much trouble."

"Don't worry about it."

We spent the rest of the morning spinning around in circles. We almost ran over a couple of swimmers in the middle of a class. I made a mental note to get in the stern next time. Melissa kept apologizing, and I kept telling her it was okay.

I was so glad when morning activities ended. Walking back to the cabin, we ran into Reb and Jennifer leaving the tennis courts. As soon as I saw them, I wished we'd gone to tennis.

"Hi, guys."

"Hi, Kelly," said Jennifer.

"What's up, Kel?" asked Reb. So far they'd both been friendly to me, but they had a way of never acknowledging Melissa's existence. I could tell they didn't like her, but I wasn't sure why. I kind of wished they hadn't seen me with her.

"How was your game?"

"Good game. Good game." Reb balanced the end of her racket on the palm of her hand.

Jennifer bent down to tie her shoelace, and we all stopped. "Yeah, for you it was. For me it was a humiliating defeat. You ought to play Tisdale or the other counselors if you want to improve your game. I'm tired of losing."

"Oh, right. Like I never lose. When I play my brother or my dad, I end up crawling off the court. Talk about humiliation." Reb tossed her racket into the air, caught it, then spun it between her palms. Obviously, she'd never lose her paddle in the water or get stuck in a canoe going in circles.

"My dad has a serve like a cannonball. Once he hit me right here"—she rubbed her shoulder—"and it left a huge bruise that stayed there forever. I told him I didn't want to play him anymore, because I was afraid one of his serves would hit me and I'd die of a hemorrhage. He told me, 'Fear's a good teacher. Gives you an edge.'"

"That's pretty mean." The second I said it, I knew I'd messed up.

"My dad's not mean! You don't even know him! He's a great guy!"

"Uh, no, I meant . . . it just sounds a little . . ." I wanted to hit the backspace and delete that last comment. Too bad real conversations don't work like IMs.

"Hey, if it weren't for my father, I wouldn't even know how to play tennis." Reb frowned at me. "My parents have always helped my brother and me to be the best. They put us in sports, music lessons, art lessons, everything—trying to find out where our talents were. And now my brother Zach just finished his first year at Brown. And I'm going to an Ivy League school too. My parents and I are already making plans."

"Reb, your parents are pretty intense," said Jennifer. "You have to admit."

"What's intense about wanting us to be good at stuff? That's not intense, that's . . . being a good parent."

"Sorry. I didn't mean anything bad about your dad," I said. I hoped Reb wasn't mad at me. Nobody said anything else. All of a sudden Melissa stopped and bent down.

"Oops. Sorry. I hate when that happens," Reb said, and I saw that she'd stepped on the heel of Melissa's sneaker and given her a flat tire.

"That's okay." We all stopped while Melissa wriggled her heel back inside her shoe. Reb sounded sorry, but then I saw Jennifer give her a playful slap.

I felt a little bad for Melissa, but I was so relieved Reb hadn't done that to me. She might have, to get back at me for that comment. Why'd she pick on Melissa, though?

Maybe because Melissa hadn't said a single word. She might as well be invisible sometimes. Sure she was shy, but she could at least *try* to take part in the conversation.

In the cabin I rummaged through my trunk and found my secret bubble gum stash. We weren't supposed to have gum, candy, or snacks in the cabins. Supposedly that stuff would attract ants. A likely story. They probably just said that to scare us. I offered everyone a piece, but Jennifer couldn't because of her braces and Melissa said no thanks. Reb took a piece, and I hoped it made up for my stupid comment.

Melissa stood in the doorway looking at me. "What should we do now, Kelly?"

I plopped down on my bunk and stared up at

Jennifer's bedsprings above me. "Nothing." It was morning free time. We had a half hour before lunch to do whatever we wanted, and I really didn't want to spend it with Melissa.

"Want to go swimming?"

"No, we just came from the lake. I don't feel like walking all the way back."

She just stood there. I was busy blowing bubbles. Reb was organizing her trunk, something she did at least two or three times a day. She hated to have anything out of place. Jennifer was brushing her bushy hair in front of the tiny mirror on the wall. Neither of them said anything.

"I guess I'll take a shower," said Melissa. There was really no good time to take a shower. In the morning we had to get up, clean the cabin for inspection, and go to breakfast, all in thirty minutes. At night we had evening program, and then we had to go straight to bed. You had to find weird times to take showers, like before lunch.

She got her shower stuff and left. Good. When she was out of earshot, Reb burst out laughing. "I thought she was gonna ask you to wash her back or something."

"Gross!" I groaned. "The thought of washing Melissa Bledsoe's pale, skinny back . . ." I made puking noises into my cupped hands, and Reb acted like she was heaving. It was kind of mean, but I'd never say that to her face. Anyway, Reb was right. Melissa had turned into a leech. We didn't have to spend every single minute together.

Jennifer looked at me. "You aren't friends with her, are you?" Her nose wrinkled.

"She's not my BFF, if that's what you're implying. I barely know her." And that was true. Melissa was okay, but she definitely wouldn't have been my first choice as a friend.

"Well, you two have been hanging out a lot. You look pretty chummy to me." Jennifer turned back to the mirror and clenched her teeth. Anytime she looked in the mirror, she made that face.

My stomach tensed up. I was dying to say something. I blew a huge bubble that popped all over my face, then I sucked all the gum back in. "It seems like you guys don't like her much."

Jennifer snorted. "Oh, you noticed that, huh? Didn't you see how obnoxious she was to me about the whole bed thing?"

"Yeah." Although I wouldn't exactly have called Melissa obnoxious.

Reb closed her trunk and plopped down on her bed. "Nobody likes her. It's because of last summer."

"What happened last summer?" Maybe now I could finally find out what was up.

Reb blew a bubble and popped it. Then I blew one. We kept making smacking noises. She was better at it than I was.

"Well, last summer we knew this girl, Heather Crabtree. She was in Melissa's cabin, and she couldn't stand her. She told us all kinds of unbelievable things about her."

"Like what?"

"Well, one time Heather and some other people wanted to short-sheet somebody, so they picked this girl Annie, just as a joke, right?"

I had no idea what she meant by "short-sheeting," but I didn't want to look like a complete idiot, so I nodded like I knew what she was talking about.

"Well, so Annie and Melissa are, like, best friends, and they both went crying to the counselor about being short-sheeted. I'm sorry, but your counselor is not your mommy away from home."

Jennifer sat on top of her trunk and looked at me. I could barely see her eyes through her bangs. "But that's not the worst thing about Melissa. Is it, Reb?"

"Oh, no. The worst . . . the WORST! Are you ready for *this*?" Reb leaned forward like she had this big secret.

I sat up and leaned forward so I wouldn't bump my

head on Jennifer's bed. I couldn't believe they were actually confiding in me, a new camper. It was cool that they felt like they could trust me.

"She used to wet the bed last summer." Reb sat back and looked at me.

I made a face like I didn't believe her. Because I didn't really, but I wasn't about to call her a liar.

Jennifer broke out laughing. "Can you believe that? Heather told us."

"Yeah. Heather said that one time she saw this big wet spot on Melissa's bed and so she goes, 'Hey, Melissa, did you have an accident?' Just teasing her, you know. But Melissa says, 'It's from a swimsuit' or something. Then she got all nervous, and she changed her sheets! Now, if she hadn't wet the bed, why'd she change the sheets?"

"That is too weird," I admitted.

"So now we're stuck with Melissa Bledsoe, a bed-wetting narc, in our cabin. Can you imagine any worse luck?" Reb groaned.

"Well, yeah. It could be worse. It could've been worse for *me*," I said. I'd just thought of a good line. I glanced out the screen window to make sure Melissa wasn't coming back.

"Yeah, how?" Reb asked.

"Jennifer wanted her to take the top bunk." I patted

the bottom of Jennifer's bedsprings. "If she had, then *I'd* be waking up with wet sheets every morning too."

"Disgusting!" Reb shouted. We all burst out laughing.

I didn't really believe that stuff about bed-wetting, and I doubted Reb and Jennifer did either, but it was something to laugh about. I was glad the Evil Twins liked my joke.

A few minutes later Melissa came back from the showers, and Reb and Jennifer tried not to laugh. I acted normal and didn't laugh. I did feel bad for talking about her behind her back. The least I could do now was try to be nice to her. But I'd have to find a way of being nice to her without doing it in front of Reb and Jennifer.

CHAPTER

6

After rest hour everyone was leaving for activities. Reb was putting on her shoes when she looked at me. "So, Kelly, what activity are you going to now?"

"Uh, I haven't decided." I held my breath for what might come next.

"Jennifer and I are going to the climbing tower with some other people. Want to come with us?" she asked, like it was no big deal, like "Hey, is this Wednesday?"— not knowing that when she asked me, my heart actually did a flip. It was like being picked first for teams.

I shrugged, because if she was going to be casual, so was I. "Uh, sure. That sounds like fun." I started to say, "I haven't been there yet," just to make conversation, but I didn't want to overdo it and look like a geek.

Melissa had walked over to the wall where the activities list was posted. She looked at me really fast, then glanced away. Reb and Jennifer were already at the door. I just wanted to walk out with them and not have to deal with Melissa. I looked at her.

"You could do the climbing tower too." I was a little nervous about asking Melissa. Reb and Jennifer had invited me, and then I'd turned around and asked Melissa without checking with them first. And now I knew for sure how they felt about her.

"Um, I don't know." Melissa stared at the activities list, considering her options.

"Yeah, want to come?" asked Reb in the weirdest tone. It reminded me of how my voice came out whenever I had to get Cheshire into the cat carrier to go to the vet's. Those were the only times he wouldn't come to me when I'd call him. Melissa just shrugged and didn't answer. I guess she didn't trust the cat carrier tone either.

Then the three of us left the cabin. I looked back once to see if Melissa was coming, but she wasn't. We *had* invited her. Anyway, she wasn't a new camper like me. She must have *some* friends from last year. She didn't need me to take care of her. I went to morning activities with her. Did that mean I had to go to afternoon activities with her too?

At the climbing tower Reb introduced me to some other girls—Darcy, Nicole, and Meredith. They were all old campers from last year. Thank God for these name tags so I could keep everyone straight. I wasn't used to meeting people and having to remember names.

"Kelly's in our cabin. It's her first year, but she's cool. She's going to hang out with us," said Reb.

What was cool about me? Whatever it was, I wanted to keep doing it. I'd just been awarded a cool badge and I didn't want to lose it.

I couldn't believe I was actually hanging out with Reb and Jennifer, and I was meeting their friends. All those girls I'd watched on the first day—at the time I didn't like them because they all knew each other, and I was alone. But now things had changed.

The climbing tower was so much fun. It was this huge fifty-foot-tall tower made out of tree trunks tied together. Some parts had netting to climb up, and at the very top there was a ledge to sit on, like a tree house. We had to wear helmets and rappelling harnesses and everything. It was *so* scary. Most of us got only about halfway up. Reb was goofing around, driving Rachel crazy. She kept acting like she was falling. We had a blast. I wondered what activity Melissa ended up going to, but it couldn't have been as fun as this one.

By the end of the day it was like I'd been hanging out with Reb and Jennifer and their friends forever. At first I kind of felt like I was holding my breath all the time. I didn't want to have another slip-up and make some stupid remark again. Also, I kept trying to think of funny things to say. Reb was really funny. Jennifer could be too, but mostly she just laughed at things Reb said. It was kind of exhausting having to be funny and careful all the time, but I knew I could do it.

Before evening program we all changed into jeans because it got really cool at night in the mountains, even in summer. I put on a sweatshirt. Reb was wearing a hoodie from Brown. I guess her brother gave her that.

When we walked into the lodge, everyone looked over and called out to us. At least it seemed that way. Reb picked out a long wooden bench for us to sit on. "Hey, Jordan, Molly. Come sit here. This is Cabin One's bench," she called. Then Melissa came in and looked at us, but there wasn't enough room. I mean, there really wasn't. The five of us could barely all squeeze on there. Melissa looked around and found a spot on the floor. Anyway, it wasn't the whole cabin. Erin and Brittany were already sitting on the floor when we came in.

Evening programs were always fun. All the Middlers were together, and we always did something like skits or games. Tonight none of the counselors were inside. The doors to the porch were closed and we could hear them rustling around out there.

Finally the doors opened, and Gloria Mendoza, a counselor in Cabin 4, came out and announced, "Presenting 'The Twelve Years of Pine Haven'!" Then a counselor named Jamie came through the doors. She and Tis were best friends. Her hair was in pigtails, and she was holding a teddy bear. To the tune of "The Twelve Days of Christmas," she sang, "My first year at Pine Haven my mother said to me, 'Don't wet the bed!'"

Reb, Jennifer, and I burst out laughing. We weren't actually laughing *at* Melissa. It was just the bed-wetting joke that made us laugh.

The whole skit was really funny. The counselors made complete fools of themselves, but you could tell they were having a great time. Rachel's line was "Don't eat a newt!" Every time she sang it, she held up a jar with a squiggly orange salamander inside. Tis had one of the funniest lines. She came out with only a towel on and sang, "Don't go skinny-dipping!" Reb kept whistling on her line. She could whistle with two fingers in her mouth. She tried to show me how, but I couldn't do it.

After the skit we were out on the porch, sitting on the upper railing with Alex and some other counselors.

She'd been Reb and Jennifer's counselor last year.

"So, my little Evil Twins are in the same cabin again this year, huh?" asked Alex. "At least *I* don't have to deal with you. You can drive Rachel crazy this summer."

"You know you miss us. You know you love us," said Reb. She stood in front of Alex and pretended to box with her.

Alex grinned. "I'm glad I don't have to put up with your evilness."

"What's evil about them?" I asked as casually as I could.

"Oh, Alex always called us that last summer. *The Evil Twins!*" Reb said in a voice like someone possessed.

"Because you were. You were always together and you were both troublemakers. Always talking too loud. Always the last two out of bed in the mornings. Always laughing and never being serious about anything," said Alex, smiling at them.

"Hey, it's camp. Why should we be serious?" Reb said.

*So that was it?* That was all there was to the "Evil Twins" nickname? Their counselor called them evil because they slept late and talked too much? I felt like a complete idiot. Why had I been so worried?

"So, are you two going to sign up for my Guard Start class?" asked Alex.

Reb glanced at me. "Maybe we'll all three sign up. What is it?"

"It's the first step toward being a lifeguard. You guys are too young to take a lifeguard class, but you can take this class."

Jennifer winced. "Do we have to swim laps? You know I hate that."

"Of course you have to swim laps, Bird Legs. It's a swimming class," said Alex.

"Don't call me Bird Legs. You're mean, Alex." Jennifer frowned and looked down at her long, skinny legs.

"Yeah, don't call my twin names, you Evil Counselor," said Reb. "*Maybe* we'll take your class. But maybe we won't."

Alex just laughed. It was obvious Reb was her favorite.

After evening program we were all walking along, just talking and stuff, when I realized Melissa was right beside us. I hadn't even known she was there.

"Gosh, there are so many stars out tonight," she said. She tilted her head back and gazed up at the sky. I looked up too.

"Wow, there are. There's a ton of them." I'd actually never seen that many stars. The sky was so black in the mountains, and you could see the stars so much better because there weren't many lights around.

"They're bee-yoo-tee-ful," said Reb.

"Yes, simply loverly," agreed Jennifer.

Now I had to say something funny. So I leaned over to Reb and sang softly, "Tinkle, tinkle little star, how I wonder what you are." Reb snorted and poked me in the ribs. Jennifer started singing it too, but louder.

Okay, it was a little mean. But I didn't think Melissa heard the "tinkle, tinkle" part.

It was crazy in the cabin before lights out, as usual. On Side B, Brittany screamed when a spider crawled down the wall. Tis picked up one of Jordan's riding boots to kill it, but Jordan shouted that she didn't want squashed spider guts all over her boots. Erin got it into the dustpan and threw it out the door. If there was ever a problem, Erin was always the one to take care of it.

All of us on Side A had stopped to watch the drama. Molly said maybe the spider had laid eggs, and pretty soon a zillion little spiders would hatch out and infest our trunks. That made everyone scream again, especially Jordan, who now had something new to stress about.

Then Rachel flashed the lights on and off as a warning. "Lights out in two minutes. Everybody in bed." It was her serious counselor voice.

"I just have one quick announcement to make," Reb said, leaping up on her cot so everybody on Side B could see her too. "Please don't anyone leave any wet swimsuits on my cot. I hate it when that happens." She bounced down on her knees like you do on a trampoline.

Jennifer and I both laughed. Everybody else looked confused.

Rachel gave her this long look like she suspected Reb was up to something. "Good point, Reb. Let's all be *courteous* and *kind* to one another. It'll make for a more pleasant camping experience."

"Rachel, with you as our counselor, how could our camping experience be anything but pleasant?" Reb said sweetly.

"Uh-huh." Rachel flipped off the lights.

Reb started singing very softly, "Tinkle, tinkle, little camper, can your sheets get any damper. . . ."

"Reb!" Rachel's voice had a warning in it.

"Hey, I'm singing myself a lullaby. It's hard to fall asleep without my mommy."

"I'm gonna write your mommy and tell her you're an 'obnoxious, disruptive influence in the cabin.'"

"She'll be so proud."

"Just tone it down."

"You betcha, Raych. Hey, can I have a night-night kiss?"

"You mean from my newt?"

"Of course! You didn't think I meant *you*, did you?"

I couldn't help laughing. Wow, what a great day. I'd met a bunch of new people, and I'd had so much fun with them. Amazingly, my mom had been right. I did just sort of make friends without even knowing it was happening.

Was I mean to Melissa? Well, we did ask her to go to the climbing tower with us. She chose not to. We couldn't force her to go along. The tinkle, tinkle stuff was a little mean, but it was just a joke. I doubted she'd even heard it.

Anyway, what was I supposed to do? Turn down Reb and Jennifer and spend the afternoon trying to drag a conversation out of Melissa? She'd be okay. She could find her own friends. That's what I'd done. It just took me a few days to do it.

# CHAPTER 7

## Friday, June 20

"Run! Here it comes!" Reb yelled. We raced down Middler Line, trying to beat the rain. We got to the screen door just when the first raindrops started falling.

"Wow, listen to it," I said. The cabin had a tin roof, and it sounded like BBs hitting a pie pan.

"I can't believe we're the only ones here," said Jennifer. "You'd think everyone would be cabin-sitting in this rain."

"Probably most people got caught some place like the lodge," Reb speculated. She and Jennifer both sat on their trunks, and I was on my bottom bunk. It was fun always having a big group to hang around with, being part of the fan club, but I liked it best when it was just the three of us.

Jennifer looked at us both. "What should we do?"

Reb's eyes widened. "Let's tell ghost stories!"

"I'm not in the mood." Jennifer shook her head.

"You mean you're scared."

"How could I be scared? You haven't said anything yet."

"Okay, good. I'll start. This is a true story, Kelly. Alex told it to us last summer. Have you ever heard of the Bell Witch?"

"No, Reb! Shut up!" Jennifer jumped up and grabbed her pillow from the top bunk. "You know how much that one scared me!" She stuck her fingers in her ears, buried her face in the pillow, and started humming. "I'm not listening!"

Reb burst out laughing. "I was just teasing. You know I wouldn't really tell it."

Jennifer hugged her pillow. "Still, you reminded me of it, and that's bad enough."

"Okay, sorry. Let's do something to take your mind off it."

"How about cards?"

"Bor-ing. Kelly, what do you want to do?"

I kind of smiled. "Why don't you read us the e-mail you got today?"

I could tell Reb was glad I'd brought it up.

Everyone in the cabin knew she'd gotten an e-mail from her boyfriend back home. "Well, okay." She jumped up and opened her trunk to get the paper. Mail came every day after lunch. Whenever anyone got an e-mail, the counselors printed the message and put it in the camper's mailbox. But we could only get e-mails, not send them, because campers weren't allowed to use the computer in the camp office.

Reb read, "'Yo, Reb! What up, chica? Hope you're having fun at camp, 'cause it's sure boring round here. So what have you been doing? I went to Big Surf with Mikey on Tuesday. We saw Lindz and Brittney. Got to go. Have fun, but not too much. Try not to miss me too much. Later. Bye. Wes.'"

Reb looked up and grinned. Okay, it wasn't wildly romantic, but at least he wrote her, and first.

Jennifer got up and stood in front of the mirror. "Pretty good letter."

"I guess," Reb agreed. "But he's trying to make me jealous, mentioning Lindsay. She's always liked Wes. She's probably chasing him while I'm at camp."

"Really?" Jennifer squinted at her reflection. "You oughta write her and tell her to keep her hands off your boyfriend."

Reb shrugged. "Well, if Wes and I break up, I'll

start going out with Daniel Cook. He's liked me since fifth grade. I thought Wes would want to break up since I was going to camp, but he didn't. He must really like me. Wanna see his picture?" She grabbed her school annual from the shelf by her bed.

Then she showed us every place Wes Mitchell appeared in the annual. He and Reb were in there a lot—they were both on the soccer and swim teams, plus Reb was on the tennis team. Reb was the class president and Wes was the treasurer. And they were both on the annual staff, except her school called it the yearbook staff. There was a picture of the two of them sitting at a table together. It looked like they were making vital decisions about which pictures to put where.

Wes was drop-dead gorgeous—the kind of guy who always made me speechless. Of course Reb would have a bf like that.

"You've got so many cute guys in your school," Jennifer said, looking at all the pictures. "I hate going to a girls' school. And wearing a uniform. And going to Mass."

"My parents thought about sending me to a girls' school too, but we decided Country Day was giving me the best preparation for college."

Jennifer rolled her eyes. "Reb, shut up. You're only

going into seventh grade. I can't believe how obsessed you and your parents are with college already. They can't even leave you alone at camp."

It was true. Reb's parents e-mailed her math problems to work on and vocabulary words to study. Every rest hour, she sat on her cot with a pad of paper in her lap and a pencil clenched between her teeth. I thought it was weird, but Reb didn't seem to mind.

"We're not obsessed with it. We're just preparing, that's all. And why are you always criticizing my parents? If it weren't for them . . ."

"I know, I know. If it weren't for them riding you all the time, you wouldn't be perfect. But you are perfect, so you'd think they'd get off your back and just let you be a kid. I thought *my* parents were tough."

Reb slammed her annual shut and threw it at the shelf. It banged against the wall and fell to the floor. We all stared at it, like we didn't know how it got there. None of us moved. The rain drummed against the roof.

I don't know how I knew what to say, but somehow I did. I looked at Reb and said, "Wow. Nice serve."

Reb looked at me and burst out laughing. "Thanks. Fifteen-love. Your service."

Jennifer and I were both laughing now too. "I can't serve like that!" I said.

"Well, of course you can't, because you're not *perfect* like me, now are you?" asked Reb, laughing. She screwed up her face and snarled at Jennifer, who snarled back.

I let out a shuddering laugh. "Well, if we're not going to play tennis, what are we going to do? We have the whole cabin to ourselves." I was so relieved we were laughing now. It could've gotten ugly.

Reb stood up and looked out the screen door at the rain. Then she looked at us with a sly grin. "I know what we can do. Let's short-sheet Melissa."

# CHAPTER 8

Jennifer actually squealed when Reb said that. "Why didn't we think of that a long time ago?"

Great. I'd barely recovered from the book-throwing incident. Jennifer and Reb rushed over to Melissa's bed. I picked up Reb's annual and put it back on the shelf. It'd been such a relief—somehow I'd been the one to make things right again. Maybe because Reb was always making jokes. I'd managed to make her laugh, and everything was fine.

But now this. It'd been days since we'd joked about the bed-wetting. We'd just left Melissa alone. What was short-sheeting, anyway? When Reb had mentioned it before, she'd just assumed I knew what she was talking about. But no way could I ask them.

"Hold on. Somebody ought to be lookout," Reb said.

"I'll do it." Hey, this was my chance. I could be lookout but still watch them.

Reb plopped down on Melissa's bunk like it was her own. It made me feel weird, because there's, like, this unwritten rule that nobody ever sits on anybody else's bed unless they ask you to, like to play cards or something. Reb was looking at all of Melissa's stuff on the wooden shelf by her bed. "Oh, how precious." She held up a stack of paper. "It says 'Melissa.'" Somebody, probably her dad, had made a border and printed up a bunch of blank sheets with her name on it. "Should say 'Dweeb.'" Then Reb stood up and smoothed out the wrinkles she'd left on Melissa's blanket.

"I can't believe we've been here a week, and we're just now short-sheeting Melissa. How inefficient of us!" Reb said with a smile.

She rolled back Melissa's blanket from the foot of the bed and then stopped all of a sudden. "I just thought of something," she said, all dramatic, looking at Jennifer. "What if she wet the bed last night?"

She and Jennifer both shrieked and clutched each other and then broke up laughing.

"Hey, c'mon," I called from the doorway. "Hurry up before someone catches us." I kept glancing out the door. Melissa might show up. Or Rachel. Then what would happen?

Reb and Jennifer got serious. They were unfolding, refolding, and tucking in Melissa's sheets. While I watched them, it hit me. Oh, *short*-sheeting! At the foot of Melissa's bunk, they folded her top sheet so it made a kind of pocket under the blanket. When Melissa got in, her feet would only go halfway to the end of the bed. Was that all there was to it? I thought it was something really bad.

I felt like an idiot for not figuring it out on my own. Well, at least now I knew.

When they got the bed made, they stepped back to admire their work.

"Now let's get out of here!" Reb shouted.

We grabbed rain jackets and ponchos, then took off running down the line. At least we were out of there. And we hadn't been caught. And it wasn't *that* bad.

It was still raining pretty steadily, and we had to jump over all the puddles because Middler Line is just a dirt path, but now it was a muddy, wet mess. We ran down the hill in the slippery, wet grass and stopped under some tall shade trees for cover.

"Where is everybody?" I asked. The whole camp felt deserted. But everything was beautiful in the rain. The grass and leaves were green, and the tree trunks were black, and the whole camp was misty and wet. It made me shiver.

All of a sudden I jumped up and grabbed one of the branches hanging right over our heads and shook it as hard as I could. All the raindrops on the branch came showering down on us. It was like our own little private rain shower. Reb and Jennifer just stood there, frozen. I had no idea what would happen next. Then Reb snapped out of it.

"You are gonna die!" Thank God she had a huge smile on her face. She dove right at me, and I screamed and ran out from under the tree. She chased me all the way down the hill, with me screaming the whole way. Jennifer was still standing under the tree.

"Jennifer, help! Help!" I yelled.

"I'm not gonna help you! I'm gonna kill you too!" Then they both caught me, and Reb dragged me toward this huge mud puddle. I was trying to get away, but the grass was so slippery. Plus I was laughing so hard I could barely stand up.

Reb pushed me right smack down into that mud puddle, and I felt the water seep all the way through to my skin. The whole seat of my jeans was absolutely soaked. I tried to stand up, but Reb had both her hands on my shoulders, holding me down.

"Ah, revenge is sweet!" She laughed evilly. "I AM your worst nightmare!"

"My butt's freezing! Let me up!" I shouted.

Reb looked over her shoulder at Jennifer. "Look who's amazingly dry," she whispered to me. "On the count of three—one, two . . ."

On three I jumped up and we both lunged at Jennifer and dragged her to the mud puddle. After Jennifer got dunked, we both turned on Reb, and by then we'd pulled off our jackets and ponchos, and we started puddle-hopping. When we got tired of splashing, we scooped the mud out of the bottom of the puddles and threw it at each other. It was amazing!

At first none of us aimed that well because we were laughing so hard. But then it was like we were psychic, and Reb and I wouldn't even have to say anything, we'd just look at each other and bombard Jennifer. Then they'd look at each other and trash me! Then Jennifer and I got Reb, and we got her good. The only part of her face not covered in mud was her eyes.

"I have never been this dirty in my *life*!" Jennifer yelled. "Is it in my hair?"

"In your hair, your ears, your nose . . . ," I said.

"Whose idea was this?" asked Reb, then threw one last mud pie in my direction but missed.

Now it had pretty much stopped raining, and people were coming out of hiding. Everybody stared at us and shook their heads like they couldn't believe it. I couldn't believe it either. Every inch of us was covered in mud. I was shivering like crazy. My wet, muddy clothes felt like they weighed a ton.

We went back to the cabin, with people staring at us all along the way. Jennifer got to the door first, and she was walking in when Rachel saw us. "Hold it right there!" She came to the door with Erin and Brittany, and the three of them stared at us with their mouths open.

Rachel shook her head. "You all can't come inside like that."

"What are we supposed to do?" yelled Jennifer.

"Go straight to the showers." Rachel made Brittany and Erin get us towels and dry clothes from our trunks. "And I would suggest showering with your clothes *on* first." Rachel handed us our stuff, trying not to touch us.

We laughed, but it was a pretty good idea, so we did what she said. We got into the showers with all our clothes on and washed the mud off; then we undressed and finished showering. My wet clothes felt like they weighed about twenty pounds when I took them off and hung them over the shower door.

We kept laughing and talking across the shower stalls. The water was so hot that it burned. I wanted to stand there in the water and steam forever.

We were friends. We really were. I'd been holding my breath all week, waiting for Reb and Jennifer to find out I wasn't really cool. But maybe I *was* cool.

# CHAPTER 9

That night after evening program, we were leaving the lodge when Reb whispered to us, "We're not going to the cabin yet. Keep quiet and follow me."

We could barely see because none of us had flashlights. Crickets were chirping like crazy. The grass was still wet from the rain, and pretty soon my sneakers were soaked. The air was a lot cooler now, and it was really damp. I could smell the wet grass.

"Reb, what's up?" Jennifer sounded annoyed since Reb wouldn't tell us anything.

"We're going to the dining hall for seconds on dessert."

"You mean we're raiding the kitchen?" Jennifer asked. Even in the dark I could hear the nervousness in her voice. Reb would be brave enough to try it, but I was with Jennifer. I was afraid we'd get caught.

"Of course not. Alex is doing it for us."

The kitchen was always open to the counselors. They could go in and help themselves to leftovers whenever they wanted. But they never gave us anything. How had Reb talked Alex into this?

"We're supposed to be in the cabin by now," Jennifer said. I was glad she'd said it because it's what I was thinking.

"Calm down. Rachel has line duty tonight, so she won't even miss us."

At the dining hall we went around back to a screen door. We could hear counselors talking inside. Pretty soon a shadow came out of the kitchen door.

"Reb?" came a loud whisper.

"Alex, over here," Reb whispered back.

Alex clicked on a flashlight and walked toward us. She was balancing two plastic bowls of chocolate pudding in one hand.

"You only brought two?" asked Reb.

Alex looked at me, then back at Reb. "Don't complain. You're lucky to get anything."

Reb gave Jennifer and me the pudding. "You all eat it. I'm not that hungry."

"No, Reb, that's okay." I tried to hand my bowl back to her. Obviously Alex hadn't been expecting me to come along. Reb and Jennifer were her favorite campers from last summer, and she still gave her twins lots of attention.

"Don't be a goof." Reb sounded annoyed. "Go ahead and take it, I don't care."

"We could at least split it."

"So I heard the Evil Twins were out making mud pies in the rain this afternoon."

Jennifer laughed. "Making mud pies of ourselves, you mean."

"Yeah," Reb said around a mouthful of pudding. "Kelly was there too. You know Kelly." Reb said it like Alex and I just needed to be reintroduced. "She's the one who started it all."

"Me?" I acted all innocent. "*You* were the one who threw me into the mud puddle."

"Which I never would have done if you hadn't shaken that branch and gotten us all soaked when we were *trying* to stay dry." She looked at Alex. "Talk about evil! This girl is the worst!"

Alex gave me a look that was a little friendlier. "Too bad I missed it."

"Yeah. We need a new name. We're triplets now."

Reb winked at me and handed me the bowl. I took it like it was a prize.

"Evil Triplets?" asked Alex.

Reb looked thoughtful. "No. Terrible Triplets."

I took a bite of pudding and handed the bowl back to Reb. I was glad it was dark. I had a stupid grin on my face.

"So—I haven't seen you guys in my Guard Start class."

"I know," Reb said. "I guess we're going to be lazy bums this summer." The thing was, we'd talked about the class after Alex mentioned it, but Jennifer didn't want to do it because she wasn't a very good swimmer. Reb was a good friend, though, not letting Alex know that part. Reb gave Alex our empty bowls. "Thanks, Allie. You're the coolest counselor in camp."

We rushed back to the cabin, since we were already late. "Oh my gosh!" Jennifer gasped. "We almost forgot! Melissa's bed!"

"Oh yeah!" said Reb. "We can't miss this!"

I'd actually completely forgotten about short-sheeting Melissa, after the whole mud fight. What if she was really upset? What if she thought I helped them? I didn't really. I just happened to be in the same room with them at the time.

"Where have you all been?" Tis asked when we came in the door.

Reb just shrugged. "We had places to go, people to see."

Tis looked at us. "Really? Care to elaborate?"

"I left my jacket in the lodge, and they went back with me to find it," I blurted out. Reb gave me a quick wink.

Molly looked over from Side B and called out, "Don't believe the Evil Twins, Tis! They were up to something devious."

"Molly, the lifeboats are leaving without you," yelled Reb. Molly drove us all crazy with her weird facts about the Titanic. "Oh, and Evil Twins? That is so last year. Nobody calls us that anymore."

I glanced at Melissa, but I had no way to talk to her without Reb and Jennifer hearing us. Maybe she wouldn't even care. We all got into bed, and Tis turned out the lights. Then Melissa made a funny noise. We could hear her kicking her covers around in the dark.

"Melissa, is everything all right over there?" called out Reb in a sugar-sweet tone. I could hear Jennifer snickering from the top bunk.

"Yeah."

"Are you sure? Need me to tuck you in, since Rachel isn't here?"

"No thanks."

"Okay. Just know that if you need anything—I'm here for you."

I felt a little bad. If I'd remembered earlier, I probably would've warned Melissa so she could fix her sheets before lights out. Maybe she didn't even mind that much. I mean, it wasn't *that* big a deal. The way Reb had talked about it, short-sheeting sounded like something really bad, but it was just a little prank.

I wouldn't mind if somebody short-sheeted me. I don't think.

*Evil Twins—that is so last year.*

I was a triplet now. Could my life get any better?

# CHAPTER 10

## Saturday, June 21

"No way am I wasting my time going to activities!" said Jennifer. Even though Rachel and Tis warned us all about no cabin-sitting, almost everyone was ditching activities to get ready for the dance with Camp Crockett. If there even *was* a dance. We still didn't know for sure, since there hadn't been an official announcement.

Reb just laughed. "I can't believe how stupid everyone's being. You think you'll meet some guy tonight and start a major, long-distance relationship? Please." She looked at me. "Want to go to archery? It won't take *all* afternoon to get ready."

I nodded. "Sure." If Reb wanted to go to archery, so did I.

Jennifer grabbed her robe and towel. "Well, it may

sound pathetic, but these dances are practically the highlight of my summer. I'm going to meet someone tonight. And I have to look incredible. So I'll see you guys later."

I was surprised she wasn't coming with us, but I was kind of glad it was just Reb and me. On the way to the archery range, I asked Reb, "Why don't the counselors just tell us if there's a dance?" All day they'd acted like it was some big secret.

"So we don't do what Jennifer's doing. Cut activities to get ready," Reb explained. "Jennifer's boy crazy. Going to an all-girls school does that to her."

I thought maybe we'd run into Darcy or Nicole or some of the other girls, but we didn't. Except for the archery counselor watching us, Reb and I had the whole range to ourselves, which was cool. But when we got back to Middler Line late in the afternoon, it was a madhouse. Every single shower had a line of about four or five people waiting.

Devon Fairchild came out of one stall. "There is not a single ounce of hot water left," she announced through clenched teeth, and everyone groaned.

"Reb, we screwed up. We should've stayed with Jennifer. Now we've got to wait in line an hour to get a cold shower," I said.

Reb swung her arm around my neck and gave me this sly grin. "We're not waiting in line for a shower. I know where there's no waiting, and still plenty of hot water."

I just looked at her but didn't say anything. We got our soap and shampoo and put on robes. We walked down Middler Line past the showers and just kept going. Then we went across the hill toward Junior Line. I smiled when I saw where we were heading.

"The Juniors don't get to go to dances, so they'll all be at activities now. Besides, those grubby little rugrats only take about two showers all summer, anyway."

She opened one of the shower stalls and turned on the faucet. Then she stuck her hand into the water and smiled at me. "Warm as bathwater."

"You are a freaking genius!"

She laughed. "I know."

So not only did we both get a hot shower, we didn't have to stand in line. Before I met Reb, I would've just been one of those girls waiting her turn. It was so cool to be friends with someone who knew how to get things done. Plus, all afternoon it'd just been the two of us, Reb and me, without Jennifer or the rest of the fan club. We'd had a great time together.

I wasn't trying to take Jennifer's place, but

sometimes I felt like Reb and I had more in common. We were both more tomboyish, for one thing. I wasn't as athletic as Reb, but I was better at stuff than Jennifer, and I thought Reb admired me for that.

Everybody was in the cabin when we got back. On Side B, Molly was doing Jordan's hair, and even Melissa was putting mascara on her pale eyelashes. Jordan's older sister, Madison, came by and warned us, "You guys better be good. The CATs will be on Porch Patrol." I had no idea what that meant. The CATs were the Counselor Assistants in Training, and Madison was one of them. They were sixteen, and they had the perfect arrangement. They were too old to be campers and get bossed around, but too young to be counselors and have responsibilities, so they could do whatever they wanted.

"It's about time you all showed up!" Jennifer yelled at us. "I'm having a wardrobe crisis! You guys have to help me." She pointed to three outfits spread out on Reb's bed. "Which do you like best?"

"The denim skirt and the pink tank," Reb advised.

"Yeah, I agree. But now what am I going to wear?" I was looking through my trunk. I just didn't pack that many nice clothes.

"Here, you can wear this." Reb pulled out a rose-colored shirt from her trunk and handed it to me. "This will look good with your dark hair."

I almost drooled all over the Abercrombie shirt.

"Don't you want to wear this?" I asked.

"Nah, I'll wear this one." She held up a pale blue Abercrombie polo. "You can borrow some jeans, too, but they might be a little long. I'm wearing my cargos."

"Oh, well, thanks, but I'll wear my jeans." I have one and *only* one pair of Abercrombie jeans. "But thanks for the shirt. It'll look great."

"I wish I was your size." Jennifer looked at us both and grimaced.

"Oh, please. You'd trade those big twins in to be *our* size?" asked Reb.

Jennifer crossed her arms over her chest. "Are they too big? Do they look freakish?"

Reb burst out laughing. "Jennifer, try to find one guy on the planet who would say, 'Hmmm, her breasts are simply too large. I find them freakish.'"

"God, I should've been dieting this week! I knew the dance was coming up!"

"Shut up!" Reb and I both yelled at the same time. Jennifer is the last person in the cabin who needs to diet. I can't believe how weird some girls get about food.

I stood in front of the tiny mirror, trying to see how I looked in Reb's shirt. Practically everything she owned had a moose on it. I had to go through massive amounts of pain and suffering just to get my one little measly pair of Abercrombie jeans.

I first asked my mom for them back in the fall. But when she saw the price tag, she almost had a seizure right there in the mall. "Absolutely not!"

So I asked for them for Christmas. That was *all* I asked for too. If they were so ridiculously expensive, maybe they should be my one and only Christmas present. When Christmas morning came, I got the jeans, but I could tell Mom wasn't happy about having to give in. She gave me this long lecture about the value of a dollar and not being fooled by designer labels, but while I sat there and nodded, I was wearing my new jeans.

"Thanks again for the shirt. I'll be really careful with it."

"Don't worry about it. You can have it if you want it."

"Oh, no! I couldn't *take* it. I'll just borrow it," I said.

"Kelly, it's a shirt. It's not like I'm giving you a kidney." She turned away, acting like it was no big deal. I could tell I'd embarrassed her by drooling over the shirt.

"Here. We should wear these so we'll be triplets." Jennifer handed Reb and me matching pink wristbands.

"At St. Cecilia's, since we wear uniforms, the hip girls all do something different to stand out. Like one day it's striped scrunchies in our hair. Or we all wear blue socks a certain way—you know, rolled down like a doughnut or just slouched. We have to sneak around the dress code since we can't wear much jewelry. You can tell who's hip and who's not by how they're accessorized."

"What cause is this? Breast cancer?" Reb asked.

"No. Our school had them made. They say St. Cecilia's, but look—I turned them inside out and wrote 'Terrible Triplets' on the other side."

Reb rolled her eyes. "Whatever." But she did put on the wristband to make Jennifer happy. I put mine on because I loved being a triplet.

By dinnertime there still hadn't been an official announcement about the dance, but everyone was all dressed up. We were having spaghetti and garlic bread, and all the old campers said that was a sure sign there was a dance. The garlic bread was supposed to be a joke—nobody would get kissed with breath smelling like garlic. None of us ate any of it.

Jordan pointed out that all the CATs were missing from their table in the center of the dining hall. Then all of a sudden, they burst through the dining room doors. They were all dressed in camo, carrying flashlights, and some of them even had branches and leaves taped to their shirts.

"Ladies and . . . ladies! We know you've been anxiously awaiting an opportunity to see some guys of the male persuasion!" When they said that, we all screamed. "Well, your wait is almost over!" they shouted. "Tonight we'll be going to Camp Crockett for an evening of song and dance!" The noise was earsplitting!

"But be careful! If those Crockett boys want you to sneak away to the bushes for a make-out session, we'll be watching to make sure that nobody leaves the dining hall porch!" Then they all started singing.

> *Porch Patrol! Porch Patrol!*
> *Start yellin' for that good ole porch patrol!*
> *If he tries to make first base, you had better slap*
> *his face,*
> *And start yellin' for that good ole porch patrol!*

So now it was official. In thirty minutes we'd be leaving to go to Camp Crockett for Boys.

They took us over in a bunch of vans and trucks. The dance was in Camp Crockett's dining hall, so all the tables and chairs had been moved to make space for dancing. We walked in, and all of us girls stood clumped together by the door. The boys were way over on the other side of the dining hall. Most of them weren't even looking at us. They were laughing and talking and acting like they were all just hanging out in their dining hall for no reason. There was a huge empty stretch of floor between the boys and us, practically the size of the Grand Canyon. How would anyone ever walk across that big empty space to get to the other side?

I could tell right away that none of *them* had spent all afternoon getting ready for this major event. I suppose they went to the trouble of taking showers. Maybe some of them had even put on clean shirts. To think we put all that energy into looking nice for these boneheads.

"I see three, maybe four guys I could dance with without throwing up," said Reb.

"Well, I'm not wasting any time," Jennifer said. "I say, 'See and be seen.'" She pushed to the front of the group of girls, where she'd be more visible. As we stood there, a few people started to dance. Reb kept making sarcastic remarks until a boy walked up and asked her to dance.

"Sure, why not?" Miss Casual. So now both Reb and Jennifer were dancing, and I was by myself. I was about to go find Erin or Brittany or one of the fan club girls when I turned around and almost fell over a boy.

"Wanna dance?"

"Okay."

I followed him out to a spot on the floor. He was okay-looking, but he never even said one word to me. When the song ended, he just walked off.

*Next*. But I didn't say it out loud.

Then I danced with two other guys—one named Brian and another guy who said his name was Franklin. Maybe he was giving me a fake name, or his last name.

But the next guy was Ethan, and he was definitely

the nicest of the four so far. He was cute. He had long blond skater hair that covered his eyes, and he was wearing jeans and skateboarding shoes. He kept tilting his head back to see out from under his hair.

After about three dances, it looked like Ethan wasn't interested in dancing with anyone else, which was fine with me.

When I saw Reb at the refreshment table, I asked Ethan if he wanted to get a drink. Reb was with a really cute guy named Cole.

"You two know each other?" Reb asked Cole and Ethan. They mumbled at each other. Guys have this weird nonverbal way of communicating.

"Well, you guys wait here. Kelly and I need to talk." Reb led me away.

"So how's it going? Do you like him?"

"Yeah, he's really nice. What about Cole? He's *cute*."

"Yeah, but he's got an ego the size of Montana. Look at Jennifer."

Jennifer was on the dance floor, still dancing with the same guy who'd first asked her. "Looks like she found her guy," Reb said with a smile. "Hey, take a look." She pointed to the dance floor. "Even Melissa found some poor loser to dance with her. He's definitely not her type."

Melissa's "loser" was kind of cute. He had dark curly

hair and a friendly face. If he'd asked me to dance, I would have. Melissa had pulled her hair back in a clip, and she had on a yellow cami and capri jeans. She looked sort of pretty.

"What's her type?" I wondered which of these guys Reb would consider my type.

"Social outcast." Reb looked around. "Now there. That guy standing over there. He looks like he'd be perfect for Melissa." She meant this skinny guy with a bad haircut and a lot of acne. "Want to do a little matchmaking?"

I looked over at Ethan. He looked bored. I didn't want to give him too many chances to find somebody else to dance with. "Maybe later. The guys are waiting for us."

When I got back to Ethan, he suggested we go out on the porch. It was dark now, but the porch lights were on. A lot of people were outside sitting on the porch's wood rails. Rachel was talking with a group of Crockett and Pine Haven counselors at the end of the porch, and when she saw me, she gave me a little wave. I didn't mind being seen with Ethan. It was definitely better than standing around with a bunch of girls, like some people were doing. And Ethan was getting cuter as the night went on.

Ethan had lots of funny stories about the guys in his cabin. I told him about short-sheeting Melissa, and he said he didn't know girls did stuff like that to each other. Then some counselors came by and made us all go back in.

When we walked in, Reb came charging over. "Hey, I've been looking all over for you! Look, Melissa and that guy aren't dancing anymore. Now's our chance to do some matchmaking."

"What happened to Cole? Where's Jennifer?" I just wanted to dance with Ethan right now. I wasn't sure what kind of matchmaking Reb was planning.

"I ditched him. And Jennifer's still attached to that same guy. So much for triplets. You and me are the Evil Twins on this one. Let's find Melissa the perfect match."

"Is that the girl you were talking about?" asked Ethan.

"Yeah." I looked at Reb. "I told him about short-sheeting Melissa. He thought it was funny."

"What are you going to do to her?"

"We're going to fix her up with somebody more her type," Reb explained. "Maybe that charming young man." She pointed out the guy we'd laughed at earlier.

"Oh, no, I got it! This'll be perfect!" Ethan's face lit up. "It's got to be Dustin Nesmith. He's in *my* cabin, and nobody can stand him. He's taken one shower this whole week, and that was because the counselor made him. Look, I'll tell him I know somebody who wants to dance with him. You tell her the same thing." Then he took off.

Reb grinned at me. "Ethan's cool. Okay, go over to Melissa and set it up. And don't act like it's any big deal for you to be talking to her."

Okay. This was weird. I'd barely talked to Melissa in days, and now I was supposed to go over and start a conversation? But I had to do it. I was a twin, wasn't I?

I walked up to Melissa with a little smile. "Hi. Having a good time?"

"I guess so." She was obviously surprised that I was suddenly talking to her again.

"Yeah, me too. I've been dancing with this guy, Ethan, and he has this friend who wants to dance with you. But he's kind of shy. He hasn't danced much, and"—she was giving me this weird look, like I had bean sprouts growing out of my ears—"anyway, he's over there. See those two guys? The one in the green shirt is Ethan, and that's his friend, Dustin."

Ethan and Dustin were across the floor, looking at us and talking. Dustin had a smirk on his face that didn't make him look at all shy. Melissa folded her arms across her chest like she had motion sickness or something.

"He looks like a nerd," she said.

"No, he doesn't." Although he did. "Do you have any idea how hard it is for a guy to ask a girl to dance? C'mon, just one dance."

"Well . . ."

Dustin was walking toward us, still with that awful smirk on his face. "Here he comes. Just don't break his heart."

I kind of pushed Melissa toward Dustin and then met Ethan on the dance floor. I was looking around for Reb and finally saw her dancing with some new guy.

"So now what?" I asked Ethan.

Ethan shrugged. "Let's just wait and see what happens. When she gets a whiff of his body odor, she'll probably throw up on him."

Melissa and Dustin danced the next few dances, and we kept an eye on them the whole time. It seemed like Reb was watching them too, but somehow she and her latest guy had ended up halfway across the room. Dustin was talking between dances, but Melissa wasn't saying much.

When the next song started, the lights dimmed. It

was the first slow dance of the night. Ethan and I sort of grabbed each other in this weird way and started slow dancing. Watching Dustin and Melissa slow dance made me wonder if *we* looked that stupid. Dustin's knees were swaying back and forth like he was skiing down a mountain. Melissa had her hands behind his back, but it looked like she was trying not to touch him.

When that song ended, another slow song started. We just kept watching the two of them, which was good. It kept us from having to look at each other. It was the first time I'd ever slow danced with a boy. I was so glad I hadn't eaten any garlic bread.

Then something happened. Dustin and Melissa were slow dancing, and he had his hands on her back. But while I was watching them, I noticed that slowly, ever so slowly, he was moving his hands farther and farther down. Just how far was he planning to go? And didn't Melissa notice?

Then all of a sudden, when his hands went too far down, she jumped back out of his arms. Everyone around them looked at them. Melissa crossed her arms and walked away. She just left Dustin standing there.

Ethan was laughing so hard that now everyone was staring at *us*. "Did you see where his hands were?" he asked.

"YES! I can't believe she didn't slap him," I said.

"I wonder if any of the other guys saw it," he said, trying to make himself stop laughing. His eyes were watering and he needed a Kleenex.

I felt bad for Melissa. I wondered if Reb saw it. I looked around, but I couldn't see her in the crowd. Dustin had wandered off to stand with some other guys. He looked like he didn't care.

Then I had a thought—had Ethan put him up to it? Maybe he bribed him or dared him to do it. He sure thought it was funny. But would he do something that mean? Or was Dustin a complete freak on his own without any help from his friends?

Pretty soon they announced that it was the last song, and then the lights went back up and we all left the dining hall to go wait by the vans and trucks. Ethan walked out with me. "That was a lot of fun. I guess I'll see you at the next dance, huh?" he asked.

Wow, that was practically like asking for a second date! "Yeah! I had a good time tonight." Because I did. And I wanted him to know it.

"Yeah, me too. I'll see ya, Kelly." He kind of squeezed my hand before he walked away to where a bunch of guys were standing.

So. A hand squeeze. For a split second when we were

saying good-bye, I had a thought. What if he tried to kiss me? Wasn't that what you did at moments like this?

But he didn't. He didn't even come close. We'd been standing about two feet apart, and that's a huge space. How do you ever even close up a space that big?

I looked around at the big crowd of people wandering around. It was dark, but you could still see from the lights of the dining hall porch. I let out a sigh. My face felt hot. I was relieved. But also a little disappointed. It's weird that I could be both at the exact same time.

I finally saw Reb waiting by the white van we'd ridden over in. She grabbed my arm and dragged me around to the other side of the van. "Did you see it? Did you see what happened?" she asked me.

"Oh, you mean Dustin and Melissa?"

"Of course! What else? Did you see how he grabbed her! Why didn't we have a camera to capture the moment?" She held out her closed fist for me to pound it. "Excellent job setting her up. I can't believe how great it worked out!"

"Thanks." I'd been a good twin. But what if Ethan had done that to me when we were slow dancing? I probably would've reacted the same way Melissa did.

Then Rachel found us and made us get into the van. Jennifer had finally shown up. "That was the best dance

I've ever been to." She sighed. She looked lovesick and stupid.

"Ah, but you missed the highlight of the evening." Reb started whispering to her so I knew she was filling her in. Rachel had turned the van around, and the wheels crunched on the gravel road. "Did everyone have a good time?" she asked.

"I had a great time," Reb yelled. "Melissa, how 'bout you? Did you have a great time? I saw you dancing a lot." She'd turned around to Melissa, who was sitting on the bench behind us.

Melissa didn't answer. I couldn't tell what she was doing, since I didn't dare turn around. Did she think it was my fault Dustin did that to her? I certainly didn't put him up to it. Maybe I should try to talk to her tomorrow.

Reb rested her chin on the back of our seat. "Mewissa. Did oo hear me? Did oo have a gweat time?" she said in this annoying baby voice.

"Yeah." That was it. That's all she said. Why did Reb hate her so much? Sure, she was geeky, but I've seen geekier. There had to be a reason. What if, when camp started, I'd fallen into the "pick on" group instead of the "be nice to" group? What if Reb had really gotten mad that day I made the comment about her father, and she'd turned on me? It just seemed so random. What a relief to be Reb's friend, instead of her enemy.

"Hey, look," said Molly. "Jockey shorts. Lots of them." We looked out the windows, and hanging over the Camp Crockett sign, this wooden arch you drive under, were all these pairs of boys' underwear. And they were pink. And there was a huge sign made out of pink construction paper that said something we couldn't quite read.

"What did it say?" asked Jordan.

"Something about 'Thanks for a great dance from the . . .' and then I couldn't read the rest," said Erin.

"I think it said 'from the Pink Team,'" said Rachel. "What's up with that, Tis?"

Tisdale shook her head like she didn't have a clue. "Tsk, tsk. I guess some Pine Haven girls were up to some mischief."

## Tuesday, June 24

When we walked into the cabin from afternoon activities, we saw this huge canvas bag sitting by the door. On Sunday we'd sent all our dirty clothes out in a bag just like this one. "Yay! The laundry's here!" said Jennifer.

We had the cabin to ourselves, so the three of us dragged the bag to Side A.

"Let's dump it all out on Rachel's bed so we can find our stuff," said Reb. She immediately started smoothing out all her clothes and carefully folding them in a stack. I've never met anyone so neat in my life.

"Hey, that's my shirt," I said.

"Jennifer, this must be your bra." Reb swung it around her head like a lasso.

"Gimme that! You freak!"

"Whose bra is *this*?" I picked up a Little Mermaid training bra covered in pictures of Ariel. When Reb and Jennifer saw it, they both burst out laughing.

"Read the name tag to see whose it is," suggested Reb.

I wasn't crazy about examining someone else's bra up close, but I looked at the tag sewn inside. "Melissa's! Isn't that so sweet?" We all cracked up.

Reb gasped and pulled something out of the laundry pile. "Here are the undies that go with it!" The three of us were practically rolling on the floor, we were laughing so hard. I felt a little bad that we were making so much fun of them because it was pretty private. I mean, I wouldn't want someone looking at my underwear and laughing. But it was just so goofy. If my mom had packed something like that for me to bring to camp, I would've burned it the first day.

"Hey, hey, HEY!" Reb yelled. She had this maniac look in her eyes. "I've got a fabulous idea! Let's fly these from the flagpole so everybody in camp can appreciate them."

My stomach had the same nervous feeling I got when a teacher was passing out a test. "I don't know, Reb. Haven't we done enough? We short-sheeted her, and then that guy at the dance . . ."

"Kelly, c'mon. Remember the pink underwear? This is our chance to do something just as funny." There was a big debate about who'd pulled off the pink underwear prank at Camp Crockett Saturday night. Some people thought it was the CAs and others said it was the CATs. Neither group would admit to it.

"We'll get caught," I said. "Everybody'll see us."

"Not now, genius. Tonight. After everybody's asleep. We'll sneak out of the cabin and do it. Then tomorrow morning, they'll be flapping in the breeze."

"It'll be great!" Jennifer agreed. "The Terrible Triplets strike again." She fingered her wristband, which she was still wearing and had insisted that Reb and I keep on too. Reb thought it was stupid. I didn't mind it. I thought it was cool we all wore the same wristband.

"Exactly," Reb said. "We haven't been very terrible lately. We'll lose our reputation. Okay, here's what we'll do. . . ."

Once Reb made up her mind about something, there was no stopping her. She really was amazing. As I listened to her, I could tell she was working out all the details in her head as she went along. And she had thought of everything.

She said we should wait till two a.m. to make sure all the counselors were back from kitchen raids. She said she'd try to stay awake, but just in case, she had a little alarm clock she would put under her pillow so no one else would hear it. She kept stressing how quiet we had to be so we wouldn't get caught.

"What about flashlights?" Jennifer asked.

"Too risky. Somebody might see the light. It's not that far to the flagpole."

So that was the plan. I felt jittery, but in a good way. It would be a challenge to sneak out of the cabin and pull off this prank without getting caught. And then the whole camp would wake up and find a Little Mermaid bra and panties flying from the flagpole. It *was* pretty funny. And anyway, nobody would know whose underwear it was. Except us. And Melissa, of course. It wasn't *that* embarrassing.

Later everyone came in and picked out their clothes. If Melissa noticed that some of her underwear was missing, she didn't say anything. We could hardly wait for night to come.

Rachel should've suspected something, because we all got in bed with no fuss. Then we just lay there in the dark, waiting. I kept shifting from my side to my back to my stomach. Lights out was ten o'clock. That meant we had a four-hour wait.

"Quit flopping around over there," Reb whispered. "I'm trying to sleep."

"Sorry." I smiled. *Good cover, Reb.* I closed my eyes and tried to be still.

And then, about fifteen minutes later, Reb was shaking me. She put her hand over my mouth and whispered, "It's time."

Good thing she'd covered up my mouth, because I kind of grunted. Two a.m.? Already? Then I noticed how quiet and still everything was. I sat up on the edge of my bed, and my head was heavy.

I'd stuffed a pair of jeans and a dark blue T-shirt under my covers, so I pulled those out and slipped them on. Jennifer climbed down from the top bunk like a burglar.

A shadow stood by the bunk beds, and even though I knew it was Reb, it still sort of freaked me out because it was so dark and I couldn't see her face at all. The shadow motioned toward the door, and Jennifer and I tiptoed behind. I could just make out the outlines of Melissa and Rachel sleeping in their cots a few feet away. I held my breath as I crept past them.

We all three stopped at the door. Slowly Reb put out her hand and pushed gently against the screen door. It opened with a soft groan. All three of us froze and waited. Nobody stirred, so Reb waved at us to go through. We slipped soundlessly through the door.

# CHAPTER 14

Whew. We'd made it outside. I let all my air out like a balloon deflating. We walked down Middler Line, the only sound our sneakers padding along the soft dirt path. It felt strange to be out in the middle of the night. The air was cool and everything was perfectly quiet, but it wasn't the same as it was during the day when everyone was at activities and the cabins were empty. You could kind of *feel* everyone asleep in the cabins. I looked up, and the sky was velvet black with a million little sparks of silver. Reb was right. There was enough light for us to see.

But when we got to the steps going down to the lodge, it was pitch-black from all the trees. Now we could barely see. We were stumbling down the stone steps when I felt a hand brush past my arm. Then there was this huge thud and a scream. I could just make out a dark form at the bottom of the steps. It was Jennifer, lying there in a heap.

"What happened?" Reb whispered at her hoarsely. Jennifer groaned in pain.

"Uh, I . . . slipped." I could hear her suck in her breath.

"Are you hurt?" Reb's voice sounded worried.

"Um, yeah . . . my ankle. I twisted it."

"Oh great! It could be sprained. We gotta get you to the cabin . . . or the infirmary. Kelly, give me a hand." She swung one of Jennifer's arms over her shoulder, and I took the other.

"Oh, stop it! It's not *that* bad. I can make it to the flagpole, at least." She pulled away from us and took a few careful steps.

"Look, I do a lot of sports, and you shouldn't mess around with injuries. You could hurt it even more by walking on it. We've got to go back."

"No way are we going back now! How can you even suggest that?" Jennifer's voice rose, and Reb and I both shushed her.

"Don't you think your ankle is more important than some stupid prank?"

I couldn't help smiling. It was sweet that she was so worried about Jennifer. She really was loyal to her friends.

"Listen. It's my ankle. I know how it feels. And I'm telling you—it's fine. I know for sure I can make it. Let's just go." Jennifer limped ahead of us. Reb reached out and grabbed her by the elbow for added support. We really didn't have very far to go. The flagpole was just past the lodge near the top of the hill.

When we got there, we all looked up to the top of it at the same time. Reb reached inside her jacket and pulled out Melissa's bra and underwear. "Give me a hand."

For some reason Jennifer and I both applauded softly, and then we laughed because we'd thought of the same thing.

"No kidding." Reb sounded annoyed. "I've never done this before."

I helped her untie the rope looped around the pole. It made my hands cold to touch the bare steel. The metal clasps on the rope banged against the pole and made a hollow clang. Next we hooked the bra through the top clasp and put the bottom clasp through one of the panty legs. Then we pulled the rope to raise the underwear up and tied the rope in place.

"Mission accomplished," Reb said, and we all slapped hands. We looked up at the underwear at the top of the pole. We could barely see it. One thing was for sure—Melissa's underwear wasn't nearly as big as a flag.

"It might be funnier if Melissa was, like, a D-cup," said Jennifer.

"Maybe we should salute and then sing 'Under the Sea.' Wait—make that 'Under the Shirt.'" Reb snapped to attention like an army guy and was about to start singing when I clapped my hand over her mouth. We all laughed.

All of a sudden Jennifer grabbed my arm. I looked at her, but she was staring at something off in the distance. "I just saw something move!"

"Where?" Reb and I both whispered. All the blood drained down my legs and I was frozen in icy terror.

"There! In front of Crafts Cabin."

"I don't see anything," Reb whispered back.

"But I did! And it was somebody. But they're out of sight now," Jennifer insisted.

"Well, let's just go," Reb suggested.

"No! They'll see us!" Jennifer hissed. She was still staring at the same spot.

"Then we should definitely get out of here!" For the first time ever, Reb actually sounded scared, and that made me feel like having a full-blown panic attack. There was somebody else out here, creeping around in the dark, maybe *watching* us?

We started moving. Should we run or walk or creep? We mostly crept. When we got to the steps by the lodge, we figured we were out of sight from any "night stalkers."

"Jennifer, how ya doing? Are you gonna make it?"

"Yeah, it's okay. It hurts a little, but I can walk on it."

"She may be okay, but I'm dying," I groaned in agony.

"What's wrong with *you*?"

"I've *got* to go to Solitary. Jennifer made me so nervous I can't hold it anymore."

"*Now*? You have to go *now*?"

"No, tomorrow morning will be just fine," I snapped back at her.

"What next?" Reb growled. "Well, c'mon. We'll be going right by there, anyway."

We stopped at the top of the steps. "You go ahead. We'll wait here."

I took short, quick steps so I wouldn't lose my grip. The lights of Solitary practically blinded me after being in the dark, and I staggered into my favorite stall—the third one on the left, which had a little poem on the wall inside: *If you sprinkle when you tinkle, please be neat and wipe the seat.*

I sat there and read that poem for the 437th time. I sighed, feeling so much better. But when I flushed, the toilet was so loud I was afraid I'd wake the whole camp. I stood still, waiting for the noise to stop. Then I stepped out of the door of Solitary and walked down the line to where Reb and Jennifer were waiting.

"Hold it!"

Every muscle in my body froze. My heart stopped and my knees buckled. All the air went out of my lungs and I stood still, paralyzed.

"Where do you think *you're* going?"

# CHAPTER 15

I think I stood frozen in that one spot for about ten minutes, maybe more. Not breathing. Not moving. A muscle in my face twitched, and I locked my knees to keep them from folding up. Slowly, ever so slowly, I looked around.

Behind me was Libby Sheppard, one of the swimming counselors. We both stood there in this little patch of light shining from Solitary, looking at each other. Good thing I'd already gone to the bathroom. I was shaking so hard now I couldn't hold my legs still.

Libby had on a sundress, and her purse was over her arm. She must've just gotten back from leave. Leave! All that careful planning—we'd never even thought of that.

"Where ya going?" Libby asked me again.

"I don't feel very good," I said, my voice quavering. No lie there. My heart was hammering so hard it felt like it was going to pop out of my chest any minute now, like an alien. If she needed more proof, I was sure I could puke my guts out right now with very little effort.

Libby frowned at me. "You don't look very good. Are you sick?"

"Yeah!" I said it a little too loudly. But maybe loud was a good thing. Maybe Reb and Jennifer would hear me and stay out of sight. Had Libby seen the underwear? Was she the one we'd seen lurking around?

If I could keep Libby's eyes on me and away from where Reb and Jennifer were hiding, maybe things wouldn't get any worse than they already were.

"Who's your counselor . . . Rachel?"

"Ah, yeah. But I didn't want to wake her up."

"Oh." Libby looked at me closely. Was she concerned or suspicious? I really couldn't tell. "Want me to walk you to the infirmary?"

"No. I mean, I feel better now. I think I'll just try to get some sleep." I put one foot behind me, ready to turn around and walk off, if Libby would just let me go.

"Hold on a second. You should probably go. There's

some kind of virus going around, you know. A bunch of girls have ended up in the infirmary. C'mon. I'll walk you down there."

Oh, great! Now would she force me to go to the infirmary? I needed a way out. I stuck my hands in my jeans pockets and looked up at Libby, trying to put a pitiful expression on my face. "Well, I'll tell you something, if you promise not to say anything to anybody, okay?"

Libby nodded, all reassuring and everything.

"Well . . . this is kind of embarrassing. I was homesick. Tonight, all of a sudden, I started missing my parents, especially my mom. All because of dinner."

"What about dinner?" Libby asked.

"Well, it was awful. Stewed tomatoes make me gag, literally. And then I'm not crazy about black-eyed peas, either."

Libby laughed.

"Anyway, I was thinking about my mom's cooking and wondering what *my* family was having for supper. And that just made me think about everything at home. I felt lonely, so I was going to the infirmary to talk to the nurse. But after I got dressed, I wasn't crazy about walking down there in the dark."

We walked over and sat down on the steps to Solitary.

"So you're sure you're not sick?" Libby put her hand on my forehead, and that actually made my chest tighten a little bit, because my mom does the exact same thing.

"No. I guess I just needed someone to talk to." I smiled at her. Might as well lay it on thick.

"You know, I was homesick my first summer at Pine Haven too."

"Really?" I asked. Wow. We were actually having a moment.

"Yeah." Libby laughed, remembering. "It was terrible. I was ten, and I hated, I mean absolutely *despised* camp. I wrote my parents all the time, begging them to come get me. But then I started having a great time, and I cried when my parents came to pick me up, 'cause I didn't want to leave."

I smiled. "I won't tell about you being homesick if you won't tell about me. Deal?"

"Deal! Well, are you gonna be okay now?"

"Yeah." I stood up and breathed. I'd managed to get out of this, amazingly. "Thanks a lot, Libby. I feel a whole lot better now."

"Sure." She gave me a quick hug, and then I headed toward Cabin 1 and she went toward Cabin 3. I prayed that Reb and Jennifer would figure it out and come back to the cabin when the coast was clear.

I tried to be as quiet as we'd been earlier, but all I really wanted to do was get in bed as fast as I could. I could see one big lump in Rachel's bed and a smaller lump in Melissa's bed, but both Reb's and Jennifer's bunks were still empty.

I got into bed and pulled off my jeans. I lay there and tried to hold my trembling legs still. Where were those guys? What if Libby caught them, too? Did Libby believe me? If she'd seen us at the flagpole, why didn't she bust me right then?

For two eternities I lay there waiting. I was about to go stark raving mad when I heard the screen door open very softly. My heart leaped in relief. Two shadows came in. They didn't make a sound. I knew it was Reb and Jennifer, but they were so quiet and so dark, it was a little scary to watch them.

I was dying to whisper to them, to find out if everything was okay. But I didn't dare. I just lay there. Reb slipped into her bed, and Jennifer climbed up to the top bunk with the springs squeaking a couple of times. It didn't matter, though, because the beds always squeak when someone turns over.

I could almost *feel* Reb and Jennifer wanting to say something to me. But not now. Too much had happened. We couldn't chance it. Talking could wait till morning. It would *have* to.

## Wednesday, June 25

The next morning, when the rising bell rang at eight o'clock, it took every ounce of energy I had to drag myself out of bed. My brain felt like it was covered with a layer of fuzz. How many hours of sleep did we get, anyway? Three? Four, maybe?

With everyone around, we still couldn't talk about our adventure, but we gave each other quick, silent looks. All I could think about was how pretty soon everyone would see a Little Mermaid bra and panties up the flagpole.

We had to do our morning chores before inspection. After I'd finished sweeping and Jennifer and Reb had made their beds and emptied the trash, the three of us took off together for the dining hall.

Thankfully, Jennifer had only a slight limp this morning.

"I'm glad you're okay," said Reb. "It'd be tough to explain how you sprained your ankle in the middle of the night. You really had me scared you'd hurt it bad."

"It's fine. I told you that last night," Jennifer replied. It was cool that Reb was so concerned about her. I knew that if anything ever happened to me, she had my back.

As we passed the lodge, we could see the flagpole. And there was Melissa's underwear, in broad daylight now. The panties were just hanging there limp, but the bra was caught in a little breeze.

"Ah, look at our hard work." Reb sighed.

The funny thing was, Chris Ramirez and Maggie Windsor walked right under the flagpole and didn't once look up. I guess some people wouldn't notice if their hair was on fire. I was beginning to wonder if maybe nobody would notice, or if people did, then maybe they wouldn't even think it was funny.

But then a group of girls walked by, and one of them, JD Duckworth, saw the underwear and started laughing. "Attention! Is anyone missing some lingerie?" She stood there and made sure that everyone walking by saw them. JD was a complete nutcase. She actually got caught by the Porch Patrol at the dance last week.

"It's so perfect that JD's the one who saw them!" whispered Jennifer.

"I know!" Reb agreed. We stopped under the flagpole with everyone else, acting totally innocent.

Reb cupped her hands over her eyes and looked up. "Why, JD—is that underwear I see?"

JD looked up too. "Why, yes, Rebecca, I believe it is. Are you missing any undergarments?"

Reb patted her chest like she was checking. "Nope. Not me. All my underwear is present and accounted for."

"Well, it's not mine, either. I think the bra belongs to somebody who's an A cup. Hey, Jessica—what's your bra size?" she yelled at this girl walking by.

As we stood there, we saw that Melissa was walking this way with a totally oblivious look on her face. Now JD was yelling at the top of her lungs, "Attention! Attention! Would the owner of an Ariel bra and panty set please report to the flagpole immediately?"

The three of us watched Melissa's every move. It was like you could read her mind. First she saw all of us standing around. Then, since we were looking up, she looked up too. Her forehead crinkled and her eyes squinted, like she was thinking, *Is that what I think it is?* Then she looked down really quick, like she didn't want to make eye contact anymore.

"Well, hi, Melissa," said Reb, all friendly. "Do you know anyone who's missing Little Mermaid underwear?" Nobody thought anything about the question, since JD had been harassing every single girl who walked by, asking her bra size. But Melissa actually jumped when Reb said that to her. She didn't make a sound, though. She looked at Reb, then she looked away, and then she took off for the dining hall without looking back.

"She must really be hankering for a bowl of Wheaties!" Reb had her elbow propped on my shoulder, and then she bent over and laughed so hard I thought everyone would suspect what was going on, but nobody did.

Inside the dining hall nobody at our table said anything about the underwear, but halfway through breakfast, Cabin 2's table clapped their hands to signal that they had a "parley-voo" to sing. Parley-voos were songs that campers made up to sing about some sort of camp news—like missing underwear.

> *Somebody lost her bra today, parley-voo.*
> *Somebody lost her bra today, parley-voo.*
> *Somebody lost her bra today.*
> *She's too flat to need it, anyway!*
> *Inky, dinky, parley-voo!*

JD was in Cabin 2, so I was sure she was the master-mind behind that one.

After breakfast somebody had taken the underwear down, but at least everyone in camp had already seen them.

"We've got to go someplace private to talk," Reb whispered to us. She was right. The three of us hadn't been alone since last night.

We decided to get our tennis rackets and go to the tennis courts. Tis and the other counselors weren't there yet, so we sat down at the end of the court with our backs against the fence. Finally we had some privacy.

"Triplets rule!" said Jennifer. She made us all touch wristbands, which Reb always thought was pretty stupid, but I thought it was fun.

"I can't believe we actually pulled it off!" I said.

"Yeah, but who took them down?" broke in Jennifer. "All that work getting them up there and then——"

"Hey, it doesn't matter, though," Reb interrupted. "If anything, it makes it more mysterious. Like, first they're up there, then they're gone."

"But Kelly, what happened when Libby caught you? We almost died when we heard her!" Jennifer gasped.

"*You* almost died! I almost wet my pants! But then I opened my mouth, and this whole involved story came out about how I was homesick and wanted someone to talk to, and blah, blah, blah. I never knew I could lie like that!"

"You did an amazing job of thinking on your feet," said Reb.

"Yeah," I agreed, loving the compliment, but I was worried about something. "But what if Libby suspects that I put the underwear up there? She did catch me wandering around in the middle of the night."

"So what?" asked Reb.

"She could tell Eda."

"Yeah, you're right." Reb sounded worried. "Then Eda would make you fly your own undies from the flagpole every day for the rest of camp, and we'd all have to stand there and salute while you raised them."

"Oh, shut up!" I gave her a shove.

Reb laughed. "The best part, though, the *best*, was Melissa's face when she saw her bra and panties flying from the flagpole! That was un-freaking-believable! I wish I'd had a camera!"

By now people were showing up, so we had to quit talking. We asked Santana Hickman to play with us in doubles. She and Reb destroyed Jennifer and me, but Reb showed me a couple of things about my serve, and it actually got a lot better.

When we walked past the flagpole after morning activities, we noticed that the flag was in place. "Do you think Melissa will get her underwear back?" I asked.

"Jeez! Who cares? It's just underwear! You act like you've never had a practical joke played on you."

"Have *you*?" I asked, because I couldn't imagine Reb ever being a victim.

"Are you kidding? *All* the time. I live with the two biggest practical jokers on the planet—my dad and Zach."

Jennifer raised her eyebrows. "Really? Like what do they do?"

Reb rolled her eyes. "Oh anything and everything. Too many to count." She paused for a second. "Like this one time—the first time we ever went skiing. I was just a tiny kid, about five I think, and I was terrified of riding the lifts. So Dad said he'd ride with me, and when we were way up high, he rocked our chair back and forth, and he looked all panicked, and he goes, 'Uh-oh, I think there's an avalanche coming!' When we got to the top of the lift, Dad practically had to peel my fingernails out of the back of the chair. He laughed his butt off over that one. And Zach, he'd pinned a note to the back of my jacket that said, 'Throw snowballs at me,' and I couldn't figure out why this group of boys kept laughing and pelting me with snowballs."

Jennifer had slowed down so she was walking slightly behind Reb. She gave me this look—her forehead wrinkled, her mouth hanging open. I looked back at her and raised one eyebrow, like, *I know! I can't believe it either!* But we both knew to keep our mouths shut.

"A few practical jokes never hurt anyone," Reb went on. "They toughen you up, keep you on your guard. I mean, just look at Melissa. Don't you think she could use a little toughening up?"

Jennifer and I were quiet, and Reb looked at us both. "Well?"

"Absolutely," said Jennifer.

I was glad Jennifer had said something, because I didn't want to answer that question. The morning had started off so exciting—I could hardly wait to see the Little Mermaid underwear in daylight. But now I had a sad feeling in my stomach. I couldn't stop picturing a little five-year-old Reb being pelted with snowballs and tormented on a ski lift by her own father. And I was still kind of worried about whether Melissa would ever get her undies back.

So Reb and Melissa actually had something in common—they'd both been picked on. But Reb had been picked on by her own family. How weird was that? Which was worse? To have your family tease you, or ds—like at school or camp? So far nobody had really picked on me, except one time in second grade this boy, Jacob Townsend, kept sticking his pencil in my hair. Ms. McCord moved him to another desk, and then he didn't bother me again.

But you just never knew when the crowd might turn on you for no reason. Anyone could be the victim. It was so hard to predict.

CHAPTER

## Friday, June 27

"Well, that was exhausting." I peeled off my grimy jeans and collapsed on my bunk. We'd just gotten back from a three-mile hike to Lookout Point.

Reb was sprawled across her cot too. Jennifer stood in front of the mirror and clenched her teeth. I wondered what kind of face she made before she got braces.

"A swim in the lake would be great right now," Reb suggested. "Can't you just feel that cold water?" Her blond hair was all sweaty and stuck against her neck.

"Yeah," I moaned. "Why don't you carry me down there and throw me in?"

Just then Melissa walked in. She kind of glanced at us like she wanted to walk right out the door again, but she didn't.

"Hi," I said, because I never wanted to completely ostracize her.

"Hi," she answered, but she didn't really look at me.

Reb sat up and waved at her like she was her BFF. "Hey there, MA-LISS-AH! So, how've ya been? Liking camp so far? Whaddaya think of the food? Been getting lots of e-mails from Mom and Dad? World been treatin' ya . . . okay?" Reb was talking really fast, like an auctioneer.

"I guess so," Melissa said, glancing at Reb and then looking away.

"Really? That's SUPER! I'm *glad* to hear it!" Reb shouted.

Melissa turned her back to us and put on her robe, then slung a towel over her shoulder. She edged out the door like she was afraid Reb was going to pounce on her.

"See ya!" Reb yelled, all cheerful, and gave her another big wave. Then she looked at us, all sad. "Gee whiz. She's not very friendly."

"Maybe we should just leave her alone." I meant it to sound like, *Yeah, you're right, she's not friendly, so let's just leave her alone*, but it didn't come out right. There was this huge silence. Jennifer looked at Reb, then me, then back at Reb.

"What do you mean by that?" Reb asked. She locked her eyes on me, and it made me nervous.

"Nothing. Just—you know, she obviously wants to avoid us, so . . ."

Reb sat there with this really straight look on her face. She didn't look mad or threatening, but she kept looking at me like she was waiting for me to say something else.

"Are we going swimming?" I asked. I got up to get my suit from my trunk.

"I don't know, Kelly. Is that what you want to do?" Reb asked.

"Yeah, I guess. If you guys want to." I tried not to look at her.

"Okay, then. Let's go." We all changed clothes, but everyone was pretty quiet. As we were leaving, Jennifer said, "This will feel good. I hope the water's freezing." She glanced at me, then at Reb, trying to read the signs.

"Yeah, me too," I said. Reb stared straight ahead. The only thing worse than her staring at me was the silent treatment.

We were walking past Solitary and the showers when Reb stopped us all of a sudden. "Do you see what I see? Over the door of Shower Number Two?" She pointed.

There were six showers in a row, each with a green wooden door and a big white number painted on it. Hanging over the door of Shower 2, we could see

Melissa's white robe and baby blue towel—the same ones she'd walked out with five minutes ago.

Reb put her arms around both of our necks, like we were in a football huddle. She was kind of smiling. "This is soooooo tempting. So, so tempting." She looked at Jennifer, then at me. "What do you say, triplets? Should we? Or shouldn't we?"

Usually Jennifer would be all over it, but this time she kept quiet and looked at me. Now, all of a sudden, Reb was her old self, and she was talking to me again.

"This is too good to pass up," I said. There was nothing else I could say.

Reb's grin was a mile wide. "Okay, who wants to do it?"

I looked at the door and then back at Reb. "I will. I'm a pretty fast runner." We were still huddled together, and Reb grabbed my shoulder, like she was pepping me up for the big play. "Okay. Try not to make too much noise. If you're fast enough, she might not even see them go."

I headed straight for the showers. My heart was beating faster. I could hear the water running inside the stall. The towel and robe were right in front of me. All I had to do was reach out and grab them. I held my hand up. I could feel Jennifer and Reb behind me, watching. With one quick move, I grabbed the towel and robe and pulled them over the top of the door. I clutched them against my chest and took off running. Did someone yell inside the shower? I wasn't sure. I was halfway down the line now, running as fast as I could. I crashed through the cabin door with Reb and Jennifer right behind me. My heart pounded in my chest, and I was gasping for breath.

I held up the towel and robe to show them. "Now what?" I panted.

Reb looked around. "Quick! Put it with the other ones!" She pointed to a stack of identical blue towels on the wooden shelf by Melissa's bed. In a rush, I folded it up and stuck it under the others at the bottom of the stack.

"What about the robe?" I yelled, holding it up and looking around.

"Just hang it up someplace!" Jennifer shouted.

I grabbed an empty wire hanger from the metal rod that was over the beds and hung the robe up with the other clothes. Then we ran out the door, crashing right into Jordan and Molly coming back from their riding lesson.

"What's with you?" Molly yelled at us, jumping out of our way.

"Nothing! Sorry!" Reb yelled as we ran down the line.

"Over here." Reb led us to some bushes between Cabin 4 and Solitary. We could see the showers from here, but we were kind of hidden from anyone walking by.

"Is she still in there?" Jennifer wondered.

"Of course she is," Reb said. "Nobody's seen a naked streak go by at a hundred miles an hour, have they?" We all laughed at the thought.

Jennifer gave us a sly look. "How *is* she going to get out of there?"

Reb shrugged. "She can just waltz right out the door anytime she wants. It's not like we *locked* her in there. Anyway, this *is* a girls' camp. Big deal if she's naked."

Jennifer snorted. "Reb, you know Miss Modest is never coming out of there without a towel on. She'll stay there till Closing Day if she has to."

"Jennifer's right. Maybe we should give them back now," I said. I have to admit—it had been a huge rush to steal them in the first place, but now . . . well, there was really no way for her to get out of the shower unless we gave them back.

"Oh, good idea," Reb said, "and then let's beg her forgiveness for short-sheeting her and flying her underwear up the flagpole."

"Well, how long should she stay in there?" I asked. I'd let her call all the shots.

"Shhh, someone's coming," Reb said. "It's Erin."

From our hideout, we could see Erin walking down the line, and as she passed the showers, she stopped and looked around. We could tell that the door to Shower 2 had opened a little, and Erin was talking to the person hidden inside. Then she looked around and walked away.

Jennifer stared at us. "She's leaving her in there?" she whispered.

"Don't count on it. She's probably getting her a towel," Reb said.

She was right. Five minutes later Erin was back, carrying a baby blue towel just like the one that had mysteriously disappeared. Then Melissa came out of the shower stall with the towel around her. Her wet hair was plastered against her head, and her ears stuck through it. She looked even more pathetic than usual. Well, at least she'd gotten out of there. She was really only stranded in there a couple of minutes.

Melissa and Erin were whispering together. "I don't know! I didn't see them!" I heard Melissa say. They went to the cabin.

Jennifer sighed. "Too bad. Fun's over."

"Not quite. It's probably just beginning. Let's go."

Back at the cabin, Reb burst through the door.

"Hey, cabinmates, what's new?" Melissa was rummaging through her open trunk, still wrapped in the towel. Molly and Jordan were on Side B, acting extremely interested in their card game.

Erin stood by the door and frowned at us. "Melissa was taking a shower, and somebody stole her robe and towel." She looked at us like, *Quit being such jerks*. Erin was way too mature to ever play any pranks like ours. I felt stupid in front of her.

"Really?" Reb gasped, all shocked. "Your things were stolen! That's terrible! Hope you had name tags in them. We'll keep an eye out for them." She had her hands behind her back, and she looked all concerned. "What'd they look like?"

Melissa slammed her trunk closed and gave Reb a killer look. "Well, it just so happens—I found both my towel and my robe when I got back." She waved to where we'd put her stuff away. She was trying to sound sarcastic, but her voice was all quavery.

"No kidding? Maybe you just forgot to take them with you, huh?"

"Oh, right! I just walked down to the showers naked! I know you guys did it. Don't deny it." She was madder than I'd ever seen her.

"Now what makes you so sure of that? We were at

the lake," Reb said. All three of us had on swimsuits.

"Oh, really? How come you're not wet?"

On the verge of hysterics, Melissa had still managed to point out this minor inconsistency in our story.

"Jennifer got her period, so we had to come back."

"*Reb!*" Jennifer slapped her on the arm, all embarrassed.

"Look, Melissa," Reb went on. "I'm just as upset as you are. I certainly don't want to see you naked." Then we walked out the door.

At least Melissa didn't cry. I was glad about that.

## CHAPTER

### Tuesday, July 1

"Hey, Jennifer, race you!" Reb and I were paddling around in one canoe, and Jennifer was by herself in another.

"You must be joking. I can't even get this stupid thing to go straight."

"How about if I paddle with you?" I offered. I looked over my shoulder at Reb in the stern. "Do you mind?"

"Fine with me." Reb made little circles in the water with her paddle.

"Let's go back to shore so I can get in with Jennifer."

"No way. That's on the other side of the lake. Just climb in. We're close enough."

We had paddled over to Jennifer, and she reached out to grab the gunwales of our canoe to pull us even closer.

I gave Jennifer my paddle and stood up slowly because moving around made the canoe rock a little. Carefully I put one foot in Jennifer's canoe and was about to bring the other leg across when she let go of the side. That made the canoes drift apart, and I lost my balance. I heard Reb yell, "Whoa!" just as I hit the water.

Green lake water swallowed me up for a couple of seconds before I could come up for air. The water was so cold it kind of shocked me, falling in like that.

"Are you okay?" Reb yelled. I'd come up between the two canoes, and I couldn't see either her or Jennifer.

"Yeah, fine," I answered. I snorted to get the water out of my nose and flipped the wet hair out of my eyes.

"Wow, that was worth seeing." Reb sounded like she was trying not to laugh.

"Just get me back in before I freeze to death, okay?"

Jennifer was trying to help me in. It wasn't easy because when I was climbing in, the canoe was tilting like crazy. Jennifer came real close to falling out on top of me.

When I finally got in and sat down, Reb and Jennifer both looked like they'd just wiped smiles off their faces. I tried to look mad, but then I started laughing, which made them both laugh too.

"I'll have to change now!" I complained. "Take me back to shore."

So we paddled back across the lake. Michelle Burns, the canoeing counselor, looked at us like we were a bunch of goofs. She was busy with serious canoers who went on river trips, and I could tell she was a little annoyed that we were playing around.

"Did you have a little trouble?" she asked us as I climbed out of the canoe.

"Yeah. Those two—they're a bad influence. I've got to change."

Reb dragged her canoe up on the bank and then waded out into the water to climb in with Jennifer. "Well, hurry. You can paddle solo when you get back."

"Aren't you coming with me?" I looked at them both.

"Hey, you're the one who needs to change, not us," said Jennifer, which made me mad. I never would've fallen in if I hadn't been trying to help her.

"Just hurry and come back," said Reb. "We'll be waiting for you."

I could tell they weren't going anywhere. I thought about just staying in my wet clothes, but it was cloudy and I was already starting to shiver.

As I walked away, I saw Libby Sheppard waving at me. She was across the lake, giving a swimming lesson. Ever since that night in Solitary, Libby had been really nice to me, smiling every time she saw me and always saying hi. I felt bad. She thought of me as a sweet little homesick camper who needed some extra attention. Little did she know I was a bold-faced liar.

I walked up the hill, my shoes squishing with every step. I was really shivering now. Thick clouds covered the sky, and it looked like it was going to rain.

When I got to the cabin, I was about to walk in when I heard something. I flattened myself against the wall and ducked down so I wouldn't be seen through the screen.

Inside, somebody was crying. Slowly I raised my head up. I pressed my forehead against the screen so I could look inside the dark cabin without being seen.

I already had a pretty good idea who it was, and I was right. I could just see the end of Melissa's bed, and she was lying there, facedown, crying into her pillow. I ducked down again to keep out of sight.

Great. I really needed to change. My clothes were absolutely sopping wet. I couldn't go back to the lake like this. But I didn't want to go in there now and face Melissa. What was wrong with her, anyway? Well, I had a pretty good idea. I stood there, trying to decide what to do. Then it sounded like the crying stopped. I was about to take off running because I was afraid she'd come out the door any second now, and she'd catch me. But then I heard her moving around inside. So very carefully, I stood up a little to peek inside again.

What I saw almost gave me a heart attack. Melissa was kneeling over Reb's trunk, digging through all her stuff! I couldn't believe it! I was catching her in the act of stealing something from Reb's trunk! But wait, that wasn't it. She was *searching* it.

She was going through all of Reb's stuff very carefully, and she looked like she was trying to put everything back where she'd found it. If she was looking for something to steal, she was being awfully selective.

Then she closed the lid. And next she moved on to Jennifer's trunk! Now I had no doubt. Melissa was definitely looking for *something*.

I couldn't believe it! I freaking couldn't believe what I was seeing. Should I go get Reb and Jennifer right now? Or just burst in and catch her in the act? Before I could make up my mind, Melissa made it up for me. Because when she'd finished with Jennifer's trunk, she moved over to mine! Now she'd really gone too far. I jumped right up and rushed for the door. I slammed the screen door open as I burst inside. Melissa was still sitting there in front of my open trunk when she turned around.

"You better shut that trunk before I slam it on your *face!*"

# CHAPTER 19

Melissa was so shocked, she almost fell right into my open trunk. I was furious! It was bad enough that I'd seen her looking through my best friends' trunks, but here I'd caught her—red-handed—looking through mine.

"What do you think you're *doing*?"

Her mouth hung open and she was still frozen, squatting there in front of my trunk. "Ah. . . ." That was all she could manage to say.

"And not just *my* trunk. I was watching you! I saw you going through Reb's and Jennifer's trunks. Are you *stealing* from us?" I yelled. I stood there, dripping wet, my arms crossed in front of my chest. I felt like I had to hold myself in so I didn't punch her.

She drew back a little, staring at me. "Why are you so wet?"

"I fell in the freaking lake! What are you doing in my trunk?"

Melissa glanced down at the open lid. One of my shirts had fallen out and was lying on the wood floor. She knew she was busted. "I . . . I lost something," she finally mumbled.

"Lost something? Well, you didn't lose it in Reb's or Jennifer's trunks, and I can guarantee you didn't lose it in *mine*!"

Melissa frowned at me. "I know this looks terrible. But honestly, I was just looking for something of mine. I've looked everywhere for it. Maybe I lost it." Then she looked directly at me. "Or maybe it was stolen."

My mouth fell open. "Okay, let me get this straight. I catch you searching all our trunks, and now you're accusing us of stealing? We would never steal anything."

"Oh, no!" Melissa yelled all of a sudden. "No, *you* wouldn't do *that*." Even though she was mad, her voice was all quavery. "But you *would* short-sheet a person's bed, and you *would* take a person's towel when she's in the shower, and you *would* fly a person's underwear from the flagpole for the whole camp to see and laugh at! You *would* do all *those* things, but you would never *steal* anything!"

She was so obviously out of line, going through our trunks. But now . . . now I couldn't think of how to turn things back around to blaming her. We just stood there, glaring at each other. There was a little puddle around my shoes where I'd dripped. My arms and legs were all broken out in goose bumps, and I just wanted to put on some dry clothes. I wasn't looking for some major fight.

"What did you lose, anyway?" I finally asked her.

"My bracelet!"

And then she started to cry. Not a little sniffle, with tears welling up in her eyes. She was bawling. Out loud. "I lost my bracelet! My grandmother gave it to me! It was hers when she was young. And she died last year!" Man. She was sobbing!

"I never take it off. Except to swim or take a shower. And then I always put it in a safe place in my trunk. And now it's gone! It's lost forever!"

I just stood there, shocked by how upset she was. I should say something. Or do something. I just didn't know what. What I really wanted to do more than anything was just walk out the door. But she was crying so hard, I was kind of scared she might hyperventilate or rupture a blood vessel or something. She sat down on her bed, and now she was holding her head in her hands and was making that hiccuping sound you make when you've been crying for a really long time.

Finally, after standing there for what seemed like an hour, with her crying and me dripping, very quietly I went over to my trunk. It was still open. I got out some dry clothes and changed as fast as I could.

Now I could leave, but I knew I had to say something. "Look, Melissa. I'm sorry you lost your bracelet. Obviously it means a lot to you. But I swear—we didn't steal it."

"Oh, and I'm supposed to take your word for it?" She looked up at me. Her face was all blotchy, and her eyes were red and swollen, but also full of anger that almost looked like hatred. "Why do you go along with them on *everything*? Why are you so *mean* to me?"

I never tried to be mean. Reb was always coming up with these ideas, and . . . I just went along with them. Melissa never seemed that upset about it, until now.

I hung up my wet clothes so I'd have something to do, but I could feel her staring at me. "It was just a few practical jokes. It's not like we hate you."

"You used to be my friend. And then you got in with Reb and Jennifer. That was the worst part. I never expected the Evil Twins to be nice, but I thought you were."

I felt like Melissa had given me a karate chop on the back of my neck. All along, I'd thought I was the nice one. But then I knew. Reb and Jennifer could have done anything—set Melissa's bed on fire, tied her to an anthill, shaved her head and made her go naked to the dance. None of that was as bad as me making "tinkle, tinkle" jokes after we'd gone canoeing together that day. It was worse. Worse for me to do what I did than anything they could've done to her. Melissa didn't expect them to be nice to her. But she'd thought for a little while that I was her friend.

All I wanted was to be to a triplet. A Terrible Triplet.

Melissa's eyes were boring through my back. I stood there with my back to her, both my feet cemented to the floor. "Want me to help you look for your bracelet?" I asked softly over my shoulder.

"Don't bother."

I didn't turn around to face her.

"Well, I hope you find it."

I walked out the door and headed toward the lake. But I could still feel that karate chop.

# CHAPTER 20

When I finally got back to the lake, morning activities were just ending, and everyone was pulling the canoes ashore.

"What took you so long?" asked Reb. "Did you get lost?"

"Really? I wasn't gone *that* long."

Reb and Jennifer came out of the shed where they'd hung up their paddles. Reb stared at me. "Are you okay?"

"Of course I'm okay. Why wouldn't I be?" Could they tell by looking at me what had just happened? Was my face still red?

Reb shrugged. "I don't know. You just look a little funny."

"I'm fine!" The last thing I needed right now was the third degree.

"Good. Then let's go."

"Go where?"

"Back to the cabin, of course. You know—hang out, wait for lunch. Do what we do pretty much every day." Reb looked at me.

"Oh, yeah. I guess activities are over now." I took a deep breath, trying to act normal. But as we walked to the cabin, my stomach was doing backflips. What if Melissa was still there?

Would she still be in the middle of a nervous breakdown? Would she accuse them of stealing her bracelet too? She wouldn't if she knew what was good for her, but she was practically out of her mind right now. Who knew what crazy thing she might try? I couldn't take any more drama. At least not in the next fifteen minutes.

I held my breath and crossed my fingers behind my back. If only I could think of some excuse for us not to go back to the cabin. But I couldn't. Anyway, they'd see right through that, and then they'd be really suspicious, wondering why I was trying to keep them away.

Reb opened the screen door and walked in first, with Jennifer behind her. When the roof didn't blow off and things didn't explode all over the place, I followed them. A quick glance around, and I saw that Molly and Jordan were on Side B, but otherwise no one else was there. I breathed for the first time in ten minutes.

"Hey, guys. What's up?" asked Reb.

"Nothing much," they answered, and since they looked completely normal, I assumed they hadn't seen Melissa crying. All our trunks were closed, and everything looked the way it was supposed to. Whew. I was so relieved I plopped down on my bunk.

"I don't know about you guys, but I need a shower," said Reb. "I smell like a frog." She opened up her trunk to get her stuff. And then she froze. She turned around really slowly and looked at Jennifer and me.

"Somebody's been in my trunk."

My heart sprang up to my mouth. I had to swallow to get it back in my chest where it belonged. I sat up on the edge of my bunk.

"What?" yelled Jennifer, all shocked. I tried to look surprised too.

Reb had this really stunned look on her face. "My stuff is moved."

"How can you tell?" I asked. It was a stupid question, because her trunk is the most organized space in the entire camp. I think she was a drill sergeant in a former life.

"Because my stuff is moved around and out of place. My clothes are rumpled up—someone's been in here."

"Who do you think did it?" asked Jennifer. The worst thing anyone could do was go through your trunk. We didn't have any privacy or any personal space, except for our trunks.

Reb just looked at Jennifer. "Do I even have to say?"

"But why? Did she steal anything?" asked Jennifer, which was a logical question.

Reb turned back, like she hadn't even thought of that. She spent about ten minutes sorting through her stuff very carefully. "I don't think so," she said, all cautious.

If Reb hadn't noticed, I never would've said anything, but she did. I opened my mouth, but the story was stuck way down in my throat, like an old popcorn kernel. I either needed to cough it up or swallow it.

"Oh my gosh, I ought to check my trunk too!" Jennifer yelled all of a sudden. She rushed over and began searching it.

Melissa might as well have left a signed note saying, *While you were out, I searched all your trunks because I think you stole something of mine. Hope you don't mind.*

"I think everything's okay," Jennifer said after examining all her stuff.

Reb looked at me. "You're awfully quiet. What about your trunk?"

"I'm just so shocked she'd be stupid enough to do this," I said.

Then I knelt in front of my trunk and looked through it. "Well, I don't see any obvious clues. It's a mess, like always." It still amazed me that Reb could glance at her trunk and tell immediately that somebody had been through her stuff. I wouldn't notice if a pack of baboons was nesting in my trunk.

"She must have done it this morning. Did you notice anything strange when you came back to change?"

*Yeah. Melissa was scrounging through your trunk like a cop with a search warrant. That was pretty strange.* "Not really," I said.

"I just know Melissa's behind this." Reb shook her head. "We've been doing stuff to her, she probably got mad, and now she's trying to get back at us."

"But nothing is missing," I tried to point out. If I could just convince Reb this wasn't such a big deal, maybe I could prevent a possible murder.

"How do we know she was trying to steal something? She could have been trying to . . . sabotage us. You know, pour shampoo on our clothes or squeeze toothpaste into our shoes." Reb closed her trunk and frowned. "I *hate* people going through my stuff. Especially here at camp where there's no privacy anyway. Anybody who'd do something like that . . ." Reb pressed her lips together. She was beyond mad. She was seething.

"What are we going to do?" Jennifer asked.

"I don't know yet. But we're *not* going to let this go."

I knew we were in for a major battle. But there was nothing I could do. I hadn't coughed up the popcorn kernel. I'd swallowed it. So there was no turning back.

When afternoon activities started, Reb watched Melissa like a hawk to see where she was going, and without even waiting for me and Jennifer to follow her, she took off after her. Jennifer and I just looked at each other like, *Oh, great. Here we go.*

Melissa walked down Middler Line with Reb right behind her. With Jennifer and me behind Reb, we looked like some weird parade. I could tell by looking at Melissa's back that she knew she was being followed. She walked with her body all tensed, and she'd turn her head a little bit like she wanted to look over her shoulder but didn't dare.

After we passed the lake, I figured out that Melissa was heading to the riflery range. We were on a dirt path that went through the woods, and all around us the locusts were buzzing in the trees. The idea of Reb and Melissa being around lethal weapons made me incredibly nervous.

Then we got to the riflery range. It was just a wooden platform with a roof over the top, kind of hidden in among all the trees. On the platform were bare mattresses for the shooters, who would lie on their stomachs and prop themselves up on their elbows to shoot. Across from the platform were the stands for tacking up the paper targets. There were girls already there shooting, and we could hear the cracking sound the rifles made.

Finally Reb caught up with Melissa and stopped her.

"I need to talk to you, Melissa."

Melissa turned around. The two of them stood on the path, face to face. Jennifer and I were a little behind Reb, keeping quiet. Melissa looked a little nervous, but she also looked kind of defiant, which was a first. "About what?"

"Somebody's been snooping around in our trunks. All our stuff's moved around and messed up. Do you know anything about that?"

Melissa glanced past Reb's shoulder and looked at me. I shook my head very slightly. The look on her face told me she'd gotten my meaning.

"Why are you asking me?"

"Gee—let's see. Somebody was snooping in my trunk, and Jennifer's trunk, and Kelly's trunk. You're the only other person on our side of the cabin. I doubt Rachel or any of the Side B guys did it. I'd say that makes you a prime suspect."

Melissa looked at me again, and I looked back at her. All she had to do was deny everything. Just keep quiet. Not admit to a thing.

"Well, aren't you a real girl detective!" she said, all sarcastic. Jennifer and I looked at each other in shock. Where did mousy Melissa get off with such a gutsy answer? But she wasn't even done.

"It just so happens I've got a mystery of my own. My favorite bracelet is gone. I think somebody stole it. Maybe the Girl Detective can solve that one." Melissa crossed her arms and looked Reb dead in the eye. The pop of rifle fire sounded like firecrackers.

Reb stared at her, obviously not having a clue what she was implying. "SO?"

"Don't you get it? Cabin 1 has two mysteries: your invaded trunks and my missing bracelet. If you solve either one of them, let me know."

Reb looked confused for a second, but then the lightbulb over her head finally went on. "Are you saying you looked in my trunk for your stupid bracelet?"

"It's not stupid. It's very valuable. A family heirloom. It was my grandmother's."

"I don't care if it's Queen Elizabeth's! Did you search my trunk?"

"Did you steal my bracelet?" asked Melissa.

"Are you asking me or accusing me?" said Reb.

"Seems like you're accusing me of trespassing," Melissa shot back.

"Seems like I have a reason to. But there's one big difference here. You've basically admitted going through my stuff. But I didn't steal your bracelet."

"Look, all I care about is getting my bracelet back. You can take anything else of mine. Anything. I don't care. But I've got to have my bracelet." Melissa's voice shook a little, and I thought she was going to start bawling again, but she didn't. "It can't be replaced. I just want you to know that."

"I did not steal your bracelet! Are you going to stand there and say I did?"

"Considering all the things you've done to me, I wouldn't put anything past you, Rebecca Callison. Not even theft."

"You're calling me a *thief*? Is that what I'm hearing?"

Was Melissa shaking? I couldn't tell. Could Reb see

that she was shaking? Melissa put her hands on her hips and looked right at Reb. "Did I stutter?"

Reb was actually stunned. I saw her freeze for a split second. Nobody ever challenged her like that. Ever. But then she recovered.

Reb's voice was a whisper. An unbelievably creepy whisper. "Excuse me, but have we met? Do you even know who I am?"

Just listening to it made me break out in goose bumps, and she wasn't even talking to me. She stepped up to within inches of Melissa's face. They were practically nose to nose. Melissa drew back a fraction, and there was sheer terror in her eyes. But she stood her ground.

"Let me introduce myself," Reb whispered. Slowly, very slowly, she reached down, picked up Melissa's hand, and shook it. "I am your worst nightmare."

And when Reb said that, I knew it was all over. No hope of a peace treaty. She'd formally declared war.

# CHAPTER 22

## Wednesday, July 2

After lunch there was a huge stampede, with everyone trying to get through the dining hall doors at the same time. We all wanted to check our little wooden cubbyholes on the dining hall porch for one thing—to see if we got any mail. Every single day I got a huge thrill at this time because I never knew—would I get any mail today?

I'd been pretty lucky all summer. Hardly a day went by when I didn't get at least one letter or e-mail. But when I reached into my mailbox and pulled out an envelope with a Camp Crockett insignia on it, I almost fainted right there on the dining hall porch. Above the insignia was a name printed in ink: Ethan Hurley.

Ethan had written me a letter! My heart was pounding so hard I could barely breathe.

It's kind of stupid, but that moment was one of the happiest in my life. I hadn't even read what he'd said, but right now, the world was absolutely perfect.

Reb and Jennifer came up beside me. I was still in a daze.

"Get any mail?" asked Reb.

I looked at her and Jennifer. "A letter from Ethan. The Camp Crockett guy." I held it up and showed them the envelope, and my hands were actually shaking a little.

"OMIGOD! OMIGOD! OMIGOD!" Jennifer screamed. "Open it!" Everyone turned around and looked at us.

Being very careful not to tear the envelope too much—I didn't want to demolish the first letter I'd ever gotten from a boy—I opened it up and started reading. Jennifer and Reb were breathing down my neck, and I kept moving to keep them from reading over my shoulder.

Hey Kelly

What's up? I guess you heard we're gonna have another dance on Sat. That's pretty cool, huh? Dustin says he's going to ask Melissa to dance again. What a stud, huh? I was in the doubles

tennis tournament last week. Me and my partner
did pretty good but we got elliminited. Hope your
having fun at Pine Haven. Camp's okay but I'm
really looking forward to my birthday in August,
plus we go on vacation to Hilton Head SC then
too. I'll send you a postcard if you give me your
home address. See ya Sat.

Ethan

"What'd it say? You are sooo lucky. I hate you," said
Jennifer.

Reb was chanting, "Read it! Read it! Read it!"

"You guys, leave me alone. Can't I have any privacy?"

"No, none. We're your sisters. C'mon, you guys
always make me read my e-mails from Wes," said Reb,
coming up to take the letter out of my hand.

"Okay, fine, but be careful with it! Don't get your
grimy fingerprints on it!"

Reb laughed and held up her hands. "Okay—we
won't lay our grimy hands on it, but hold it still so we
can read it."

So I held the letter for them while they read it. When
they'd finished, Jennifer sighed. "Should I write Curtis?
Just to let him know I haven't forgotten him?"

"Sure, if you want to," I said, but I never would've had the nerve to write Ethan if he hadn't written me first. "But what should I do now? Should I write him back?" I had to play things just right. I didn't want to screw this up.

"Yeah, definitely," said Reb. "Just to let him know you got it. But keep it casual, like he did. Like, 'Yeah, the next dance is coming up. Guess I'll see you there.' Casual."

Jennifer nodded. "Reb's right. You should write him, but don't make a big deal out of it."

I nodded and sighed. It was a *huge* relief having friends advise me on the next move. I was so glad I had Reb and Jennifer.

Reb grinned at me, hooking her arm around my shoulder. "That's cool he wrote you. It's definitely a sign he likes you."

I tried not to smile as I carefully folded the letter and put it back in its envelope. "You guys will help me figure out what to say?"

"Absolutely."

All during rest hour, I lay on my bunk and scribbled out different drafts of letters to Ethan. I figured Jennifer was working on a letter on the top bunk to her Camp Crockett guy too, because I could actually hear her pen scratching on paper. Melissa was on her cot, her back to the rest of us. She seemed to be napping, but maybe she was faking it so she didn't have to look at us.

Reb was lying flat on her back, staring up at the rafters. That was weird. She wasn't preparing herself for Harvard or Yale, like usual. Since yesterday, Reb had become totally obsessed with how to get back at Melissa. Things had gotten even more tense. Yesterday Melissa had told Rachel about her missing bracelet, and Rachel gave the three of us the third degree. Reb was furious.

"Give me a lie detector test! Get me a stack of Bibles to swear on!" she'd yelled. I wasn't sure if Rachel believed us or not. She'd made us all search the cabin— under the bunks, in the corners, behind all our trunks. But of course we didn't find the bracelet.

All of a sudden Reb sat up with a big grin on her face and got a pad of paper out of her trunk. Was she going to help me write my letter? Or work algebra problems?

"What're you doing?" I whispered, but Rachel shushed me.

Reb had this excited look on her face. "I've got it!" she whispered back. Another shush from Rachel. If we said anything else, she'd keep us ten extra minutes after rest hour. She was a regular slave driver at times.

When the bell rang, Melissa sat up, put her shoes on, and left. She'd definitely been faking. I knew she was still really upset about her bracelet. But what could we do? We hadn't done anything.

Jennifer and I waited for Reb, but she still sat cross-legged on her cot, writing away.

"Okay, ladies. Out the door. You'll be late for afternoon activities," said Rachel.

"I gotta finish this letter to my mommy. I'm telling her what an inspiration and role model you are, and obviously that takes a long time," Reb answered, not looking up from her paper.

"Move it. Out the door. Rest hour's over." Rachel was afraid that if she left us in the cabin, we'd cut activities and wind up cabin-sitting.

"All done!" Reb announced happily. She folded up the paper and stuffed it into her shorts pocket.

We walked down Middler Line in the crowd of girls, but Reb said she needed to stop in Solitary. When she came out, she looked around and said, "Let's go back and get our tennis rackets. We forgot them."

But obviously we weren't going back for our rackets. By now the cabin was empty. Reb plopped down on her cot and looked up at Jennifer and me with that same huge grin on her face.

"Kelly's love letter got me thinking. I know what we're going to do to Melissa."

Reb pulled the folded papers out of her pocket and looked up to make sure she had our attention. Then she cleared her throat and started reading:

Dear Dustin,

I bet you're surprised to get a letter from me. I can't believe I'd ever be brave enough to write to a guy, but here goes. You may have gotten the idea that I didn't like you. Well, you're wrong. With the next dance coming up, you're all I've been thinking about. Although I'm practically dying of embarrassment telling you all this, I really like you. But when we were slow dancing, I was so nervous I could barely talk to you.

I know I walked away and left you standing there, and I feel so stupid. But that was my first slow dance, and I was a little nervous about it. I'm hoping to see you Saturday, and maybe we can dance again. And this time, during a slow dance, I promise I won't walk away. Maybe we can go out on the porch. The counselors here always joke about being on Porch Patrol, but they can't watch us every second. I've never kissed a boy, but I'm hoping that will change. Soon.

See you Saturday.

Love,
Melissa Bledsoe

Jennifer shook her head in amazement. "Are you really going to mail that?"

"Of course! Isn't this the *perfect* revenge? I knew I'd come up with something. I just didn't know it would be this good."

Jennifer looked in the mirror and said to her reflection, "I would die if somebody sent a letter like that to a boy from me. I don't know which is worse—sending it to a boy you like or to one you can't stand."

"Melissa would never write a letter like that," I pointed out. Reb couldn't seriously be thinking about sending it. This was way too much.

"I know that. But how does Dustin know that?"

"What do you think he'll do when he gets the letter?" wondered Jennifer.

"At the dance he'll be all over her. He'll make her night miserable!"

"I don't know, Reb. It's almost too much. Haven't we done enough to her already?" I asked.

"Too much? *Too much?* I'll tell you what was too much. Going through our trunks was too much. Calling us thieves and liars right to our faces was too much. Telling Rachel we had something to do with her missing bracelet was too much. You think this is too much? Hey, the way I see it, I'm letting her off easy."

I was actually kind of scared of Reb at that moment. Her face was all red and flushed. She looked mad at *me*. I kept quiet.

Reb looked at me steadily. "We're together on this, aren't we? We're triplets, right?" She held up her wrist-band to remind me. She usually thought the whole wristband thing was stupid, but now of course it was all for one, and one for all.

What could I say to that? The one thing I'd learned was how hard it was to say no to Reb.

"We'll always be triplets," said Jennifer, holding out her arm to show her wristband. I nodded and held out mine, too. But I felt like a traitor. The weird thing was, I felt like a traitor to everyone—Reb, Jennifer, and Melissa. But who was I betraying? I couldn't betray everyone at the same time. So who was it?

Reb seemed satisfied. She looked around. "Remember that personalized paper we saw when we were short-sheeting her? Let's use some of that." She found the stack of paper on the shelf by Melissa's bed. It had a border of little purple flowers around it, and across the top in type like cursive handwriting it said, "From Melissa."

"Perfect! Absolutely perfect!" Reb took a couple of sheets off the stack. "She probably won't miss these," she added with a grin. Then she sat cross-legged on her cot while she copied the letter onto Melissa's stationery. It was so believable this way, with Melissa's name on it. But then, that's the way Reb wanted it.

When she was done, she looked up at us. "Okay, if we mail it tomorrow, Dustin should get it Friday. He won't have time to write her back, but he'll have plenty of time to think about her before the dance on Saturday." She nodded her head, all satisfied that this was going to work great. "This is going to be the best revenge ever!"

## CHAPTER

## Saturday, July 5

"Does my hair look okay?" Jennifer asked again. It was the fifth time at least.

"No, it looks terrible. You really oughta go to the bathroom and fix it," I snapped.

Jennifer winced. "Jeez, what's with you?"

"Look, I'm sorry. I've told you it looks fine. Would you please stop asking?"

It wasn't her fault. We were all waiting in the dining hall for the Crockett boys to walk in. I was a nervous wreck. Reb, on the other hand, was absolutely cool and calm. She'd set her trap. Now all she had to do was sit back and watch.

But I didn't want to watch. I didn't want any part of it.

All day yesterday, I'd wanted to tell Melissa about the letter. But the day was all weird because of the Fourth of July. We didn't have any regular activities. We had a capture-the-flag game in the morning and a counselor hunt in the afternoon. Then everybody went skinny-dipping, and for dinner we ate hot dogs and ice cream outside on the hill and watched fireworks over the lake.

It should've been fun, but I kept walking up behind Melissa and then not doing anything. It was horrible. It was like needing to sneeze, but not being able to. I wanted to tell her. I just couldn't get it out. I'd be standing right by her, and I'd think, *Hey, Melissa.* But nothing ever came out. Plus Reb and Jennifer were always close by.

Anyway, maybe it was better *not* to tell her. Maybe nothing would happen. Maybe Dustin wouldn't do anything. Maybe Melissa would never even find out. If nothing happened, then it would be better if she never even knew the letter existed.

When the boys walked in, everybody got all excited. Right away I saw Ethan in the crowd. Should I walk up to him? Or wait for him to see me? Luckily he saw me and kind of waved. But then he just stood there talking to some guys.

Okay, what was up? Did I sound stupid in my letter?

Was he leading me on? What should I do? But then he walked toward me. Whew. I'd die if he ignored me.

"Hi, how ya doing?" he said. He was wearing an over-size striped polo and cargo shorts with big pockets. His hair looked even blonder than before.

"Good. I got your letter," I said, which was like the stupidest thing in the world to say, because I'd written him back. Obviously he already knew I'd gotten his letter.

"Yeah, I got yours, too."

"Cool. I wasn't sure if it would get there in time." Why was everything out of my mouth sounding absolutely ridiculous? I hadn't been this nervous at the first dance.

"Yeah, it did—yesterday. Thanks for writing back."

Then we didn't say anything for a few awkward, long moments, since we'd completely used up that topic of conversation.

"Oh, hey! Guess who else got a letter—Dustin! Melissa wrote *him* a letter!"

I cringed. Was this stupid letter going to ruin my evening with Ethan? "Oh. He told you about it?"

"Told us about it? He made us all read it about a hundred times. He wouldn't shut up about this Pine Haven babe who's in love with him. Nobody could believe it."

"Really?" I paused for a second. Should I tell him?

He'd find out eventually. "Can you keep a secret?" I asked. It gave me an excuse to lean close to him. He smelled like Axe, and from now on, whenever I smelled that, I would always think of Ethan Hurley. "The letter's a fake. We wrote it."

"*You* wrote it!" he yelled.

"Shhh!" I grabbed his arm. I loved having an excuse to grab his arm. "Keep it down! Reb wrote it. It was her idea." Might as well give credit where credit was due.

"But the sheet of paper said 'Melissa' and everything."

"Yeah. We lifted some of her personalized stationery to make it look legitimate."

"Wow! You guys are too evil!" Ethan marveled. "It did seem unbelievable that a girl would be so crazy about Dustin." He looked at me and nodded admiringly.

"Here you are! Do you want to miss *everything*?" Reb almost knocked us over when she ran up to us. "Dustin's going to move in on Melissa any second now!"

"But Reb, this is *your* project. I'm not going to spend the whole evening following Melissa and Dustin around. Why don't you get Jennifer?"

"Jennifer won't let what's-his-face out of her sight. It's me and you on this."

"Hey, and me!" said Ethan. "Kelly told me about it.

That's amazing! And Dustin fell for it. We all did. The whole cabin really thought Melissa wrote him."

Reb's eyes lit up. "You mean he told all his friends about it? Perfect! Things are going even better than I planned! Look—there's Melissa."

She was standing by some other girls, and Dustin was a few feet away. He'd obviously seen her, and now it looked like he was working up the nerve to go up to her. Finally he walked up, put his arm around her back, and tapped her on the far shoulder. She actually turned to the other side to see who it was, then looked around to see him standing next to her.

Melissa didn't say a word to him. But Dustin was talking. She kind of nodded, like she was listening to him jabber away. Then they started to dance. I couldn't believe it. She'd dance with this guy after what he did the last time? Maybe because all the songs now were fast. He wouldn't have a chance to grab her.

"Why don't *we* dance too?" I asked Ethan.

"You can't take off now," Reb protested. "Things are just getting started."

"Reb, I'm not going to watch their every move all night just in case Dustin burps in her face or something. There's nothing to see now."

"Just don't let them out of your sight. I'll be

watching them too," Reb told us.

At least we were dancing. It ought to give Reb some satisfaction that she'd managed to get Dustin and Melissa together too. Maybe if they danced a few dances together, she'd call it even. And then Melissa would never even know about the letter.

After a few songs, I'd almost forgotten about Melissa and Dustin. I was having a great time with Ethan, just like before. Then Reb came up behind us and grabbed me.

"Let's go. They're at the refreshment table now."

"Really? Let's go see which flavor cookie she picks out—chocolate chip or shortbread."

"Seriously. We need to go over there. Something's about to happen."

I rolled my eyes. "Reb, what do you expect? You think Dustin's gonna tear her clothes off? Or is Melissa gonna spit in his eye? They're *together*. What more do you want? Why do you think something else is going to happen?"

Reb just smiled at me. "Because I'm going to make it happen."

# CHAPTER 24

Ethan looked at me. "Come on. Let's see what she's up to."

Reb walked right up to Dustin and Melissa, standing by the refreshment table. Ethan and I went up too and got some drinks. Melissa obviously hated this guy. She looked like she just wanted to get away from him. Dustin didn't look too thrilled either. Melissa had been so crazy about him in "her" letter, and now she'd turned into a cold fish. If Reb expected some excitement from these two, I figured she'd be disappointed.

"Hey, Melissa, how's it going?" Reb asked, all friendly. But not in the tone she usually used with Melissa. She really sounded nice this time. Melissa tensed up when Reb approached her. She had the look she always had with Reb—like she was ready to break and run if Reb pounced on her. Obviously, she was suspicious that her worst nightmare suddenly wanted to have a chat with her.

Reb leaned close to Melissa. "So, are you having a good time?"

Melissa looked at her cautiously, then looked back at Dustin. "Not really."

Reb looked surprised. "Not really? But you two have been together all night. I think you make a cute couple."

Melissa looked nauseated. "I can't stand him. I want to get away from him."

Reb smiled at Ethan and me. "Well, if you don't like him, you shouldn't have written him that love letter."

Melissa looked at her. "I didn't write him."

"Oh, c'mon. Don't be embarrassed. Kelly wrote Ethan, too. It's no big deal to write a boy. But you really led Dustin on, Melissa. You shouldn't have written all that stuff if you don't really like him."

"What are you talking about?"

"Ethan says Dustin let everybody in the cabin read it. Oh, and your 'Melissa' stationery? What a sweet touch that was."

Melissa froze. She looked at me, then at Ethan, then back at Reb. "My stationery?" She looked over at Dustin, still standing by the refreshment table stuffing a cookie in his mouth. "What did you *do?*"

"It was your letter. Don't you remember all the stuff you wrote to Dustin? It was just a couple of days ago. Have you forgotten already?"

Melissa was about to walk off. Then she stopped and looked at Reb. "What did you . . . ? Tell me what you did." I could see tears welling up in her eyes.

Reb looked at Ethan. "Melissa can't seem to remember what she said. But Dustin read it to your whole cabin. So, Ethan. Do you remember any good parts?"

"Uh, yeah. I think I do." Ethan went right along like he and Reb had planned this for weeks. "You said something about how the Porch Patrol can't watch us every second. And you were hoping for your first kiss."

Melissa stood there with her arms crossed, trying to look tough, or mad, or something. "So. You wrote that guy a letter and signed my name to it. And you did it on my stationery. Very funny. Ha, ha." It was a good strategy to act like she didn't really care. It might have worked, if it hadn't been for the tears that she just couldn't stop. Melissa was about to turn and run, and I wanted to grab her and make her stay. I knew I had to stop her. I had to keep her from running away in tears.

And then something happened inside me. It felt like

jumping off the high dive. Something inside me said, *Okay, go.* My breath flew out of me and my stomach rose up inside me and I was flying through space, waiting to land. But I had jumped.

"That's not what happened," I said. I walked over to Dustin and grabbed him. "That letter you got from Melissa? She didn't write it. It was a fake," I said in front of him, Ethan, Melissa, Reb, God, and everybody else.

"Kelly!" Reb yelled. But I kept going.

"Melissa didn't write it. I wrote it."

Now everything was in fast-forward. Reb was grabbing me, trying to pull me away, trying to get me to shut up. Dustin was about to choke on his chocolate chip cookies. Melissa had stopped crying and was just standing there, caught in the headlights. I had no idea what Ethan was doing. It felt like everybody around us was watching us. Maybe they were. Maybe it just felt that way.

"I wrote it!" I was yelling. It seemed like I said that about fifty times. It seemed like I'd been shouting that all night.

"Kelly, SHUT UP!" Reb also yelled that a lot.

I don't remember everything too well. It was pretty out of control. At some point Dustin said, "I don't believe you. It had her name right on it!"

"I took some of her stationery to make it look real."

"You're lying!"

"Shut up!"

"Then ask her. Ask her what it said. She doesn't know, because she never even saw it!"

"What'd it say?"

"I don't know! I didn't write it," Melissa insisted.

"Shut up!"

"It starts off, 'I bet you're surprised to get a letter from me. I can't believe I'd have the nerve to write a guy, but here goes. . . .'"

"Maybe she read it to you before she mailed it."

"But she didn't! She didn't know anything about it! I took her stationery! I wrote it! I mailed it!"

"Shut up! *Shut up!*" A hand kept trying to cover up my mouth. Reb's, I guess, but for some reason I kept thinking it was Ethan's. "It was a joke! It was just a stupid practical joke! I'm sorry." I said that to everybody. To Melissa, Dustin, Reb. Everyone.

"SHUT UP!" Reb roared in my face. Would she slap me? She might have. But somebody dragged us out the door. Was it Ethan? Jennifer?

It was Rachel.

"Girl fight!" A loud meowing noise. Then laughing. Out the door, on the porch, out in the gravel beside the dining hall. Not even dark yet. How could it not even be dark yet?

"*What* . . . is the problem?"

Reb and me standing there. Like we were about to box. Breathing so hard. Both of us. Her face so red. Was my face that red? It felt hot. Where was Ethan? Was Jennifer out here too? People were watching us from the porch. The outside air felt so cool.

"You ruined it! You ruined everything!" yelled Reb.

"Calm down. What's this all about?" asked Rachel.

"I'm sorry! Look, I'm sorry, okay? I'm sorry. It just went too far," I said.

"It was perfect! You ruined it!"

"You guys settle down, or I'll send you to the cabin and you'll miss the rest of the dance. I'll take you there myself," said Rachel.

"It just needed to stop! It had to stop! I didn't blame you."

"I HATE YOU! GOD! I HATE YOU! NO FRIEND HAS EVER TURNED ON ME LIKE THAT!"

Lightning bugs were coming out of the grass. Crickets were chirping.

A beautiful summer evening.

I wished I was anywhere else but here.

CHAPTER 25

## Monday, July 7

I couldn't believe how beautiful the view was from up here. I was sitting on a bench on the porch of Middler Lodge. In the distance I could see the blue misty mountains, and in front of them were dark green mountains. Then there was a strip of mountains that were light green from the sunlight. Above the mountains, the sky was a pale blue with soft, cotton-ball clouds. Too bad I didn't have my camera.

I could hear Molly and Jordan talking inside the lodge because the big wooden doors were open. Melissa was in there too. Rachel and Tis had sent us all down here before dinner to plan for the talent show coming up in a few days. Every cabin had to enter at least one act, and even though we all swore we were completely untalented, they made us come down here anyway. Brittany and Erin got out of it because they were packing to go on the hiking honor trip tomorrow with Rachel and all the other superhikers. Honor trips were for people who'd worked really hard and done very well at one activity.

I had no idea where Reb and Jennifer were. Jennifer and I were still wearing our wristbands. But what was the point? Reb had stopped wearing hers. On Sunday morning I'd seen her take it off and toss it into her trunk like, *I'm done with that*.

We weren't triplets anymore.

On Saturday Reb and I never went back to the dance. I didn't get to see Ethan, but in some ways that was good. I'd probably never see him again. That made me really sad. He was supposed to write me from Hilton Head too. But I never had a chance to give him my home address. Who knew what he thought of me now? He probably laughed about our "cat fight" with all his friends afterward. Maybe he didn't. I hope he didn't.

After our huge fight, Rachel took us both back to the cabin. She tried to get us to talk, but neither one of us would tell her anything. By that time I was crying. Reb didn't cry. She sat on her cot with her back to us and refused to say a word.

"Is this over some boy?" asked Rachel.

"No," I said, wiping the tears away. "Well, kind of." It was easier just to lie about it.

"Well, no boy is worth losing a friend over. You two are best friends. You have to work this out."

I nodded and glanced over at Reb's back. Was I really Reb's best friend? I always thought Jennifer was and I was her second-best friend. I'd always wanted to be in first place.

Rachel left us alone because she had to go back to the dance. She probably thought it would give us a chance to make up.

Reb sat on her bed with her back to me, not moving. She was a statue.

"Would you please talk to me?" I said in this really whimpering, teary voice. I wished I could stop crying. She hated people being all weak and wimpy.

She just got up and walked out the door. I had no idea where she went that night. But I know she didn't go back to the dance, because I asked Jennifer about it later and she said she never saw her.

Since Saturday night Reb had not said one single word to me. Even though we slept five feet away from each other and ate at the same table together, I had become invisible.

I could hear Jordan and Molly inside the lodge talking.

"No, I got it. How about this?" Jordan was saying.

"You know, you're really good at this," said Molly. They were probably annoyed that I was sitting out here and not participating. But they knew Reb and I were in the middle of a huge fight.

"What do you think, Melissa?"

"I liked it the second way. That's the best one."

"Kelly?"

Without even turning around, I could tell it was Melissa.

"Mind if I come out?"

I looked over my shoulder and shrugged, like I didn't care what she did. She came out on the porch and stood by the railing.

"Um, I just wanted to thank you. For standing up for me."

I rolled my eyes. "Yeah, no sweat."

"No, honestly—thanks. I really appreciate it. I thought it was really brave. The way you took the blame. In front of everyone. Because I know *you* didn't write it."

I just shrugged. I really did not want to talk about this. Couldn't she tell? I was not trying to be brave. I've never been brave. I've never taken the blame for anything in my life. Even stuff I *was* guilty of. That was the weird part. It was so unlike me. I just didn't want to blame Reb.

"I know Reb did it. You couldn't be so mean. She did everything, and you and Jennifer just went along with her. Like with everything else. She was always the one who did everything. She's the meanest person I've ever met in my entire life."

I just sat there, fiddling with my wristband. I wondered when I should take it off.

"So are you and Reb still mad at each other?"

"What do you think?"

"Well, you're better off. Some friend she is to turn on you like that. I guess you see that now. I'd rather have a scorpion for a friend than Reb Callison."

"Melissa, shut up! You think losing my best friend makes me better off? Reb hates me now, and it's all your fault!"

Melissa drew back. "My fault?"

"Yes, your fault. If you'd had a spine, you would have stood up for *yourself*. Why didn't you ever stand up for yourself? That's why Reb kept picking on you."

"You were the ones who wrote the letter! I didn't even know anything about it!"

"If you hadn't gone through our trunks, Reb never would've written that letter! Can't you just face the fact that *you* lost your bracelet, and we had nothing to do with it?"

Melissa's mouth hung open. "I just . . . all I was trying to do was thank you. . . ."

"Fine! You've done that! Now can't you leave me alone?"

Melissa backed away. "Why are you so mad at *me*? I was hoping we could be friends. . . ."

"We can't be friends!" I yelled at her. "I only did that at the dance because I felt sorry for you. Rescuing you cost me *my* best friend. That was too high a price to pay. If I had it to do over, I'd keep my mouth shut!"

Melissa backed through the open doors to the lodge. "You're just as bad as Reb!"

"What happened?" I could hear Molly and Jordan asking her.

Mumble, mumble, mumble. Somebody came to the door and looked at me, but I didn't turn around.

"Well, we've got to finish this." Blah, blah, blah. Thank God Jordan and Molly had discovered some hidden talent.

I felt bad for yelling at Melissa. I hadn't meant to; it all just came spurting out like soda from a shaken-up can. It wasn't really her fault. We did pick on her. But they were just pranks. At first. Then it got worse. If she hadn't searched all our trunks and called us all thieves, things wouldn't have gone this far.

Was that true, what I said? If I had it to do over, would I keep my mouth shut?

I honestly didn't know the answer to that.

## CHAPTER 26

## Tuesday, July 8

It was time to end this. This silent treatment stuff was kind of understandable for the first day or two, when we were both still so upset and mad, but we couldn't go on like this forever. This was the last week of camp.

I made up my mind. I'd be the first to break the ice. When morning activities started, I followed Reb. Jennifer saw what I was up to and caught up with me.

"Hey, where ya going?"

"I'm gonna try to talk to Reb."

Jennifer sniffed. "Good luck. I've tried talking to her, but she just won't open up. I've never seen her like this. I know she feels really, really bad about all this. I can tell she wants us all to be friends again."

"Really?" I was surprised, because that sure wasn't

the impression I was getting. Reb treated me like I was invisible. "Then maybe it'll help if I make the first move?"

Jennifer frowned. "I don't know. You know how she can be. You want my theory?"

I nodded.

Jennifer leaned close to me, talking just above a whisper. "I think she's embarrassed. That's why she's not talking to anyone, always doing things alone now. That's why she avoids me and won't even look at you."

"Embarrassed about what?" I didn't get it. Reb sure didn't act embarrassed to me. She seemed mad. I got the feeling she really hated me.

"That she went too far with the whole letter thing. And that she got so mad at you. She's embarrassed about the way she acted, Kelly. But you know how she is. She's so proud, so afraid to ever let down her guard and admit she's not absolutely perfect about everything. She'd rather walk barefoot across hot coals than admit she made a mistake."

"Then it will help if I try to talk to her," I said.

Jennifer shrugged. "Maybe." But she didn't sound very convinced. "Want me to come with you?"

I shook my head. "Thanks, but . . . it's kind of just between me and Reb. You don't mind, do you?" I didn't want to leave Jennifer out, but I did feel like I needed to talk to Reb alone.

"No. I know what you mean. Just tell me what happens, okay?"

After Jennifer walked away, I caught up with Reb. I was really nervous.

"Hey. Can I talk to you for a second?" My heart was actually pounding.

Reb stopped walking, but she didn't turn around.

"Are we . . . are you never going to talk to me again?" She just stood there and didn't say anything.

"I'm sorry. I told you that the other night. I'm sorry I messed up your whole revenge against Melissa. Maybe I should've just stayed out of it." If Jennifer was right, if Reb was embarrassed, maybe it would help if I apologized.

"Can't we be friends again? I said I was sorry."

Reb still hadn't turned around. She didn't seem embarrassed. She seemed mad. She wouldn't even look at me. Maybe Jennifer read her all wrong.

"You know," I went on, feeling like a complete idiot, "Saturday's the last day of camp. Then we all leave. And we won't see each other till next year. If all of us even come back next year."

The more silent Reb was, the more I felt I had to

talk to fill up the empty space. I felt like there was one right thing I could say that would put everything back the way it was. That would make us friends again. I just wasn't sure what that one right thing was. But I guess I figured that if I kept talking, maybe I'd hit on it, by accident.

"I want us to be friends again."

Finally Reb turned around. She looked right at me, for the first time in days. But she didn't say anything. She just stood there, silent.

"Can we?" I asked.

"Leave me alone."

Then she walked away.

I don't know how long I stood there.

I watched her walk away. She didn't ever turn around. I felt like a cartoon character who'd just been hit with an anvil. I was flattened. But I couldn't throw the anvil off and pop back to my normal size. It was like I could feel a real weight on my chest crushing me, squeezing all the air out of me.

*That's it*, I kept thinking. *It's over.*

I started to walk. I couldn't see anything around me—no trees or grass or anything. My legs moved, but I had no control over them. I didn't know where they were taking me. I didn't care. Good thing that legs will work like that sometimes, that they'll take you some-place and you don't have to think about it. Somehow I was on the road that went past the camp store and down to the riding stables.

Then, for some reason, I veered off and started walk-ing through the trees till I was away from the road. I didn't want anyone to see me. I didn't want to see any-one. I wished that I was the only person in the whole world.

I eventually stopped walking and found a flat rock to sit on. I don't know how long I sat there. I don't know when I started crying. I honestly don't know if I was there for ten minutes or two hours.

I couldn't believe it was over. Jennifer had read it all wrong. Reb wasn't embarrassed about anything. She just hated me, that's all.

I tried to hate her, too. What was her problem? She *was* kind of mean.

What was I saying? She was incredibly mean. If you weren't her friend.

But before all this happened, she'd never been mean to me. Even when camp first started and she didn't even know me. She was nice to me. Nice to me, mean to Melissa. I'd been so freaking relieved that it'd worked out that way, that she'd chosen me as a friend. And then we started picking on Melissa. Was that the only thing that bonded us together? If we stopped picking on Melissa, was that the end of our friendship?

Melissa was right about Reb being the meanest person she knew. But she was wrong about one thing. *I'd rather have a scorpion for a best friend than Reb Callison.*

Not true. Reb was a good best friend.

Or at least she had been.

She tried to teach me to whistle, helped me with my serve. She read the letter I wrote to Ethan and gave me advice on it. She let me borrow clothes for the dance. A really good friend. It wasn't just picking on Melissa that made us friends. There was more to it than that.

This was my worst nightmare.

I put my head down on my folded-up knees and cried and cried and cried. I cried till I thought I was going to throw up. I cried till I was shuddering every time I breathed in. I cried till I was just so *tired* that I finally stopped.

I sat up and wiped my runny nose on my shirt. I still had on my wristband. I should take that stupid thing off. We even swam and showered with them on, because they were made of that rubbery material.

I slipped the wristband off my wrist. The ink where Jennifer had written "Terrible Triplets" had faded, but I could still read it. I drew my hand back, ready to toss the wristband into the woods. But I didn't. I looked at it for a while, then I slipped it into the pocket of my shorts. Maybe Reb would notice I wasn't wearing mine anymore and feel bad. But then maybe she wouldn't even care. She was done with me.

Even though I was absolutely miserable, it was nice out here in the woods, sitting on this rock. It was all shady and cool under the trees. And birds were flittering about in the branches and making little noises. Everything was so quiet. I could hear people's voices every now and then, but from really far away. After a while I even heard the bell ringing, way off in the distance.

I didn't move. Was it the bell for lunch? Or just the end of morning activities?

Then I made a decision. I'd stay here. I wouldn't show up for lunch, and I'd still be gone by rest hour. Eventually, everybody would realize I was missing.

Then they'd be worried. The counselors would ask everyone when they saw me last. Everyone would start searching the camp. They'd never think to look out here for me. If people came around, I'd duck in the bushes and hide. Maybe I'd even stay out here all night. It was warm enough. It's not like I'd die or anything. Maybe in the middle of the night, I could sneak back to the dining hall and steal food.

At some point they'd have to call in the police. Maybe they'd drag the lake, thinking I might've drowned. They'd bring in search dogs. Big German shepherds and bloodhounds, barking and pulling on their leashes. Rachel would go through my laundry bag and give them a piece of clothing I'd worn. Hopefully a shirt and not something embarrassing like underwear.

Reb would feel really bad. She'd be organizing all the search parties. She'd be wringing her hands and crying. "If I could just talk to her," she'd say. She'd make everyone keep looking long into the night. "We've got to find her! She's my best friend!"

Yep, that was the plan. That's what I decided to do.

I lay there in the dark, listening to all the night sounds. Frogs were croaking like crazy. All the little tadpoles that were in the lake when camp first started had grown tiny arms and legs a couple of weeks ago, and then they'd lost their tails, and pretty soon they were just little frogs. Frogs make a lot of noise at night.

I was glad it was dark. Nobody could see me. Everyone else was quiet too. I could hear Jennifer rolling around above me. Usually we all whisper a little after lights out, but lately we'd stopped doing that.

I heard Reb sniff in the cot next to me. Was she crying? Doubtful. She probably just had a stuffy nose.

I didn't stay out in the woods, obviously. I didn't even stay there till lunch. I got hungry. Plus, after a while it got kind of boring and I started feeling all itchy, like I was getting chigger or mosquito bites. At lunch everyone acted like things were completely normal. None of them realized how close they'd come to having some major drama over a missing camper.

I let out a sigh, then wished I hadn't. Had Reb heard it? One reason this was so hard to deal with was the fact that we live with each other. It's not like back home. At home, if you have a fight with a friend, you can avoid each other for a while. But at camp everyone eats together, dresses together, sleeps together. There's no avoiding each other.

That's why we all got to be such good friends so fast. It really is like sisters. It's just all so *intense*.

I heard Melissa sit up. I could see her profile in the dark. Then she plopped back down again. Was she asleep? I did feel bad for her. Every free minute she had, she looked for her bracelet. She'd taken everything out of her trunk and searched through it dozens of times.

At lunch we sang this song,

*Five more days of vacation, back to civilization,*
*Back to father and mother, back to sister and*
*brother,*

*Back to sweetheart and lo-uh-ver!*
*I don't want to go home!*

"Five more days!" Molly had groaned. "I can't believe camp will be over in five more days. I'm so depressed, I can't think about it!"

"I know," Melissa said with a sigh. I looked at her, and she must have seen me. "I have five more days to find my bracelet. Then it's lost forever."

Reb had eaten her grilled cheese sandwich like she hadn't heard any of it. That stupid bracelet. None of this would've happened if it weren't for Melissa's missing bracelet. Okay—maybe she was sort of justified for suspecting us. She'd probably always blame us. She'd probably go home and tell her mom that these girls picked on her all the time and stole her grandmother's bracelet. She'd never accept the fact that she'd lost it. She said she never took it off, but obviously she did. Maybe it just fell off. Maybe the catch on it broke. Once the setting fell out of my mom's wedding ring. Just one day it was there, and then the next day it was gone. She never found that, either. Boy, did that cause a lot of drama.

How could I ever get Melissa to believe me? Whatever. Let her go on thinking we did it. I didn't even care anymore.

## Wednesday, July 9

When I woke up, it took a few seconds for the dream to come back to me. Reb, Jennifer, and I were all talking. Reb had something in her hand. I knew it was Melissa's bracelet, even though I never saw it. Reb was smiling.

"Okay, who wants to do it?" she asked.

"I will," I said. The one thing I remember about that part was how happy Reb was and how glad I was to be her friend.

Then I was kneeling in front of my trunk, and I was afraid Melissa would come in and catch me so I was moving really fast. I was really nervous and excited. I opened my trunk, and there was this little secret compartment in the side of it. It was like my wooden jewelry box at home, the way the lid opened up. But in the dream, it was actually built right into the inside of my trunk. I put the bracelet in there, then closed it up. I was so glad it was hidden. There was no way anyone could tell a secret compartment was there.

Then Reb and I were together. "Good job!" She was so happy with me.

"She'll never find it," I told her.

Omigosh! What a freaky dream!

I looked around. The light was gray. I could barely see. But it wasn't dark any more. It was just starting to get light outside. Everyone was still sound asleep.

I tried to go back to sleep too, but I never did. I lay in bed, rolling around. When the rising bell rang and I was getting dressed, I actually looked around inside my trunk for a secret compartment.

There wasn't one.

After breakfast Reb took off to tennis by herself. Jennifer and I went to the climbing tower. Poor Jennifer. She'd tried talking to Reb too. "I hate that we're not triplets any more!" she kept saying. She was the only one who still wore the wristband. But all her attempts to play peacekeeper failed. Reb just didn't want to talk to anyone.

I felt so depressed at the climbing tower. It reminded me of that first afternoon when we all hung out together.

Everything was different this week anyway. Camp was winding down. Lots of people were gone on honor trips as a reward for working really hard at one activity, and the counselors didn't care anymore whether we just goofed off.

"I know Reb feels really bad that you guys aren't friends anymore."

I looked down at Jennifer, who was a few feet under me. "Did she say that?"

"Well, no. But I can tell she's thinking that. I think she's depressed."

I shook my head in disbelief. "She's not depressed. She just hates me."

"Oh yeah? Then why won't she talk to me, either? She doesn't hate *me*. I'm telling you—she's miserable, but she just doesn't know how to fix things."

"I don't believe that for a minute. We've both tried talking to her. If she wanted to fix things, she should've just talked back."

"This may sound weird, but I think not talking to anyone is her way of punishing herself."

"I doubt that." All I knew was that camp was almost over. And if things didn't get better soon, they'd never be resolved.

Jennifer and I didn't go all the way to the top. We slid

down our safety ropes and unstrapped our harnesses.

"I had the weirdest dream last night." That dream had been haunting me all morning. I couldn't get it out of my head. I hate dreams like that, that you can't forget about. That you can still *feel*, late in the day, long after you've woken up.

I told Jennifer my dream, and I even admitted to her that I'd looked for the secret compartment. She laughed at that part. The one thing about the dream that I really still felt was what good friends Reb and I were, and how happy we both were.

"Maybe it means I should look in my trunk," I said. "I mean, what if it is in there? By accident? What if it fell in there or something and I never even knew it?"

Jennifer looked skeptical. "Maybe."

"Maybe I should go back to the cabin and take all my stuff out. . . ." I stopped dead still, absolutely frozen.

Jennifer stopped and looked at me. "What?"

I could barely breathe, I was so excited.

"*What?* What's wrong?"

I still couldn't speak. It hit me. Just like a bolt of lightning.

"Kelly! What is wrong?"

"Jennifer." I grabbed her by the shoulders. "I think I know where to look for it."

CHAPTER 29

In a flash we were back in the cabin. Nobody else was there. The whole way back Jennifer kept begging, "Will you tell me?" But I wouldn't. I was afraid to say it. Afraid I'd jinx it.

"Okay, where? Where?" she asked, now that we were back. I had a few places that I wanted to look. First in the cabin, and if not there, then one other place.

I walked over to where raincoats and a few other clothes were hanging on the metal rod over the beds. Hanging up with all the other stuff was one item I wanted to check. Melissa's white bathrobe.

"Oh!" Jennifer exclaimed, as I pulled the robe off the wire hanger. I dug inside one pocket. Nothing. I was almost afraid to reach inside the other. I put my hand inside and felt around.

Nothing.

I looked inside both pockets. Nothing. I shook the bathrobe. Nothing.

I felt this incredible sinking feeling. Jennifer stood there with her arms crossed. "Well, it was a good idea."

I looked around at Melissa's shelves. "There's a few more places," I said. On the wooden shelf by Melissa's bed was a stack of baby blue bath towels. When Jennifer saw where I was heading, she actually sucked in her breath.

I picked up the first towel and carefully unfolded it. Nothing! There were four more. With each one I unfolded, I felt more and more disappointed. If it wasn't here, there was still one other place to look. Around the shower stalls. I picked up the last towel and unfolded it and was just about to put it back down when I saw something.

A glint.

I turned the towel over. There, on the other side of it, was a bracelet.

"Kelly! Omigod! There it is! You found it!"

I held up the towel. The clasp of the bracelet was caught in a loop of the terry cloth. I looked at

Jennifer. Neither one of us could believe it. Very carefully I unhooked it from the towel and held out the bracelet in my hand for Jennifer to see.

Her mouth was still hanging open, this dopey grin on her face.

"You found it! I can't believe it! You actually found it!"

I closed my hand tight around the little chain of gold and smiled back at her.

"Yeah. I found it."

CHAPTER

"That is the weirdest thing that I have ever seen in my entire life." Jennifer's eyes were locked on mine. She rubbed her hands across her arms and shivered. "It's like you're psychic! Are you psychic?"

I shook my head. I was still holding my closed fist up in the air. "I never was before."

"How did you do that? How did you know where to look?"

"I didn't. I just . . . all of a sudden . . . I don't know. Something reminded me of when we took her towel."

We both looked at Melissa's towels, all rumpled up now. It'd been stuck inside the towel at the bottom of the stack. I thought about how she probably did the same thing I did—used the same couple of towels all the time, and then when they came back clean from the laundry, she'd fold them and put them at the top of the stack. The ones at the bottom might not ever get used.

"If I didn't find it there, I was going to check the showers next. It was just luck. Just pure luck."

Jennifer shook her head in amazement. "I still can't believe it. Wait till you tell her. She'll be so happy."

"Yeah," I agreed. "But first . . . first, let's tell Reb about it."

We found Reb at the tennis courts. She was smashing serves across the net to Tis, like a shot out of a cannon. Her face was total concentration, and she didn't even see us at first. Jennifer stayed by the edge of the court, but I walked right across it, with complete disregard for proper etiquette.

When Reb saw me coming, she stopped in mid-serve.

"Come here. I've got something to show you." Then I walked off. I didn't look back. I just assumed she'd follow me.

"Ah, excuse me?" I heard Tis say.

"Sorry. Go ahead. Help Santana and Jessica," Reb yelled back at her.

I smiled. Reb was following me.

I walked over to the hill by the tennis courts overlooking the lake and sat down in the grass. Jennifer sat down beside me. Reb walked up to us, holding her racket. She stopped right in front of me.

She didn't look mad. She *did* look interested. But she didn't say a word.

"Look what I found." I held my hand out and opened it up.

Reb looked surprised. She stepped forward like she wanted to touch it, but then she stopped.

"Go ahead," I said. I held it out to her and she took it from me. She held it up between her fingers.

"We just found it. Five minutes ago."

"*You* found it," Jennifer corrected.

"Where?" Reb sounded curious. Very gently she handed the bracelet back to me.

"Folded up in Melissa's towel. The one we took . . . the one I took from the shower that day."

"Huh." Reb made a little surprised noise.

"Kelly is psychic. Reb, it was the freakiest thing. You should've been there. We were in the cabin—"

"I'm not psychic."

Reb's mouth twitched a little. Was that a smile? "You did find it, though."

"Yeah. And I'm really glad. But I also feel totally guilty."

"What for?" she asked. She was still standing there in front of Jennifer and me, holding her racket. I wished she'd sit down with us. I wanted to pat the grass next to me to make her sit down, but I didn't. The sun was behind her back, and her face was a shadow.

"Well, we kept telling her we didn't take it. But in a way we did. At least I did. If I hadn't stolen her towel, she never would've lost it. It was all my fault."

Reb gazed at the lake off in the distance. Was she still going to give me the silent treatment? Tell me to leave her alone? None of us said anything. Finally, Reb cleared her throat. "You mean—if I hadn't made you take her towel, she never would've lost it. So I guess it was all my fault."

"I'm not blaming you."

She glanced at me, then looked back at the lake. She was swatting her leg with her racket. "I know you're not."

There was another long pause. I didn't know what to say, and Jennifer didn't seem to either. Reb was so quiet. She didn't seem mad, though. She seemed to be in some kind of trance.

"I guess we should give it back to her," I said finally.

Reb nodded, but she kept looking at the lake.

"Will you guys come with me?" I asked softly.

"I'll pass," said Reb, still staring at the lake. I felt so disappointed—I'd hoped that maybe this would fix things somehow. But I guess I was wrong.

I looked at Jennifer. "How about you?"

Jennifer sighed. "I hope you don't mind, but . . . I think you should do it. You're the one who found it. And you're better friends with her."

"I was never really friends with her."

Jennifer put her head down on her knees. "Well, you were nicer to her than we were."

That wasn't saying much. *I never expected the Evil Twins to be nice, but I thought you were.* Maybe now I really could be the nice one.

I stood up and brushed the grass off the back of my shorts. I had to go find Melissa.

Riflery was her favorite activity, so I checked there first. And Melissa was there. This was my lucky day. There were about five or six girls lying on the mattresses on the platform, propped up on their elbows to shoot. But Melissa was sitting up. I watched them for a few minutes. Jamie, the riflery counselor, asked me if I wanted to shoot some targets, but I told her I was waiting for someone.

When the shooters were done, they all laid down their rifles and went to get their targets. Melissa was walking back, looking at her target, when I went up to her.

"How'd you do?"

"Oh, uh, pretty good." Melissa looked up at me, all surprised.

I glanced at the target. She'd hit three bull's-eyes and two bullets in the nine-point ring. That was forty-eight points out of fifty. "Wow! That's incredible! How come you sit up, though?"

"Oh. I passed that progression, so now I sit. The next position is standing."

"That's really good." It was so good, I couldn't believe it. I was really impressed.

"Aren't you going to shoot?" Melissa asked.

"Um, no. Actually, I came to see you. Look what I found." I reached in my shorts pocket and carefully took out her bracelet.

Melissa clutched her chest and gasped. *"My bracelet!"* Then she reached out for it. Her hands were shaking. "You *found* it! Oh, I can't believe it! I never thought I'd see it again! I've been hoping and praying. . . . Thank you! Thank you!"

"Well . . . don't thank me. It was my fault."

Melissa was trying to put it on her wrist, but it was kind of awkward because it's a one-handed motion, so I helped her with it. She looked at me, all curious. "What do you mean?"

"Um. Well. Remember that day we took your towel? I was the one who grabbed it. And that's where I found it. Inside your towel."

"Inside my towel?" Obviously Melissa wasn't really following me, but she looked like she didn't really care. She was so happy.

"Yeah. When I found it, it was actually stuck to the towel. The clasp was caught on it. I guess when I took your towel, the bracelet must've been lying on it. It got stuck to the towel. And then I put the towel back on your shelf. With the bracelet stuck to it."

Melissa nodded, like she was remembering. "Yeah. It *was* around that time when I lost it. I remember I was so mad about my towel and robe being taken, and then I couldn't find my bracelet, and I thought, 'What a terrible day!'"

"I didn't see the bracelet, Melissa. I swear I didn't. It was an accident. I really didn't mean to hide it from you. If I'd known where it was, I would've given it back to you sooner. I'm really sorry."

Melissa was smiling. She obviously didn't care. She

had her bracelet back and that was all that mattered.

"The funny thing is—it was with your stuff all along. You'd have found it eventually. At least when you got home and unpacked your trunk."

"Oh! I still can't believe it! I am *so* happy! It would have killed me if I'd lost it forever. It's so important to me."

"I know. I'm really sorry."

"Oh, it's back now! That's all I care about. Thanks, Kelly! Thank you so much."

"You're welcome."

She didn't hate me. I was a little surprised. She had every right to. I walked away, relieved that at least the missing bracelet was found. But I still felt bad. Melissa had put up with a lot. If all that stuff had happened to me, what would I have done?

I wasn't sure. I was glad I didn't have to find out.

## CHAPTER 31

"Boo!" Reb stepped out from behind a tree right in front of me, and I jumped. We were in the little patch of woods near the riflery range. She must have followed me, or maybe she was waiting for me. She was still carrying her tennis racket, and Jennifer was nowhere in sight.

We stood there looking at each other for a second.

"Did you give it back to her?"

"Yeah."

Reb nodded. "Did she blame you? You know, for the whole towel thing?"

"No, not at all. She was just so glad to get it back."

"I knew she would be."

We walked up the wooded path together. Neither

one of us said anything. I wondered if I should say something. Reb didn't seem like she was mad anymore. It was like the ice had thawed and she'd become unfrozen. She was just Reb again.

"You're a good person."

I stopped walking and looked at her. "What's that supposed to mean?"

Reb kind of smiled and didn't stop to wait for me. "It's not an insult. It's a compliment." She was walking ahead of me.

"Oh." I started walking again. "Thanks."

"I'm not." Long, long pause. "A good person, I mean."

I didn't know what to say to that. We were just walking along, not really looking at each other. "Sure you are."

"Not always."

"Well, nobody's a good person all the time," I said.

"True." Silence.

"It was just jokes. Just practical jokes. You know. Camp stuff. For fun. I mean, look at her. She's such a wimp. If you can't take a little heat at summer camp, you'll wilt in the real world."

I didn't say anything. Maybe I nodded a little.

"There's something about her that annoys me. She's

just so . . . *nerdy*. She's so quiet, it's like she's afraid of her own shadow."

"She's good at riflery, though. She just shot a forty-eight."

Reb shrugged. "Whatever. I guess everyone's good at *something*. Anyway, I thought I was doing her a favor. Toughening her up a little."

"I doubt she's any tougher now than when camp started," I said.

"Maybe not. I guess I didn't really do her any favors, huh?"

Then she didn't say anything for a long time. She walked along, swinging her racket.

Then all of a sudden, really abruptly, she said, "Are we friends again?"

"I hope so. I want to be."

"Are you still mad at me?" she asked. She was walking ahead of me, whacking away the branches on the path in front of us like she was clearing it with a machete or something. I felt like we were in a jungle.

"Reb, I was never mad at you. Are you still mad at me?"

She kept swinging her racket. Left, right, left, right. "Are you sure you don't hate me? Think you'll ever forgive me? Think you could lower yourself to be friends with me again?" she asked over her shoulder.

"I forgive you." Whack, whack, whack. "Do you forgive *me*?" I yelled at her. She was way up ahead of me now, far up the path. Walking faster and faster.

"Do you hate me?" she asked. It seemed like she was asking the trees.

"No."

"Do you like me again?"

"Yes," I answered. I almost said, *I never stopped liking you*, but I didn't. That's not how she wanted me to play the game.

"Can you lower yourself to be friends with me?" she asked the woods around us.

"Yeah, I can," I said out loud, to the trees. "I'll just have to lower myself."

# CHAPTER 32

## Friday, July 11

"I'll never take it off again. They'll bury me in it," Reb said solemnly, slipping the pink wristband over her hand.

"Oh, shut up! Stop making fun of me. I'm just so happy we're all triplets again," said Jennifer.

I was too. Good thing I didn't throw my wristband away in the woods, because now we were having a "banding ceremony," as Jennifer called it.

"And now for the wall signing." Jennifer pulled the cap off her Sharpie and handed it to Reb. Reb looked at the marker. "Am I supposed to say some sort of incantation first?"

Jennifer smacked her arm. "Shut up and sign."

Reb sucked on her lips to keep from smiling. "At

least you're not making me do it in blood." She wrote her name on a bare spot on the wall, then handed me the marker. I signed my name under hers; then Jennifer signed her name and wrote "Terrible Triplets" across the top. Next summer we could all come back to Cabin 1 and see where we'd signed our names.

"Good," said Jennifer. "Okay, now we can get ready for the Circle Fire." She went to her shelf and got a can of bug repellent. Pretty soon the whole cabin was engulfed in a stinky fog.

"Let me warn you guys in advance. I'm going to cry my eyes out. I do every year," said Jennifer.

"Some people actually cry?" I asked. Everybody had been talking about how sad the Circle Fire was going to be. I didn't really get it.

"Some people? Try everyone. Everyone cries," Jennifer told me.

"Even the counselors? Even Eda?" I asked. I dug through my trunk for my white Pine Haven polo. I'd never admit this to anyone, but I actually liked wearing the uniform—white polos with a green Pine Haven logo and white shorts. We only had to wear it on Sundays and special occasions, which wasn't too bad. And it made me feel like I was part of something. Just like the wristbands did.

"Some counselors cry. Eda never cries, but almost every single camper does," said Jennifer.

I looked at Reb. I couldn't imagine her crying. She was too cool. She must've read my mind, because she said, "It's not like all the other campfires. The Circle Fire's different. Everybody's all serious. It's the time to say good-bye."

Molly and Jordan walked in, and instead of going over to their side like they usually did, they came over and sat around on our side, and a few minutes later so did Erin and Brittany. We were all still talking about the talent show the night before.

"Good job, guys," said Reb. "Sorry we didn't help you out too much."

"Yeah, it was great. A lot better than if we'd been involved, I'm sure," said Jennifer. We did feel bad that all of us on Side A had dumped the talent show on the B girls, but they did a really great act. They dressed up like Tarzan and Jane and a couple of monkeys and did a dance routine. It was freaking hilarious. It ended up being one of the best acts.

"Thanks, guys," Molly said. "We owe it all to Jordan," which was kind of a joke, because Jordan got sick and had to go to the infirmary. She almost missed the whole thing. Poor Jordan. There was always something to stress her out.

The screen door banged and Melissa came in. When she saw us all sitting there, she froze for a second, like she didn't want to come in.

"Hey, what's up?" asked Molly.

"I was just going to get dressed," said Melissa. "What's happening with the CAs? Did anyone hear?" At least Melissa was trying to interact with the rest of us.

"I heard none of them are getting hired back next year," whispered Jordan.

"No way!" whispered Brittany. "That's so unfair!"

"I'm not sure that's true," said Erin. "I think everyone's saying that, but I doubt Eda will actually be that tough on them."

It was a huge deal. All the CAs, including Tis, had been caught in a prank against Camp Crockett, and the rumors were that they were in huge, huge trouble with Eda. We didn't even know what had happened for sure. Some people said they'd been caught at Camp Crockett late at night in the middle of the prank. Some people said they hadn't actually left Pine Haven yet, but were in a van on their way over there when Eda found out about it. None of us knew what had happened, and Tis would hardly say a word. She was obviously upset about it, but she wouldn't tell us what happened.

"That would suck so bad if they couldn't come back

next year," said Reb. "I'm coming back until I'm a counselor. I plan on working here every summer till I graduate from college."

We all said we wanted to come back next year too. Even Melissa chimed in and said *she* was coming back. I found *that* hard to believe. Maybe she said it because we were all saying it. Or maybe she really did want to come back.

Reb and Melissa didn't look at each other, of course. Ignoring each other was probably the best they'd ever do. At least it was better than open warfare.

All of a sudden, Rachel's face appeared, pressed up against the window screen. "Ah, look at my little chickadees! All here together. I can't believe you're all leaving the nest tomorrow. That makes me so sad!" Her face was scrunched up in a fake cry.

"Where's Tis? Are the CAs getting fired?" asked Jennifer.

Rachel came inside and plopped down on her bed. "They're not getting fired." She had on her green polo that the counselors wore.

"Are they going to get hired back next year?" asked Molly.

Rachel shrugged and didn't say anything. We could tell she didn't really want us to ask her about it. She kept changing the subject, talking to us about how we were going home tomorrow and asking if we had everything packed. And then it was time to go.

So all of us in Cabin 1 walked down to the Circle Fire together. It was just before dark, and the light was really soft and gray. We could see a few lightning bugs light up here and there above the grass. The Circle Fire was at Lakeview Rock. It was almost like a rock cliff that you could walk out on, and it was big enough for the whole camp to sit on. If you walked to the edge, you could stand there overlooking the lake.

By the time we got there, the big campfire was already lit and a bunch of campers were sitting down in a circle around it. We all sat down together. Gloria Mendoza, a counselor in Cabin 4, was softly playing one of Pine Haven's mellow songs on her guitar. The smell of wood smoke filled the air. I could feel the heat from the fire on my face, but the air on my back was nice and cool.

We started off singing songs, but none of the rowdy, loud songs that we sang in the dining hall during meals. We sang serious songs about sisterhood and friendship. Reb and Jennifer were right. Everyone was all quiet, and the mood was pretty solemn. It was like the fire hypnotized us. We were all just singing and staring into it, listening to it pop and crack.

People took turns standing up and giving speeches about what camp meant to them. Eda tried to balance things out by asking old campers and new campers to say something. A few counselors gave little speeches too.

I sat there and looked around at everyone. I couldn't believe that this was really our last night of camp. Tomorrow we'd all be going home. No wonder everyone cried at the Circle Fire. I had to come back next year. And the summer after that. That was the only way I could stand to leave tomorrow, if I knew that camp didn't have to end forever.

Now some of the counselors were opening up cardboard boxes and passing around little white candles to all of us. Then Eda stood up to give her speech. "Every summer since 1921, girls just like you have been coming to Pine Haven. And every summer when it's time to say good-bye, we have a Circle Fire. Good-byes are difficult, but they're necessary."

By that time pretty much everybody was crying. Some girls were just sniffling and looking red-eyed, but others were really sobbing. We all had our arms around each other's shoulders. Eda stuck a long wooden match into the fire to light it. Then she lit her candle and turned and lit the candle of the counselor standing next to her. Then the counselor passed the flame to the girl next to her, and we kept passing the flame around from one person to the next. Finally, after the flame had been passed all the way around, all our candles were lit.

"Every summer we all come together for one month, which always seems to fly by much faster than we want it to. While we're all together, we form a whole. We're the girls and young women of Pine Haven. It's that sense of togetherness that makes our camp such a special place. But tomorrow we'll leave Pine Haven to go back to our homes and families. The campfires will all be out here."

Then Libby, my old friend from Solitary, and another counselor picked up shovels and threw dirt onto the fire until all the flames were out. That made everything a lot darker, except for all our little candles.

"Tonight, on our last night at camp, I'd like you to think about what each of your flames has added to the fire at Pine Haven. And also think about what the fire at Pine Haven has added to each of your flames."

Then Eda stepped back, and we all just stood there, really quiet, holding our candles in front of our faces. With the whole camp there, we made a really big circle. You could see the flames flickering a little, and now with the fire out, the night air felt really cool. In the candlelight, everyone looked alike. We were all wearing our white polos and holding candles. It was strange that you sometimes couldn't even tell who was who. But I liked it. It was really pretty and nice.

Now we started to walk away from the campfire. We could walk around with our candles for a while before we went to the cabins. But we couldn't talk. That was the tradition. From now till tomorrow morning, we couldn't say anything. We had to respect the tradition and keep silent. As people walked away, all the lights from the candles bobbed up and down. Pretty soon you could see them all over the hill. I couldn't believe how beautiful the night looked, with all the little flames scattered all around. Down by the lake, you could see candles along the bank, and the lake itself looked like black glass.

I walked along with all the other Cabin 1 girls back up the hill, tilting my candle forward a little so the warm wax would drip in the grass instead of running down my arm. I was still sniffling. Jennifer was right. Everyone had cried. Even Reb got pretty teary toward the end. By the time we got up to the cabin, we blew out our candles and got undressed and into bed without turning on any lights.

Silent and dark and sad. That's how I'll always remember the last night.

## Saturday, July 12

"I promise I'll e-mail all of you at least once," said Brittany. "But if you don't write me back, I won't keep bugging you, so . . ."

"I'd rather IM," said Molly. "Or text, except my parents refuse to buy me unlimited, so I have to pay for all my text messages."

That was pretty much the conversation at breakfast—what was the best way to keep in touch: by phone, e-mail, or some variation. I was just trying really hard not to puke. The smell of oatmeal and greasy link sausages didn't help any. Just thinking about the ride home in the car through those windy mountain roads made me queasy.

But once breakfast ended and we went outside, the

fresh air calmed my stomach a little. All the counselors were wearing their green Pine Haven polos and white shorts so they'd look official for the parents. The last day. Tonight I'd be sleeping in my own bed at home. I dreaded having to wait around for my parents to get here. I just wanted to snap my fingers and be home.

Everything was as bustling as it had been on the first day. A truck full of Camp Crockett counselors pulled up, and the guys hopped out to help move trunks and carry stuff. Already a few cars were driving up the gravel road. Pretty much the entire camp was standing around on the hill, waiting.

"I can't believe this is really happening," moaned Jennifer. "We're leaving. This is the end. Tomorrow we won't even see each other, and then the day after that . . ."

"Shut up, all right? We get it," Reb snapped at her. "It's bad enough. You're just making it worse."

The two of them were leaving for the Asheville airport at eleven o'clock. My parents had said in their last e-mail that they'd be here sometime in the middle of the morning, whatever that meant. I refused to look at my watch.

It was horrible. We said good-bye to Erin first, and some other people, and then some more people.

Somehow Brittany left and we didn't even get a chance to say good-bye to her. Then Rachel came and found us and said that Melissa was leaving.

"Don't you want to say something to her?" she asked us before walking off to greet Melissa's mom.

Jennifer looked at Reb and me. "How about, 'Sorry we ruined your life. Hope you don't turn psycho'?"

Reb tried not to smile. "What do you think, Kel? Should we say anything to her?" She was pretty much the same old Reb as before, except now she seemed to ask my opinion more than she used to.

"Wouldn't hurt to say good-bye," I suggested.

We walked over to Melissa's car. Tis and Rachel were giving her a hug, and Molly and Jordan were there too, telling her to have a good year and they hoped they'd see her next summer and blah, blah, blah.

Melissa got into her car and closed the door. She was probably glad to be leaving early. She saw me through the half-open window and smiled and waved. I noticed she was wearing her bracelet. I waved back and smiled too.

"Good-bye!" we all yelled as the car turned around in the gravel and drove away.

At least we'd said good-bye to her.

Jennifer shrugged. "Well, that wasn't so bad."

"No, but this is going to be." Reb pointed to a blue van where Eda stood with her clipboard. It was the eleven o'clock van to the Asheville airport. She was starting to call off names.

"God, this sucks. We've got to go," said Jennifer, on the verge of tears.

"I forgot something!" Reb said all of a sudden. "In the cabin—hang on a second!" She took off and was halfway up the hill before Jennifer and I even figured out what was going on.

Jennifer looked at me. "What's she doing? She couldn't have left anything. . . ."

"I know. She checked and rechecked everything about fifty times," I said. We started up the hill after her to see what she was up to, but she met us on the way down.

"It's all good," she assured us. And then she winked at me.

"What was it?" asked Jennifer.

"My Little Mermaid bra. I forgot to pack it."

Jennifer rolled her eyes. "Whatever."

When we got to the van, Jennifer and Reb were the last ones to get in. They said good-bye to Tis and Rachel and everybody else, and then they looked at me.

Reb grabbed the two of us. "Okay, let's not get

sappy. We know we'll keep in touch. And then next summer . . . it'll be the Terrible Triplets, same as always, right?"

Her voice was all hoarse. We touched wristbands, and for once Reb didn't roll her eyes. Then they both hugged me, and I was already jealous that the two of them at least got to ride together to Asheville, but I was going to be left all alone. Jennifer was sobbing. Reb's eyes were red. I had snot coming out of my nose. I wish I could cry more gracefully.

Then they got into the van and the doors were closed. I didn't stay to watch it drive away. I was running up the hill to the cabin. Everything was a blur of green.

I still needed to take my sheets off my bed and stuff them into my trunk. When I burst through the screen door and saw how empty everything was, that just made me cry harder. But then I stopped.

There was something on my pillow.

It was a shirt, all folded up in a neat square. And a piece of folded paper on top.

It was Reb's Abercrombie shirt—the one she'd loaned me for the first Camp Crockett dance. I picked up the sheet of Pine Haven stationery covered in Reb's neat handwriting.

Hey Kelly,

Sorry about the way things have been between us this week.

And about all the mean things I said to you. I think you've forgiven me, but I just wanted to let you know I was sorry. Anyway, we are friends. FOREVER. And don't you forget it.

                                                    Reb

P.S. It's not a kidney, but I wanted to give you something.

P.P.S. Triplets Rule!

I actually hugged the shirt. Not because it was an Abercrombie shirt either. I didn't even care about that. I took off my T-shirt and slipped Reb's shirt on. Then I pulled the sheets off my bed and crammed them into my trunk.

But the last thing I put in was Reb's note on top. That way when I opened up my trunk at home that evening, it'd be the first thing I saw.

Up next—What happens
when Judith Duckworth decides
to become JD at camp?


Find out in
ACTING OUT!

# Summer Camp Secrets
## ACTING OUT

Katy Grant

# Summer Camp Secrets

For my three favorite people—
Eric, Jackson, and Ethan.
You guys are my world.

# Acknowledgments

I am so grateful to Andréa Mendoza, who, as a recent Guard Start grad, let me interview her repeatedly, answered my many questions, and read the manuscript, offering me her advice. Her expertise and knowledge were an immense help as I wrote this book.

Also, thanks to Barbara Parsons, who read this manuscript and, as always, gave me sage advice, support, and insight. She is far more than a critique partner; she is a true friend.

And thanks to my gaming consultants—you know who you are.

# CHAPTER 1

## Sunday, June 15

This was it. I was about to leave my past behind me and start my new life. All I had to do was say good-bye to my family and get on the bus.

My mom clutched my arm. "Promise me you'll wear your headgear," she said, loud enough for twenty people to hear. Was that the most important thing she had to say to me before I left for a whole month?

"Mom! I told you I would. Stop asking me." We were in a huge crowd of parents and kids, all hugging and saying good-bye.

I looked around at the girls near me. One girl had on a ton of eye makeup, and she kept looking at her nails. They had that stupid white line painted across the top. The girl beside her was chatting away about something.

Another girl stood with her parents, not saying anything. She held a unicorn backpack in front of her like a shield.

"We'll e-mail you tomorrow to see how you're doing, but you'll have to write us back by snail mail, so I packed some envelopes and stamps for you," said Mom.

"Okay, thanks." I tried to sound grateful instead of annoyed, since she'd told me this three times already. She had her arm around me, and she wouldn't let go. It wasn't her fault she was being so clingy. This was my first time away from home.

"Gimme a hug, darlin'." Dad grabbed me away from Mom and squeezed my guts out. A couple of the other dads looked up at him. He's six foot four, so he's easy to spot in a crowd. "Have a great time. And don't worry about us. We can take care of ourselves."

I nodded but didn't say anything. I wished he hadn't said not to worry. How could I not? But maybe I'd have a break from worrying about my family for a while.

Then Adam hugged me. "Have fun, munchkin. Don't get eaten by a bear."

"I won't!" I laughed and hugged him back. He's fifteen, and he's already six foot one. I was going to miss being called munchkin. I felt small around my dad and brothers, but most of the time I felt like a giant freak, since I'm so tall for a girl. "Thanks for coming with us," I told him, but then I wished I hadn't said it. It made it sound like I was mad at Justin because he was still in bed when we left. I'd had to say good-bye to him at home.

"I guess I should go," I said. The bus engine was rumbling, and stinky gas fumes filled up the whole parking lot. Mom hugged me one more time and then finally let me go so I could get in line. I looked at the sign on the front of the bus. CAMP PINE HAVEN. Cool. My new life was about to begin.

I stood in line, smushed between girls in front of me and behind me. I kept my tennis racket pointed down so I wouldn't bop anyone in the knees. Somehow the girl with the unicorn backpack had ended up in front of me, only now the backpack was on her shoulders and pressed against my stomach.

I looked back at my family and waved before going up the steps. Mom smiled but she was blinking a lot, so I knew she was about to cry. Dad and Adam waved back.

We all shuffled down the bus aisle. Girls were cramming pillows, backpacks, and other junk in the overhead storage bins and holding up the whole line. By the time I made it halfway down the aisle, all the front seats were full. So what? I wanted to sit in the back anyway. I walked past the eye makeup girl and her friend, past the unicorn backpack, and was about to sit next to a girl with a long brown ponytail when she stuck her hand over the empty space and said, "It's taken."

The girl in the seat behind Ponytail said, "You can sit here."

"Thanks." I shoved my tennis racket and backpack in the overhead bin and plopped down in the seat next to her. She smiled at me. She was African American, and she had on little wire-rimmed glasses, a yellow tank top, and daisy earrings. She was really tiny. She probably didn't weigh more than seventy pounds dripping wet with rocks in her pockets.

"I'm Natasha."

"Hi," I said. She glanced at me like she was waiting for something. The bus was moving now, and the driver was trying not to mow down all the parents still standing in the parking lot.

"What's your name?" she asked finally.

That was an easy question. Ordinarily. Most people know the answer to that by the time they're two. I almost gave her the wrong name, out of habit. But then I remembered who I was supposed to be.

"JD. That's what everyone calls me," I heard myself saying.

It felt so strange to say my new name out loud. Now that I'd told one person, there was no turning back. I'd have to stick to my plan.

"Nice to meet you, JD." She cleared her throat. I could tell she was a little on the shy side, but I still liked her. "What does JD stand for?"

I stared at her like I was in a trance. What was I supposed to say to that? I thought I could just tell people to call me JD and they would. Did they have to know my whole boring life story?

I tried to think of something funny. "Just Dandy!" I said. It wasn't that funny, but it was better than the truth. Natasha looked at me like I was speaking Portuguese.

"Okay, I'm kidding. That's not what it stands for." I stalled, trying to think of a better answer. The bus made a wide turn and I gripped the seat in front of me to keep from sliding over and smashing Natasha against the window.

"You want to know what it really stands for? It's pretty embarrassing."

Natasha's eyes got bigger. "Oh, you don't have to tell me."

"No, I don't mind. My first name is January and my middle name is December. Crazy, huh? I have really weird parents. You know, the New Agey type. It could've been worse. At least they didn't name me Apple."

Natasha smiled, which made me feel bad about telling her such a goofy story. But it was part of the plan. I wanted to make sure no one at camp ever knew my real name.

Judith Duckworth. I've always hated my name. It thounds like I'm lithping when I thay it. Mom named me after her grandmother. She was crazy about her grandmother, and she thought naming me after her would be a great way to honor her. Too bad my great-grandma's name wasn't Ashley.

I'd never told anyone to call me JD before, but that was about to change. I'd tried to come up with some kind of nickname for myself, but I didn't want Judy—that sounded old to me—and Ducky was even worse. I figured initials would be pretty good. And I liked the way they sounded. JD. That was *sooo* much better than Judith. Already my life was improving.

Natasha looked at me. "Are you nervous about going to camp?"

"No. Why should I be? I think it'll be fun."

She smiled and scooted her glasses up on her nose.

"You're braver than I am. I'm nervous about meeting a lot of new people."

"You know what my dad said about going someplace where nobody knows you? He said I should think of it as a fresh start."

Natasha nodded like that made a lot of sense. My dad also said camp would give me a break from all the stuff our family has been through, but I didn't mention that.

A fresh start. That was what I was most looking forward to. Going someplace where nobody knew me.

Fifth grade was when I first realized how boring I was. That was the year Chloe Carlson came to our school. You'd think being the new girl would be hard, but it wasn't for this girl. From Day One all the boys were in love with her and all the girls wanted to be her friend. Part of it was her name. How could you be anything but cool with a name like Chloe Carlson? Her parents obviously knew what they were doing. They didn't name her something random like Bernice. Or Judith.

This year, in sixth grade, I tried to act like Chloe. I made funny comments in class and I tried to be everyone's friend, but it didn't really work. Everybody stared at me and said, "Why are you acting so weird?"

So when my dad said camp would be a fresh start, I figured it was time for a personality makeover. Then I had this great idea. I'd borrow Chloe's personality while I was away at this summer camp in North Carolina, and she'd never even have to know.

While I talked to Natasha, I tried to think what Chloe would do if she was on this bus right now. She'd say something funny loud enough for everyone to hear. I just wasn't sure what that funny thing would be.

"Do you have any brothers or sisters?" asked Natasha. Now the bus was making a humming noise, and everyone was pretty quiet, talking to the people next to them.

I thought about it for a second. I could tell her anything—make up an older sister or a baby brother. But I decided to go with the truth. I didn't want to act like Justin and Adam didn't exist. "Yeah. Two brothers. Both older. What about you?" At least I could tell her that and she wouldn't say, *Oh the football stars at Central High? THEY'RE your brothers?*

"I'm an only child."

"Really? What's that like?"

Natasha shrugged. "Okay, I guess. It's all I know. I think that's why my parents are sending me to camp. So I can see what it's like to live with other kids for a change. But I'm really going to miss them. The three of us are very close."

"Hey, we've got a whole month without parents," I said. "It'll be great." Then I did the craziest thing I've ever done in my life. I stood up and yelled really loud, "Hey, everyone, let's hear it for a whole month without parents!" Then I whooped, the way I would at Justin's and Adam's football games. "Woo-hoo! Woo-hoo!"

When everyone turned and stared at me, I smiled and waved, like I was glad to be making a fool of myself. Then I slid back down in the seat. Natasha's eyebrows were way above the rims of her glasses.

"Sorry. Didn't mean to cause a scene," I told her. I could tell she hadn't expected me to do that. *I* hadn't even expected me to do that. Chloe wouldn't have done something *that* stupid. I hoped I wasn't blushing. It felt weird being the center of attention—like I was wearing someone else's shoes instead of mine. It didn't seem to fit right.

"It's just that this bus ride is pretty boring, don't you think?" I asked Natasha, acting like I was used to being the life of the party. "I mean, look at everyone. They're all half-asleep. We should liven this place up. I know! Let's sing 'A Hundred Bottles of Beer on the Wall'! Everyone loves that song!" Maybe the more I acted this way, the faster I'd get used to my new self.

"No, they don't," said the ponytail girl in the seat in

front of us. "Why don't you do us all a favor and shut up?" she added over the back of her seat. The friend she'd saved a seat for turned around and gave me a dirty look too.

I had no idea what to say to that. For one thing, nobody would ever tell Chloe Carlson to shut up while she was being funny. And if anyone ever said anything slightly sarcastic to her, she always had a quick comeback. Always. I tried to think of something, but my brain was frozen.

The ponytail girl had turned back around. She figured she'd shut me up for good. I did feel pretty silly. I wasn't very good at acting this way. I felt like covering my face with my hands, so I did, but then I got inspired.

I sat there with my face covered up and pretended to cry. I let out these loud *boo-hoo* sounds. "I don't have any friends!" I sobbed, loud enough for everyone around me to hear. Then I looked up at Natasha. "Will you be my friend if I pay you a buck?"

That's when the girls behind me started to laugh. "I'll be your friend for five bucks!" somebody yelled.

"Twenty for me!"

Natasha shook her head and grinned. "I had no idea I was inviting a crazy person to sit beside me. JD, of course I'll be your friend, and you don't need to pay me a dollar." She looked over the back of the seat. "I'll do it for free!" she said.

"My first friend!" I yelled. "I actually have a friend now!" The two girls in front of us had put their pillows over the tops of their heads to cover up their ears. "And I've got some enemies, too!" I shouted.

Natasha cracked up laughing. I could only imagine what my friends back home would've said. *Judith, what's wrong with you? You never act like this.*

Maybe Judith didn't. But JD did.

"We're finally here!" said Natasha when we turned onto a gravel road and passed a sign that said CAMP PINE HAVEN FOR GIRLS. She jiggled her knee up and down as she looked out the window. We passed a lake and some tennis courts. There were tons of people all around and a lot of cars lined up along the road.

When we got off the bus, a bunch of counselors were waiting for us and yelling directions. They all had on matching green shirts, so they were easy to spot. They broke us up into age groups, and Natasha and I found out we were both in the group called Middlers—ages ten to twelve. That made us the oldest in the group.

Then a lady with a clipboard asked us our names. When it was my turn, I said, "JD Duckworth," like I'd always been called that. She looked at her list and didn't seem at all confused. "Okay, JD. You're in Middler Cabin Two A."

Then Natasha said, "Natasha Cox."

"Hi, Natasha. You're in Middler Cabin Three B."

Natasha and I looked at each other. "Can't we switch? We're best friends. We really need to be together," I said.

The lady shook her head. "Sorry, cabin assignments have already been made. But you'll still see a lot of each other." She smiled and moved on to the next girl.

Natasha and I walked over to where all the luggage from the bus was piled up. "I can't believe it. We just get to know each other and we're already split up," I said.

Natasha pushed her glasses up her nose. Now that I was standing next to her, I saw that she only came up to my shoulder. "I know, but like she said, we'll still see each other a lot."

Some guys wearing red T-shirts that said "Camp Crockett" helped us carry our trunks to the cabins. It was weird that the camp made everyone bring trunks to keep all their stuff in, but that's what the letter had said to do. Plus they gave us a list of what to bring and told us to put name tags in all our clothes. When my mom was getting my things ready, I felt like I'd joined the army.

We had to climb up a big hill to get to where the cabins were. I was glad I only had to carry my tennis racket and backpack.

"It sure is pretty here, isn't it?" asked Natasha. It was a sunny day, and everything was so green. There were trees everywhere, big rock formations, lots of hills, and off in the distance, bluish-colored mountains. All the buildings were wooden, and the whole camp looked like it should be on a postcard or something.

At the top of the hill we came to a long row of cabins. "Well, I guess this is good-bye—for now," said Natasha when we got to the door of Cabin 2. She looked scared.

"Okay. I'll see you later." It was too bad we couldn't stay together.

The guys carried my trunk in and left it inside. When I walked in, a counselor with curly blond hair said, "Hey! Are you my camper? I'm Michelle!"

She was obviously a counselor because she looked older, and she was wearing one of those green shirts, but I was about three inches taller than she was. I'm five foot six, and my doctor says I'm still growing. If I keep growing till I'm eighteen, I figure I'll be six-nine eventually.

"I'm JD. JD Duckworth."

She frowned a little like she'd never heard of me, but then she said, "Oh, okay. Nice to meet you, JD!" She had a great grin that made her eyes crinkle up.

The cabin was awesome. It had screens all around it, so it felt really open and breezy. And there were bunk beds. I've always wanted bunk beds. Justin and Adam had them a long time ago, but they each have their own room now.

"This is cool," I said, looking around at everything. The walls and floors were wooden, and girls had written their names all over the place.

"Wow! 1981!" I yelled. I pointed to a spot on the wall that said JENNIFER H. 1981. "That is so amazing! These cabins are that old?"

Michelle laughed. "Yeah. And guess what? My mom went here when she was a kid. And some people have grandmothers who went here. Can you believe it?" Her eyes crinkled again. "I'll send my daughter here too—if I have one."

Two other girls were already in the cabin, and while we were all trying to get everyone's names straight, another girl came in.

"Here. These will help us get to know each other faster," said Michelle. She handed out name tags. They were made out of little round slices of wood with a plastic string, but when I saw mine, I almost had a heart attack. It had JUDITH written on it. So much for keeping my old name a secret.

I held it against my stomach. "I need a new one. One that says 'JD.'"

"No problem! I'll just change the old one." Michelle took a marker from a shelf beside her bed and wrote "JD" in big red letters on the back of the piece of wood. Then she hung the string around my neck with the "JD" side showing. "How's that?"

"Good. But can I see the marker for a second?" I asked. I took off my name tag, scribbled over JUDITH so no one could read it, and then put it back on again.

All the other girls were watching me, but I didn't care. I was officially JD now.

"What's your real name?" asked one girl.

"Josephina Delilah," I said, coming up with the weirdest name I could think of. "Terrible, huh? That's why I go by JD." Michelle smiled, and I knew she wouldn't give away my secret. Having initials as a name would be fun. I needed to think up lots of crazy names to tell people when they asked me what JD stood for. It would add to the mystery if nobody ever knew for sure.

Off in the distance we heard a bell ringing, and Michelle called out, "Hey, that means it's time for lunch.

Everybody follow me, and I'll show you where the dining hall is."

A lot of parents were still wandering around, and I sort of wished my parents could've seen the camp, but I was glad I'd taken the bus. I never would've gotten rid of my mom. I kept my eye out for Natasha till I spotted her walking with a group of girls. "Hey, let's sit together at lunch!"

"JD! I was looking all over for you. How do you like your cabin?"

"I love it, and I've got a great counselor. She's really friendly." It was so exciting to see the whole camp. I loved how woodsy and outdoorsy everything looked.

"Yeah, I like mine, too." She leaned close to me. "I'm not as nervous now."

I patted her back. "See, I told you this would be a fresh start."

But when we got inside the dining hall, we found out we couldn't sit together because we had to sit with all the people from our cabin. Michelle took me and the other girls to our table and introduced us to Alex, the counselor in Cabin 2B. She had deep blue eyes and light brown hair pinned up off the back of her neck. She was really pretty, but she didn't smile at all, so I was glad I was on Michelle's side of the cabin.

"Welcome to *Pain* Haven," said a girl with her elbows propped on the table and a sneer on her face. Her name tag said KATHERINE. "For all you new campers: This place bites. I've been coming here since I was seven. I should know."

"Nice," Alex said, frowning at her. "Maybe they'd like to decide for themselves." She looked at the rest of us. "I've been coming here since I was eleven. It's a great camp. I'm on the swimming staff."

"I'm canoeing, by the way," said Michelle, waving and smiling from the end of the table. "Katherine! We're going to have a terrific summer!"

Katherine rolled her eyes. "Whatever."

Lunch was great—tacos and fruit salad. I'd always heard that camp food was lousy, but I ate three tacos, and they didn't kill me. They didn't even make me queasy.

After lunch, Michelle pointed out different things as we walked back to the cabin. She said the oldest girls were called Seniors and the youngest were Juniors. We were right in the middle. "That's the camp office, and behind it is the infirmary, where the nurse is. That's the Crafts Cabin, and the stables are down that road."

One weird thing was the bathrooms. They weren't inside the cabins; instead there was a building called

Solitary with a bunch of sinks and toilets in it, and there was another outdoor building for the showers. It had a roof and shower stalls, but it was still like you were showering almost directly outside. I felt like we were really going to be camping out for the whole summer, and that would definitely be fun.

Back in the cabin, Michelle told us to pick out which beds we wanted. The cabin had two big rooms, A and B. Four of us were on Side A, and Alex was in charge of four girls on Side B. Luckily, Katherine was on her side of the cabin.

"I'll take a top bunk if nobody else wants one," I said. I'd been hoping for the top as soon as I saw the bunk beds.

"Then I'll take a bottom," said Courtney. Her hair was the first thing I'd noticed about her. It was hard not to. Here was this tiny person with a head of honey-colored hair so thick and wavy it looked like a lion's mane. She unpacked some sheets and started making up the bottom bunk below me.

"I guess I'll take the other top," said Lauren. Her blond hair was practically white, and she wore it in a short ponytail. The back of her shorts said "Dancer."

Amber, a girl with long brown hair and a nose that looked squashed, took the other bottom bunk. "This is my third summer, so let me know if you guys have any questions." She had a sweet smile, so I felt bad for thinking of her as the flat-nosed girl.

"Well, it's my first year, but I made one friend on the bus. She didn't want to be friends at first, till I paid her a buck. Oh, and I made several enemies, too!" I said. I realized I was talking too loud.

"How?" asked Amber, her forehead wrinkling.

"Just by being me!" I told her. I felt like I was auditioning for a play. I had to make a big impression so I'd get the part. The others looked at me like they didn't know what to think. Everyone started making up their beds. Was I ever going to pull this off? Did they think I was funny or just obnoxious?

I opened my trunk to get out my sheets, and the first thing I saw was my headgear on top, with a note from my mom. *Hi, sweetie! Remember: 14 hours a day! Love, Mom.*

Groan. At least she didn't call me Judith. Most of those hours were at night, but I had to put the thing on in the evening, and then I'd take it off when I woke up. I wished I could go the whole month without wearing it, but I'd probably go home and find out my teeth were permanently crooked. My cousin had such a bad bite, she had to have her jaw broken and then wired back together again.

So then, just to be stupid, I took out my head-gear and put it on, in front of everyone. I fluffed up my hair and declared, "Don't hate me because I'm beautiful!"

Luckily, everyone laughed, including Michelle.

"Do you only wear it at night?" asked Courtney from her bottom bunk, looking at me sympathetically.

"Mostly. My orthodontist calls me 'Beaver Face.' I'm his favorite patient."

Again I got laughs, so I figured I'd keep the stupid thing on for a while. I would never have let anyone see me in this back home. I'd been wearing it since February, and I'd missed Elise Rutherford's sleepover because my mom called her mom and told her to make sure I wore it. I pretended I had the flu.

"This is great! You guys are already getting to know each other!" said Michelle, watching us all as she sat cross-legged on her cot against the wall. Over on Side B, Alex's group was hardly talking at all.

Mom had carefully packed my trunk, but she'd put my sheets and towels at the very bottom. I piled a bunch of clothes and stuff on the floor beside me, trying to find the new striped sheets she'd bought for me.

"Oh, are those pictures from home? Can I see?" asked Michelle.

I looked down and saw my photo album peeking out from under my pile of stuff on the floor.

"Um, sure," I told her. What else could I say, now that she'd seen it? I handed the album to her and hoped she'd look through it and then give it back. The less everyone knew about my family, the better. I unfolded my sheets and climbed up to the top bunk to make my bed.

"Who are these guys? Are they your brothers?" she asked, flipping through the pages. I glanced down and saw that she was looking at Justin's and Adam's football pictures.

"Uh, yeah. They both play football," I said, deciding to leave it at that. I was wrestling with the sheets, so it was easy to act distracted.

"What positions do they play?"

From the top bunk, I could see the newspaper articles I'd cut out and pasted inside. One had a picture of Justin jumping up to catch a pass, and another had a picture of both of them together. I'd been so proud of them when those pictures were in the paper.

I climbed down and sat on the edge of Michelle's cot.

"That's Adam. He's fifteen, and he's a safety. He'll be on the junior varsity squad next year. And Justin's seventeen. He's a tight end." I could tell her a little about them. She didn't have to know *everything*.

Michelle read the headline. "'Central High Brothers Both Powerhouse Players.' Such cuties!" she said, even though they looked all sweaty and grimy in the picture.

"Do you like football?" I asked.

"Uh, that would be *yes*. I guess I didn't tell you where I go to college." She jumped up and pulled out an Oklahoma Sooners T-shirt from her trunk.

"Oh wow, great football school. Did you go to any games last year?"

"Every home game. I had season tickets. So I bet these guys will be getting football scholarships, huh?" she said with a big grin.

I shrugged. "Maybe." I just wanted to get off the subject of my brothers and football. I hadn't planned on telling anyone about that stuff.

"Maybe? Don't be modest." She nudged me with her elbow. "They're obviously both talented. They may be the next Manning brothers!"

I shook my head. "I wouldn't go that far. Anyway, they're not quarterbacks."

"Manning brothers?" asked Courtney. Michelle winked at me and grinned.

"You know—Peyton and Eli. They're both NFL quarterbacks." I wondered if I should tell her what "NFL" stood for. Who hadn't heard of the Manning brothers?

Just a few months ago my family did joke around about how maybe one day the boys would both be playing in the NFL, but nobody said that anymore. Not since what had happened this spring.

A bell rang and Michelle told us that now we all had to go to the lake to take swim tests. Everyone pulled swimsuits out of their trunks and started changing.

I was glad I could finally put my photo album away. I stuck it under a bunch of clothes at the bottom of my trunk. Why'd I even bring it along in the first place? I thought I'd want to look at it if I missed my family. But I could already tell I wasn't going to miss them that much. I had a whole month away from them, and I wanted to make the best of it.

I took off my headgear and found my new red one-piece in my trunk. I never wore bikinis because they made me look like a cow.

I really wanted my JD plan to work. So far, so good. But I had to make a big first impression. By the end of the day, I wanted a lot of people to know me. I still remembered Chloe's first day at my school. Everyone had said, "Have you met the new girl?" Now all I needed to do was to get everyone at this camp talking about the girl named JD.

The tough part was figuring out exactly how to do that.

CHAPTER 3

Michelle took all the Cabin 2 campers down to the lake together. Alex had left early since she was on the swim staff. Besides Katherine (or Miss Sunshine, as I silently thought of her), the other Side B girls were Mei, Isabel, and Meredith.

I looked at Mei's name tag and called her "Mee," but she said it was pronounced "May," like the month. She was Asian, but when her parents were helping her carry all her stuff into the cabin, I'd noticed they were both Caucasian, so I figured she was adopted.

Isabel had dark frizzy hair and freckles on practically every inch of her body. At lunch Meredith didn't eat the tacos because she was a vegetarian. She knew Michelle from last year, and she talked to her the whole time about canoeing.

I kept my eye out for Natasha, but I didn't see her anywhere. I looked at all the Cabin 2 girls, and they seemed pretty okay. Except for Katherine, who complained about how she'd done this stupid swim test every year.

"Great! It'll be easy for you," Michelle said, putting an arm around her shoulders.

Katherine wriggled away. "I hope I drown."

Of all the girls, Amber seemed most my type, or *Judith's* type—quiet but friendly, and a little . . . well, blah. If we'd met at school last year, we probably would've been best friends. Courtney, on the other hand, reminded me of Chloe Carlson. She was cute and bubbly like Chloe, but so far she didn't seem to have a killer sense of humor like Chloe, which was good. If she and I got to be friends, we couldn't both be cracking jokes all the time. I scooted up so I could walk close to her.

When we got to the lake, Michelle took off to say hi to some old friends, and we all sat down around the edge to wait our turn. Lots of girls were already waiting. A wooden dock jutted out over the lake, and Alex was standing at the end of it in a blue-and-white striped bikini, holding a clipboard and watching some girls in the water.

The test looked supereasy. We just had to jump in, tread water for five minutes, and then swim across the lake. And the lake wasn't very big, so it wouldn't be tough swimming across it. I figured it was maybe forty or fifty yards to the other side.

While the other girls talked, I thought about how Chloe would make some funny remark right now and crack everyone up. But I had one big problem. Chloe was naturally funny. I wasn't. It was like being born color-blind, or having one leg shorter than the other. I had a humor deficiency. Sure, it made things tougher, but that meant I had to try harder.

I stared at the water, trying to think of something funny to say. A group of girls dove off the end of the dock and started treading water. I could see some tiny things swimming around near the edge of the lake. At first I thought they were fish, but they didn't have tails. They were little dark blobs darting around in the water. Oh, they were tadpoles.

I jumped to my feet. "Shark! Shark!" I yelled at the top of my lungs. When everyone looked at me, I shrugged and sat down. "Oops! Sorry. It's just a stick. My bad."

It seemed like one of those moments on TV when everything freezes. All of a sudden about a hundred eyes were all looking at me. My heart thumped in my chest. I wished I could take it back. I felt so silly. How could funny people stand this kind of attention?

Alex blew her whistle and made the girls in the water swim up to the dock and climb out. Then she spun around and marched over to us. The other swim counselors had turned around to look at us too.

"WHO SAID THAT?" The sun was behind her back, and as she hovered over us, all we could see was this dark shadow.

Nobody said a word. Not one person was going to tell on me. *That* was pretty cool. I'd never done anything to purposely get in trouble before, and I couldn't believe that all these strange girls I'd just met already had my back.

"I asked you all a question. I know the girl who yelled that was sitting over here." The shadow leaned over us, and now we could see Alex's face, all dark and scary. "If I don't find out who it was, every one of my little Cabin 2 campers will swim an extra lap across the lake."

I had no idea what would happen next. There was a long silence while Alex waited for someone to say something. Amazing! They still wouldn't tell on me.

So that was when I did it. I crossed my arms and pointed at Lauren on one side of me and Courtney on the other. "I did it," I said, but I still pointed at the two of them. I heard Courtney let out a puff of air.

"Okay," said Alex, in a *now we're getting somewhere* tone. "So you're the wise guy. You think water safety is something to laugh at?"

She was being so lecturey, I couldn't stop myself. I held my hand over my eyes to shade them from the sun, and I threw her a salute and said, "Yes, Sergeant, I do think water safety is something to laugh at. I laugh at water safety every single day."

My heart would not stop pounding. I'd never been a smart mouth before in my whole life. It felt like jumping out of a plane. It was scary and exhilarating, and I didn't know how I was going to land.

Alex stood over me, staring me down. I could hear someone behind me trying not to giggle. "We'll see how funny it is. On your feet. You'll take your test now. And you'll swim two laps across the lake instead of one."

She led me over to where the other girls were standing on the end of the dock. They were all dripping wet, watching Alex yell at me, and I felt bad for making them stand there, because a couple of them were shivering.

I turned to look at the others sitting by the lake edge. I made a funny face behind Alex's back to show I didn't mind getting in trouble, and Courtney gave me a tiny, two-fingered wave. I was a little scared, but I'd definitely gotten noticed.

"Okay, ladies, this comedian is the one who interrupted your swim test. Apologize to these girls for making them stand here and wait."

I looked at all the girls dripping there on the end of the dock. "I'm vewy sowy I intewupted yowah swim test. Pwease fowgive me," I said. A couple of them had to hold back smiles.

What could Alex do to me? She looked at me like she wanted to drown me, but instead she yelled, "In the water!" and blew her whistle right in my ear.

I dove off the end of the dock, mainly to get away from that whistle. The water was icy cold, but when I came up for air, I started treading water right away, to warm myself up. The more I moved, the less cold I felt. Alex timed us with her watch. When five minutes were up, she told us all to swim across the lake. "Two for you," she said, pointing at me. "And if you cause any more trouble, we'll make it three."

I put my face down and started doing the crawl stroke. I was glad to be in the water now, out of the center of attention. I wasn't sure I could think up anything else funny to do. So I had to swim an extra lap. So what? There were worse ways to be punished. I figured

I'd do them really fast to show her I didn't care.

I kept my head down and breathed on every fourth stroke, the way Justin had taught me. Every now and then I'd look up to see how close I was. Pretty soon I'd made it to the other side, where another counselor with a clipboard was waiting on the edge of the lake. She smiled at me when I came up for air. She probably hadn't heard all the trouble I'd caused on the other side.

"Wow, you are some swimmer," she said. "Look at the rest of your group!"

I looked back, and the other girls were barely halfway across. I didn't know I'd gone *that* fast.

"Are you on a swim team in your hometown?"

"Nope. I've just always been a pretty good swimmer." I flipped my hair out of my eyes.

"You should think about taking the Guard Start class. It's for really good swimmers who aren't old enough to start actual lifeguard training. Think you'd be interested?"

"I don't know. Maybe." I'd never thought about being a lifeguard. I didn't really want to take any swimming classes. What I wanted to do this summer was get good at tennis, but she was being so nice to me, I figured I should at least act interested.

"What's your name and cabin number?" she asked.

"JD Duckworth, Middler 2A."

She flipped through some pages till she found my name and put a check mark next to it. "Okay, JD. I'm Libby. You passed the test with flying colors. And give the Guard Start class some thought. Classes begin tomorrow."

She sure was a lot nicer than Alex. "Will you be teaching it?" I asked.

"No, but don't worry. One of us on the swim staff will be."

She told me I could get out and dry off, but I said I had to do one more lap. "I was goofing around before the test, and Alex got a little mad."

Libby smiled at me. "Well, that shouldn't be a problem for you." I took off across the lake again, going even faster this time. Partly it was to get back at Alex, but partly I was showing off. Even if I didn't do the class, it was still pretty cool that she was amazed by my awesome swimming skills.

By the time I made it across the lake, the Cabin 2 girls were just jumping in for their test. I climbed the ladder at the end of the dock and shook myself off. Alex kept her eyes on the girls in the water. "Can I go now?" I asked, trying to be polite. I'd caused enough trouble for a while. She nodded and didn't look at me.

I was walking away to get my towel when she blew

her whistle. I thought she was after me again, but when I turned around, she was on her knees, yelling at someone. "Are you okay? Do you need the flotation?"

Now everyone was rushing over to see what was going on.

"Everyone out of the water!" Alex yelled. I could see one girl trying to keep her head above water, but she was definitely panicking. She went under and came up again, coughing like crazy. It was Isabel, the quiet one on Side B. The rest of the girls climbed up the ladder at the end of the dock, one by one, watching Isabel the whole time.

"Girls, move it!" yelled another counselor. She'd run up with this big red foam thing and she tossed it to Alex, who threw it out to Isabel. By now, everybody at the lake was watching.

Isabel grabbed the floaty thing, and Alex pulled her over to the dock. Then she grabbed her under the arms and sat her on the edge of the dock. Isabel sat there and coughed while Alex leaned over her. "Why'd you jump in if you can't swim? You should've told me you can't swim!" she shouted.

It took every ounce of energy I had to keep from running over to Alex and pushing her into the lake. How could she be so mean? It was bad enough that the poor kid had to be rescued, but did she have to embarrass her in front of everyone? Poor Isabel.

Alex turned around, and her face was as white as a new pair of gym socks. She looked pretty freaked out, but that still didn't give her the right to yell at Isabel.

Katherine had her hand over her mouth, snickering. "What a loser!" she said to Mei.

"Shut up, or I'll push you in," Mei hissed at her. I liked that girl. She was tiny, but she had the personality of a firecracker.

I wrapped myself up in my towel, then sat down on a big rock to wait for the other girls to finish. I finally saw Natasha, sitting about twenty feet away with the girls from her cabin. Isabel came and sat beside me on the rock. She wouldn't look at me.

"Don't worry about it," I told her. "Just shake it off."

Isabel nodded but kept staring at her toenails.

When the other girls finished their test, we all walked back to the cabin together.

"Wow! You were amazing," said Amber. "Way to show up Alex!"

"I told you I made enemies on the bus. Looks like I've made one more!"

"Thank you so much for admitting you were the one who yelled that," Lauren said. "I thought she was going to bust all of us." Her blond hair looked even whiter when it was wet and the sun was shining on it.

"Look, there's something you guys need to know about me," I explained. "I'm always causing trouble. Trouble is my middle name." I said it like I believed it.

"I thought it was Delilah," said Amber.

"Nah, I was just kidding about that. JD really stands for Juvenile Delinquent!" They all laughed. I couldn't believe it. If getting in trouble got me this much attention, it was worth it. If I could keep this up all month, my personality makeover would be a huge success. It was only the first day, but already I felt more like JD than Judith.

# CHAPTER 4

## Monday, June 16

"Prevention, fitness, response, leadership, professionalism." Alex held up one finger at a time and ticked off the five areas she wanted us to remember. "Those five areas will be our focus for the next four weeks."

Off in the shallow end I watched the nice counselor Libby with her advanced beginner class, working on back floats. They were mostly Juniors, eight or nine years old, and then poor Isabel, stuck with all the little kids. Isabel had been so embarrassed about having to be rescued yesterday, but right now I wished I could switch places with her.

There was a long silence, and I looked up to see why Alex had stopped talking. She stared at me with her arms crossed, and the rest of the class was looking at me too.

"Do I have your undivided attention now?" snarled Alex. I nodded and wrapped my towel more tightly around my shoulders. Boy, she really hated me, but the feeling was completely mutual. I almost died when I found out *she* was teaching the Guard Start class. Why couldn't it have been Libby?

Alex kept talking and I tried to listen. Six of us had signed up for the class, and I was glad that most of them were from my cabin: Courtney, Mei, and Lauren. Besides us there were two other girls, Claudia and Shelby. We were all huddled up with our towels wrapped around us like blankets. It was only nine thirty, and it was freezing out here. Okay, maybe not quite freezing, but it was probably in the sixties at least. When we woke up this morning, the cabin felt like a refrigerator, and we'd all worn jackets and sweats to breakfast. I had no idea the mountains got so cold at night.

"I have to warn you that the final test will be really demanding," said Alex. "You'll have to tread water for two minutes without using your hands, swim five hundred yards without stopping, and retrieve a ten-pound object from a depth of ten feet."

Courtney poked me in the ribs, and I glanced at her. Her eyes widened, and I raised my eyebrows. It did sound pretty hard. Five hundred yards—that was like swimming five football fields.

"I have another Guard Start class with Senior girls who are thirteen and fourteen, but most of you are twelve. So you're all a little young." She paced back and forth and locked her eyes on each one of us as she talked. "I fully expect that some of you won't be able to hack it, and you'll drop out. A few of you might get all the way through the class, but maybe you won't pass the final test. If you do pass, your next step will be taking a lifeguarding class when you're fifteen." She stopped in front of us and crossed her arms.

"You'll also be expected to complete thirty service hours—helping out with swimming lessons for the little kids. So this class is going to be a lot of hard work. Anyone who's not ready to give it her all should leave now."

I jumped to my feet and waved to everyone. "I guess this is good-bye! Have fun!"

Alex stepped aside to let me pass, but I felt someone yank my towel from behind. It was Courtney. "She's just kidding." She and Lauren pulled me down and made me sit between them. Courtney held on to my towel like she didn't trust me to sit still.

I could have easily walked away. Who needed this?

I didn't even want to be a lifeguard, so this class was a complete waste of time for me. I'd wanted to go to the climbing tower this morning, but Courtney and Lauren had dragged me here instead. They thought the class sounded cool, and then Mei wanted to do it too. So I came along, mostly to be with them. They seemed like the type of girls Chloe would be friends with.

Alex was staring me down. "You're welcome to go. Why don't you leave now before you waste another minute of my time?" Courtney gripped my towel tighter, so I kept quiet and didn't move.

"Are you staying or going?" Alex asked, boring a hole through me with her blue death-ray eyes.

I shrugged. "I might as well stay. I'm dressed for the part." I opened and closed my towel really fast. Mei bit the edge of her towel to keep from smiling. Alex turned away and started blabbing about the five areas again.

It felt scary being the troublemaker. But if I was going to try this out, camp was definitely the place to do it. I'd thought about it a lot since Alex had yelled at me yesterday. What could she do to me? What could any of the counselors do to me? It wasn't like school, where you got called to the principal, or got detention, or got a note sent home to your parents. The worst thing they could do to me was send me home, but I'd have to do something major, like set the cabin on fire, to have *that* for a punishment. And I wanted to be a comedian, not an arsonist.

When Alex finished jabbering, she gave us all workbooks, and we did exercises in them called "Safety First" and "Know Your PFD: Personal Flotation Device." Then she told us all to get into the water to swim laps. "Four laps, ladies. Across the lake and back, two times." Then she pointed to me and said, "JD's doing five laps today. Just to show me how committed she is to the class."

Alex blew her whistle and we lined up to dive in. I went second after Lauren, and when I came up for air I was gasping from the cold.

"How is it?" asked Mei from the dock, her arms folded across her chest and her shoulders hunched. If she was cold now, the water was really going to wake her up.

"Fr-freezing!" I yelled. The water was so frigid it made my head ache.

"Colder than yesterday?" asked Courtney.

"Yes!" Lauren and I shouted at the same time.

Alex blew her whistle at us. "Stop complaining and start swimming!" One by one, the others dove in. After everybody had screamed and groaned and gotten over the shock, we all started across the lake.

"I'm never going to make it," said Courtney when she came up for air. Her teeth chattered, and her lips were pale.

"Sure you will. It's not that far," I told her.

"No, I mean everything. This class. There's no way I'll ever pass it."

"Me neither," said Mei, bobbing up beside us. Her black hair looked like it was painted on. "I thought I was a good swimmer, but she scared me to death back there."

I looked back at Alex standing on the dock with her whistle between her teeth, ready to blow it if we made a wrong move. "Hey, Alex. Instead of sucking on that whistle, why don't you swallow it instead?" Of course she couldn't hear me, but everyone else could. They all laughed at my joke, so I kept going.

"I think Alex needs a nose ring," I said. "Then she could hang her whistle from it. Wouldn't that be a nice fashion statement?"

"JD, stop!" gasped Lauren, treading water just enough to keep her head up. "I can't swim and laugh at the same time!"

"No, don't stop," Courtney said, blowing water out of her nose. "It'll take our minds off how cold we are."

"These are the five areas we'll be working on this

summer: Marco Polo, belly flops, cannonballs, hand-stands . . ."

"That's only four," Mei pointed out.

"And making Alex so mad she swallows that whistle!"

Just then we heard the whistle blow. "Stop horsing around out there!" Alex called across the lake.

Everyone cracked up, so then I said, "Hey, guys, let's all turn around and neigh at her. C'mon, on the count of three . . ."

I counted to three and then spun around in the water and neighed at Alex on the end of the dock, but we were so far away from her now, there was no way she heard me. No one else did it, but the others sure laughed their heads off.

"This class is going to be fun with you in it," said Claudia, the girl who'd looked bored when Alex was talking and who'd kept checking her watch the whole time.

"Yeah, I was about to leave when she went on and on about how hard it was going to be," put in Shelby, a skinny girl with bangs covering her eyes. "But when you stood up and made a big joke of it, I decided to stick it out."

"I fully expect half of you to drown before the class

ends," I said, making my voice growly like Alex's. "And the rest of you better be willing to dedicate your lives to this class or I'll shoot you at sunrise."

"That's just how she talks!" Mei laughed.

"Somebody better tell her this is *summer* camp, not prison camp," I yelled. It was so much fun to laugh at Alex while we were on the other side of the lake. She couldn't reach us out here.

"You should tell her that," Lauren suggested. "It would be so funny if you got out of the water and said that to her!"

"Yeah! Do it!" everybody else was telling me.

"Maybe I will," I said.

"No, don't, JD. You've made her mad enough for one day," warned Courtney. "She'll kick you out, and we all want you in here with us or we'll never make it."

"Okay, fine. I'll try to be good, but it won't be easy." I put my face down and swam faster because I didn't want the rest of them to see my big, goofy smile.

It was working! Boring Judith Duckworth had disappeared, and I was JD, the funniest girl in the class now. But what if I ran out of jokes? I just hoped I could keep up this act forever. Or at least till camp was over.

# CHAPTER 5

## Friday, June 20

"See, isn't this better than going to activities?" asked Courtney.

"Definitely," I said, trying not to flinch. She pushed my cuticles back with this little tool that looked like a shovel for a Barbie doll.

"How'd you learn to do this?" My other hand soaked in a little pan of warm water. We were sitting on Courtney's bottom bunk, and she had all these instruments lined up on a towel. It looked like she was about to perform surgery on me.

"Just from watching people do them and getting them myself. Haven't you ever had a manicure?" she asked.

"Nope. This is my first." And probably my last. It was

a lot more painful than I thought it was going to be. "Now what are you doing?" She picked up a tiny pair of scissors and grabbed my fingertips.

"Hold still. I have to trim your cuticles. Then we're ready for polish." She looked up at me. "When we're done with your nails, I'll pluck your eyebrows for you."

"Oh, fun! Then you can pull out my toenails with a pair of pliers. I'm *glad* we didn't go to tennis."

Courtney laughed. "Thanks for cabin-sitting with me. You aren't worried we'll get caught, are you?" We were supposed to be at activities right now.

"I never worry about breaking rules. Rules were made to be broken," I bragged.

"That's what I like about you, JD. You're such a rebel."

When Courtney said we should cabin-sit for the afternoon, she tried to talk Mei and Lauren into hanging out with us, but they *were* worried about getting caught, so they went to riflery. Part of me wanted to go with them, because I hadn't been there yet. There were so many cool activities I hadn't tried yet, like rappelling and kayaking, and I'd only been to tennis once. What did it say about me that I'd rather shoot a gun than get a manicure? That I wasn't very good at being a girl. That was something I needed to work on.

"Besides, it's not like they'd punish us if they did catch us," Courtney went on. "They'd just send us to an activity." She buffed my nails with a big pink buffer.

"Exactly. People are always so afraid of getting in trouble. We're brainwashed to follow the rules from the time we're in preschool." I hoped that if anyone did catch us, it would be Alex. I liked Michelle, and I didn't want to be a troublemaker for her. Alex was a different story.

"Do you get in trouble a lot at school?" asked Courtney.

"Oh, yeah. I'm always causing trouble wherever I go," I said, trying not to blush. If only she knew.

"I wish I could be more like you."

"That's ridiculous! Just be yourself," I blurted out. Easy for me to say.

"I wrote some of my friends and my boyfriend Andrew about you. About how you're the life of the Guard Start class and how your jokes get us all through it."

"That's cool." I couldn't believe all the nice things she was saying. I watched her stroke on the red polish she'd picked out. It was a little extreme for me. For Judith. But I figured JD liked extreme colors.

"So do you have a big group of friends you hang out with back home, too?" she asked. It surprised me that she said "too." I had met a lot of people at camp, but I didn't really think of myself as having a big group of friends.

"Yeah, I guess. There's Chloe, Nick, Haley, Jordan, Seth, and Jenna," I said, naming all the popular kids in my school. "We go to the mall and hang out at the food court," I lied. They went to the mall. I once saw them there when I was shopping for new shoes with my grandma.

"Are you going out with any of those guys?" she asked.

"Well, Seth and I were going out, but we broke up. He was way too clingy—texting me about thirty times a day. I couldn't breathe from all that attention." That was exactly what I'd overheard Justin's girlfriend Sarah say about her old boyfriend. Who knew that line would come in handy sometime? "So now Nick and I are going out. He gives me my space."

*You're lying. You don't have a boyfriend. You're not popular. And your real name is Judith. Quit putting on this act.*

I kept waiting for Courtney to say that, but she just nodded. Every day I expected someone to walk up to me and say, "You're not fooling any of us."

But I was. Apparently. No matter what huge lie I told people, they all seemed to believe me. Why was I even doing this? Courtney already liked me. I didn't have to exaggerate for her.

"That's how Andrew is too," Courtney was saying. "We go out—but in a group. So there's no pressure. He's only sent me one e-mail this whole week. Which is fine with me, because if he was writing me every day, it'd be too much. You know?"

"Exactly," I said. Courtney blew on my nails to dry them. I had to admit, the polish made them look so much better. "Nick hasn't even written me yet, but then I haven't written him, either."

Nick D'Angelo was the cutest guy in my class— dark curly hair, dark brown eyes, and this devilish grin that made him look like he was always up to something. Drool. In my dreams I was getting mail from Nick D'Angelo.

Mail came every day after lunch, and Eda, the camp director, would print out e-mails and stick them in these little wooden boxes on the dining hall porch. Courtney got a stack of e-mails every day from her friends. I'd gotten several e-mails too, but mostly from my family and only a couple from friends. *Girl*friends.

Mom, Dad, and Adam had all sent me e-mails, but Justin hadn't. Mom and Dad both wrote, *Justin sends his love*, and Adam wrote, *Justin told me to say hi*, but I wondered if he really did. I had no idea how he was doing and what was going on back there, because none of them would tell me. They all made it sound like life was great. I knew that wasn't true.

Letting Courtney pluck my eyebrows made my eyes water, but it took my mind off Justin and my family. I felt bad that I could forget about them so easily. All week I'd been having so much fun, I'd barely thought about them. I knew that was one reason my parents had sent me to camp—to give me a break from all the stuff our family was going through. But I still worried about them. I couldn't help it.

"Now let's get some ideas for hairstyles," said Courtney, grabbing a stack of magazines from her trunk for us to look through. "I've been thinking about cutting my hair. Do you think I should?" She pulled her mass of wavy hair together on the back of her neck to give me an idea of what it would look like short.

"You've got great hair," I told her. "You should keep it long."

She sighed. "Maybe so. If I cut it, it would be curlier than ever."

We flipped through the pages of those magazines for probably an hour, with Courtney stopping on almost every page to comment on makeup and clothes and hair that she liked. It was the most boring hour of my life, but I tried to act interested. I really needed to get better at all this girl stuff. What was wrong with me? Why didn't I find this stuff interesting?

"Oh, I love that look," said Courtney, pointing to a model in a black miniskirt with lace leggings.

"You'd look good in that," I told her. I'd look like a gorilla if I tried to dress like that, but Courtney was so petite, she could pull it off. She was probably a size one or zero. Maybe she was even a size minus one, if there was such a thing.

I was a size nine in juniors, and my shoe size was eight and a half. Mom told me she thought my feet wouldn't grow any more, but what if they did? What if I ended up with a size thirteen? Did they even make women's shoes that big?

Courtney sat up and looked out the screen windows. "Omigosh, JD! Look!"

The sky had turned dark gray, and the cabin was all shadowy and dim. We ran to the screen door and looked outside. Rain started pelting down in buckets. Streams of water poured off the roof, and pretty soon a little river had formed in front of the cabin.

"Now I'm really glad we didn't go to activities!" I yelled over the sound of the rain pounding against the cabin roof. Since the cabin had so many screens, it was almost like being outside in the rain—we could smell the wetness and feel it in the air, but with the roof over our heads, we were nice and dry.

Then we saw people running down Middler Line, trying to get to the cabins. One dark figure came crashing through our door as we jumped out of the way.

It was Amber, and she looked like she'd been dunked in the lake. Her hair hung in wet strands like black vines, and her riding boots were covered in mud. She took riding lessons three times a week, and it seemed like she was always wearing those boots.

"It's pouring!" she shouted.

"We noticed!"

Mei and Lauren were the next to show up, both of them completely waterlogged; then Isabel came running in, her eyes wide and her bare legs splashed with mud. Everyone changed out of their wet clothes. I put on my blue hoodie, and Courtney wrapped up in a fuzzy yellow sweater. The whole cabin felt ten degrees cooler from the rain.

Lauren rubbed her blond hair with a towel. "I'm so glad this camp has cabins! Last summer I went to dance camp, and we slept in tents. It rained for three straight days and everything we had got soaked."

Pretty soon everyone came over to Side A, and we all sat around on Courtney's and Amber's bottom bunks.

Mei saw Courtney's magazines and picked one up. "I know—let's play a guessing game. I'll hold up a picture of a model and you guys guess 'real' or 'not real.'"

Everyone laughed. Amber covered her face with her hands. "Don't show me any of those pictures! Whenever I look at models, I want to run out and get plastic surgery."

"Oh, Amber! How can you say that?" asked Courtney, hugging her stuffed monkey.

"Uh, hello? Have you seen my nose?" Amber looked around at all of us. "Look, you guys. I know I've got a funny-looking schnoz. You don't have to pretend it's not there." Now I felt awful that I'd always thought of Amber as the flat-nosed girl.

Mei tossed the magazine away in disgust. "You do not need plastic surgery! We should burn these. All they do is make perfectly normal people feel bad about themselves."

"Don't blame it on the magazines. Anyway, all I need to do is look in a mirror to see what's wrong with my face," Courtney said.

"You?" I exclaimed. "You have a cute face, gorgeous hair, and a tiny body. You're perfect from head to toe!" It came out sounding kind of mad, but I'd meant it as a compliment.

"I am not! I hate my cheeks!" Courtney snapped at me. I couldn't tell if she was mad about the "perfect" remark.

I looked at her face and then at her backside. "Which pair of cheeks don't you like?" Everyone burst out laughing, but I wasn't trying to be funny. There was nothing wrong with either set of her cheeks, from what I could tell.

Courtney slapped her face with both hands. "I hate how fat and round my face looks. I wish there were exercises to make my face lose weight."

"You do not have a fat face," we all yelled at her, but she sucked in her cheeks to try to make her face look thin.

"Everyone has something they don't like about themselves," said Lauren. "I can't stand the way my voice sounds."

"What's wrong with your voice?" asked Amber.

"It always sounds hoarse, and I have to clear my throat all the time, and sometimes it comes out sounding squeaky."

Amber sniffed the air. "You guys—do I smell like the barn? I just came from my riding lesson. I love horses, but I'm always afraid they make me smell."

We all told her she smelled fine. I couldn't believe all the weird things people thought were wrong with them. Maybe they were all just making something up— saying they didn't like stuff about themselves so they wouldn't seem conceited. I'd always assumed most girls felt okay about themselves. I thought I was the only one who was so aware of all my flaws.

"When I was about four, I wanted Caucasian eyes," said Mei. "I didn't like that my eyes looked so different from my parents' eyes. Now I'm fine with my eyes, but I hate my ears."

"Why? What's wrong with your ears?" I asked.

"They stick out."

"They do not!" Courtney said.

"Yeah, they do. That's why I always wear my hair down. To cover them up."

Katherine came banging through the door and glanced at all of us hanging out on Side A. Then she went to her side of the cabin without speaking to anyone.

"Uh, Katherine, want to join us?" called Amber, who never wanted anyone to feel left out.

"NO!" she bellowed from across the cabin. We all looked at each other and smiled. We didn't exactly feel deprived of her company.

Isabel and I were the only ones who hadn't said anything yet. If I had to list all the things I didn't like about myself, it would take all week. I didn't like being the size of a linebacker around all these girls who were so petite that a strong breeze would blow them away. I'd recently been reminded of how bushy my eyebrows were and how disgusting my fingernails looked most of the time. Plus my entire wardrobe looked like I was

♥ 55 ♥

stuck in PE class, 24/7. All I ever wore were basketball shorts and T-shirts in assorted colors. It would take me a lot less time to tell what I *did* like about myself.

But what I hated most about myself was the one thing I couldn't mention—my boring personality. What if right now I told everyone that all week long I'd been putting on an act? It would be the perfect time to do it.

"I hate all my freckles," said Isabel softly. "And of course I'm not good at anything. And I'm short."

"Well, I hate being tall!" I declared, jumping off Courtney's bottom bunk. I banged my head against the springs of my top bunk, and everyone burst out laughing. That was the second time I'd been funny without trying to be. I pulled my blanket off my bunk and wrapped it around my head like a shawl.

"The only thing I could model would be next year's tents. I have a great career ahead of me as a plus-size model." I strutted around between the bunks with the blanket over my head, like I was on the runway. "The paparazzi will tell me to say 'Moo' before they take *my* picture!"

Everyone was laughing but Courtney. "JD, you are not fat!" she insisted.

True, I wasn't fat. Mom always called Justin and Adam her "big, strapping boys." She never called me strapping, but that's what I was. We all had the same genes.

"No, I'm not fat. I'm strapping! I could play tackle football just like my brothers, and I wouldn't even need shoulder pads." It was a little embarrassing to admit how much I hated my size, but at least I was getting noticed. Judith would've sat beside Isabel like a lump and never would've said a word. At least as JD, I got laughs.

The door banged open and Michelle and Meredith walked in. "Hey. What are you guys up to?" Michelle asked.

"Has it stopped raining?" asked Lauren, because they looked pretty dry.

"Yep. Finally," Meredith said. "We were stuck in Senior Lodge. We just saw an awesome mud fight."

Michelle looked at me with the blanket around my head. "Are you cold?"

"We were naming all the things we don't like about ourselves," explained Amber.

"My thighs," said Michelle, without missing a beat. Then she frowned at all of us. "Wait a second. What kind of conversation is this?"

"Well, Lauren thinks I'm a cow, and Mei thinks Courtney's ears are too Caucasian. Isabel said Amber's breath smelled like a horse, and Amber said we all needed plastic surgery." I was pointing fingers at everyone and talking really fast. I hoped everyone would laugh. Luckily, they did. Courtney hit me with her pillow.

Michelle plopped down on her bunk and folded her legs up. Meredith sat on the end of her bed. "Oh, if only you cuties could see yourselves the way I see you! Instead of dissing each other . . ."

"We weren't! We were dissing ourselves," Amber corrected.

Michelle nodded. "Whatever. Instead of dissing anyone, let's all go around and tell each person what we like most about her."

Lauren fell backward on the bunk. "That's corny. Let's not."

"No, we should! I think it's a great idea," said Amber.

"Me too," I said. "I'll start with Amber." I turned to face her. "You are so sweet, and I can tell you're a great person to have as a friend." I felt bad for thinking that Amber would've been a good friend for boring Judith, but JD should hang with Courtney instead. Now the two of us were always together with Lauren and Mei. I wondered if Amber felt left out. "Plus, I think your nose looks mahvelous," I added, because I felt the pressure to keep it funny.

Then everyone else said nice things about Amber. She was an easy one to do. She always had a good attitude about everything. She just went to her riding lessons and wrote poetry during rest hour. Then we picked Courtney, and everyone mostly complimented her on her looks, obviously, but I told her I liked how she was always saying nice things to other people. "And your cheeks look mahvelous," I assured her.

What I wanted to do was hug Courtney and thank her for picking me, Judith Duckworth, to be her friend. Before camp, I never would've thought I could have a bff like Courtney. Sometimes I wondered why she liked me, but then I'd remember. She liked JD. She didn't even know Judith.

Michelle said she liked Mei for her spunk, and I said I liked how she always did the right thing. What I meant was, I thought it was great how she always stood up for Isabel when Katherine was mean to her, but of course I couldn't say it that way.

"You're really good at keeping the peace," said Mei to Meredith, even though she'd missed most of the conversation.

Meredith had a funny way of putting her hands on her hips and saying, "This is not a crisis" any time anyone got upset or mad. Mei was good at sticking up for Isabel against Katherine, but Meredith kept things from getting out of hand in the first place.

Lauren got embarrassed when it was her turn. People mentioned her oh-so-blond hair and limber dancer's body. Amber grinned at me and said, "I think Lauren's voice sounds mahvelous."

"Oh, snap! Now what do I say?" I wailed. "Lauren, out of the whole Guard Start class, you try harder than anyone." She rolled her eyes and looked out the window. "I mean, I like how dedicated you are to the class. I could learn something from you." This morning Lauren had been the last one to finish her laps. She'd gotten mad at us all for clapping when she finally made it to the end of the dock.

When it was Isabel's turn, everyone said nice things about her personality, which made me mad. Did they have to be so obvious? Courtney had gotten so many compliments about her looks, and now they were going on and on about Isabel's personality. Why didn't they just put a bag over her head? "Isabel, you have beautiful eyes and a great smile," I said. She looked at me and grinned.

"I have a lot of respect for Isabel. She really has a desire to succeed," said Michelle, smiling. We all admired the way Isabel worked so hard at learning to swim.

"Now it's your turn," Amber said, pointing at me.

"You are the funniest person I've ever met in my entire life." Everyone else agreed, so I felt like a million bucks.

Little did they know I wasn't really funny, at least not naturally funny. All week I'd worried about running out of jokes. How long could I keep this up? Every single time there was a pause in the conversation, I'd think, "Say something funny now," and I was always afraid I'd draw a blank.

"You have a great personality," said Isabel, so softly I could barely hear her.

"Thanks!" But should I take credit for a good personality that wasn't even mine? I'd given up trying to act like Chloe; I couldn't do it. JD was a lot louder and more obnoxious than Chloe and not so quick and clever with the comebacks. But my new personality was warmer and fuzzier than Chloe's, more like a big teddy bear. Chloe had a way of cutting people down to get laughs. It seemed like I mostly made fun of myself.

"And you're a great athlete. So stop calling yourself a linebacker. I wish I had half your strength and endurance," said Lauren, looking at her fingernails the whole time.

Michelle grinned at me. "What I like most about JD is her sensitivity."

I had no idea what that meant, but I liked the way it sounded.

Camp was so much fun. It was hard to believe we'd only been together for a week. It seemed longer. Being around a bunch of girls was a lot different from my life back home with a house full of boys. Maybe this was what it felt like to have sisters.

# CHAPTER 7

## Saturday, June 21

"I have absolutely nothing to wear tonight," I said, looking at the pile of clothes I'd pulled out of my trunk. It was such a girl thing to say, but it was true. Luckily, my brothers weren't around to hear me or they'd never stop teasing me.

"Maybe you can borrow something of mine," offered Amber. She'd just come back from the showers, and she was still wrapped up in a towel.

"Are you a size nine?" I asked.

"Uh, I wear mostly five." She shrugged and smiled at me hopefully.

"Thanks anyway," I told her.

"I'm glad we did our nails yesterday," said Courtney. "One less thing to worry about today."

We were one hour away from having a dance with the boys from Camp Crockett. Everyone in the cabin was rushing around getting ready.

"Should I wear my hair down?" asked Lauren as she brushed her hair in front of the little mirror on the wall. All week I'd never seen her without her blond ponytail.

"I think you should," Courtney said, squeezing next to her to look in the mirror while she put on some mascara. "And I can't wait to see you dance tonight."

"Oh, please. I bet none of those guys can move at all," snorted Lauren. She had shown us some dance moves this morning when we first heard there might be a dance tonight. She was an awesome dancer. "I've been taking lessons since I was four," she'd told us with a little smile.

"Well, I'm ready," Mei announced, coming over to Side A. She had on a pink skirt and a white shirt, and she looked adorable. "Think these guys will actually dance with us?" she asked, trying out some of the steps Lauren had shown us. "Or will they stand around and ignore us?"

"They'll ignore us. They're all jerks," we heard Katherine say from Side B.

"Way to look on the bright side, Katherine," said Mei over her shoulder.

"I always get nervous before dances. I'm not good at talking to boys," Amber admitted.

I slammed my trunk shut. "Why would you be nervous talking to boys? Boys are . . ." I tried to think of the right words. "Boys are like dogs. They're smelly and playful and they scratch themselves a lot."

"Omigosh, JD!" gasped Amber. "You always crack me up. 'Boys Are Like Dogs.' That would make a great title." She grabbed a spiral notebook from beside her bed and jotted something down. Maybe I'd given her inspiration for a new poem.

"So you're saying you don't get nervous around boys?" asked Courtney, looking at me skeptically.

"No, I don't. Remember, I have two brothers, and their friends are always hanging around our house at all hours of the day. I know how to talk to boys," I said. Justin and Adam had two friends I was totally in love with—Ben and Ryan. They thought of me as just a little sister, so I could tease them and punch them in the arm and pull their hair. I never got nervous around those guys.

Lauren turned away from the mirror. "So, you want to give us any advice?"

"Just watch a pro in action tonight," I bragged. "I'll have a boyfriend before the night is over."

"Oh, really?" said Mei.

"Okay, JD. If you say so," Lauren said.

Obviously they didn't believe me, and I couldn't really blame them. What was I saying? But now I had to follow through.

"What about Nick?" asked Courtney.

I came so close to asking "Nick who?" until I remembered that in my fantasy world I was going out with Nick D'Angelo. "Well, what Nick doesn't know won't hurt him, will it?" I said.

Michelle and Alex came in and asked us why we were all dressed up. "Do you guys know something we don't know?" asked Michelle with a sly grin.

No one had said for sure yet that we were having a dance. They worried that if they made it definite, we'd all be so excited we wouldn't go to any activities all day, so they kept us in suspense until the last moment. At least if there wasn't a dance I'd be off the hook for finding a boyfriend.

"We were tired of looking like slobs all week," said Courtney, batting her eyelashes at Michelle.

"I seriously have nothing to wear!" I yelled.

"Want to borrow something of mine?" asked Michelle, saving my life.

"Oh, you mean there *is* a dance tonight?" Lauren said.

Michelle looked at me and smiled. "I never said that! JD can borrow my clothes anytime."

We looked through her clothes until we'd picked out a pair of chocolate-colored cargos and a tan tank. I rolled the pants legs up so they didn't look too short. "Then layer this on the top." She handed me a short-sleeved shirt with a tiny flower print. "Leave this shirt unbuttoned. What do you think, everyone?" She spun me around for inspection.

"You look great, JD!" said Amber.

"Here, wear these earrings," Lauren offered, bringing me a pair of little gold hoops. "And I've got a necklace for you too." She squinted while she put her earrings in for me.

"When you're done with her, bring her to me so I can do her hair and makeup," said Courtney, putting on lip gloss in front of the mirror.

"Oh, thank God I've got an entire pit crew to dress me! I could never do this on my own!" They all laughed, but it was true.

While Courtney styled my hair and did my makeup, everyone else stood around and watched. When she was finished, she wouldn't let me look in the little mirror. "Let's go to Solitary, where you can really get a good look."

We all trooped down Middler Line to the bathrooms. Courtney grabbed my arm as we went through the doorway. "Close your eyes." She led me over to the full-length mirror next to the row of sinks and stopped. "Okay, open."

I opened my eyes and looked in the mirror at someone who looked like a really good version of me. "Wow!" I said. Lauren, Amber, and Mei stood behind me, grinning. "Thanks, guys! I couldn't have done it without you. And I seriously mean that."

Solitary was packed with other girls using the sinks and pushing for a turn in front of the mirror, so we left for the dining hall, since it was time for dinner anyway.

"Garlic bread, anyone?" asked Michelle with a grin, passing the plate around our table. I took two pieces, but Courtney frowned at me.

"You think that's a good idea right before a dance?" she asked.

"What? Too many carbs?" I wondered.

"No, goofy. Garlic. If you want to gargle half a bottle of mouthwash, go ahead."

In the middle of dinner the CATs (Counselor Assistants in Training) came in clapping and singing. I loved the CATs; it was their job to make sure all the campers were having a good time. They were sixteen, so they were kind of in between campers and counselors. When they announced that we were going to Camp Crockett for a dance, the whole dining hall went crazy.

"But be careful!" the CATs yelled. "If those Crockett boys want you to sneak away to the bushes for a make-out session, we'll be watching to make sure that nobody leaves the dining hall porch!" Then they sang this crazy song, holding flashlights and shining them all over everyone.

> *Porch Patrol! Porch Patrol!*
> *Start yellin' for that good ole Porch Patrol!*
> *If he tries to make first base, you had better slap*
> *his face,*
> *And start yellin' for that good ole Porch Patrol!*

When they'd finished singing and sat down at their table in the middle of the dining hall, Lauren asked, "Are they really going to the dance dressed like that?" They were all wearing camouflage T-shirts and pants, and they had leaves and little tree branches stuck in their hair and taped to their clothes.

"They sure are," said Alex. "So don't let them catch you."

"You mean they'll be watching us? Has anyone ever gotten caught?" I asked.

"Of course not," said Katherine. "They sing that same stupid song every year. Who would want to be seen with any of those Crockett creeps?"

"The point is, while you're at Camp Crockett you're not to leave their dining hall. And if anyone does try to leave, the Porch Patrol will stop you. So I expect you all to act like young ladies this evening!" warned Michelle.

So nobody had ever been caught by the Porch Patrol. Wouldn't *that* be a great way to make a name for myself? Maybe no one had ever been caught because no one had ever tried to sneak away.

But wasn't there a first time for everything?

# CHAPTER 8

When we walked into Camp Crockett's dining hall, I saw Natasha hanging out with her new bff, Ashlin. I ran over and gave her a hug like I always did whenever I saw her. It was sort of sad that Natasha and I had different sets of friends now.

Lauren, Mei, Courtney, and I were all standing together. All the boys were across from us, and so far no one was dancing, even though the music was playing.

I decided I needed to work fast. I couldn't stand around waiting for some guy to find me. I had to go to him. Most girls were hoping to dance with some cute guys and maybe even meet someone they really liked. That didn't matter to me. I just needed to make it look like I'd found a guy who liked me.

I looked at the crowd of boys. There sure were a lot of shrimpy guys who went to this camp. I wanted to find someone who wasn't a foot shorter than I was, and judging by the looks of this crowd, that wasn't going to be easy.

The guys stood around talking to each other. Every now and then one of them would look over in our direction, like they were checking to see if we were still there.

"See anyone you like?" asked Courtney.

"Maybe. How about you?" I said.

"Yeah. See the guy in the green Hurley shirt? He keeps looking over here."

"Hey, you in the green shirt. Come over and dance with my friend," I said, kind of loud, but not loud enough for him to actually hear me.

"JD, stop!" hissed Courtney. "Try not to embarrass all of us, please!"

"Oh, don't worry. I won't embarrass anyone but myself. Why don't you all just watch and see how it's done?"

I walked straight over to where three guys were standing. Two of them were close to my height. When they saw me coming toward them, they all got panicked looks on their faces, like they didn't know what I was going to do to them. Most girls didn't realize that boys were scared of us half the time.

"Hey, guys. Wassup?"

"Hi," one of them answered. The other two just stood there.

"My friends dared me to come talk to you guys. They didn't think I'd do it, so help me out here, okay?"

"Sure," said the talker of the group.

"I'm JD, by the way."

"Oh. I'm Lance." He was around my height, and he wore glasses and had a really severe case of bed head.

"I'm David," said the other tall guy. He had braces and a buzz cut, and his face was beefy and round.

"I'm Michael," said the short guy. He wasn't really that short, just not as tall as the rest of us.

"What's JD short for?" asked Lance.

"Jamaica Daytona," I said, looking at him with a straight face.

"What a weird name. No wonder you go by your initials," Michael said.

"Well, my parents love the beach. Good thing they're not into mountains or I might've been named Everest Rushmore." It was a lot of fun telling crazy stories to people. Amazingly, they always believed me, or at least they hardly ever questioned me.

The guys looked at me like they didn't know what to do next. I glanced over to where my friends were, and they were all watching me. When Courtney saw me, she raised her eyebrows. I had to make this look good. Time to bring up the one subject that every boy in the world was interested in.

"Wow. This dance pretty much sucks, doesn't it?" I asked them.

"Yeah," they all said at the same time.

"You know what would make this a really good dance? If we had a room with a long row of TVs and about five or six different game systems," I said.

"Oh, sweet!" groaned Lance, like he could picture a setup like that.

Michael and David nodded. "That would be awesome."

"So which systems do you guys have?" I asked.

Then all three of them were talking at the same time. Wii, PS2 and 3, DS, PSP, Xbox 360—they rattled them all off. I stood in the middle and let them talk. I glanced across the dining hall and saw Mei's jaw drop.

"Yeah, have you ever played Twilight Princess on Wii?" I asked Lance. He was the one I liked best. Behind his glasses, I noticed he had beautiful gray eyes, and when he smiled, he had a dimple in the side of his cheek.

"Oh! I don't have it, but my friend Gabe does. It's pretty tight."

"I've got it for GameCube," said Michael. "My favorite part is when you're battling the monkeys."

"On Madden, do you guys ever set a player's weight as high as it'll go and his speed at zero so he can barely move?" I asked.

Lance let out a loud cackle. "I love doing that! One time I made this one player really weak. He tried to catch a pass, but he fell over and couldn't get up!"

The four of us spent at least ten minutes talking about all our favorite games and what levels we'd gotten to on all of them. Then I said, "Hang on a second, guys. I need to talk to my friends, but I'll be right back."

I walked across the dining hall to my crew. "Wipe that smirk off your face!" said Lauren when I walked up to her.

Mei grabbed me by both arms. "How? How? Just tell us how you did that!"

"What were you guys talking about, JD?" asked Courtney. "You sure had their attention."

I shrugged. "Nothing, really. Just guy stuff. Look, I gotta go. My boys are waiting for me. Do any of you want to dance with one of them?"

"I'll take the cute one," Courtney said.

"The one with the dark hair? That's Michael. I'll see what I can do." It didn't surprise me that Courtney would pick Michael. He was the cutest of the three, but I still preferred Lance's gray eyes. Plus he was taller than Michael.

Then I walked back over to the guys. "Look, guys, I know it would be a lot more fun to stand around and talk about video games all night, but my friends are bored. So why don't you come over and meet them? You don't have to dance or anything."

I walked off like I assumed they would follow me, and they did. I'd never been the one who's always telling other people what to do, but the weird thing was, it worked. At least most of the time. It seemed like most people spent a lot of time waiting for someone to tell them what to do. I figured I might as well be the one who did the telling.

While my friends were introducing themselves to the guys, I decided it was time to put my plan in action. I leaned over to Lance and said, "I don't like to dance, do you?"

"No, I suck at it," he answered. He had really long legs, and he moved like he wasn't used to walking on them yet.

"Hey, want to go out on the porch? It's pretty stuffy in here."

Lance shrugged. "Okay, sure."

He followed me outside to the porch, where a bunch of people were hanging out and talking. Some people were sitting on the rails and others were just standing around. It was almost dark. Crickets were chirping, and a few moths fluttered around the porch lights.

"So, do you know any good cheat codes for the Sims?" I asked.

"Yeah, freeall, fisheye, midas. You enter them by holding L1, L2, R1, R2."

While Lance chattered away about the Sims, I glanced around. Besides a bunch of campers, a few Crockett and Pine Haven counselors were out here too, but I didn't see any of the CATs. Did that mean they weren't really on Porch Patrol? Had the whole thing been a joke? If we walked away from the dining hall right now, would anybody notice us?

"It's a pretty nice night out, isn't it?" I said. "Feel like taking a walk? I've never been to Camp Crockett before. You could show me around."

My heart started pounding a little when I said that. Getting caught *sounded* like a great idea when I'd first thought of it, but now that it was time to actually go through with it, I wasn't so sure.

Lance scratched his ear. "Uh, I don't think we can

leave. The counselors told us to stay around the dining hall for the whole dance." His feet kicked against the porch rails.

"Really? That's weird. I wonder why they'd even care. Have you ever played Destroy All Humans?" I asked. Think, think, think. What excuse could I make for us to leave the dining hall?

Lance went off on what a great game that was. I noticed there were steps at either end of the porch. The ones we were closest to were by the parking area, and there were lights shining on all the Pine Haven vans and trucks we'd come over in. At the far end of the porch, though, there weren't any lights. And there weren't very many people hanging out there either. If we did try to leave, that should definitely be our exit.

"It's sure crowded out here. Let's move down there where there aren't as many people." I headed for the far end of the porch and Lance followed, telling me about the time he leveled out all of Rockwell's buildings. So far we hadn't broken any rules, but my heart wouldn't stop pounding. It was easy for me to talk about what a rule breaker I was to everyone. Now it was time to really prove it. But how could I convince Lance to go along with me?

Maybe I should tell him I needed to make a phone call. I had a poor sick grandma in the hospital who might not make it through the night. Couldn't he help me find a phone somewhere?

"I have this old copy of *Tips and Tricks*. It has a strategy guide that helped me get through all the levels of that game," said Lance.

"Really? I would *love* to see those. Do you remember any of them?" I asked. How exactly does one get from the subject of aliens conquering Earth to a poor sick grandma? *My poor grandma used to love watching me use my disintegrator ray to reduce my enemies to dust. But she's really sick now, and . . .*

"Well, it's in my cabin. I brought a stack of *Tips and Tricks* with me in case—"

"It's in your cabin?" I said. "Can I see it? Please, oh please? I've been stuck on level eighteen forever. I've gotta see that guide!" Okay, now this just might work. I felt a little braver now. I reminded myself that JD didn't get nervous when it came to getting into trouble.

"Uh, I don't think we're supposed to—"

"Oh Lance, don't tell me you're one of those nerdy guys who's always worried about following all the rules. I know you're not like *that*." I was down the steps before he could get another word out. "Which way is your cabin? We can be there and back in ten minutes. Nobody will ever know we're gone."

I walked fast, going in the opposite direction of where all the counselors were at the other end of the porch. It was pretty dark now, and I hoped we wouldn't get all the way to Lance's cabin before *somebody* saw us. It would be okay to get into a little trouble, but I didn't want to cause a huge uproar. Lance trotted to catch up with me.

"No, really. I think we should—"

"Is this the way?" I pointed down a dirt path that looked like it might lead to some cabins.

"No, that goes to the Mites cabins. I'm a Newt. Our cabins are that way, but—"

"This way? I'm so glad you brought those magazines with you. Looking at strategy guides will be so much better than being stuck at this dance." I couldn't really see his face in the dark, but he was at least keeping up with me now. The grass was all dewy and wet, and the crickets were singing like crazy.

"Uh, JD—I'm not sure we can—"

"C'mon. Don't be so nervous!" My gosh, were all boys this shy? If they got this stressed over showing a girl their strategy guides, how did they ever get up the nerve to kiss someone?

"Hey! Where are you guys going?"

Finally! We turned around, and the beam of a flashlight bounced across our faces. All I could see were two dark forms standing there, shining a light in our eyes.

Perfect. The Porch Patrol really was on duty after all.

# CHAPTER 9

I recognized them when they got a little closer: Madison Abernathy and Lydia Duncan. They were still dressed in camouflage.

"What are you two doing?" asked Madison. She was really pretty, with long dark hair. She had a few leafy twigs sticking out all over the place.

"Uh, we . . . uh," stuttered Lance. His mouth hung open, and the light reflected off the lenses of his glasses. Now I felt bad for getting him into trouble.

"We were just going for a walk," I said. "Lance was showing me the Camp Crockett sights." I gave them both a big smile. No way could I tell them we were on our way to his cabin.

"No, you're not," said Lydia. "You guys know you're

not supposed to leave the dining hall. Get back to the dance."

"Are we in big trouble? Please don't tell Eda," I begged. Actually, I didn't care if she told Eda or not. The more people who knew about it, the better.

"Just get going." Madison shone her flashlight at us one more time, so I couldn't see their expressions. Did they think it was funny they'd caught us? Or were they mad? Their voices had been all stern-sounding. When we walked past them, I wanted to grab Lance's hand so it would look like we were up to *something*, but I didn't want to make the poor guy faint.

"Uh," said Lance. He was still speechless.

"Hey, it's okay. They won't do anything to us," I whispered to him. Madison and Lydia walked behind us, like they didn't trust us to find the dining hall on our own.

When we got back to the porch, it seemed like there were about twenty or thirty people watching us as we walked up. I bumped against Lance a couple of times to make it look like we were a real couple who'd been caught making out in the dark. He scooted over each time I did it, though, so I stopped.

Maybe I should've smeared my lip gloss before everybody saw us. Why didn't I think of that before? Chloe Carlson would've thought of that. Wait a second, Chloe

Carlson wouldn't need to smear her own lip gloss; the boy she was with would've done it for her. But so what? Chloe wasn't the one who got caught this time. *I* was. And things couldn't have been more perfect. It was exactly like I thought it would be.

"Lance! You da man!" a boy yelled from the porch. Somebody whistled as we walked up the steps. I had a little smile on my face as everyone watched us. Lance stared at his shoelaces the whole time.

When we walked into the dining hall, a Camp Crockett counselor gave us a long, intense look; then he walked toward us. I was afraid he was Lance's counselor, and now he was going to yell at us for leaving the dining hall. But for some reason, he was looking right at me. He didn't even notice Lance was there.

"Hey, don't I know you?" he asked.

The second he said that, I recognized him. Brandon Matheson, a guy who used to play football at Central. A teammate of Justin's!

What was *he* doing here? I did not want to be recognized by anyone from home! Especially not in front of Lance. If Lance hadn't been with me, I would've taken off running in the opposite direction.

Brandon pointed at me. "I got it! You're a Duckworth, aren't you? Yeah! I remember you from all the practices!"

"Oh, hi," I said. *Now, bye. See ya later. Adios, amigo.* "You're Brandon, right?" I asked him through my clenched smile. His hair was longer than it used to be, and he looked a little older.

"Yeah, that's right. So you're going to Pine Haven, huh?" asked Brandon.

"Uh, yeah." My head bounced up and down like a bobblehead. Maybe we could keep the topic of conversation on camp instead of football. "You're a counselor, I guess. That must be fun. What's your activity?" Lance looked back and forth between me and Brandon. So far he hadn't missed a word of this conversation.

"I'm on the hiking staff. Hey—how's Justin doing?"

"He's doing great! I'll tell him I saw you. Wow! He'll really be surprised. This is Lance, by the way. Brandon's from my hometown." Maybe now we could say our good-byes and walk away. I held my breath and hoped that Brandon wouldn't say anything else about Justin and football in front of Lance.

"Hey, dude. What's up?" Brandon said without even looking at Lance. He was completely focused on me, unfortunately. "Well, I heard what happened. What a shame. I couldn't believe it." He said it in a sorry-your-dog-died kind of voice.

So he *had* heard about what happened. I was hoping

that maybe if he was away at college, he didn't know all the gory details. No such luck.

"Yeah. Well, things are okay," I said, my head bobbing up and down like crazy. "So you're in college now?"

"Yeah, I just finished my first year at Auburn. I'm playing lacrosse now."

"Really? Cool. Lacrosse is a great sport." *In fact, let's talk about lacrosse from now on, and not speak of football ever again.*

"Yeah. I didn't get a football scholarship. I considered trying out as a walk-on, but I'm an engineering major, and I really needed time for my studies. With lacrosse, I can play a sport without it taking up all my time."

I nodded. Obviously, Brandon had been bitten by the chatty bug seconds before he'd run into us.

"Hey, listen. Tell your brother I said hi. Hope everything works out for him. I was real sorry to hear what happened. It hurt the whole team."

"Okay, thanks. I will. Bye, Brandon!" I took two steps back, hoping he wouldn't say anything else before I could finally get away.

But he was done. He walked off.

*Oh my God!* My heart hammered in my chest. My face felt flaming hot. All I wanted to do was get as far away from Brandon Matheson as I possibly could. I pushed through the crowd of people, not even caring at this point if Lance was still following me or not.

How was it possible that I'd been recognized when I was two hundred miles from home? And that the person who recognized me not only knew Justin, but used to play football with him? What were the odds? Brandon Matheson, of all people! And when did he turn into such a yakker?

"Uh, JD?"

I spun around to see Lance trailing along behind me. "What?" I snapped at him.

Lance drew back like I'd spit in his eye. "What was that all about?"

"Oh, Brandon. He knows my brother. Used to play football with him. Are you as thirsty as I am?" I took off toward the refreshment table at a mad run. Lance tried to keep up with me.

"What was all that stuff about 'I heard what happened'?" asked Lance. Boy, he'd certainly gotten curious all of a sudden.

I stopped at the refreshment table, grabbed a cup of red bug juice, and gulped it down. "Oh, that. Justin got injured. Pulled his quadriceps. He might not be able to play next season."

"Oh." Lance took a drink of bug juice and looked around. "I wonder where Mike and David are."

I let out a sigh and concentrated on getting my pulse down from rapid to normal. My hand holding the paper cup was shaking, so I crumpled it up and tossed it into the trash can.

It wasn't a total lie. Justin had pulled his quadriceps once during his sophomore year, and he missed the last two games of the season. I was so relieved Brandon hadn't blabbed too much about what had happened. Lance didn't need to hear that. No one needed to hear that.

"Is it true?"

I spun around to see Katherine beside me. "I heard you and some guy got caught by the Porch Patrol." She gave Lance a quick look and then sneered at me.

"Yeah. So?" I did not feel like dealing with Katherine right now.

"So what you were doing?" she asked.

"Katherine, if you want the latest news, check the headlines every day." I stomped off through the crowd of dancers. Lance ran up behind me.

"Sorry about that. I didn't know we'd get in trouble," he said.

I slowed down as we weaved in and out of the

people on the dance floor. "It's okay. I don't mind," I told him over my shoulder. Poor guy. He'd put up with a lot tonight. "Anyway, it was my idea to leave the dining hall in the first place, remember?"

We moved over to the edge of the dance floor and sat in some chairs along the wall. "Thanks for hanging out with me tonight. I had a great time," I told him. "Too bad we couldn't have played a few levels of Destroy All Humans."

"Yeah." Lance nodded. He sat with his feet sticking way out, and a couple of people stumbled over them as they walked by. He was tall and goofy, but I still liked the guy. He really was a good sport. "I've never met a girl who knows so much about video games. I didn't even want to come to this dance, but it turned out pretty okay."

By now everyone was slow dancing, and we sat there and watched them. Now I was wishing I hadn't made all those comments about not liking to dance. Lance would be okay to slow dance with. He had beautiful gray eyes and he was fun to hang out with, and he'd followed me all over the place tonight.

Maybe at the next dance. Hey, if I could convince him to leave the dining hall, it couldn't be that hard to figure out how to get him out on the dance floor.

When the dance ended, everyone crowded through the doors to go outside.

"Sorry I got us in trouble," I told Lance. "Maybe I'll see you at the next dance?"

"Sure. See ya later!" He'd found David and Mike, and they were dragging him away, asking a bunch of questions. I wondered if he would tell them what we were really doing. Probably. He didn't seem to have a clue what the Porch Patrol was really there for.

When I walked up to the truck that would take us all back to camp, everyone swarmed around me.

"So you really got caught?" asked Mei. "Was it the guy with the glasses?"

"What were you doing?" Lauren asked.

"JD, you *have* to tell us what happened!" said Courtney.

I plastered a huge grin on my face and said, "I don't kiss and tell!" Then I refused to say another word, even though they kept pumping me for more info.

It would've been a perfect night if it hadn't been for Brandon Matheson. It was bad enough that Lance had witnessed that little meeting. What if one of my friends had been with me when I ran into him? Or Michelle? Almost every day Michelle asked me more questions about Justin and Adam. I wished she'd never even seen those pictures of them playing football. There was no way I could tell her I didn't want to talk about my own brothers.

"Climb in!" yelled Jerry. He was Pine Haven's hiking guide, and he'd driven the white truck we had to ride in. We all piled into the back and sat on the benches that lined the sides and the back of the truck.

"So, are you going to tell me about it?" whispered Courtney.

"I will, but not now," I said. At least Brandon hadn't called me Judith. Maybe he didn't remember my name. I was only Justin's kid sister to him.

The truck rumbled down the road, and everyone laughed when we passed under the Camp Crockett sign, because there was pink underwear hanging all over it. I could pull off being JD at camp, but when camp was over, then what?

There were times when it felt like I'd always been JD. Sometimes I completely forgot about my old life as Judith. Until it would come sneaking up on me, like Brandon Matheson. *Don't I know you?*

No, Brandon, you *don't* know me. And Courtney, Lauren, Mei—they don't know me either. How could they know me?

They don't even know my name.

## CHAPTER  10

## Monday, June 23

"So how would you rate him, on a scale of one to ten?" asked Mei.

"Oh, I'd say about a seven," I said. I kicked with my feet under water so I wouldn't splash everyone around me.

"A seven? Is that all?" Courtney asked, swimming up beside me. Out of everyone in the class, she was the one who was most able to keep up with me. But when we swam laps, I didn't go fast. It was more fun for all of us to stay in a group and talk.

"Okay, an eight, then," I said. "Wait up for Lauren, you guys." We all slowed down so Lauren could catch up to us.

"Don't let me hold everyone else up!" Lauren snapped

at us when she got closer. We all felt bad that she had such a hard time. She tried her best, but it was always a struggle.

"JD, admit it. Nothing happened between you and that guy," said Claudia. "I bet he didn't lay a hand on you. Or a lip!"

The whole class cracked up over Claudia's lip remark. She obviously saw through me, more than anyone else. I hadn't exactly lied about what happened when Lance and I got caught by the Porch Patrol on Saturday night. Everyone had just assumed we'd been kissing. Of course, saying "I don't kiss and tell" whenever anyone asked me about what happened probably had a little something to do with it.

"Okay, whatever. Believe what you want to believe," I told the others. "Maybe Lance and I weren't kissing when those two CATs caught us. And maybe his breath didn't smell like Skittles."

"Like Skittles? His breath smelled like Skittles?" asked Shelby, pushing her bangs out of her eyes.

"Yeah, but I didn't mind," I said. "He did have a pucker like a fish, though." Now everyone was laughing over my remark. Poor Lance. He really was a nice guy, and I didn't plan on making fun of him. I was just trying to think of something funny to say. Good thing he'd never know I'd said that about him.

"Only JD would be crazy enough to get caught by the Porch Patrol," said Courtney.

"Yeah! I couldn't believe the way you walked over and started talking to all those guys. You definitely have a way with boys, JD," Mei said, paddling beside me.

"What's all the discussion about?" yelled Alex as we swam up close to the dock. "Everyone out on the side. We're going to work on reaching and throwing assists today."

Alex told Claudia to jump in and show signs of distress. Then she demonstrated how to do a reaching assist by lying on our stomachs on the dock and reaching out with an arm, and then holding on to a rung of the ladder and reaching out with a leg. Next she threw a ring buoy out to Claudia and pulled her in.

"Okay, now I want you guys to try it in pairs. Claudia, out of the water. Courtney, you jump in and Claudia will do both a reach and a pull assist with you."

The rest of us sat on the edge of the dock to watch the exercise.

"You guys want to know something?" whispered Mei, hugging her towel around her shoulders. "I've never been kissed. Pathetic, huh?"

"No, it's not!" I said. "Look, it's really no big deal. It's not like I saw fireworks or anything." I dangled my feet over the edge of the dock, my toes touching the water. I watched a few little tadpoles dart up to the dock and then swim away.

"Well, I haven't really been either," Lauren confessed. The sunlight made her squint, so she kept her hand in front of her eyes. "Except for Will Thurmond. He kissed me on the playground when we were in second grade. But I'm not sure that really counts. It was on the cheek."

"Sure it counts," I told her. "If you want it to."

"Ugh!" she groaned. "If Will Thurmond counts as my first kiss, I'm even more pathetic than you are, Mei. He was always having nosebleeds!"

"This guy kissed me at my school's fall festival last year," said Shelby. "We were in the haunted house. I was *so* not expecting it. We'd just stuck our hands in bowls of Jell-O and spaghetti, and then all of a sudden—smack!"

We were all laughing, but I felt sort of bad. It was fun getting so much attention for being caught by the Porch Patrol. That part had gone exactly the way I'd hoped it would. And now my reputation as a rule breaker was really growing. But if my friends were going to get a complex over it, I wasn't sure it was worth it. I didn't want Lauren and Mei to think something was wrong with them because they'd never been kissed.

Because I hadn't either. I hadn't even had a peck on the cheek by a second-grade nosebleeder. Last year I'd been shooting hoops with some boys during recess. I was guarding Jacob Zinner when I noticed that *his* breath smelled like Skittles, and for a second I'd wondered what it would be like to kiss him. *That* was the closest I'd ever come to being kissed. Just thinking about it.

"Good job!" yelled Alex from the water. "Okay, now let's have Mei and Lauren."

Lauren and Mei took a turn while Claudia and Courtney came over and sat down. "What were you guys laughing about?" asked Courtney, dripping all over us.

"Oh, nothing," I said. I wanted to get off the subject of Lance and kissing for a while. Shelby and I scooted over to make room for them to sit down beside us.

"Oh, JD—I almost forgot to tell you. Yesterday during rest hour, Michelle was writing mommy letters," said Courtney, wrapping herself up in her towel.

"So?" I asked. Michelle had asked us all about our favorite activities so she could write the weekly letter home to our parents, telling them how we were doing.

"So—what if she tells your parents you got caught by the Porch Patrol?"

Claudia shook her head. "Nah, she wouldn't do that. Eda doesn't want the counselors to say anything bad about us to our parents, unless there's some real problem." She looked at her watch. "Fifteen more minutes." Claudia was always counting down the minutes till class was over, like she had someplace better to be.

"Anyway, it wouldn't surprise my parents that I'd gotten in trouble," I said. "You know what I always say—rules were made to be broken."

But Courtney had me worried about something. I had to remember to tell Michelle to call me Judith in the letter home to my parents. If she wrote something like *JD is working very hard in her Guard Start class*, they wouldn't know who she was talking about. And I'd have to find a time to tell her when nobody else was around.

Also, mentioning the letter home to my parents made me feel guilty. I'd barely thought about my family for days. I was so completely caught up in my camp life.

It seemed like I had always woken up to the sound of a big bell being rung and the feel of cool mountain air drifting in through the window screens. Every morning we cleaned the cabin, ate breakfast, and went to activities. Then it was lunchtime, rest hour, and more activities. Then dinner, evening program in Middler Lodge, and bed. I loved the pattern of every day. It was like a school schedule, only everything centered around fun instead of work. It seemed like I'd swum in this lake hundreds of times, and I'd sat on this dock and gazed at these mountains my whole life. It was amazing how easy it was to put my family and my old life out of my mind.

Shelby and Courtney cheered for Lauren and Mei while they did the exercise. Lauren splashed water at us. She seemed to think it was a pity remark when we told her she did a good job at something. The truth was, she was really good at doing the service hours and helping out with swim lessons. And she was always the first to finish the workbook exercises we had to do. It was only the swimming part she had trouble with.

"What's up with you? You look so serious all of a sudden," said Courtney, shading her face with her hand while she stared at me.

If I went more than five minutes without cracking a joke, everyone looked at me and asked me what was wrong. It was just what I'd always worried about—that I'd run out of funny things to say and then everyone would find out the truth. There were times when I wanted to yell, "I'm sick of this!" and go back to being Judith.

"Why'd you have to mention the mommy letters?" I asked her. "I miss my mommy." At least now that I'd thought about her for the first time in days, I missed her. "Don't you miss your mommy?"

"Of course," Courtney said.

"I miss my mommy, oh yes, I do, I miss my mommy, and I'll be true!" I started singing to the tune of one of the camp songs. "When she's not with me, I'm blue, I'm blue-hoo," I sang in a really deep voice, "oh, Mommy, I miss you!"

"Keep it down before Alex hears you," Claudia told me.

"Good idea," said Courtney, giving me a look and jerking her head to the side.

"What? Don't you like my singing?" I wailed. "Is there anything wrong with being a loving daughter singing a song to my mother? Huh? You got a problem wit' dat?" I shook my fists at the rest of them. But they were all acting like I'd just cursed my mother's good name or something. Shelby stared out at the lake. Claudia and Courtney both glared at me. For some reason, nobody liked my joke.

"Huh! What's wrong with this crowd?" I went on. "I happen to love my mother. Ouch!" Courtney had poked me in the ribs as hard as she could. "What? You don't love your mother?" I asked her.

"JD, shut up," Claudia warned. "Your joke's not

funny, so drop it. I can't believe Alex hasn't heard you yet." She glanced at her watch again.

"Shelby, don't you miss your mommy?" I asked.

Shelby stared at the lake and didn't move a muscle. It seemed like Claudia and Courtney were frozen too. Why was everyone being so quiet all of a sudden?

Then Shelby looked at me for the first time since I'd started the mommy joke. Tears welled up in her eyes. "Yeah, I do miss my mom. A lot." Then she slid off the end of the dock into the water.

Alex looked up to see what was going on. "Shelby! Out of the water till it's your turn!" she yelled.

"Sorry, I slipped," Shelby called, bobbing to the surface.

Claudia and Courtney both grabbed me at the same time. "You idiot! Don't you know Shelby's mother is dead?" hissed Claudia.

"Boy, JD! How many signals do I have to give you?" whispered Courtney. "I kept trying to shut you up!"

"Oh," I said.

"I told you to drop it," Claudia went on. "But you just kept going. You really know how to run a joke into the ground."

Shelby was taking her time climbing up the ladder. When she came out, she stood dripping on the end of the dock with her back to us and her arms crossed.

"I didn't know," I whispered to them. We all stared at Mei and Lauren as they finished their exercise with Alex. None of us said anything else. Shelby didn't move.

I sat there with my feet hanging off the edge of the dock, feeling like the biggest jerk in the world. Of course I'd heard their signals. I knew they were trying to shut me up; I just didn't know why. But I kept going. Sometimes when I could tell my jokes weren't funny, I'd get louder instead of letting it drop. Judith was never loud and obnoxious. And she'd never hurt anyone's feelings, either.

Finally Alex made Mei and Lauren get out, and it was Shelby's and my turn. Shelby jumped in, and when she came up, she still wouldn't look at me. I lay down on the dock and reached out to her with my arm first. Shelby swam up and took it quickly.

"Not so fast! Remember—you're in distress and the lifeguard has to help you out," said Alex.

Then I climbed partway down the ladder and offered her my leg. When she was almost up to me, I slid down into the water beside her.

Alex blew her whistle. "No! Stay on the ladder! This is a reaching assist from the side of the pool. Or in this case, a dock."

"Sorry, I slipped!" Then I whispered, "Shelby, I'm sorry." She nodded, but she wouldn't look at me.

Next she swam away from the dock and showed signs of distress, and I had to throw the ring buoy out to her. She grabbed it and I pulled her in.

"Good. Now switch places and Shelby is the rescuer. In the water, JD."

When Shelby climbed out of the water, I whispered to her again. "I didn't know. I never would've said that if I did. Don't you know what JD really stands for? Justa Dimwit." Shelby wiped her bangs out of her eyes and gave me a little smile.

But when I jumped off the end of the dock to be rescued, I had a heavy feeling in my chest, like a weight. I didn't like being boring old Judith. But at times I wasn't crazy about JD, either.

## CHAPTER 11

## Friday, June 27

"There is no way Alex will make us swim in weather like this!" groaned Mei. "Maybe she'll cancel class."

"Don't count on it," muttered Lauren. It was a foggy, misty morning, and we were all walking to the lake wearing nothing but swimsuits and flip-flops with our towels wrapped around us. Everybody else had left the cabin bundled up in jackets.

"I wish I had a wet suit. The freezing lake water is definitely the worst part of that class," Mei went on.

"No, Alex is the worst part, and I'm the best part!" I shouted. "If I wasn't in this class, you'd all die of boredom!" I twirled around in circles with my towel stretched out like a cape.

Courtney laughed, because she always appreciated

me. I kept spinning in circles as we walked down the gravel road to the lake. "This is fun. I'm getting seriously dizzy. I may puke, and then maybe Alex will excuse me from class."

"No, she'll say, 'Wipe that puke off your chin and jump in the water!'" said Lauren.

I stopped spinning because I saw Natasha and her friend Ashlin walking up behind us. I staggered over and almost crashed right into them.

"Natasha! My first friend!" I threw my arms around her and squeezed her in a bear hug.

"Hi, JD. How are you?" she asked, patting me on the back a little because I wouldn't let her go.

Then I hooked my arm around her shoulder and glared at Ashlin. "How much did you pay Natasha to be her friend?" I demanded. "Five bucks? Or ten? Because she was my friend for free!"

Natasha wriggled away from my arm and patted me on the shoulder. "Calm down, JD. Yes, she's crazy, but she's really harmless," she told Ashlin.

Then Natasha and Ashlin walked away, disappearing into the fog. Natasha always put up with me hugging her all the time and calling her my first friend, but I could tell she was a little tired of my act. Maybe she wasn't the only one. When I didn't get laughs, I never knew what I should do. I wondered if Chloe Carlson ever told jokes that fell flat.

When we got to the lake, mist was rising from the water, making it look spooky and cold. Alex walked up and said in a surprisingly quiet voice, "Lauren, can I talk to you for a second?"

Lauren didn't look at all surprised. In fact, she had an expression on her face like she knew exactly what was coming next. The two of them walked away from us and talked quietly together. Lauren looked small with her towel wrapped around her shoulders.

"What's up?" Claudia whispered, taking a quick peek at her watch.

"I don't know, but I don't think it's good," Courtney whispered back.

"She'd better be nice to her, or I'll give her a knuckle sandwich," I murmured. We all whispered to each other and kept our eyes down, not daring to look in their direction. Every single one of us tried to act like we didn't know what was going on.

Then Lauren looked at us before she walked away from the lake. Alex came toward the rest of us with a frown on her face. "Okay, ladies. Today I want to work on CPR," she informed us, her voice still soft. She walked over to a storage shed near the end of the lake.

We all looked at each other but kept quiet. Everyone was so serious. It was like someone had died.

Alex came back, dragging a dummy under one arm. It had a head, arms, and a body but no legs. She stretched it out in front of our little semicircle.

"This is Clyde P. Ripple," she said. "Clyde has just been pulled from the water and is unresponsive. I've alerted another lifeguard to call 911. Now I'm going to check to see if Clyde is breathing." She knelt over the dummy.

"Poor Clyde!" I wailed. "Looks like another shark attack victim!" The whole group was so gloomy, I figured I had to liven things up. Mei and Courtney snickered and looked away.

"He's not breathing," said Alex in a loud voice, like she hadn't heard me, "so now I'll begin to administer CPR. I first check for foreign objects in his mouth."

"Spit out your gum, Clyde!" I whispered loudly.

Alex's lips pressed into a thin line. "Then I tilt his head back to open his airway."

"I hope Clyde's a good kisser," I said.

"JD, shut up," said Alex. "Now I'll do two puffs of air and turn my head to watch his chest rise."

"If Clyde doesn't make it, let's have a burial at sea," I suggested.

Alex stopped and looked at me. "You're about to push me too far. This is your second warning."

"Ruh-roh, Raggy!" I said in my best Scooby-Doo voice.

"This is CPR, JD. This is a lifesaving procedure. Not only are you missing out on all this information, but you're preventing the rest of the girls in class from learning it too. If I hear one more crack out of you, you're gonna leave and not come back." Alex stared me down and I kept quiet. Then she turned her attention back to Clyde.

"Crack," I whispered to Courtney, just to get in the last word. I truly didn't think Alex would hear me, or maybe I thought she'd ignore me like she often tried to do.

Alex stood up and pointed. "Leave. You're out of this class. I don't want to see you back here again."

Nobody looked at me, and I didn't look at them, either. Everything was deathly quiet. I stood up and wrapped my towel around me. Alex still pointed, like I'd asked her for directions and she needed to show me the way. I walked away from the group; the only sound I could hear was my flip-flops smacking against the wet grass. I walked past the shallow end of the lake where Isabel was taking her swimming lesson. Hardly anyone was out in canoes this morning,

♥ 107 ♥

partly because of the weather, and partly because a group was leaving soon for a river trip.

For the first time all summer, I was by myself. The only time I was ever completely by myself was in the showers or in Solitary, but even then somebody was usually in the stall beside me. I walked back up the gravel road, past the dining hall, and then up the hill toward the Middler cabins. I didn't see any other campers wandering around because everyone was at activities. The fog was starting to lift, but the whole camp still felt quiet and deserted.

At least I could go back to the cabin and change into some warm clothes. Lauren was probably there, and we could cabin-sit for the rest of the morning. I couldn't wait to tell her I'd been kicked out of class too. Maybe it would make her feel better. Why couldn't the two of us have switched places? Lauren really wanted to do well, but she wasn't a good enough swimmer. I couldn't have cared less, and yet everything we did was easy for me. It wasn't fair.

I passed Middler Lodge, where we had evening programs every night after dinner. It was empty now, and the big doors stood open. I didn't really care that I'd been kicked out. I never wanted to do that class in the first place. I only took it to be with my friends. All those girls were hoping to be lifeguards some day. Not me.

When I got to our cabin, at first I thought nobody was there. Lauren wasn't on Side A, which meant she must've changed clothes and then left for some other activity. Too bad, because I'd really wanted to talk to her. I opened my trunk to find some clothes.

"What are you doing here?"

I turned around to see Katherine standing in the entry way. "I could ask you the same question," I said, turning my back on her so I could change.

"I thought you had that swim class."

"I used to. Alex kicked me out." I pulled a sweatshirt over my head.

"How come? What'd you do?" asked Katherine.

"Nothing. I made Alex mad. I kept telling jokes and wouldn't shut up."

Katherine made a snorting sound. "It figures. Look, let me give you some advice. You're always trying to be funny, but you're not. You put on this big act like you're a real troublemaker—getting caught by the Porch Patrol and all that. Big whoop. You're trying to be something you're not."

I closed my trunk but didn't turn around. It was like Katherine had read my mind. What else did she know about me?

"At least everyone likes me," I said over my shoulder. "My whole cabin hasn't turned against me." From Day One, Katherine had been hard to get along with, and then she'd started teasing Isabel because she couldn't swim. Now none of us could stand her.

"Oh, boo-hoo, I'm so sad that I don't have any friends," said Katherine, wandering back over to Side B. She was obviously annoyed that I'd interrupted her morning of cabin-sitting all by herself. I was glad she was going to leave me alone.

I climbed up on my top bunk and stretched out. *You're always trying to be funny, but you're not.* Partly that was just Katherine being her crabby self. But then maybe part of it was true. I'd seen other people roll their eyes when I cracked jokes. And this morning even Natasha seemed tired of my act; she'd always liked me before.

I turned over on my side and stared at the wall. JD WAS HERE. I'd written that last Sunday, the day after the dance, when everyone was still talking about me and Lance. I was feeling pretty darn good about myself then. I reached out and touched the rough wood of the cabin wall.

I'd been able to keep up the JD act for almost two whole weeks. But now everything was falling apart. I got on people's nerves, I hurt people's feelings, I tried to be the life of the party, but instead I just made a fool of myself.

And I'd finally pushed Alex too far. Why didn't I keep my mouth shut? I'd wanted to get one more laugh in. And maybe part of me wanted Alex to kick me out. Now I could finally do the activities I really wanted to do, since Guard Start wouldn't be taking up all my time.

But then I'd also written my family about the class and told them how good I was. I didn't even have to lie about that part; it was true. And Michelle had told them the same thing in the letter she'd sent. What was I supposed to tell them now? *Oh yeah, you know that pre-lifeguarding class I was taking? I got kicked out for cracking jokes, so I didn't finish it.* How was I ever going to explain that? *But Judith, that's so unlike you.* And did my parents really need another kid disappointing them? Hadn't they already been through enough with Justin?

I grabbed my pillow and buried my face in it. As much as I hated to admit it, Katherine was right about one thing. So much for trying to be something I wasn't. I should've known this would never last. Maybe it was time for me to make JD disappear.

"JD!" Courtney and Mei came bursting through the screen door looking for me. I'd been waiting for them. I knew they'd come looking for me as soon as class ended.

"Hi." I sat up on my top bunk and looked at them. Courtney had a *what am I going to do with you* look on her face. Mei stood there with her arms crossed.

"We've got to fix this," said Courtney. "It's bad enough we lost Lauren. We can't lose you, too."

"I've got to tell . . ." *I've got to tell you guys something. My name's really Judith. And before camp, I had the personality of a doorknob. My brain's worn out from thinking up jokes. I'm going back to my old self. Maybe you'll like me or maybe you won't.*

"Yes! That's exactly what I was thinking! You've got to tell Alex you're sorry. If you apologize to her, maybe she'll let you back in the class," Courtney suggested.

"Hey, where's Lauren?" asked Mei. "We need to talk to her, too."

"I haven't seen her," I said. I cleared my throat and tried to start again. "Listen. I have a confession to make."

The screen door banged open and Lauren walked in. She was wearing the same shorts with "Dancer" across the backside that she'd worn the first day. She climbed up to her top bunk, then propped her chin on her hands and stared at all of us. "Well, go ahead and ask. I know you're all dying to know."

"Okay," said Mei, leaning against the metal bunk frame and looking up at her. "What did Alex say to you?"

Lauren let out a sigh. "Actually, she was really nice to me, if you can believe it. She said I was doing great with all the service hours and workbook activities, but she didn't think I'd be able to swim five hundred yards. Big surprise."

"Was that all?" Courtney asked.

"She said I could keep coming to class to learn as much as I could, or I could try again next summer."

She tugged on her blond ponytail and shrugged. "It's nothing I didn't already know. I've been worried about passing that test since the first day. Now I'm off the hook." She picked up her pillow and hugged it.

"Well, guess what?" I said. "I'm out of the class too. I finally pushed Alex over the edge."

"What happened?"

Everyone was looking at me. "We were all mad about the way she treated you, and so Alex was standing at the end of the dock watching everyone in the water. I walked up behind her . . . and pushed her over the edge!"

Lauren hid her smile behind her pillow.

"Yeah, she was blowing her whistle at me the whole way in, but as soon as she hit the water, it got water-logged and only made a noise like this." I made wet raspberry noises with my lips. By now, all three of them were laughing.

"So then she swam over and tried to climb up the ladder, but I planted my foot right on her forehead and said, 'Oh, no you don't!'" I stuck out my foot to demonstrate how I'd kicked the imaginary Alex back under.

"So then she was fighting mad. I jumped in and landed on her back, and she kept trying to throw me off, but I hung on for dear life. Then Courtney got on

Mei's back, and Shelby got on Claudia's, and we had the most vicious chicken fights you've ever seen in your life." Courtney and Mei were actually bent over laughing now. "Sorry you missed it, Lauren. It was actually a pretty useful class. Alex and I won, by the way. Then she kicked me out."

"Shut up! You guys aren't the only people in this cabin, you know!" yelled Katherine from Side B, because we were all laughing so loud.

"Sorry, Katherine! I'm just over here NOT being funny, and everyone's laughing at how NOT funny I am!" I shouted. Okay, maybe I'd been a little hard on myself. On JD. She seemed to be her old self again. Or was that her new self?

There was a tap at the door. "Hey. JD? Courtney?" A face pressed against the screen. It was Shelby, and Claudia was with her.

Mei ran over and opened the door for them. "We have visitors!"

Claudia and Shelby came in. "JD, you have to apologize to Alex. She'll probably let you back in if you settle down. You're the best swimmer in the class," said Claudia, and Shelby nodded.

Wow! I couldn't believe it. I'd always thought I'd gotten on Claudia's nerves, and I didn't think Shelby was too

115

crazy about me either since that stupid mommy song.

"Nah, she hates me. She's hated me since the swim tests, when I yelled 'shark!' She's glad to get rid of me."

"Are you okay?" Shelby asked, looking up at Lauren.

"Oh, sure. I'm a lousy swimmer, but I'm okay."

"You're not a lousy swimmer. And you're a great dancer," said Courtney.

Lauren looked at her and grinned. "Well, that part is true."

"So are you going to do it?" asked Shelby, looking up at me on my bunk. "If you apologize and you're really sincere, she'll probably give you a second chance."

"Why should she? I've been wasting her time all summer," I told them all.

"Because despite what a hardnose she is, she's all about swimming. And you are definitely her star student when it comes to skills," Claudia explained.

"It's true," agreed Courtney. "Look, at the very least, you kinda owe her an apology anyway. What's the worst thing that could happen? She turns you down, and you're still out of the class. But maybe this way, you might get back in."

It was great that they all wanted me to come back. It made me feel wanted—which, considering the way I'd been feeling an hour ago, was pretty nice.

But a part of me felt the same way Lauren did. Now I was off the hook for the class and I didn't have to go anymore. No more icy plunges first thing in the morning. No more spending all my mornings at the lake helping out with swim lessons to do all my service hours. No more wasting my time pretending I was really interested in becoming a lifeguard. I hardly had any time for tennis or rappelling and rock climbing, all the other stuff I'd so wanted to try.

They were all looking at me with these puppy-dog eyes.

"Do it," urged Lauren. "You are the best swimmer."

"Okay, okay! I'll do it for my fans!" I said, sliding down from my bunk and taking bows left and right.

Then I grabbed Courtney's shoulders. "But there's one thing I have to know. Clyde? Did he make it? Did he pull through?"

Courtney clapped me on the shoulder and shook her head. "I'm afraid not. We buried him at sea, just like you requested."

I collapsed on the floor and bawled fake tears. But I hadn't been this happy since the Porch Patrol incident.

# CHAPTER 13

## Saturday, June 28

"Now's your chance!" Courtney whispered to me as she brushed her hair.

"No! We'll be late for assembly!" I whispered back. I was putting away my toothbrush after brushing my teeth in Solitary.

"You're stalling!" she hissed at me.

"Okay, fine. I'll try to talk to her, but don't be surprised if she brushes me off."

The bell had just rung for assembly on the hill. The whole camp was supposed to be there for the flag raising.

Courtney gave me a stern look as she walked out the door. Lauren and Mei had already left. Alex, Isabel, and I were the only ones still in the cabin.

"Uh, Alex?" I asked, walking over to Side B. "Could I please talk to you for a second?"

"Now? It's time for assembly." She was changing clothes after coming back from her Friday night leave. All the counselors got one night off every week. It was the first chance I'd had to talk to her since class yesterday.

"It's really important," I told her.

Alex glanced at Isabel tying her shoes. "You'd better go. You're going to be late."

Isabel rushed out the door and left us alone in the cabin.

"Let's go. You can talk to me on the way," she said. We walked out together. Alex walked fast, and I had to hurry to keep up.

"Um, I want to apologize for yesterday," I started off. "I know I've caused a lot of trouble in class. And yesterday was really bad." We turned by Middler Lodge, and we could see the whole camp already sitting in the grass out on the hill. The flag raising hadn't started yet.

"I know CPR is really important. I shouldn't have been goofing off and distracting everybody while you were trying to teach it." There, that sounded pretty good. And it was even sincere.

"Okay," said Alex. She'd slowed down, but she hadn't really looked at me yet.

"I know I've been a real slacker. I'm sorry about that. You *are* a good teacher." I hadn't planned on saying that last part, but then I realized it was true. She was strict, and most of the time I didn't like her, but she was doing a good job.

"I really have learned a lot in the class. We all have. You obviously really care about teaching us the right methods."

Alex stopped walking and looked at me. "Yes, I do. And you've been one frustration after another for me, JD."

"I know. I'm sorry." Now I really did feel bad about being such a troublemaker. My number-one goal had been to get laughs and make everyone think I was this amazingly funny and popular person. I'd never really thought about how much harder I made her job.

Eda, the camp director, was walking up the hill with the CATs who were about to raise the flag. It was a good thing there wasn't underwear up the flagpole like there had been a few days ago. When I saw it, I was so bummed I hadn't thought of doing something funny like that.

"Is there any way you'd let me back in the class?" I blurted out. "I promise I'll totally calm down and won't cause any more trouble at all. I swear!" I crossed my heart to show her how much I meant it.

Alex edged down the hill closer to the rest of the crowd, and I followed her. She let out a long, tired sigh. "You know, this all sounds really nice and sincere, but I'm not sure I can trust you to behave. So far, you've shown me nothing but disrespect. You hardly ever listen, you crack jokes when I'm talking. You don't act at all interested in really learning anything, JD."

Well, she had me there. "You're right. I wasn't really that into the class. I mainly took it to be with my friends. But now I'd like to try to finish it. I'm pretty good, I think."

"Everyone please stand for the flag raising," announced Eda, and so we had to shut up. I still wasn't completely convinced I wanted to spend even more time on the class. But at least I'd done what the others wanted me to do. I did apologize. And I did ask to get back in.

Alex and I stood at the back of the crowd and watched while the CATs raised the flag. Then we had to say the pledge. When we were done, everyone sat down, and Eda began the announcements.

"We'll talk about this when assembly's over," Alex told me. Then she moved over to where Libby and some of the other swimming counselors were sitting, leaving me stuck all by myself. Courtney, Mei, and Lauren were way in the front. I saw Courtney looking around for me in the crowd, but she didn't see me back here.

Saturday was the only day the whole camp got together for an assembly. Besides Eda's announcements, different counselors stood up to let people know about upcoming trips out of camp. I sat there and listened and wondered what Alex would decide.

When assembly ended, I moved through the crowd and met up with everyone else.

"Did you talk to her?" asked Courtney.

"Yeah. I apologized. And I even asked if I could get back in, so I hope you're happy."

"Well, what did she say?" Mei asked.

I rolled my eyes. "She didn't. The flag raising started and we had to stop talking. She *said* she'd talk to me about it later."

"There she is! Go talk to her now!" Mei gave me a push in Alex's direction.

I walked over and stood near Alex, waiting for her to finish her conversation with the rest of the swimming counselors. When she was done, she looked at me.

"I guess you want an answer." She frowned at me.

"If you just give me another chance, I swear I'll really change." We walked away with the rest of the crowd. Everyone was scattering in different directions.

"I want to talk to you about something," said Alex.

"Okay," I agreed, feeling a little nervous. We were approaching Middler Lodge, and Alex motioned me to follow her.

"In here," she said.

The lodge was a big stone building with high ceilings and wooden rafters, a moose head over the fireplace, and a wide porch around the outside. Alex made me sit down on a wooden bench, but she stood the whole time.

"You're the worst possible student a teacher could have."

I'd always known she didn't like me, but I didn't think she hated me that much. How was I supposed to respond to that?

"You know why?"

"No," I said. I'd always thought I was at least good at the swimming part, even if I sucked at the listening part.

"Because, JD, of all the students in the class, you have the most potential. But you're the biggest screwup. I'd rather have ten Laurens who can't swim more than a hundred yards but who really care about the class and give it their all."

"I know." I looked down at my hands. I knew that what she was saying was true.

"You're the best swimmer in your class, and I think you're probably better than the group of Senior girls I'm teaching too, and they're all a year or two older than you. I've seen fifteen-year-olds in lifeguarding classes who aren't as strong as you are."

"Really?" I knew I was good, but I had no idea I was *that* good.

"Absolutely. But so far I haven't seen any desire from you at all. I wish I could take your skills and give them to Lauren, because she had more desire than anyone."

"I know!" I said, looking up at her. "That's just how I felt yesterday morning!"

"So if I let you back in, what's going to happen?"

"I'll stop causing trouble. I'll listen—for once."

Alex shook her head and sighed. "I would love for you to finish the class."

"Really?" I'd figured she was glad to get rid of me.

"Of course. I want everyone to finish. I'd hoped Lauren would at least stay in and keep learning, but she decided she'd rather wait till next year to try the class again. And that's okay. All I want to do is to prepare every single person in my class to become a good lifeguard."

"I promise—you won't even recognize me in class from now on. It'll be like I'm a completely different person," I managed to say with a straight face.

Alex raised her eyebrows. "Okay. But one tiny slip-up, and I don't ever want to see your face again."

"Thanks, Alex!" She let me go, and I raced up the steps toward our cabin. Everyone else would be happy to hear the news. And I was good at something, really good. Wouldn't my parents be thrilled when I wrote them about that?

**CHAPTER 14**

## Monday, June 30

"Today we're going to do a submerged rescue," said Alex. "What do you think that means?"

"When you're under the water?" guessed Mei.

"Well, yes. It's when your drowning victim has gone under, and you have to go underwater to complete the rescue." Alex kept talking, explaining how this was different from a rescue where the victim was splashing around and still conscious. I sat quietly and listened.

For once I felt like I could relax. I didn't have to be "on" the whole time, trying to come up with a joke. Everyone knew I was on probation, and one slip-up would get me kicked out again. It was great to finally have an excuse to be good.

Alex demonstrated how we were supposed to swim

down to our victim and wrap the rescue tube around her before bringing her up to the surface.

"Okay, let's pair up. One of you will be the victim, and the other is the rescuer. If you're the victim, I want you to go under toward the bottom of the lake and then float there. When the rescuer approaches you, stay passive, like you're unconscious."

Claudia threw me a quick glance, like she expected me to make a joke about that. I looked back at her with my lips pressed together as if they were glued shut.

Shelby and Courtney were the first ones to try it. Shelby dove in, came up for a quick breath, and then did a surface dive. Courtney stayed on the dock, holding the red foam rescue tube and waiting until Alex blew her whistle. Then she wrapped the tube around her waist and jumped in.

Alex had told us that the tricky part would be forcing the tube underwater. It was made to float, and so it took a lot of strength to get it to submerge. We watched Courtney struggle with it. She looked like she was wrestling a giant hot dog. Meanwhile, poor Shelby was probably turning blue near the bottom of the lake.

After a couple of minutes Shelby bobbed to the surface and took a breath. "What's going on?" she asked.

"Sorry. This is really hard," said Courtney.

Alex told Shelby to get out for a few seconds while she jumped in and showed Courtney how to submerge the tube. But even after watching Alex, Courtney still had trouble doing it.

"Okay, let's mix things up a little." Alex climbed up the ladder and handed me the tube. "Courtney, this time I want you to be the victim."

Courtney dove under and stayed there. Alex signaled me to jump in and save her. I wrapped the tube around my waist and jumped in, bobbing up again quickly because the tube made me float. Then I pulled the tube into the water vertically the way Alex had shown Courtney.

The tube started to float back up, but I forced it down with all my strength. Once I had the whole thing below the surface, it was a little easier to control. I kept a firm grip on it while I swam down to where Courtney was floating.

Now the tricky part was getting the tube in between me and Courtney. It kept trying to float up to the surface. And I could only hold on to the tube with one hand because I had to grab Courtney with my other arm. After a few seconds I had the tube in place, and I swam back up to the surface, bringing my victim along with me.

When we both came up, everyone applauded and cheered. "Excellent! That's exactly how it's done!" said Alex.

Then she made me get out and demonstrate to everyone how I'd done it. I felt pretty good that I'd done it right the first time. After I gave them all a few tips, she sent Mei and Claudia in to try it. Mei was the rescuer, and she had as much trouble getting the tube under as Courtney had.

In fact, everyone had a hard time with this exercise. It was one of the hardest things we'd done so far. Every time someone was struggling, Alex told me to get in and show them how to do it. At first I thought it was pretty cool that she was asking me to show everyone how to submerge the tube. But then it occurred to me: She wasn't letting me help her teach the class. She was being especially hard on me to make sure I knew she was the boss. It didn't take long till I was completely exhausted.

So this was how it was going to be. She'd let me back in the class, but she was going to torture me the whole time. Why did I want to put myself through this?

"Okay. That's enough for today. I'll see you guys during free swim, right?" Alex asked us as we got our towels and dried ourselves off. She expected all of us to show up later to do some of our service hours, helping the swim staff lifeguard during free swim.

"Yes," Shelby and Courtney replied. The rest of us groaned.

We were walking away when Alex called me back. "JD, I want to talk to you for a minute." My shoulders slumped. Why couldn't she leave me alone?

When Mei and Courtney tried to hang around and wait for me, Alex told them I would catch up with them later, so they left me alone with her.

"You thought I was pretty hard on you today, didn't you?" she asked me.

"Yes," I said, looking her in the eye. I had to obey her. I didn't have to like her.

"You know why I asked so much of you?"

"To keep me in line. Maybe to punish me a little for causing trouble in the past."

"No, that's not it at all. You're the only one who could do that exercise so easily. Maybe I do expect more of you, but that's because you can do more. I doubt Mei ever would've been able to submerge that tube if you hadn't kept showing her how."

I didn't say anything. "Well, that's all I wanted to say. You did a great job today. For the first time you performed up to the level of your ability."

Then she let me go. As I walked away, I couldn't help smiling. Now I knew how Justin and Adam must feel, being the best at something. When camp was over, I could brag to both of them about what a great swimmer I was. I knew they'd be proud of me.

But then I wondered, would hearing about my great success make Justin feel even worse about his own problems?

# CHAPTER 15

## Friday, July 4

"Every cabin needs to enter at least one act. You've got almost a whole week to get ready, but first you guys should decide who's going to enter," said Michelle.

"I nominate JD!" Courtney called out.

"Great idea! She'd be perfect!" said Amber.

"Wait a second, you guys!" I told them. "I didn't agree to this."

"Oh, JD, you'd be great!" exclaimed Michelle. "What kind of act are you going to do?"

"Something funny," Amber said. "If JD's doing it, it'll definitely be funny."

One minute Michelle was explaining to us that a talent show was coming up next week. The next minute *I'd* been picked to represent the whole cabin.

"Are any of you guys talented?" I asked, jumping up on Michelle's bed and looking over at Side B.

"Not me." Isabel shook her head.

"I can whistle," said Meredith.

"I could do impressions of all the people in camp I hate," offered Katherine.

"You do it, JD," said Mei. "You're the obvious choice."

I plopped down on Michelle's bed. "What if I don't want to? What if I say no?"

"Well, somebody needs to step up, because every cabin is supposed to participate. So be thinking about it. Make it fun," Michelle said. "Now all you guys need to go to the dining hall so Alex and I can hide."

On the way to the dining hall we saw a bunch of counselors wandering around. They were waiting for us to go inside before they went to their hiding places.

The best part about the Fourth of July was that we didn't have any regular activities all day, which meant we got a day off from Guard Start. This morning we'd had a capture-the-flag game with the Juniors and Middlers playing against the Seniors. We won. Now it was time for the counselor hunt.

Inside the dining hall Eda explained the rules to us. "Counselors can hide anywhere on the camp property, but they cannot leave camp. No hiding in the stables, either, because it bothers the horses. Each counselor is worth a certain number of points based on how many years she's been at Pine Haven. When someone in your cabin catches a counselor, tell her your cabin number so you'll get credit for those points. Once a counselor is caught, she'll come back here to the dining hall. The cabin with the most points wins."

Then Eda made us sing three or four camp songs to give the counselors plenty of time to hide. Some of the camp songs I actually liked, but one of them that Eda made us sing was so sappy and stupid, it always made us laugh. It was called "Camp Days!" and it was to the tune of "My Bonnie Lies Over the Ocean."

> *Pine Haven, we'll always remember*
> *For friendships so wholesome and true.*
> *Pine Haven, you gave us our girlhood,*
> *Forever, we'll love only you!*
> *Camp Days! Camp Days! We frolic and skip in the*
> *dew, the dew!*
> *Camp Days! Camp Days! We frolic and skip in the*
> *dew!*
> *Your mountains inspire us to greatness,*
> *Your streams fill our pure hearts with song,*

*Your trees make our souls sing with rapture,*
*Pine Haven, to you we belong!*

When we got to the chorus about frolicking and skipping in the dew, I held my arms over my head and did some funky moves to make everyone laugh.

*Pine Haven, when we have to leave you,*
*The sorrow we feel will be great.*
*Our hearts pine for you all the winter,*
*Pine Haven, to us you're first-rate!*

Mei had her hands over her ears when we sang the chorus for the last time. "That's the stupidest song ever. Where did it even come from?"

"I think someone made it up about seventy years ago," I told her. Eda opened the dining hall doors, and we all rushed outside.

"We should split up," suggested Lauren. "We'll cover more ground that way."

"Good plan. Plus it's hard for eight people to stay together," I said.

"How about the little Guard Start clique all stay together, and the rest of us rejects will be another group," Katherine said, wiping sweat off her forehead and flicking it at Isabel. It was a hot, sunny afternoon, and already we were all red-faced and sweaty.

"I'm not in the Guard Start class any more, Katherine. So I guess I'm with you rejects," said Lauren. She took a couple of steps toward Katherine, who backed away.

"No one's a reject," Meredith said. "Look, these are the teams. Me, Amber, Katherine, and JD will be together, and Isabel, Lauren, Courtney, and Mei in the other group. And remember, we're all working together for Cabin Two, right?"

We all agreed that was a good way to split up the cabin. It evenly divided the A and B sides and broke up our "little Guard Start clique." And it kept Isabel and Katherine apart. Meredith was the best. She'd probably grow up to be a hostage negotiator.

"I know a great spot where a bunch of counselors always hide," Amber told us. "Over in the woods near the camp store." So our group took off in that direction, with Amber leading the way.

I knew it wasn't any big deal, but I couldn't stop thinking about the talent show next week. Had I really been picked to do an act for it? It was pretty cool that everyone automatically pointed to me and said I should be the one to do it. That never would've happened to Judith.

"Do you guys really think I should be in the talent show?" I asked. "Be honest. Because if somebody else wants to do an act, I don't mind."

"I think you're perfect for the talent show, JD. You have the best sense of humor of anyone in the cabin," said Amber.

"Yeah, you do it. Nobody else wants to," said Katherine as we walked along. The sunshine made everything look wavy, like a mirage. "If you guys really want to catch some people, we should hotwire one of the counselors' cars and drive downtown to Sonic. Half of them are down there now drinking cherry limeades while we get heat stroke looking for them."

"They can't leave camp, Katherine," Meredith reminded her.

"They cheat, you lamebrain. Some people never get found. Caroline Heyward? She's worth fourteen points, and nobody's ever found her. Why? Because she and a bunch of counselors jump in their cars and leave camp before we're even out of the dining hall."

"But what kind of act should I do?" I asked. I felt like everyone had dropped the talent show in my lap and told me to figure it out for myself.

"You'll think of something. It'll be great. Don't worry about it," Meredith assured me. "I hope we find Alex and

Michelle. Together they're worth seventeen points."

We were at the edge of the woods now, and Katherine was complaining about ticks. "Just what I need—a raging case of Lyme disease."

"Oh, don't think of the woods like that," said Amber. "'Deep green in summer, golden in fall / Barest in winter, spring blooms for all.' That's how I like to think of the woods." We crept through the underbrush, keeping our eyes out for any signs of people hiding.

"That's nice. Where'd you hear that?" I asked her.

"Oh, that? Uh, I made it up. It's part of a poem I wrote about trees." She blushed a little. Amber spent almost every rest hour either reading poetry or writing some of her own. I'd never thought of writing poetry as something to do for fun.

"I see someone!" yelled Meredith. We crashed through tree branches and caught Gloria, a counselor who worked in the Crafts Cabin. She'd been hiding behind a vine-covered tree stump.

"We got you! Middler Cabin Two. How many points are you worth?" I asked her, as she stood up and brushed leaves out of her hair.

"Uh, just one," she said. "This is my first year." She gave us a little smile, like she was sorry she wasn't worth more.

Gloria walked away to report back to the dining hall, and Katherine nodded knowingly. "See. The rookies don't know any better. They actually hide in camp. One lousy point. What a waste of time."

"Shut up, Miss Sunshine!" I snapped at her, but Meredith quieted me down and we kept looking.

Our group actually did pretty well overall. We found five counselors who totaled twenty-two points. At five o'clock the bell rang, and we all went back to the dining hall.

"We caught four people," Mei announced when we met up with the other half of Cabin 2. "They were worth nineteen points."

"Cool, that gives us a grand total of forty-one," said Meredith. But it still wasn't enough to beat out Senior Cabin 7, which won with fifty points.

"Senior Cabin 7 will be first in line for ice cream at dinner," announced Eda to the whole dining hall. "And tomorrow you can all sleep late, because you get a day off from inspection!" They all cheered while the rest of us groaned in envy. Getting a day off from cleaning the cabin was one of the best rewards to get. Our cabin kept getting demerits during inspection, thanks to Katherine.

Nobody found Caroline Heyward, the counselor worth fourteen points, but Michelle got caught down near the archery range by Junior Cabin 3, and Middler Cabin 1 found Alex near the campfire circle, so at least we knew *our* counselors hadn't cheated.

There was a big fireworks show planned for that night, so instead of eating in the dining hall, we had dinner out on the hill—hot dogs, baked beans, chips, and lemonade in little Styrofoam cups. A lot of campers were already lined up in front of the long food tables, and others sat around in groups in the grass, eating off paper plates. Once we got our food, we all found spots in the grass to sit down.

I couldn't stop thinking about what Michelle had said earlier.

"Hey, guys. About the talent show Michelle mentioned. Am I . . ."

"Yes, you're doing it," said Courtney, like that was the end of the discussion. She reached down and carefully picked up a ladybug from a blade of grass.

"Well, okay. But what should I do?" No one but me seemed to consider this a big deal.

"Whatever you want to do. You'll come up with a great idea, JD. You've got such a fabulous sense of humor," Courtney assured me. She blew softly on the ladybug, and it opened its wings and flew away.

"I could use some help. Maybe all four of us could

do something together. We just need to think of something." After all, Michelle hadn't said only one person had to do the act. Doing it as a group would be a lot better. At least some of the pressure would be off me that way.

"I get stage fright," said Mei, licking the barbecue seasoning off her chip before popping it into her mouth.

"And I'm not funny," Lauren put in.

"Well, it doesn't have to be funny, does it?" I pointed out. "We could do . . ." My brain strained to think of what kind of act the four of us could do, but nothing came to me.

"Yeah, but funny is best. Funny always works," said Mei. "My school has a talent show every year, and sure, some kids play the violin or sing, but the acts people remember are the funny ones."

"Like what? I really need some ideas."

"You'll think of something. You've got a whole week to plan it," said Courtney.

"Yeah, it'll be great. I bet Cabin Two wins the talent show with JD as our act," Mei predicted. "Then maybe we'll get a day off from inspection like those Seniors in Cabin Seven."

I had this horrible tense feeling in the pit of my stomach. It was like a teacher had just announced a big research project due next week, and half our grade was riding on it.

How would I ever come up with an idea? And what if I couldn't think of anything? Then what? I could see myself up on a stage, standing all alone in a spotlight with a silent audience staring at me, waiting for me to do something. *Something funny*. But my mouth felt like it was full of cotton, and my feet were two lead weights, glued to the stage.

I was going to bomb. There was no doubt about it.

## CHAPTER  16

## Saturday, July 5

"Come on. We're your friends. You *have* to tell us," pleaded Mei.

"There's no secret to it, really," I said. "Just walk up to one of them and start talking. That's all I did the last time." I glanced at my reflection in the little mirror on the wall. We were all making last-minute touchups before leaving for the dining hall. Tonight was the second dance with Camp Crockett. This time the boys were coming to Pine Haven. I was just glad to have a break from worrying about the talent show for a while. And I was looking forward to seeing Lance again.

"But what did you say to them? You had to talk to them about *something*." Mei kept pumping me.

"You're definitely holding out on us," said Lauren. "I

helped you guys with some dance moves. The least you could do is tell us how you got all those boys to start talking."

All afternoon my friends had been trying to get me to reveal my secret. It was fun to keep them all guessing. It was like being the only one who knew a cheat code to a game that would get me to a certain level. If I kept it a secret, I would continue to amaze them with my abilities. On the other hand, if I did tell them, they'd all be grateful.

"Okay, you guys. I'll tell you. But don't go telling everyone. There's one subject all boys are interested in," I announced. They all stopped primping and looked at me.

"Sports?" asked Lauren.

"Girls?" guessed Mei.

"No. I mean, lots of them are interested in sports and girls, but the one thing that all boys are into"—I paused for effect—"is . . . video games."

"Video games?" Courtney said. "*That's* your secret?"

"But I don't know anything about video games!" Mei groaned.

"Start off by asking them what systems they own and what their favorite games are," I told her. "Then ask them what games they want to buy. All guys have a video game wish list." I gave them a quick briefing about systems and games. They didn't really need to know that much, as long as they could ask the right questions.

"We'd better go," said Courtney. "A lot of girls are already down there." We left the cabin and walked down the hill toward the dining hall.

"So what are you and Lance planning this time?" asked Lauren. "If you elope, should we write to your parents and tell them?"

I tried to think of something funny to say, but I was stumped. A few people had been teasing me, asking if I was going to get caught by the Porch Patrol again. I didn't really know what to say. How was I supposed to top getting caught during the last dance? That was the trouble with having a reputation: People expected a lot from you.

"I have to behave myself tonight," I said finally. "Michelle warned me to be good." That part was true. After the first dance, Michelle had pulled me aside and grilled me about what Lance and I had been up to. I'd sworn to her that he hadn't laid a hand on me, that we'd just talked about video games all night and he'd offered to show me his *Tips & Tricks* magazine. She hadn't looked very happy with me, though, and today she'd told me not to pull any "stunts" like last time.

"I thought you said this guy kissed like a fish," said Mei. "Do you really want to see him again?"

"Yeah, I do. He happens to be a very nice guy," I said, regretting my fish pucker joke. Tonight my goal was to get Lance to slow dance with me. And not because I wanted to impress everyone. Last time I'd been so concerned about working on my reputation, I hadn't even danced a single dance. Tonight that was going to change.

Inside the dining hall we had to wait around for the boys to arrive. When they started coming in, I looked for Lance, but he wasn't the first guy I saw.

Brandon Matheson came walking in with a group of boys who must have been from his cabin. As soon as I saw him, I stepped behind Courtney. I hoped her hair would hide me, and it did a little, but it didn't help that I was a head taller than she was.

Brandon! I hadn't even thought about him. I'd have to dodge that chatterbox all night! I pretended I was scratching my forehead and managed to peek through my fingers in his direction. He wasn't looking over here. The last thing I needed was for him to start talking to me again when all my friends were around.

"JD, there he is!" said Courtney, and for a second I thought she was talking about Brandon. But it was Lance she was pointing to.

"Let's go tell him he kisses like a fish!" said Mei, really loud.

I grabbed both her arms and squeezed. "Don't you dare! I'll never speak to you again! *And* I won't tell you any more stuff about video games."

Mei burst out laughing and wriggled away from me. "Calm down. I'm just joking with you."

Courtney and Lauren were laughing too. "I've never seen you so worried, JD. It's not like you," Courtney said.

I was about to snap at them all, *Maybe you don't know me as well as you think*. But I stopped myself and tried to act casual. "Look, I'm gonna go say hi to him. If you need any help, just come ask me."

I left them and squeezed through the crowd of people to get to Lance. He was with Mike and David again, and when they saw me walking toward them, David punched Lance in the arm.

"Hi, guys," I said.

They all said hi. Lance smiled, and his dimple appeared in his cheek. I loved that dimple. And I noticed something else about him. The reason he had such gorgeous eyes was that he had really long eyelashes. I wondered what he'd look like without his glasses. I was glad to see that tonight he'd actually combed his hair—no more bed head.

We talked for a few minutes, and then luckily, David and Mike walked off. Lance and I found some chairs to sit in on the edge of the dance floor.

"Hey, do you like the *Ratchet and Clank* games?" asked Lance.

"Sure, I've played the first one, Going Commando, and Size Matters. Which one's your favorite?" I asked him.

The only problem with getting guys on the subject of video games was figuring out how to get them off it later. We talked about *Ratchet & Clank* for about ten minutes until Courtney came over.

"JD, I need to talk to you!" She insisted that we talk in private.

"What does WoW mean? This guy keeps talking to me about it," she whispered when we'd walked away from where Lance was sitting.

"Oh, that's *World of Warcraft*. It's an online game. You play it with other people online, and tons of people are really into it. Some even get addicted."

Courtney let out a sigh. "Okay, thanks. At least I know what the heck he's talking about now." She walked off, and I went back to Lance.

But then less than two minutes later, Mei found me because *she* had a question. "Hey, JD—what's FPS?"

"That's first-person shooter. It's a game where you see everything through a character's eyes, but you don't actually see the character himself. The other type is third-person shooter. In those games you can see the character onscreen," I explained.

"Oh, I get it. Thanks!" Then Mei looked over to where Lance was sitting and said, "Hey, Lance, JD says you're a . . ." She looked at me with a wicked grin on her face, and my heart stopped. "Nice guy!" she yelled before she walked away. I took a deep breath and waited for my heart to start up again. I knew she was just teasing me, but it still freaked me out.

"Want to go out on the porch?" asked Lance when I walked over to him. "It's really hard to talk over the music. And don't worry. I won't take one step off the porch tonight." He held up his hands like he was surrendering.

"Okay, sure," I said. We went outside, but the second we were through the doors I regretted it. Brandon Matheson was out here with a group of Crockett counselors.

I spun around and almost knocked Lance down as he walked up behind me. "Oh, sorry. You know what? I need to get a drink first."

We went back inside and headed for the refreshment

table. Lauren came running up to me. "Hey, this really works! I asked this guy what his favorite video games were, and he's been talking to me all night. And he's a pretty good dancer!" Then she took off to find her dancing gamer.

Well, at least Lauren was having a great night. So far Lance and I hadn't danced even one time. I had to get him to dance to at least a couple of fast songs before I could try to convince him to slow dance.

"Good song, huh?" I yelled at him when a Black Eyed Peas song started up. It was really loud. "I actually like to dance to this song. Do you want to . . .?"

Lance looked at me and shook his head. "Uh, no thanks. I really can't dance at all."

"Oh, I can't either really, but my friend Lauren— you know the one with the blond hair? She showed us a couple of . . ." Just then Mei walked past me with a guy and made a fish-lips face at me.

Lance saw her and laughed. "What's wrong with your friend?"

"She's . . . uh, she has asthma. She makes that face sometimes. I guess it helps her breathe better." Okay, that was the last straw. That girl was getting no more video game info out of me tonight.

"You ready to go outside now?" Lance asked.

*That depends. Is Brandon Matheson out there waiting to talk my ear off?*

"Are you sure you don't want to dance just one time? Come on. Just one dance." I took his arm and sort of dragged him out on the floor.

"I hate this," Lance groaned. "I'm going to look really stupid."

"Oh, you, me, and fifty other people," I assured him. We were moving to the music when a bunch of people started yelling by the refreshment table.

"What is that all about?" Lance asked, stopping to watch.

"Don't worry about it," I told him, but Lance and everyone around us had all stopped to gawk at Kelly Hedges and Reb Callison screaming their heads off at each other. It was so bad a counselor came and dragged them out.

"Wicked! I love watching girls fight!" said Lance.

Great. Brandon Matheson, gaming consultations, and now a fight. What next? A flood and a couple of plagues?

"Forget about them. Just listen to the music," I told him. Lance did manage to dance with me a little after that, but then he wanted to sit down again.

So we did. And for the next half hour, we didn't

move out of those seats. When the slow songs started, we kept talking. But I didn't have the nerve to ask Lance to get up and dance with me. I knew he didn't really want to. But I wasn't sure if he was embarrassed about slow dancing in general, or if he didn't want to slow dance with *me*. If I were cute like Courtney or little like Mei, then would he have wanted to? Was any boy ever going to like me for myself? If I was JD around my friends, should I be JD around boys, too? Or someone else? And who? Who should I be?

Pretty soon the dance was over, and all the boys were walking out. "Bye, JD! It was fun talking to you," Lance said, right before he walked out of my life forever.

"Bye, see ya later," I told him. But I probably wouldn't. I felt bad for using him at the first dance. All I'd cared about was impressing everyone with how cool I was. But what good did it do making everyone think we'd been kissing when nothing had happened?

Maybe one day I'd get a real kiss from a real boy. Maybe then I wouldn't care what everyone else thought about me. I'd only care what I thought about myself.

## Monday, July 7

Hi, everyone!

Thanks for the e-mails. I love getting mail!! Swim class is going great. We take the final test on Wed. and I'm pretty sure I'll pass. Guess what? I'm going to be in the talent show in three more days! My cabin picked me to be in it. All my friends think I'm really funny.  I've got a great

I'm not sure what I'll do for an act, but it'll be funny.

I'm going to fall flat on my face and embarrass myself in front of the whole camp then everyone will find out I'm not funny I'm a fake nobody even knows my

Tell Justin I hate his guts cause he hasn't written me one stinking time all month!! HES NOT THE ONLY ONE WHO HAS PROBLE

I crumpled up the paper and stuck it under my pillow. Then I rolled over so I was facing the wall. Since it was rest hour, I didn't have to talk to anyone. I could just lie on my bunk and act like I was asleep.

I had a headache. And a chest ache. It felt tense and tight, and it had been like that all day. All through breakfast, through swim class, through lunch. The talent show was three days away, and I still had no idea what I was going to do for it.

Then I got two e-mails in my mailbox after lunch, one from Mom and Dad, one from Adam. But nothing from Justin, of course. Why would he bother to write me?

The bell rang, and everyone got up from their bunks and started moving around. I kept my eyes shut and tried to make my face relax.

"Is she asleep?" someone whispered. It sounded like Michelle, but it might've been Amber.

A floorboard creaked and a trunk lid opened, then closed. I heard someone tiptoe over to my bunk. I could feel someone standing by the edge of my bed.

"JD? It's time to go to activities." A hand patted me on the back.

I thought about faking it and acting like I was still asleep, but I didn't want to overdo it. Campers never took naps during rest hour, only counselors. "Naps are my favorite college elective," Michelle had told us once.

I sat up and blinked. Michelle was standing on her tiptoes, looking up at me in my top bunk. "I don't feel well," I said, making my voice sound scratchy. Courtney and Lauren were watching me. Amber sat on her bunk, pulling on her riding boots.

"Are you sick too?" Michelle asked. Meredith had gone to the infirmary yesterday. There was some kind of virus going around.

"I don't know. Maybe." I wanted to get out of afternoon activities, but I also wanted to avoid a trip to the infirmary.

Michelle put her hand on my forehead. "I don't think you have a fever."

I shook my head. "No, I don't have a fever. I just feel so *tired*." I fell back on my bunk and rubbed my eyes.

"We did have a really hard class this morning," murmured Courtney so Alex wouldn't hear her from Side B. "We each had to rescue our partner. Then we swam *eight* laps." It was the most we'd ever had to do.

"Maybe you should take it easy this afternoon," said Michelle.

I nodded and rolled over.

"I hope you feel better," Courtney whispered. I heard Michelle telling Alex I needed to sleep.

When the screen door banged shut for the last time, I kept still and waited to make sure everyone was gone. Then I sat up and looked around. I was so glad to be alone.

I pulled out the crumpled-up paper from under my pillow and tossed it toward the trash can by the door, but I didn't make it. Too bad, or that definitely would've been a three-pointer. I hopped down from my bunk and went to pick up the paper. I wadded it into a really tight ball and tossed it in.

I'd write to them later. Maybe tomorrow, when I felt better. When I wasn't so depressed. And worried.

*Justin had a doctor's appt. today. He really is going to pull through all this and be just fine*, Mom had written in her e-mail. It sounded like she was trying to convince herself instead of me. Adam didn't even mention Justin. I wondered if they were still fighting with each other all the time, or even worse, not speaking at all. For a long time Justin wouldn't even talk to Adam; he blamed him for what happened.

A whole month at camp was a good break for me, but camp was over on Saturday. Then I'd go back home to . . . everything.

I climbed back up on my top bunk and stretched out. It was sunny outside, but inside the cabin, it was always shady and kind of dark. There was a warm, piney smell coming in through the window screens, and insects were making buzzing noises outside.

My old name tag was lying on the shelf next to my bunk. We hadn't worn these in weeks, because we all knew each other now. I picked it up and looked at it.

JD. The other side was just a dark red smudge where I'd marked it out. I couldn't see the JUDITH at all. But I knew it was there. I held the name tag by the string and flicked the little oval slice of wood with my finger. It spun around. JD. Smudge. JD. Smudge.

What if I'd just been myself? What if I hadn't pretended to be something I wasn't? What would camp have been like for Judith, instead of JD?

"Judith. Judith. Judith Duckworth." It felt funny to say my name out loud. "Judith, how did you manage to screw up your life so much?"

In three more days JD was going to get up onstage and have absolutely nothing to do.

*What happened, JD? We thought you were funny.*

*Sorry, you were wrong. Oh, and by the way, the name's Judith.*

I hung my name tag around my neck with the smudge side facing out. That was all I was. A smudge. A nobody.

Then I covered my head with my pillow and started to bawl.

CHAPTER 18

When I heard the screen door open, I wiped my nose.
I'd stopped crying by that time, but I was still pretty
sniffly. I lay still on my bed, facing the wall. I didn't
really want anyone to see me like this.

From the footsteps, I could tell it was Amber. She
tried to be quiet, but her riding boots clomped against
the wooden floor. So I sat up and looked at her. "It's
okay. I'm not really asleep."

Amber's forehead wrinkled up when she saw me.
"Are you okay?"

"Yeah." I guess my face was all blotchy from
crying.

Amber sat on her bunk and pulled off her boots.
"Are you not feeling well, JD?"

I fell back on my bed. "No! I feel awful!" Then I couldn't help it. I started to cry again.

"Is there anything I can get you? Want me to walk you down to the infirmary?" she asked softly.

"No. I'm not sick. I'm just . . . having a bad day." I needed a Kleenex. Michelle had a box beside her bed and I sat up and looked at them. Amber was a mind reader. She went over and pulled one out of the box and brought it to me.

"Thanks, Amber." She was such a sweet girl, but our little Guard Start clique was always together, and nobody from our cabin ever hung out with her much. I knew she had friends—horsey friends. All the girls who took riding lessons were a clique of their own. But maybe Amber and I could've been close friends, if I hadn't overlooked her.

"You're the nicest girl in the cabin," I said.

Amber rolled her eyes and smiled a little. "Oh, please."

"You are. Katherine's the meanest, Isabel's the quietest, Meredith's the fairest, Mei's the feistiest. . . ."

"You're the funniest!"

"No, I'm not!" I sobbed. I was crying my eyes out. It was like the pipes had burst. All the water was gushing out, and I couldn't do anything to stop it. The Kleenex was a shredded piece of fluff. Amber ran and got me a handful.

"I am not funny," I said again. I blew my nose three times. I hadn't cried this hard since I was a little kid. Now I even had the hiccups.

"How can you say that? You are so funny. You're one of the funniest people I've ever met!" She smiled at me. I could tell she really meant it too; she wasn't just trying to cheer me up.

"Amber, I'm . . . I have a secret. I've got to tell someone. If I don't, I think I'm going to explode." I held my breath, trying to make the hiccups stop.

Amber's eyes widened. "Okay."

"I'm . . . all summer I've been trying to be . . . I'm really nothing like everybody thinks I am. That's not the real me. I know I'm always cracking jokes and being a big goof and a real loudmouth." I took a deep breath. It was so stupid that I kept hiccuping. "But before camp, I was *nothing* like that. I was always pretty quiet. I always followed the rules. I was more like"—I started to say *more like you*, but then I stopped myself—"more like Isabel."

Amber's mouth twitched in a half smile. "You were like Isabel?"

"I was! Only maybe not as shy. I was *boring*. Nobody ever noticed me."

"Well, you're not like that now!"

I slid off my top bunk and went over to the mirror. I looked terrible. My eyes were all puffy and red. My face was blotchy. I turned and looked at Amber. "This is just an act! I'm not even JD. That's not my name. Before camp, nobody ever called me that."

Amber frowned. "Did they call you Josephina?"

"No!" I couldn't help laughing. She'd remembered that stupid made-up name from the first day. "I made that up too. My real name is Judith. That's what my family calls me, my friends back home, all my teachers— Judith. Not JD." I crossed my arms and looked at her. There. I'd said it. I'd finally told somebody the truth.

Amber stared back at me. She shrugged a little. "Well, okay. Is that the big secret?"

"Yes! Don't you think it's terrible that I've been pretending to be something I'm not? That I even lied about my name? That nobody at this camp really knows me?"

Amber frowned again. "What have you been pretending to be that you're not?"

"Funny!" I huffed. I threw up my hands. "Crazy! Wacky! A troublemaker! I'm not really like that. Don't you get it?"

Amber raised her eyebrows. "Oh, I get what you're saying. I just . . . don't know what the big deal is. You are funny, JD. You *are*. And so nobody's ever called you JD till now. So what? You're JD to us."

I sat down on the edge of her bed. "But it's a lie. All summer I've just been pretending."

"Maybe that's how it started out. Maybe you were putting on a big act in the beginning, but don't you think you're JD now?" Amber asked.

I stared at a patch of sunlight on the floor. "I don't know." I didn't tell her about trying to be like Chloe Carlson. Now it sounded really silly that I'd wanted to borrow someone else's personality for the summer. "I'm not sure who I am. I'm not really Judith anymore. But JD's just an act. I'm . . ." I started to say "Smudge" because that's who I felt like. A rubbed-out nobody. But that was so ridiculous I started to laugh. I still had the stupid name tag around my neck with the smudge side showing. I took it off and tossed it up to my top bunk.

Amber smiled while I sat there on her bed and giggled. One second I was bawling my eyes out, and now I couldn't stop laughing. Couldn't she see what a mess I was? I finally got ahold of myself.

"And now I'm supposed to do something for the talent show, and I'm going to bomb! I've got to come up with some kind of funny act, but I can't think of anything!"

"You won't bomb. You'll be great."

"Amber! Haven't you heard a word I've said? Do you know how hard I try to come up with funny things to say? It's not like they just pop into my head. I sit there and strain my brain. It's like trying to remember all the state capitals. And then sometimes I can't think of anything funny, and Courtney or Lauren will look at me and say, 'What's wrong with you? You're being so quiet.'"

Amber reached over and patted my leg, because I'd practically been shouting at her. "But it works. You do come up with funny things to say. A lot. You may think that you're not naturally funny, but you really are when you try."

I closed my eyes and leaned my head against the metal bed frame. "What am I going to do for the talent show? I have to get out of it."

"Maybe I can help you."

I opened my eyes and looked at her. "Will you do an act with me?"

"Well, I'll help you think of something to do. You're the actor, remember?"

"Okay, if you can come up with something funny for me to do, I'll do it. I don't mind being up on stage and making a fool of myself, as long as I get laughs. Can you write me a funny poem or something?"

"Funny poem," said Amber slowly, giving it some thought. "What about a song?"

"Yes! Anything!"

Amber bit her lip and smiled. "I need some paper. What if we . . . yeah, you should definitely do a funny song. I'll write the words and you can sing it." She grabbed a spiral notebook and a pen from the shelf by her bed.

"Can I read some of your poems?" I asked.

"Oh, they're not funny. Maybe sometime. Yeah, maybe later. But let's work on this for now."

"Amber, I just want you to know that you are saving my life!" I told her. I let out a huge sigh. For the first time in days I felt like maybe this would all work out.

Amber had a look on her face like the wheels were already starting to turn. "What if we wrote a song kind of like . . ."

The screen door banged open, and the entire Guard Start class walked in. Even Claudia and Shelby.

"Hey! Are you feeling better?" asked Mei.

"We've got great news!" Courtney said.

"What?" The only great news I could think of was that Alex had canceled class for tomorrow.

Courtney was all smiles. "Lauren thought of a great idea for the talent show. We're all going to do a hip-hop routine, and she'll choreograph it for us!"

The whole Guard Start class stood there with huge smiles on their faces, and Amber and I looked at them.

"Well?" asked Courtney when I didn't say anything.

"You've been whining for days about how you needed some help thinking up an act," said Lauren.

"This way you don't have to do it alone. We'll all do it together," added Shelby.

"I'm not much of a dancer, but they talked me into it," Claudia said. "It'll be fun."

"And I have *the* most amazing routine for us to do," said Lauren. "It's one that my sister's high school spirit line did. It had people talking!"

"Why?" I asked.

"Because of the moves. And the music. You have to see it. It's really wild."

"I can't dance," I said. Amber clutched the spiral notebook to her chest. She had a polite little smile on her face, like this was the first time she'd heard anything about a talent show.

"I'll teach you. Don't worry. We've got three days to work on it. We'll practice every spare minute we have." Lauren did a couple of spins across the floor.

"That's a great idea, you guys!" said Amber. She tucked the spiral notebook back on her shelf.

"No, it isn't," I said.

Lauren stopped spinning. Everyone stared at me.

"I mean, yeah, it is a good idea, but Amber was going to help me think of an act too."

"Oh," said Courtney.

"Okay," said Mei. Everyone looked at Amber. Nobody said anything.

"Oh, no, we were just . . . we hadn't really thought of anything to do yet," stammered Amber. "You all do the dance routine. Can I watch you practice?"

"Sure," said Lauren, standing in the middle of the floor with her arms crossed. There was a really long pause while we all looked around at each other.

"So . . . what do you want to do, JD?" Courtney asked.

JD. I was JD again, like I'd always been. Why did I pick Amber, who I barely knew, to spill my guts to? What if I'd picked Katherine instead? Then there'd be a giant banner hanging from the dining hall: JD IS A FAKE! LET'S ALL HATE HER NOW!

"I don't know," I said.

"Well, I think you should do the dance routine," Amber told me. "Honestly, JD. I said I'd help you, but I really didn't have any ideas. And Lauren already has something planned out." Amber smiled at me, that sweet smile. I bet it sucked being the nicest person in the cabin sometimes.

"Whatever," I said.

"Well, we don't want to force you to do it," Lauren said, barely keeping the sarcasm out of her voice. "Do something else. I was only trying to help you out." She kept her arms crossed and watched her toes wiggling in her flip-flops.

I wanted to tell everyone the truth. Just get everything out in the open once and for all. Maybe I'd even tell them all about Justin, too. Then I wouldn't have any more secrets and I could stop all this pretending. I could be me again. Whoever that was.

But Amber had barely blinked when I told her. Was it really such a big deal after all?

"Thanks, you guys. I really appreciate it. Let's do it! This way I won't be by myself. But let me warn you—I dance like a gorilla."

Lauren looked up at me and smiled. "You won't when I'm through with you!"

## Tuesday, July 8

"Okay, Claudia and JD, you're both still a little late on that part. Let's break it down." Lauren lined up Claudia and me beside her and showed us one more time. "Now with the music." She nodded at Amber, sitting on the floor next to the iPod speakers. Amber started the music again.

Claudia and I followed along with Lauren while the others watched us.

"Bounce, bounce, together left, together right, shoulders and foot," Lauren called out over the music. She signaled for Amber to stop the music. "Much better. Claudia, you were right on the beat that time, and JD, you just need to pick up the tempo a little more."

I wiped my sweaty face on my shirt. I had no idea

that dancing was such a workout. "Are you sure you don't want to slap a gorilla suit on me and let me prance around while the rest of you do the real dancing?" I asked.

"You're getting it. I can't believe what a good job all of you are doing, considering how little time we've had. Okay, let's take a short break."

We all collapsed on the floor or found seats on one of the wooden benches. We had the whole lodge to ourselves since it was morning free time. A nice breeze blew in from the open doors and windows and cooled us off a little.

"I was wondering," Shelby started off, "if maybe we should tone this down a little?"

Lauren wiped her face with a hand towel. "What do you mean?"

"Well, this dance. It's pretty—extreme. Don't you think maybe it's a little much for the camp talent show?" asked Shelby from where she sat on the floor.

"That's why we're doing it," said Lauren. "It'll be the talk of the night!"

There was no doubt about that. When Lauren had shown us the dance routine she'd planned, we'd all watched her openmouthed. Some of the moves were . . . well, shocking. Just the way we were supposed to shake and move and strut. We even had to do this one part where we totally stuck out our hips. It was hard for me not to laugh every time we did that, because I felt so embarrassed about it.

"When my sister's spirit line did this for the first time, the crowd went wild. The guys, especially. They were all whistling and howling," Lauren had told us.

We'd all agreed we could see why. Lauren had said that some parents had complained about how "mature" the routine was.

"What time is it, Claudia?" asked Lauren.

Claudia looked at her watch. "Ten after one."

"Okay, we've got another twenty minutes till lunch. Let's run through it a few more times. On your feet, ladies!" She jumped up and clapped to get us all motivated.

We all got to our feet and took our places in the two lines Lauren had put us in. At least she'd had enough sense to stick me in the back. "Heads up, eyes forward, backs straight! Music!" Lauren yelled, and Amber turned on Lauren's iPod again so the music came blaring out of the little white speakers.

We did the whole routine from start to finish without Lauren making us stop at all. I did my best to keep up with everyone and not stomp around like a defensive lineman. Amber sat on the floor, hugging her knees and watching us.

"Okay, good! Very good! Much better," said Lauren. "Now let's work on the body roll." She stood with her back to us, talking over her shoulder. "Foot, knee, hips, stomach, chest, then knees in, knees out," she directed, demonstrating the roll for us as she talked. "And remember, when you get to the chest pop, really hit it hard. Pop! Like that."

Amber started the music again, and we all worked on the body roll. When we did the left spin, I saw Alex standing in the open doorway, watching our every move. Oh, great, just what we needed right now—an audience. But I had to get used to the idea. Alex was only one person; in two nights we'd be performing in front of the entire camp.

When the song ended, Amber paused the iPod, and Alex strolled into the lodge. "Excuse me. What do you think you're doing?"

"Practicing for the talent show. Michelle told us we could use the lodge when nobody was down here," said Lauren, lifting up her blond ponytail so she could drape the towel around her neck. Michelle and Meredith had both left this morning for the canoeing honor trip—the reward that all the canoers got for working so hard this summer.

Alex stood in front of us with her arms crossed. "Oh, the problem isn't *where* you're practicing; it's *what* you're practicing."

Lauren shrugged. "A dance. What's the big deal?"

Alex looked at all of us. "The big deal is the type of dance you're doing. Don't you think it's inappropriate?"

"In what way?" Lauren asked innocently. I was so glad to let her do all the talking. I'd had enough run-ins with Alex to last me the whole month. The rest of us kept quiet, watching the two of them.

Alex frowned at us. "It's . . . it's way too edgy. Where'd you even learn dance moves like that?"

"My sister's spirit line did this same routine. It happened to be a huge hit at her high school," said Lauren, conveniently leaving out the part about the parents who'd complained about it. Courtney and I exchanged quick looks. Mei watched a granddaddy longlegs scurry across the wood floor.

"Uh-huh," Alex said. "Well, it's one thing for girls who are sixteen and seventeen to perform those moves. But you guys are only twelve years old."

"Oh, please!" Lauren protested. "We're not babies."

"What if we changed some things? Cleaned it up a little?" asked Courtney.

Alex shook her head. "No. Even that wouldn't help. Nothing about this routine is okay."

"Why? What's so bad about it?" asked Lauren.

"Do you really want to perform dance moves like this in front of Eda? I mean, think about it. What if your parents were in the audience? Wouldn't you be embarrassed to be dancing like that in front of them? And may I remind you that there will be Juniors watching you, and they're only eight and nine years old? Do you think you're setting a good example for them?"

"Alex, please. We just want to do a really cool dance routine. We're not trying to set an example or anything," said Lauren.

"I don't want you guys performing this act. You can do a dance routine, but not using any of those moves! Got it?" She gave us all the death-ray glare.

Lauren nodded but didn't say anything. Alex slowly looked us all up and down one more time before she walked out of the lodge. We all sat there, frozen. We didn't want to speak until we were sure she was gone.

Mei tiptoed over to the open door and checked to make sure the coast was clear.

"I can't believe it!" huffed Lauren. "If only she hadn't seen us."

"What should we do now?" Shelby asked. We all looked at each other.

"I guess we'll have to figure out a new act," I said. "We still have a couple of days. We can come up with something." I glanced at Amber sitting by the iPod speakers, and she gave me a little smile.

Lauren glared at me. "Do I know you? Since when do you listen to Alex?" Everyone else was looking at me too.

"Oh, come on, you guys. You know how much trouble I got into with her. She kicked me out of class once already."

"Yeah, but that was class. This is the talent show. It's not the same. I can't believe you of all people would care about what Alex says," Lauren retorted.

I didn't say anything at first. Everyone waited for me to respond. "Maybe I'm tired of being the rule breaker." I wasn't that crazy about doing the dance in the first place. Alex telling us not to do it seemed like a good way for us all to get out of it.

"Oh, great timing! Now all of a sudden you're gonna be the good little girl and not do this dance because Alex says it's too . . . 'edgy.'" Lauren put air quotes around that last word and rolled her eyes in disgust.

"Hey, she's got a point, JD," said Courtney. "All

summer you've been the rebel, and we've watched Alex yell at you. Yes, she did kick you out of class, but then she let you back in. And anyway, class will be over by the night of the talent show."

"True. If we do the dance, what's the worst she can do to us?" asked Lauren, looking right at me. How many times had I made that same comment? Now it was coming back to haunt me.

"She'll be mad," Shelby said.

"And none of us has ever seen Alex mad before, so won't that be a shocker!" Mei put in.

"We can clean it up a little. Then we can say that we did listen to her," suggested Courtney.

"I just don't want the rest of you to get in trouble," I said. My gosh, what was happening here? I'd started a revolution! Maybe next they'd want to overthrow Eda and take over the whole camp.

"Don't worry about us," Courtney said excitedly. "I've never been a rebel before. Come on, guys. Let's do it! This is our chance to make a big name for ourselves. Imagine the reaction we'll get!"

Lauren nodded with satisfaction. "Now you're talking!"

Claudia smiled. "It might be kinda fun. Our way of getting back at Alex for being so strict with us all summer. It's just dancing. It's not like we're letting anyone drown if we don't listen to her this time."

Shelby kept quiet. Amber sat by the iPod speakers, listening to all of us.

"What do you say, JD?" asked Lauren. "Are you in or out?"

Everyone turned and looked at me. I'd created monsters. Five rebellious, rule-breaking monsters.

I didn't want to do the dance. I wanted to tell them to go ahead and do it without me. But I'd gotten them all into this. I couldn't abandon them now. If they were going to get into trouble, I had to be in there with them.

I forced my mouth into a smile. "Like I always say—rules were made to be broken."

# CHAPTER 21

## Wednesday, July 9

"Before we get started, I want to congratulate all of you on your hard work. You were all good swimmers to start with, but now you're well on your way to becoming lifeguards." Alex kept talking, telling us how proud she was for all the time we'd put into the class. We sat quietly and listened. What would she be saying about us tomorrow night after the talent show?

The five of us sat lined up on the dock. Lauren had also come down to cheer us on—she was sitting over by the edge of the lake. Now that she was busy choreographing our dance, she didn't seem to mind dropping out of the Guard Start class. "Instead of being a lifeguard when I'm a teenager, I can spend my summers teaching dance," she'd told us. When Courtney had said she could do both if she kept working at it, Lauren had shrugged. "Maybe." She seemed happy with who she was. *Dancer*. It said so right on her shorts. I wondered what my shorts should say.

"Okay, let's start with treading water," Alex announced. We all stood up to dive in. At least it was a nice, sunny morning so the water didn't feel quite so cold.

Once we were all in, Alex timed us with her watch. We only had to tread water for two minutes, but we couldn't use our hands, so that made it a little harder. Still, this part was the easiest. Alex blew her whistle when the time was up.

"Great. Now the weight retrieval," she said. We all climbed up the ladder and stood dripping at the end of the dock. Alex picked up a ten-pound black block and held it in front of her. "Watch closely, everyone. I want you to see where it goes in." Then, with both hands, she heaved it out into the water. It made a big splash and disappeared. "Who's first?" she asked.

I knew I could do it, and I thought maybe watching me dive down for the weight would make everyone else see that it wasn't that hard. But I didn't want to be a show-off.

Claudia stepped up. "I'll go."

"Okay, great. Dive in."

Claudia dove off the end of the dock while we all waited and watched. After a minute she came up sputtering. "I can't even see it!"

"It's okay. Look around and see where you are and remember where it went in. Take a deep breath and try it again. You can do this," Alex assured her.

Claudia paused while she got her breath. Then she dove under again. This time she came up after a minute or so and announced, "I see it. But I didn't get it yet."

She went under again while we waited. Alex looked at us all. "I got to do this test in a clear blue swimming pool. I'll admit it's much, much harder doing it in a lake. But lifeguards have to train in all kinds of water." She watched for Claudia to surface.

This time when Claudia came up, she had the weight with her. She swam up to the edge of the dock like an otter, with her head above water and her hands below the surface. When she got to the ladder, she hoisted the weight up and dropped it on the dock with a thud. I could see the muscles in her arms trembling as she did it. Then she climbed up the ladder and knelt beside us, gasping for air.

"Don't worry," she panted. "It's . . . not . . ." She didn't even bother to finish her sentence.

"Great work! Okay, go relax for a while," Alex told her, and Claudia stumbled over to sit with Lauren on the rock.

"I'll go next," I offered. I watched while Alex heaved the weight back into the water, and then I sprang off the end of the dock. As I swam deeper, the water temperature changed. I passed from cool water into really cold water deep below the surface. And down here, the visibility was really bad. Claudia had stirred up dirt at the bottom of the lake while she'd groped around for the weight. I couldn't see much of anything. I had to feel around until I found it.

When I felt my fingers touch something smooth, I grabbed it and started kicking toward the surface. But the closer I got, the heavier the weight felt. I was almost up when I felt it slipping out of my hands. My hands flailed around wildly, trying to grip it again, but it was gone.

So I surfaced and took a breath. "I dropped it! I was almost up when it slipped!" I shouted. I was so frustrated that I didn't get it on the first try. I tried to stay right above where I knew the weight had fallen.

"It gets heavier as you get closer to the surface," yelled Alex from the dock.

"I noticed!"

I took long, deep breaths and then did a surface dive

to go under again. This time I didn't worry so much about seeing the weight. Instead I did it mostly by feel. When I had it in my hands again, I crouched on the bottom, then pushed up with my legs as hard as I could, clutching the weight against my midsection. I shot up to the surface a lot faster this time, and I was able to keep a firm grip on the weight. I paddled over to the dock and lifted it up.

"Excellent!" Alex said.

After I got my breath, I told the others what I'd figured out—to feel for it instead of trying to look through the dark, muddy water. And to hold it against your body and use your legs to kick off from the bottom.

"Very good advice," agreed Alex.

Shelby went next, and we were all amazed that she got it on the first try. We cheered like crazy when she came up and plopped the weight on the dock. "That really helped!" Shelby told me with a grin as she climbed up the ladder. "Thanks!"

Mei was next. It took her three times, but finally, on the last try, she had the block in her arms.

After Courtney's turn, Alex asked us if we were ready to swim the five hundred. We had to do a total of ten laps back and forth across the lake. Four laps had to be the crawl, two laps had to be the breaststroke, but the rest could be any combination. This part wasn't timed, but we did have to do all the laps without stopping for very long.

The thing I liked about swimming was that after a while, I'd fall into a rhythm, and then it wouldn't even feel like I was swimming at all. It was almost like walking someplace when you weren't paying attention to where you were going. It took a long time to get tired out when you were walking, and that was how swimming was for me, if I took it slow and steady.

All kinds of thoughts passed through my brain. Sometimes little bits of a song would pop into my head, or I'd remember parts of a conversation. At times I'd count one-two-three-four as I did my strokes. It was almost like being hypnotized. Swimming a bunch of laps always made me feel good. At the end I'd be tired, but it was a good kind of tired.

We'd all started off in a group, but now everyone was spread out. Sometimes I'd feel someone near me, but other times it felt like I had the lake to myself.

When I was on the sixth lap, I switched to the breaststroke, just to give myself a change of pace. Now, with my head forward when I came up for air, I could see things a little better than when I was turning to the side to breathe on the crawl. I watched as Alex and the dock got closer and closer with every breath.

By the tenth lap, I'd really slowed down, and I switched back to the crawl again. I took long, slow strokes in the water so I could rest as I finished up. When I was within thirty feet of the dock, I let myself glide up, just kicking with my feet. Then I reached the ladder.

Alex gave me her hand as I climbed up. "Congratulations! You've passed," she told me. I looked back to see everyone else still in the water. I felt kind of lightheaded, but other than that, I wasn't too tired.

I sat on the rock with Lauren and waited while the others swam their laps. "How does it feel?" she asked me.

"I'm glad it's all over."

One by one, the rest of them finished their laps. "Congratulations!" Alex shouted at each person as she climbed out. She was all smiles, and she looked so proud of us. When the class first started, I'd really thought that Alex was out to get us all—me especially. She'd been so strict, and she never smiled. But now I realized that all along, all she'd cared about was teaching us so that we'd do well in the class.

"That's it! Congratulations, everyone!" Alex whooped and applauded for all of us, and so did Lauren. It was hard to believe that all our hard work was finally behind us.

Alex told us we could go change into dry clothes. For once, we didn't have to stay at the lake after our lesson to do service hours.

"I knew you'd all pass," said Lauren. She looked happy for us. "I hate to say this, but—we have to rehearse after lunch."

We all groaned, because after such an exhausting morning, we weren't looking forward to another work-out. But the talent show was tomorrow night. We really needed some more practice.

"Bye, Alex! See you at lunch," I yelled to her as we all walked off wrapped up in our towels. She had really helped us all get through the test—telling us what a good job we were doing and encouraging us through the tough parts.

Today she was our proud teacher. But that might all change by tomorrow night.

**CHAPTER 22**

## Thursday, July 10

"JD, I need to talk to you about something," said Michelle, just as we were all leaving for morning activities.

"Okay," I said, knowing that anytime someone started a conversation like that, it couldn't be good. Courtney, Mei, and Lauren stood by the door waiting for me.

"She'll just be a second," Michelle told them. They all walked out the door, looking at me over their shoulders as they left. Michelle waited to make sure they were gone. Then she sat cross-legged on her cot and patted a spot beside her for me to sit. She gave me her big grin, her eyes crinkling at the edges.

"What are you doing for the talent show tonight?" Michelle had been away for two days on the overnight canoeing trip, so she was out of the loop.

"Oh, I'm doing something with the whole Guard Start class," I said.

"What is it?"

"A hip-hop dance. Lauren taught it to us." I didn't like where this conversation was going.

"Really? Because Alex told me she saw you guys rehearsing. And she said the dance you were doing was totally inappropriate for girls your age." Michelle spoke in a soft voice. It reminded me of my mom reading me a bedtime story when I was four.

"We changed some things, though. She thought some of the moves were too 'edgy,' but we took those parts out," I said, trying to believe what I was saying.

Michelle patted my hand and then held on to it. "JD, listen. I don't want you girls doing anything at the talent show that might be inappropriate."

"But it's just a dance. And Lauren's sister did this same routine with her school's spirit line and the audience loved it," I said. I pretended that Lauren was talking instead of me.

"Fine, but remember that you'll be in front of the whole camp. Eda, all the younger girls—everyone." Michelle looked me right in the eye. "I trust you to have good judgment, JD. You're a real leader for all these girls. They'll listen to you. Please don't do anything that would be an embarrassment for anyone." She gave me this really intense look, and I nodded. I wanted to turn away. It was so hard to look at her.

Michelle stood up and gave me a hug. "Okay, that's all. Go find your friends."

I walked out of the cabin with my head spinning. I felt like Michelle had hypnotized me or something. I knew I would do anything she asked me to. I ran down the hill to where the whole Guard Start group was waiting for me.

"What happened?" asked Courtney.

I didn't say anything at first. Michelle's words still bounced around inside my head. *Good judgment. A real leader.*

"Well? What did she want?" Mei asked. "We knew something was up just by the way she sounded."

I looked at all of them. "We can't do the dance."

"What?" cried Lauren. "No way! The talent show is tonight!" I noticed she had her iPod and speakers with her.

"I guess Alex told her about watching us rehearse and how 'inappropriate' it was. So Michelle doesn't want us to do it."

"Wait a second," said Claudia. "Did she specifically say, 'Do not do the dance'?"

"More or less."

"She used those exact words?" Claudia went on.

"She made it very clear that she didn't want us to do anything that might be embarrassing."

"I'm not embarrassed by it," said Lauren. "I think it's an awesome dance."

"Me too," said Courtney. "I don't think it's inappropriate. Or embarrassing."

"Look, you guys. Both of our counselors have pretty much forbidden us to do this act. We really can't go through with it," I said. *They'll listen to you.*

"Yes, we can," Lauren argued. "Aren't rules made to be broken?" She raised her eyebrows and looked at me.

"What's the worst they can do to us?" asked Mei. "Camp is over on Saturday. "What are they going to do—give us detention? Fail us? Send us to the principal's office?"

"Yeah, JD. Why are you so worried about getting in trouble all of a sudden? Doesn't JD stand for 'Juvenile Delinquent'?" Courtney asked.

Why had I made that speech so many times this summer? I just had to brag about what a troublemaker I was.

"Come on. We need to rehearse. I've already asked one of the Senior counselors if we can use their lodge to practice. Just so we don't have anyone snooping around." Lauren turned and walked away. Claudia followed her. Shelby, Mei, and Courtney stayed put.

"Are you coming?" asked Courtney.

"No."

That was the answer I wanted to give. And it wasn't because Michelle and Alex didn't approve. I didn't want to do the dance. For once, I didn't make a decision based on what everyone else might think about me. I made it for myself.

Lauren and Claudia stopped. They turned around and looked at me. All eyes were on me. Nobody said anything. I realized my toes were cold from the dewy grass. I only had on flip-flops. Everyone was waiting for me to say something else.

"I'm not going to do it," I said.

Shelby cleared her throat. "Me neither."

Lauren stood in front of us with her arms crossed. She gave us a long look. Then, slowly, she nodded. "Fine. The four of us will do it without you." She turned away.

"I don't think you should," I said. My arms were crossed too.

"Well, that's your opinion," said Lauren. Then she and Claudia walked off. Mei and Courtney hadn't moved.

"Come on, JD," Courtney begged, her voice just

above a whisper. "Do it with us. If you're part of the act, it won't be such a shocker. Everyone expects something crazy from you."

"Let's do something else," I suggested. "Something they won't get mad at us about."

"It's too late for that," said Mei. "We've worked so hard at this. All of us."

I looked at the grass in front of me. "No. I'm not going to do the dance. And I don't think you guys should either."

There was a long pause. The four of us stood there. Lauren and Claudia were now almost out of sight.

"Well, I'm sorry you feel that way. I still want to do it," said Courtney.

"Me too," said Mei. Then they walked off, leaving Shelby and me standing there.

Shelby pushed her bangs out of her eyes and looked at me. "Think they'll get into big trouble if they go through with it?"

"I don't know. I have no idea what's going to happen," I said.

So much for being a leader everyone would listen to.

Amber—

Hey!! Guess what? This morning Michelle told me she doesn't want us doing the dance. Now Shelby and I aren't doing it, but the rest of them still are. I know it's totally last minute, but I was thinking—maybe I should come up with a different act??!! What do you think? I don't want everyone else to get in trouble. Got any ideas?? I'm desperate!!! See me after rest hour—k? THANKS!!

JD

I folded the piece of paper into a triangle-shaped paper football and took aim. I flicked it toward Amber's bottom bunk, but it missed and landed on the floor. She still saw it, though, so she reached down and picked it up. Lauren gave me a look from her top bunk, but I kept my eyes on Amber, watching her unfold the piece of paper.

When she finished reading it, she looked up at me with wide eyes. "Well?" I mouthed to her. She shrugged her shoulders, then gave me an okay sign with her fingers.

Rest hour had just started, so we all had to lie there on our bunks and be quiet the whole time. Michelle was asleep, as usual, so I might have been able to get down from my bunk and go talk to Amber, but I didn't want to chance it.

I felt pretty rotten that I was asking Amber for help now. We had only a single afternoon to figure something out. Maybe it was too late.

Amber opened her spiral notebook, and I watched her flip through the pages and start writing. She looked up at me and smiled. I let out a sigh. At least she was going to try.

All through rest hour, Amber scribbled away. The only sound in the cabin was her pen scratching across the page.

When the bell rang and rest hour was over, Lauren, Mei, and Courtney left together without saying even one word to me. So had I lost all my friends by making this decision? I guess they felt like I'd abandoned them.

Michelle sat up on her cot and rubbed her eyes. "Come on, you two. Get moving. Time for activities."

I slid off my bunk and looked at Amber. "I am so sorry to put you on the spot like this at the last minute. If you don't think there's enough time, it's okay."

Amber closed her notebook and bit her lip. "Well, I admit it's not going to be easy to pull this together. But you know that day I said I would help you? I already had an idea then. That's what I've been working on during rest hour."

"Great! Amber, thank you so much! So what's your idea?"

"Well, like I said the last time, I think you should do a song. A funny song. I've been working on the lyrics, but I still need help on some parts. But here's the problem. I can't work on this now. I have to go to the stables and watch a friend jump her horse this afternoon. So can I meet you later?" She was already pulling on her riding boots.

"Absolutely," I told her. What a relief that she was even going to try to help me.

"But I need you to do a few things while I'm at the stables. Can you go to Crafts Cabin and get a bunch of brown yarn? As much as they can spare."

"Um, okay," I agreed. "What's it for?"

Amber smiled shyly at me. "I'll tell you later. And then, do you know Jamie Young, the riflery counselor? She's in Cabin Three."

"Oh, yeah. I know her. She's my friend Natasha's counselor."

"Okay, go find Jamie and ask her if you can borrow her Hawaiian shirt. It has parrots on it."

"Yarn and a Hawaiian shirt. Gotcha." These were weird requests, but if Amber had told me to find the horn of a unicorn, I would've done it.

"I'll meet you back in the cabin around four o'clock. We have a ton of work to do, but I think it's a pretty good idea."

"Oh, Amber! Thank you, thank you, thank you!" I left the cabin to go round up the stuff she wanted. I couldn't wait to find out what she had planned for me. Maybe I could knit while I danced the hula. Anything, as long as I had an act to do.

CHAPTER

"Are you nervous?" asked Amber.

"A little," I admitted. It was the whole waiting part that was hard. I figured once I was onstage, JD would take over and I could be my crazy self. Or my crazy made-up self.

"You look great," Amber said.

"Thanks! It feels like Halloween." I shook my brown yarn locks. I just hoped my wig would stay on. Amber held the Slinky dog for me.

All the people doing acts were crowded outside the kitchen doors at the back of the dining hall, waiting our turn. Inside, the whole camp was watching as one act after another went onstage. Through the screen windows we could hear a Junior girl playing "Yesterday" on the piano. She was pretty good, considering she was only eight.

Lauren, Mei, Courtney, and Claudia were all waiting out here too, but some Senior girls stood between our two groups. All day I'd barely seen or spoken to my friends. Was this how camp was going to end—with those guys not even talking to me, and with Amber as my new bff? Everything was so mixed up and weird.

"I guess Lauren's group is going through with it," I whispered to Amber.

"I guess so," she whispered back. "Maybe they cleaned it up, like they said they would. Maybe it won't be too outrageous." That was Amber—always looking on the bright side. The group was dressed in matching white shorts and pink tanks. I'd seen them going around to different cabins today, borrowing the clothes they needed.

Then I looked over and saw Mei wiggling through the crowd toward me.

"I'm not going through with it," she announced when she reached me.

"What?" I asked. "How come?"

Mei shrugged and bit her lip. "I just . . . I'm not sure what's going to happen. Michelle and Alex will definitely be mad. What if we really do get into trouble?"

I glanced over at Lauren and the others. The dance group was now down to three. I could see Lauren's furious expression. Courtney was talking to her and gesturing.

"I'm gonna go talk to them," I said, pushing through the crowd to get to them.

"Oh, hi, Benedict. How's it going?" Lauren glared at me as I walked up.

"Hi, guys," I said, ignoring her remark. "If you don't want to do your dance, it's okay. Just let me go on and make a fool of myself, all right? I'll be Cabin Two's act."

"This is all your fault!" snapped Lauren. "The only reason I suggested doing this dance in the first place was to help you out. And then you go and desert us! Now nobody wants to do it!"

"Then let me do it!" I shot back. "You guys can pull out!"

"I don't want to pull out! I want to do the dance! We spent hours and hours working on it." Lauren threw up her hands while Courtney and Claudia stood silently by, looking helpless.

Mei and Amber came over to us. "Lauren, just let it go. JD has something funny planned," Mei told her.

"What a waste! All that time we spent! And for what? Nothing! You're all a bunch of wimps." Lauren pointed at me. "You started this. If you hadn't backed out, none of the others would have."

She was right. It was my fault. If I could've thought of an act on my own, none of this would've happened. And now everything was falling apart.

"Look, let's . . ." Everyone stared at me, waiting for me to say something. There they all were, in their little matching outfits. And they were all good dancers. If only Alex hadn't seen us rehearsing that day. If only Michelle hadn't hypnotized me into being a good girl this morning. Would it be so bad if they did the dance? What was the worst that could happen?

"What if . . . why don't we do them together? I'll do my act onstage, and you guys can all be my backup dancers," I blurted out. It was the only thing I could think of.

"What? We're supposed to go on in about five minutes!" yelled Lauren. "We don't even know what you're doing for an act!" She looked me up and down. I had on Jamie Young's Hawaiian shirt with parrots all over it and three packages of brown yarn hanging on my head. It was supposed to look like long wavy hair.

"I'm singing 'Camp Days,'" I told them. "Amber made up funny lyrics for me. I'm doing a Weird Al imitation," I added, in case they didn't recognize me.

"'Camp Days'?" asked Mei. "'Camp Days! Camp

Days! We frolic and skip in the dew, the dew'? You're singing that song?" Her jaw dropped.

"Yeah! It'll be funny! You guys back me up. Come on! Let's do it!"

"No way!" said Lauren. "No way are we going to go out there and dance to some stupid camp song without any real music! It'll mess up the whole routine!"

"Middler Cabin Two? Where's the act for Middler Cabin Two?" shouted Lydia Duncan, one of the CATs. They were organizing everything, telling people when to go on.

"Over here!" called Amber, waving the Slinky dog over her head.

"You guys are next. I need you over here by the door. As soon as the juggler finishes, you're on."

"No, we can't be next!" Courtney yelled across the crowd to her. "We're not ready!"

"Yes, we are!" I yelled back. Then I turned to the rest of them. "You guys, please! This will work! I'm going out there and I'll sing 'Camp Days' while all of you dance behind me. Can't you imagine how funny that will be?"

"The dance we're doing is *not* funny," Lauren insisted. She had her arms crossed, and she looked like she wasn't going to budge.

I grabbed her shoulders. "Lauren, listen. If you do the

dance the way you practiced it, everyone's gonna freak. But if you do it while I'm singing some ridiculous song, it'll give the whole camp a chance to see your amazing choreography and the group's awesome moves. And no one will get upset about it. Trust me."

Courtney nudged her with her elbow. "It might be a good idea. We all know the dance by heart. We could do it without any music at all."

"I can't believe this is happening," said Lauren, shaking her head.

"Cabin Two! Front and center!" Lydia called.

"Hey, if we're all going on, what about Shelby?" asked Claudia.

Shelby! Oh my God, we'd completely forgotten about her. Since she'd backed out of doing the dance, she was sitting in the audience with all the other campers.

I turned to Amber. "Can you go find her? Tell her what we're doing and get her to dance with us."

"She's not dressed for it," Lauren reminded me.

"We'll figure something out," I said. I pushed my way through all the other girls standing around till I reached the kitchen door where Lydia was waiting.

"Okay, as soon as the applause stops, I'll announce you, and then you guys go on. Does your act have a name?" Lydia asked me.

"Uh, the Dancing Fools," I told her, saying the first thing that came to mind. The others had joined me, and we were all outside the door.

"We can't go on now," said Claudia. "What about Shelby?"

"I'm not going on at all," Lauren insisted. "I'm not a dancing fool."

"We need a few more minutes," I told Lydia. "Can you send someone else on next?" I begged her.

"We'll go," said a couple of Senior girls standing behind us, dressed in togas.

"Fine. As long as the show goes on," Lydia said, disappearing with them through the screen door.

Just then Michelle appeared with a can of Coke. "Amber told me you might need this," she said. "Drink up."

"Oh, yes! You're a lifesaver." I grabbed the can and took three big gulps. Amber had remembered to ask Michelle to buy me a drink from the counselors' vending machine.

"Hey, where's our liquid refreshment?" asked Mei with her hands on her hips.

"Do you need to burp too?" Michelle asked.

"What are you talking about?" cried Mei.

"No, you don't need to burp! Just dance!" I told her before taking two more swigs.

Amber came dashing up with Shelby. "I found her!"

"Shelby, you're all dancing behind me while I sing," I said in between swallows of Coke. The pressure was starting to rise.

"She's not dressed!" Lauren protested.

Shelby had on a gray Pine Haven sweatshirt and denim shorts. "Stick her in the middle. It'll be fine," said Mei.

Lydia came out of the kitchen door. "Dancing Fools, are you ready now? Because you're next." Inside, we could hear the applause for the last act.

"We're ready!" I said, handing Michelle the empty can. I was about to explode.

"Wait! Your dog!" yelled Amber, tossing me the Slinky dog. It had a stuffed head and backside, but its middle looked like a plastic accordion.

I followed Lydia through the kitchen to the swinging door that led to the dining room. Through the door I could hear the sound of a couple hundred people shuffling around in seats and making noise. The rest of the girls crowded up behind me.

Lydia went through the door and announced, "And now, from Middler Cabin Two, please welcome The Dancing Fools."

Everyone applauded as I rushed out on the stage. It

was just a wooden platform at one end of the dining hall. All the tables had been moved out, and the audience was sitting in long rows of chairs.

There was only one problem. I was all alone. I could see Courtney peek through the swinging door, and the others were standing behind her, still arguing. Or at least it looked that way. Were they not going to follow me? Should I go ahead and start singing without them? There was a long pause while I stood there, clutching the Slinky dog and looking at the door. I could hear a couple of snickers.

Then Courtney, Mei, and Claudia came running out. They got more applause, but it was pretty obvious that none of us knew what to do. Mei kept motioning to Lauren and Shelby while we all looked at the door. Again I heard some laughter.

"We really did rehearse this!" I said loudly. I got several laughs, and then the door swung open and Lauren and Shelby ran out. Lauren's face was beet red, but I doubted anyone in the audience could see it. They all lined up the way we'd done in rehearsals. Shelby stood in the middle in her Pine Haven sweatshirt, and with two girls in pink tanks on either side of her, it looked like we'd planned it that way.

I took a deep breath and walked to the edge of the

platform. "Tonight we'll be performing a lovely camp tune you're all familiar with. It's called 'Camp Days.'" I made loud throat-clearing noises and held up the dog like an accordion. I heard Lauren count off in a whisper, and the girls began to dance as I sang to the tune of "My Bonnie Lies Over the Ocean."

> *Pine Haven, I try to forget you.*
> *Your meals give me gas all night long.*

I let out the huge burp that had been building up inside me. A roar of laughter exploded across the dining hall.

> *Your lake makes me freeze all my toes off.*
> *Tadpoles in my suit—that's just wrong!*

By now I had to shout over all the noise of people laughing. I pumped the dog's belly like an accordion while my backup dancers strutted behind me.

> *Camp Days! Camp Days! We frolic and skip in the dew, the dew!*
> *Camp Days! Camp Days! We frolic and skip in the dew!*

*Mosquitoes and gnats have attacked me.*
*A spider laid eggs in my bed.*
*I think there's a bear up in that tree.*
*The frog in my trunk might be dead.*
*Camp Days! Camp Days! We frolic and skip in the*
*dew, the dew!*
*Camp Days! Camp Days! We frolic and skip in the*
*dew!*
*Pine Haven, we're trapped here all summer.*
*I want to take showers alone.*
*This camp life is really a bummer.*
*Oh, Eda! We want to go home!*

The wild moves that Lauren had taught everyone now looked really funny with me singing this ridiculous song. Nobody could be offended by the dancing now.

I realized that the group was only partway through their dance, so I started again at the beginning, pumping the accordion dog like crazy. When I got to the line about tadpoles in my swimsuit, I wriggled and jumped around. The whole dining hall was going wild. I'd never had such a big response.

When I got to the last verse, the dancers had stopped, and they stepped forward on either side of me.

❤ 207 ❤

We all sang the last lines, *"Oh, Eda! We want to go home!"* together.

By that time, people weren't just applauding; they were stomping their feet and cheering. We took our bows and then ran back through the swinging door.

Amber was waiting for us on the other side. "That was awesome! It was amazing! It looked like you'd rehearsed it for weeks!"

We all slumped over on the stainless steel sinks and countertops around the kitchen. I couldn't believe we'd done it. It was over, and it'd been huge.

Lauren wiped beads of sweat off her forehead. "Good job, everyone." Then she looked at me and burst out laughing. "The crowd loved it! We're Dancing Fools!"

CHAPTER 25

## Friday, July 11

"Mei Delaney, JD Duckworth, Claudia Ogilvie, Shelby Parsons, and Courtney Prosser." Alex read off our names, and everyone clapped politely as we went up to get our certificates.

She shook hands with each of us as she handed out the pieces of paper—one was a Red Cross certificate that said we'd passed the Guard Start class, and the other was a Pine Haven certificate that read, "In Recognition of Special Accomplishments in Swimming."

We were about to sit down when Alex stopped us. "I'd also like to recognize Lauren Haigler for her accomplishments in swimming this summer. Lauren completed thirty service hours, and she was a great help and inspiration in our swimming program."

♥ 209 ♥

Alex motioned Lauren to come up and join us. I could see that half-annoyed, half-embarrassed look Lauren always got whenever people complimented her, but she came up beside us, shook hands with Alex, and accepted the Pine Haven certificate.

We all sat down and took our places while the awards assembly went on. Since tomorrow was the last day, we were having a special Friday assembly on the hill.

I sat by my friends and clapped for other people as they received different certificates. Meredith got one for canoeing, and Isabel got one from Libby Sheppard for learning how to swim this summer. Some people got awards for tennis, and some got them for hiking and rappelling. I felt a little bummed that I'd never gotten around to doing all the activities I'd wanted to this summer.

But I was glad I'd finished the Guard Start class. Not only finished, I was the best swimmer in the class— Alex had said so herself. That was a great feeling— knowing that I was really, really good at something. My family would be so proud of me. I still hadn't decided if I ever wanted to be a lifeguard, but finishing the class made me feel like I'd accomplished something all on my own that had nothing to do with being JD.

When the counselors finished giving out certificates

for activities, Eda had a few awards of her own. She announced the winners for the talent show, and the Dancing Fools all had to go up and receive certificates for getting second place.

When they had announced the winners last night at the end of the talent show, we had all screamed our lungs out. We'd been happy just to get through it; it had never even occurred to us that we might come close to winning.

Everyone cheered and hooted as Eda handed us our certificates. When the applause died down, I said, "The Dancing Fools want to thank Amber Cummings for writing such great lyrics! Amber, come up here!"

Amber was sitting in the grass beside Michelle and Alex, and she covered her face with her hands when I mentioned her name. But Michelle nudged her, and Amber came up and joined us. "We never could've done it without Amber!" I yelled over the applause. And that was true. She'd come through for all of us.

We all sat down again and listened as other awards were given out. It'd been so much fun working on the song with Amber. I couldn't believe what a great idea she'd come up with. Basically, she'd written all the lyrics during rest hour yesterday, which amazed me. I only added a few things: the part about freezing in the lake and getting tadpoles stuck in your swimsuit. And Amber had written the last line as "Oh, Mommy, we want to come home!" but I thought about Shelby and the way she'd felt when I'd made that stupid mommy joke. So I'd suggested changing the line to "Oh, Eda! We want to go home!" and Amber had agreed to it.

Now people were saying that from now on, everyone at camp would sing our version of "Camp Days" instead of the sappy original. We all thought that was pretty cool. And everyone had raved about how good the dancers were, and how funny it was to mix those moves with that goofy song.

"Now we'll go ahead with regularly scheduled activities today. Then tonight we will have the final Circle Fire," announced Eda.

Meredith stopped us as the crowd stood up and started walking away. "Hey, guys, it really was a great act. But why'd you keep the chorus the same as the original?"

"Are you kidding me? How could we improve on frolicking and skipping in the dew?" I asked.

Then Michelle walked up. "I am so proud of all my campers! You guys did a great job." Then she grabbed my arm and pulled me aside. "Thank you," she whispered.

"For what?" I asked.

"For taking care of things. For making sure that your act was appropriate." She smiled at me. Courtney and everyone else wandered away while Michelle and I talked.

"Believe me—it all came together at the last minute," I told her.

"Well, however it happened, I'm glad it worked out. I can't believe camp is over tomorrow!" Michelle groaned.

"I know," I agreed. "I don't want to leave. I wish I could stay here forever. I love this place."

"Oh, come on. Camp is great, and we're all going to be sad saying good-bye, but look at the bright side. You'll be so happy to see your family tomorrow."

"Yeah, I will be," I said. Then I looked at her. "But my family's a mess." If there was anyone I could tell this secret to, it was Michelle.

Her eyebrows went up, and she waited for me to go on. I'd never talked about this to anyone.

"We're having a lot of problems now. I'm glad I've been away all summer. In some ways I don't want to go home." I looked at her. "Do you think that's terrible?"

"No, of course not," said Michelle. A little line appeared between her eyes. "Do you want to talk about it?"

"Yeah, I think so. But not here." A lot of people were still wandering around after the assembly.

Michelle nodded. "Let's go someplace private."

So we went to Middler Lodge and sat out on the porch. The view was beautiful from up here, with the blue mountains off in the distance. And today was a sunny day.

Michelle kept quiet and waited for me to talk. I was glad we were sitting on a wooden bench looking out at the view. That way I didn't have to look at her.

"Well, you know all about my brothers and how they're big football heroes?" I asked. Michelle nodded. "That's how it used to be. But it's not that way anymore. Not since this spring."

Michelle looked concerned. "Did one of them get injured?"

"No," I said. Injuries they could recover from. "No. It was Justin. He got caught using steroids."

"Oh," said Michelle very quietly.

"Yeah. And guess who turned him in."

"The coach?" she asked.

"No. Adam told on him. He went to the coaches and told them first, before he even told my parents about it. It was a huge scandal. Everybody in the school knew about it. It was in the newspaper. We live in kind of a small town, and during the fall everything revolves around Friday night football. The whole town was talking about the Duckworth brothers and what happened at Central High."

Michelle blew a long breath out. "I can imagine. It must have been terrible."

"It was. Everybody took sides. Some people said the coaches knew about it but looked the other way. A lot of people were mad at Adam for telling on Justin. Adam said he did it because he was afraid Justin might have bad side effects from the drugs. But then Justin said Adam only narced on him because he was jealous. You know, Justin's older and stronger and bigger. I think maybe Adam was a little jealous."

"Well, for whatever reason he did it, Adam did the right thing," said Michelle, glancing at me. "Steroids can cause so many health problems. It was dangerous for Justin to be on them. You know that, right?"

"Yeah, I do. But it's messed up our whole family. People have broken windows in our house—they drive by at night and throw rocks. And one time when I was walking home from school, a reporter jumped out from behind a bush and asked me if I knew my brother was 'on the juice.'" I tried to tell that part without crying.

Michelle put her arm around me and patted my

shoulder. Now I really felt like crying. "So that's why I'm not looking forward to going home. Sure, I love them and miss them. But I don't want to go home to all that. My parents sent me to camp so I could get away from everything."

I felt like I'd just run a mile. I was so exhausted and relieved. I took long, deep breaths. I actually did feel better, now that I'd finally told someone my big secret.

"Well, it can't be easy," Michelle said. I could tell she was trying to think of the right words. "Things will get better over time. How's your brother doing now?"

I shrugged. "It's hard to say. He hasn't written me all summer. He's been pretty withdrawn from our whole family. I think he's depressed. We're not sure if he'll be allowed to play football next year. But that's all he cares about. If he's not a football player, he doesn't know"—I stopped talking because I realized Justin and I had something in common—"he doesn't know who is."

For most of his life Justin had been a football player. He'd played since he was a little boy, starting out in Pop Warner. It was like Lauren having "Dancer" on her shorts. Justin wore his jersey and that was who he was. But now what?

"It's a tough lesson for him," Michelle admitted. "Hopefully, he'll be able to move on and get his life back on track."

I nodded. Then I started crying. I felt guilty for saying I didn't want to go home. What would my family think if they heard that? But I dreaded having to go back and face everything. There was nothing I could do, though. I couldn't stay at camp forever.

Michelle kept quiet and patted me on the shoulder till I calmed down. My nose was runny, but I didn't have anything to blow it on. Michelle stuck out her arm and offered me her sleeve, which made me start laughing. "Go ahead! I can always wash this shirt later!" she said cheerfully.

"I am not going to blow my runny nose on your shirt!" Now I couldn't stop laughing.

"Want me to pull some leaves off the trees, then?" she asked, looking up at some tree branches just a few feet away from the porch.

"NO! I'll just sniffle." I took a deep breath. I really did feel better. "Thanks, Michelle."

She looked at me and smiled a little. "Are you sure you're okay now?"

"Yeah. I really am." We got up and left the porch. I went to Solitary and washed my face before anyone could see me.

Everyone was waiting for me in the cabin. "Where'd you go?" asked Courtney.

"I was talking to Michelle about something," I told her. Nobody said anything about my face, so I figured all the crying signs were gone.

"So what activity should we go to this morning?" Lauren asked. "Since nobody has to go to the lake and swim laps."

"How about tennis?" I suggested. They all thought that was a weird choice, since we'd barely played all summer, but they agreed to go with me.

The four of us walked out of the cabin swinging our tennis rackets. "Would you guys have liked me if I wasn't always cracking jokes and getting into trouble?" I asked suddenly.

"Of course," said Mei. "But it's hard to imagine you not doing those things."

"What if I said that before I came to camp, I had a completely different personality?"

"What if I said that my biological parents were from outer space, and they sent me to this planet because our home planet was about to be destroyed? And here on Earth, I have special powers," said Mei.

"Like what?" asked Courtney.

"I can do this!" Then Mei started doing all the steps from the dance routine, which made Courtney and Lauren crack up.

"Hey, you stole *my* special powers!" Lauren yelled, and bumped Mei out of the way with her hip so she could do the dance.

"I'm trying to tell you guys something!" I cried. They all stopped and looked at me. "If you'd met me before camp, you wouldn't even recognize me."

"Why? Did you used to be four-six instead of five-six?" asked Courtney.

"No. I just act very different at home than I do here. That's all."

Lauren shrugged. "Well, we all do."

"Do any of you even know that my real name is Judith?" I asked.

"Judith?" Mei covered her mouth with her hand and snickered. "*Judith?* I've never heard that one before!"

"Well, it is," I said firmly. "And I want you all to start calling me that."

They burst out laughing. "Okay, Judith. Whatever you say," Mei agreed.

Not one of them even acted surprised. They didn't seem to get what I'd just told them. "I'm not joking about this, you guys! At home I'm this quiet, boring girl named Judith Duckworth. But when I came to camp I decided to change that, and so I told everyone to call me JD. But I'm not JD. I'm Judith.

Tomorrow we all go home, and I have to go back to being myself."

Lauren pretended to smack my back with the tennis racket. "Look, JD—or Judith. Or John Jacob Jingleheimer Schmidt. We're your friends, no matter what we call you."

"Yeah, but . . ." How could I explain it so they'd understand?

Courtney solemnly put her hand on my forehead. "Do you feel okay, Schmitty?"

"Problem solved! Let's call her Schmitty from now on!" said Mei.

I felt pretty silly. Maybe my whole personality makeover wasn't such a big deal after all. They didn't even care! "Stop calling me Schmitty! Call me . . . whatever. I guess it doesn't matter."

Courtney shook her head and whispered to Mei and Lauren, "I'm really worried about Schmitty. She's not herself today."

"I am myself! I think. Let's just go play tennis and have fun, okay? It's our last full day together."

I did feel like myself. And maybe Lauren was right. Maybe it didn't matter what they called me. Whatever name I went by, somehow I would manage to be me.

## Saturday, July 12

I hated the way the cabin looked exactly like it had on the first day we got here. All the mattresses were bare, and everybody's stuff was packed away. That day I'd been so excited. Now I was just depressed.

But I had one last thing to do in the cabin before leaving. I took a pen out of my backpack and climbed up on my top bunk. It didn't seem like my bed anymore, because now my sheets and blanket were packed. I found the spot on the wall where I'd written JD WAS HERE. Under it, I wrote JUDITH WAS TOO! I tried to make my handwriting look different. I thought about how maybe years from now, some camper would read those two messages and not even realize they were written by the same person.

Then I capped my pen and stuck it into my back-pack. My trunk had already been carried out by some Crockett counselors. I took one last look at everything before I walked out of the cabin for the last time.

Everyone was waiting for me on the hill. I'd told them I needed to go to Solitary. Courtney had said she'd come with me, but I'd told her to stick around with the others in case she missed saying good-bye to someone. I wanted to be alone when I signed the wall.

"Katherine just left," Courtney announced when I walked up to them.

"Oh, darn, I wanted to give her a big hug!" I joked.

"She said she'd e-mail you the second she got home," Mei assured me.

Michelle and Alex walked up. "They're starting to load the bus," said Michelle, and my heart dropped all the way down to my toes. That meant I had to leave now.

"I hate this!" Courtney said, burying her face in her hands. "I'm going to cry all day today!"

Last night had been bad enough. We'd all cried our eyes out at the Circle Fire. How could camp be over already?

Everyone walked with me to the bus. A big crowd of people was standing around, and everyone was hugging and crying and saying good-bye. I hated all the good-byes. But I was glad that my parents weren't coming to pick me up. I'd watched Isabel's mom when she was saying good-bye to all of us. Isabel had cried, and that made us cry. Her mom looked so upset that her daughter was reacting to going home by bursting into tears.

One by one everyone stepped up to say good-bye to me. Alex hugged me—Alex the slave driver, who was always frowning at me. "I'm really proud of you," she said.

"Oh, shut up!" I blubbered at her. I could take her being strict. I couldn't take her being proud of me.

"Take care, sweetie," said Michelle, giving me a big, long hug. "I'll be thinking about you. Everything will be fine. Write me or call me if you ever need to talk." Her eyes were all teary when she let go of me.

Then Mei, Lauren, and Courtney said their good-byes. It was all a big blur. We hugged and cried and promised to keep in touch. I felt like my heart was breaking. These guys had seen me through my JD experiment, without ever really knowing it.

"I'm going to miss you so much!" sobbed Courtney.

"Maybe we can visit each other during the school year. All four of us," I said, wiping away tears.

Just as I was about to go up the steps, Amber ran

up and gave me a hug. "Thank you. You're my favorite poet," I told her.

"I'm so glad you were in my cabin this year," said Amber. "You made it the most fun summer I've ever had here." That should've made me feel good, but I wished we'd gotten to know each other better. At least we'd had fun together with the talent show. I was glad about that.

Finally I walked up the steps. All of the bus windows were down, and girls were hanging out of the windows, still waving good-bye. I took an empty seat in the middle on the left side, so I could still look out the window and see everyone.

Then I saw Natasha getting on the bus, and I waved at her to come to my seat. "You can sit here. I promise I'll behave myself, and I won't sing any songs."

Natasha grinned as she put her stuff in the overhead bin and sat down. "I was hoping you'd sing 'Camp Days' for me!"

"Oh, that! I meant I wouldn't sing 'A Hundred Bottles of Beer on the Wall.'"

"Well, I never got a chance to tell you what a great job you did in the talent show. I told everyone you were my first friend!"

"Really? Cool. I'm glad everyone liked it. But it was really a group effort."

The driver closed the doors and started the engine. Natasha and I both stood up and waved to everyone one more time. Courtney, Mei, and Lauren did a few dance steps for me before the bus started pulling away. All three of them were still crying.

"I had a great summer," I said to Natasha.

"Yeah, me too," she agreed.

Now that camp was over, who should I be when I got home? Should I go back to being Judith like nothing had ever happened? Or maybe be somebody else? When would I know for sure who I was?

The bus rumbled down the gravel road and then turned onto the highway. We still had a long trip ahead of us. But I knew my family would be waiting for me at the bus station, and they'd all be so happy to see me. Maybe even Justin would come with them this time.

"You think you'll come back next summer?" Natasha asked me.

"I hope so," I said. "But I don't know for sure." There were lots of things I didn't know for sure. I sat back in the seat and looked out the window.

Maybe someday I'd know all the answers. Maybe someday I'd know exactly who I was.

I'd just have to wait and see.

Up next—Can Darcy and Nicole's
friendship survive the summer?

# Find out in
# FRIENDS FORNEVER!

# Summer Camp Secrets

## FRIENDS FORNEVER

Katy Grant

# Summer Camp Secrets

## FRIENDS FORNEVER

For my own BFF, Susan Moore,
whose friendship, counsel, love, and an
incomparable wit have always sustained me.
And will always—forever.

# Acknowledgments

Special thanks to my editor Liesa Abrams, whose enthusiasm over this subject matter gave me inspiration through every step of the writing process. I still remember a phone conversation between us when I had only presented her with a few rough pages outlining a story about best friends. Liesa was bubbling over with excitement for this idea, and as I began writing, I kept coming back to her words of encouragement whenever I struggled with the plot or blocked over a passage. All I had to do was remind myself, "Liesa loved this idea!" and I was able to work my way around the rough spots as I wrote. For each of the Summer Camp Secrets books, she has been with me every step of the way, but for this one in particular, Liesa made me feel that this book would become a story that would really speak to my readers.

Thanks to Steve Williams, whose knowledge of rappelling and climbing helped me as I wrote the climbing tower passages. Steve patiently explained basic climbing techniques and answered all my greenhorn questions.

Finally, I want to thank my husband, Eric, and my sons, Jackson and Ethan, for continuing to live with me while I wrote this book. Whenever my frustration levels rose, I would snarl, "These books don't write themselves, you know!" They would immediately pitch in and do their share of housework, laundry, and meal preparation. You guys see me at my worst, and you still love and support me. I am eternally grateful for that.

## Sunday, June 15

It was the best day of the year! In one hour we'd be arriving at Camp Pine Haven, and I'd finally get to see Nicole again. I sent her another message.

How much longer 4 u?

Idk
i think bout 30 min
how bout u?

Mom sez 1 hr
u r gonna get
2 PH 1st

Probly

cant wait 2 get off this stinkin bus!


Guess wat

i have a huge secret 2 tell u


"Don't your fingers get tired?" asked Mom from the driver's seat.

"Not really," I said. "You're dropping me off first, right?"

Mom looked at me in the rearview mirror. "No, sweetie. We're dropping Blake off first. We'll get to Camp Crockett before we get to Pine Haven."

"No way! That'll take too long," I groaned as my phone chimed. I read Nicole's text—she was begging me to tell my secret, but I texted back that she'd have to wait.

I tried to reason with Mom. "Look, if you go to Pine Haven first, you'll only have to stop for fifteen minutes. Just unload my stuff, say good-bye, and go. Then you guys can spend extra time with Blake if you want."

Blake was totally focused on his PSP game. I could tell he was nervous about going to sleepaway camp for the first time, even though he was trying to act all cool about it.

"You mean we have to come to a complete stop when we drop you off at Pine Haven?" Paul asked from the captain's chair next to Mom. "Our plan was to drive past really slow and let you jump out. We'll heave your bags to you through the window."

"Sounds great to me," I said, typing a reply to Nicole. She was telling me about the obnoxious girl sitting behind her on the bus who was trying to get everyone to sing "One Hundred Bottles of Beer on the Wall."

"Darcy, it makes more sense to stop at Camp Crockett first, because we come to it before Pine Haven. If we take you first, we'll have to double back."

I sighed. "Well, how long is that going to take? I need to tell Nic exactly when we're getting to Pine Haven."

Mom glanced at her watch. "I'll have you there by one thirty."

"One thirty! But that's two hours away! You said we'd be there in an hour. It's not going to take a whole hour to drop off Blake."

Mom gripped the steering wheel tighter and didn't answer me. Blake didn't make a sound from the backseat. Paul kept quiet too and looked out the window.

Bad news
now mom sez well get 2 PH n 2 hrs!

Y so late?

I tried to text Nicole back to explain about taking Blake to Camp Crockett first, but when I hit send, I got a NO SERVICE message.

"Oh, great! Now I don't even have service!" I snapped my phone shut and tossed it on the seat beside me.

"Oh no, a crisis," Blake said, still not looking up from his game. "You and Nicole can't talk to each other for two whole hours. You'll never make it."

"Relax, kiddo." Paul turned around to smile at me over the back of his seat. "Enjoy the beautiful scenery. Listen to these mellow tunes. Talk to your mom and me. Remember, we won't get to see you two for a whole month."

He gave me a wink and I smiled back. Paul draped his arm around Mom's neck, and she loosened her grip on the steering wheel a little. They were still newly-weds, and they acted like it. Always holding hands and smiling. Saying "I love you" about fifty times a day. It was a little too much PDA for me, but I was glad they were both so happy.

I stared out the window at all the green trees. The road twisted back and forth into hairpin turns as the van climbed higher and higher up the mountain road. I could feel my heart starting to pound. Almost there! Two more hours and I would be back at camp. Back with all my friends. Back with Nicole.

*Finally!* I'd really thought this day would never come.

From the back bench, Blake looked up and swallowed. He had sweat on his upper lip, and his face was pale. "How much longer?"

"Mom, I think he's going to puke." Mom looked in the rearview mirror.

"I'm not gonna puke. I'm just tired of being in this stupid van."

"Get yourself a cold drink, dude," Paul advised. "It'll settle your stomach."

Blake scrambled over his seat and pulled a can of Sprite out of the cooler in the back.

"Can you get me one too?" I asked.

Just then my phone chimed and flashed a message from Nicole. "Hey! I have service again!"

U still
there?

Ya

lost srvice 4 awhile

Me 2

I texted Nicole again about how we had to go to Camp Crockett first to drop off Blake, but then right after I sent it, I lost service *again*.

I hoped she got my message. Otherwise, she'd get to Pine Haven and be out of her mind waiting for me to arrive.

At least it hadn't been a whole year since Nic and I had seen each other. Over the winter break I'd gone to visit her at her mom's for New Year's Eve. I had hoped Nic could come to Mom and Paul's wedding in February, but her mom said we'd just seen each other the month before. Then we tried to plan a visit over our spring breaks, but they fell on different weeks, so that hadn't worked out either.

I don't think even one day went by when we didn't text or IM each other, but I was still dying to see her. And tell her my secret. I was so excited about it, I had almost given in and texted her about it, but I decided to wait. It would be so much more fun to tell her in person.

While I sipped my Sprite, I kept checking every few minutes to see if I'd gotten service back. I held my phone above my head to try to get a signal. But no matter how much I waved my phone around, it couldn't find a cell tower. About twenty minutes later we were driving under the big, arching Camp Crockett sign. Blake sat forward with his arms propped on the back of my bench, looking at everything out the window.

"You are going to have such a great time. Trust me. Every single second you'll be doing something fun." I grabbed his arm and squeezed it.

"Ow! Stop it, Darcy," Blake said in a really whiny voice that made him sound like he was six, not ten.

"Sorry. Hey, look at the lake. Pretty cool, huh?"

It was actually kind of fun to see Camp Crockett in the daylight. I'd been here a few times in past summers when Pine Haven had dances with the Crockett boys, but it was usually almost dark when we came over.

We found a parking spot along the side of the road and climbed out of the van. All around us were Camp Crockett counselors in red T-shirts, and boys, boys, boys everywhere we looked.

Why had I complained about having to come here

first? This wasn't going to be bad at all.

Mom and Paul left to find someone in charge, while Blake and I watched all the activity. I got more than a few looks from guys who probably felt like I was invading their all-male space. We watched old campers give each other hand slaps, high fives, and fist pounds. That sure was different from Pine Haven, where we all hugged each other.

"Don't worry. You'll make friends really fast," I told Blake.

He frowned at me. "I'm not worried."

Mom and Paul called us over to a group of counselors and introduced us to two of them, Brandon and Rob.

"How's it going, Blake?" asked Brandon, the cute, dark-haired one. He gave Blake a firm handshake. Blake threw his shoulders back a little; he loved the whole male-bonding, handshake thing. Brandon and Rob helped us get Blake's stuff out of the rooftop carrier, and then we headed to Newt Cabin 4.

Camp Crockett had animal names for their age groups—Mites, Newts, Bobcats, and Bears. At Pine Haven we had only three age groups, and the names were kind of boring—Juniors, Middlers, and Seniors. And Camp Crockett called their dining hall the mess and their bathrooms the latrine. I'd always thought it was weird that at Pine Haven the name for our communal bathrooms was Solitary.

Brandon talked a lot, telling Mom and Paul all about where he was from and where he went to college. I couldn't wait to see the inside of the cabins.

I felt like a spy, sneaking around on foreign territory. *Camp Crockett cabins—where few girls have gone before.*

In a lot of ways their cabins were just like ours— wooden buildings with screens all around the top half, two big open rooms called Side A and Side B, and bunk beds and metal cots. Also, there was graffiti all over the wooden walls inside, just like at Pine Haven. Only the outside of their cabins looked different from ours. Theirs were painted a pale green; ours were just plain wood.

"Okay, I did it right this year and packed the sheets and blankets on top," said Mom, opening Blake's trunk so she could make up his bunk.

Now that the excitement of being inside a boys' cabin had passed, I was dying to leave. I was sure that Nicole was already at camp by now, waiting for me. "After this, can we go?" I asked, as softly and politely as I could.

Mom frowned at me as she tucked in Blake's sheets.

After Blake's bunk was made, Mom and Paul wanted to inspect every single inch of Camp Crockett under a magnifying glass.

Finally, after two or three millennia, they were ready to leave.

I knew from experience that Blake's number one priority now was not to cry. I didn't hug him, because he hates when I do that anyway. I just touched his arm. "Hey, I'll see you in about a week at the first dance. Write me whenever."

Blake rolled his eyes. "Don't hold your breath." Then Mom hugged him too tight and too long. What was she thinking? That was a good way to send him right into a bawling breakdown.

Paul smacked him on the back. "Remember what we talked about, okay?"

Blake smiled and nodded. "Yeah, thanks. I will."

Hmm, that was interesting. I guess Paul must've had some kind of heart-to-heart with Blake recently. That was pretty cool. He was good about stuff like that.

I tried not to knock anybody over in my rush to get back to the van.

Finally, finally, finally!

Now I was just minutes away from my first day of summer camp! If I didn't die of excitement on the drive over.

# CHAPTER 2

I felt like I was going to explode as we drove down the shady, tree-lined roads toward Pine Haven. This summer camp hidden away in the green, wooded mountains of North Carolina just so happened to be one of my favorite places on the planet. All year long I'd been dreaming about this day. I even had a countdown clock on my blog. When I'd set it up, there were 286 days till camp started. One by one, I'd waited for all those days to tick down.

I tried my phone one last time, but it still couldn't get service, so I gave up and handed it over to Mom. It didn't matter anyway; I was sure that Nicole was already at camp waiting for me.

When at last we saw the wooden sign by the

entrance, I actually screamed out loud. "We're here! We're here!"

"Try to show a little enthusiasm, won't you?" Paul chuckled. Last year he'd come along with Mom to drop me off, so he knew the whole routine.

I gripped the seat and stared out the window, soaking in everything I could—the lake, the tennis courts, the archery range, the path through the woods that led to the riflery range. Senior Lodge, the dining hall, Crafts Cabin, even the infirmary next to the camp office was a wonderful sight. It all looked exactly the same!

"Everything looks so beautiful!" If I had to describe Pine Haven in one word, it would be green—green woods, green grass, a lake shimmering green from all the trees surrounding it. Deep, lush green everywhere I looked.

Mom slowed the van to a crawl as we got to the main part of camp. I saw familiar faces everywhere I looked. As soon as Mom stopped the car, I threw open the door and jumped out.

Lunch had just ended, and everyone was coming out of the dining hall.

"Darcy! Darcy!" I heard people screaming my name from all different directions. All at once I was surrounded by Boo Bauer, Abby Harper, Amber Cummings, Jordan Abernathy, and Molly Chapman.

"Omigosh, it's so good to see you!"

"What cabin are you in?"

"When did you get here?"

We were all hugging and talking at the same time. Then out of the crowd I saw Nicole trying to push through everyone to get to me. "Hey, back off! She's *my* best friend!" Nicole shouted, and everyone laughed and let her squeeze through.

Nicole and I hugged and bounced up and down. "I thought you'd never get here! We got our request— we're in the same cabin again!" she screamed at me.

"We are? Thank God! Who else is with us? Who are our counselors?"

The whole group of us started up the hill. Nicole and I were in Middler Cabin 3 with Libby Sheppard and Jamie Young as our counselors, but none of the rest of the group was in our cabin. During the past two summers, we'd all been together at one point.

"Has your mom left already?" Nic asked me when we were halfway up the hill.

"Omigosh! I completely forgot about them! I kinda abandoned them the second we got here."

Nicole and I left the group and ran back down the

hill to the road, where Paul was unpacking my stuff from the rooftop carrier. Mom stood beside him, shading her eyes and trying to find me in the crowd.

"Darcy!" Mom exclaimed. "Can you please stay with us? You need to carry some things too, you know. Hi, Nicole. You've grown a couple of inches!"

Nicole grabbed my sleeping bag. I carried my duffel and let Mom and Paul get my trunk.

"Sarah Bergman and Whitney Carrington are both in our cabin, but everyone else is new," Nicole told me as we walked back up the hill.

We couldn't stop talking about who was in which cabin, who hadn't come back this year, and which of our old friends Nicole had already seen. By the time we got to Cabin 3, I felt halfway caught up on everything.

"See, I saved the singles for us," said Nic, pointing to the two cots that were side by side next to a set of bunk beds. She'd already made her bed with the same pink and red polka-dot sheets she had last year.

"Perfect!" I tossed my duffel on the empty cot next to hers. "It'll be easier for us to talk after lights out."

It was a madhouse inside the cabin, the way Opening Day always is, with everyone meeting each other, bringing in luggage, and unpacking their stuff. Libby was busy talking to my parents, and I gave Whitney a big

hug. She was on Side B with Jamie and three new campers. Whitney was already giving them all a briefing on
some Pine Haven traditions. Then I met Patty Nguyen,
the new girl on Side A.

Totally unexpectedly, I had a sudden rush of . . . I
guess it was homesickness. Only it wasn't for home;
it was for the way things were last year with our old
cabin. Sure, there were old friends around, but it was a
different mix of people from last year. And there were
four new people. I just wished everything could be
exactly like it was last year.

"I'm on the swimming staff, and my cocounselor,
Jamie, is in charge of the riflery range," Libby was telling
Mom and Paul. I could tell my parents liked Libby right
away. She was really mature; after all, she's twenty-two,
definitely one of the older counselors at Pine Haven.
Plus, she's got a smile that wins everyone over as soon
as they meet her.

I knew Mom wanted to make my bed for me, but I
could do it myself. "You guys really don't need to stick
around. I know you have a long drive back," I told them.

"And don't let the door hit us on the way out, huh?"
Paul said with a laugh. "Do us a favor, okay? Lie to us
and tell us you'll miss us?" He put his arm around my
shoulders and gave me a squeeze.

I hugged him back. "You know I will. I'm just so excited to finally be here!"

Mom gave me a big hug and kiss. "Remember—you promised us a minimum of two letters a week."

"I know. I promise. And you guys send me lots of e-mails too. Especially if you have any big news." I smiled knowingly at her.

Paul gave me one last kiss. "We love you, kiddo. Have a great time."

"I love you guys too. Bye!" I walked out the door with them and waved as they walked down Middler Line. I was a little sad to see them go, but I could hardly wait to have my first long conversation with Nic.

When I went back inside, she was sitting on her cot, giving me the look I knew so well—one eyebrow raised, one corner of her mouth twisted down in a frown.

"What's up?" I plopped down on the end of her cot. With my parents out of the way, Libby now focused on helping Patty make up her bunk.

"Paul. Your new 'dad.'" Nicole made quotation marks in the air with her fingers. "All that hugging and kissing and 'we love you, kiddo'? Darcy, how can you stand it?" She grabbed my arm sympathetically. "Who does he think he is?"

"Oh come on, Nic. He is my stepfather now, you know."

"Exactly. With the emphasis on *step*. Is he going for a Father of the Year Award or something? Richard never acts like that with me, thank God. And he and Mom have been married for three years."

"Paul's just the huggy type," I explained. "I don't mind it. He's not my father, but he's still a member of the family."

"Wow, he didn't waste any time, did he? He and your mom have been married—what? Three months? And now you're all one big happy family?" Nicole rolled her eyes like she couldn't believe Paul would be so bold.

"It's four months, and yeah, we are one big happy family. You say that like it's a bad thing." I couldn't believe it! Here Nicole and I were, together for the first time in six months, and we were . . . not exactly fighting, but close.

Nic shook her head and smiled. She must've been thinking the same thing about where this conversation was going, because now her tone was completely different. "It's so great to finally see you! You're already tan. And your hair—I love it longer."

The tan I couldn't do much about. Blake and I both have Mom's Italian complexion. My hair had been short last summer, but I've been letting it grow. It's dark brown and it curls like crazy, but the longer it gets, the more it straightens out. I've always envied Nic's pencil-straight, caramel-colored hair. She can wear it up, down, in braids, or in a ponytail, which was how she had it today.

"Thanks. Cute earrings," I said, looking at the tiny hearts in her ears. "Hey, those look familiar. Did I give those to you?"

Nicole laughed and touched her earlobes. "Not exactly. You left them at my house when you came for New Year's Eve, remember? I was going to mail them to you, but I never got around to it. Then I planned to bring them to camp, but I was so afraid I'd forget them that I stuck them in. Want 'em back?"

"Don't worry about it right now." We both laughed. Last summer I'd come home with half of Nic's clothes in my trunk, and she had a bunch of mine. We swap back and forth so much we sometimes forget which clothes are whose.

"Are you trying to torture me or something?" Nicole asked. "Ten minutes we've been together and you still haven't told me your big secret."

"Oh! Sorry, I was totally distracted. But first I need to go to Solitary. Come with me."

We took off out the door to the bathrooms in the building between Cabins 3 and 4. I wanted to talk to Nicole in private without everyone else hearing us. I went to one of the faucets and washed my hands.

"Hey, this reminds me of when we shaved our legs for the first time." Last summer Nic and I bought plastic razors and a can of shaving cream at the camp store and then shaved in this room. Instead of sinks, Solitary has long troughs all along the walls, so we had to stand at the trough with one leg hooked over the edge so we could reach the faucets. Afterward we had a massive shaving-cream fight. Mom was not thrilled when she found out I'd shaved. She thought eleven was too young.

"Yeah, great memory." Nicole held up both hands like she was about to choke me. "Will you tell me already?"

I grabbed a paper towel from the dispenser, then tossed it into the trash barrel. "Okay. I've been absolutely dying to tell you. Mom and Paul have been talking about having a baby!"

Nicole gasped. "Oh, no! That's horrible! You've got to stop them."

My mouth fell open. "What? Are you kidding me? I am so excited, I could scream! It's incredible! It's amazing! I'm going to be a big sister!"

Nic crossed her arms and glared at me. "You're already a big sister."

"Blake doesn't count. Well, I guess he counts, but it's not like I remember him as a baby. A baby, Nic! We're going to have a sweet, precious, adorable little baby in our family!"

"Precious? Adorable? Do you have any idea how much babies cry? Sweet? Wait'll you get a whiff of the first dirty diaper." Eyebrow up, corner of the mouth down.

"Oh, don't be so negative! Every time I go to the mall, I go straight to the baby clothes section. I hope it's a girl! What do you think of Vanessa? Or Madeline? But a boy would be fine too. Colton. Don't you think that's a cool name? And then there's the nursery to decorate. . . ."

"Yeah, if it's a girl, you'll probably have to share your room with the squealing little darling."

"Who cares! The only thing is"—I grabbed Nic's arm—"Mom's worried about whether she can get pregnant at her age, and if there'll be any complications. I heard them talking about it." Those worries absolutely terrified me.

"Oh, good point. Maybe it won't even happen."

"Nicole! How can you say that?" I was hoping she'd comfort me.

"Darcy, you need to be realistic. Things might not be all sunshine and roses."

"But they might," I insisted. "Mom didn't have any trouble with Blake or me. And she's really healthy. Anyway, that's my big secret." Why did I need to convince Nicole to be happy for me?

"Well, I hope for your sake everything will turn out okay," said Nicole.

Walking back to the cabin, she bumped me with her hip and I bumped her back. Nic and me together again at Camp Pine Haven for another incredible summer. That definitely made me smile.

CHAPTER 3

On the afternoon of every Opening Day, all the campers
had to go down to the lake and take a swim test, whether
it was our first year or our fifth. I'd always thought that
was strange; I mean, if we proved we could swim last
summer, why would we have to do it again?

Nic and I had just gotten back to the cabin after our
mandatory first-day swim tests when Sarah Bergman
arrived.

"Oh, yippee!" she said, spotting the bottom bunk. "I
get to fold myself up under here every night?"

At five foot five, Sarah towered over the rest of
us. All the girls in our cabin were twelve, but Sarah
could've easily passed for fifteen. Her dark hair was
pulled back in a French braid. Her forehead was usually

wrinkled up in a really serious expression, like she was concentrating on solving a complicated math problem.

"Hey, it could've been worse. The new girl, Patty, picked the top bunk. At least you're not climbing up there every night," I told her. Nicole and I pulled out dry clothes from our trunks and changed out of our wet swimsuits.

"Where's Miss Whitney Louise Carrington?" Sarah asked in a perky voice that was supposed to be an imitation of Whitney. Even though Sarah mocked Whitney constantly, they were still best friends.

"I think she's giving all the newbies the grand tour," said Nicole.

"My mother was a camper at Pine Haven from 1977 to 1981, and my grandmother was a camper from 1951 to 1960," Sarah said in her chirpy Whitney voice. Nic and I fell over laughing. We were definitely in for a fun summer with Sarah around.

"So four new campers? What are they like?" asked Sarah, hunching over to sit on the bottom bunk.

"Well, let's see—I've already mentioned Patty in the top bunk. Seems nice. Kinda quiet, though. She's Asian, long dark hair. I think she's going to be really easygoing. The other three are on Side B with Whitney—Ashlin, Natasha, and Claudia."

"Natasha was on the bus with me," added Nicole. "She sat behind me with that really obnoxious girl."

"But Natasha seems like a real sweetie," I pointed out. "She's very petite, glasses, African American. You can tell she's a little freaked over meeting all these new people. Now, is Claudia the one with dark hair?" I asked Nic.

"No, that's Ashlin. The first time I saw her, I thought she was somebody's little brother. Girls who are that flat-chested shouldn't wear their hair so short," said Nic.

Okay, that was a little mean. "Like you and I have so much to brag about," I said. "So Claudia must be the one with reddish hair—long, parted in the middle. She seems sort of . . ." I tried to think of a way to describe my first impression of Claudia.

"Bored," Nic put in. "This may be her first summer at Pine Haven, but she told us at lunch that she's been to three other summer camps. She's not exactly a newbie."

"And Whitney already has them all under her spell? Amazing!" Sarah snorted.

"Need any help getting your bed made?" I offered.

Sarah groaned and closed her eyes. "Don't bother. I just want to veg for a while." She stretched out on her unmade bunk.

Since we had some free time before dinner, Nic and

I left Sarah to chill while we went up and down Middler Line, trying to find all our old friends.

"Look, there's Alex! And Jennifer's with her!" I said. Alex was our counselor from last year, and Jennifer was our old cabinmate. We all had a happy little reunion in front of Cabin 1.

"You got braces!" I said, and Jennifer moaned and gritted her teeth.

"Two months ago. I hate them."

"Where's Reb?" asked Nicole. That was Jennifer's BFF.

"Not here yet! Can you believe it? She had a really late flight."

"I'm just so glad I've got a whole new batch of *good* campers this year," Alex teased us. "I hope they don't give me as much grief as I had last year."

That homesick feeling hit me again, like a wave in the ocean when you weren't expecting it. If only I could relive last summer, with everything exactly the same.

"Oh, really?" I asked. "Well, Libby Sheppard and Jamie Young are our counselors, so Nic and I got someone decent. For a change." Teasing Alex made the feeling go away a little.

When I looked up, Mary Claire, Nicole's eight-year-old stepsister, was walking toward us. When she saw Nic and me with our friends, she stopped and acted like she wasn't sure what to do next.

"Mary Claire! Hi! Remember me?" I walked up and gave her a little pat on the arm. I'd met her a couple of times when I went to visit Nic. Mary Claire's dad was married to Nicole's mom. Usually it was just Nicole and her mom and stepdad living together, but Mary Claire stayed with them two weekends a month. "Nicole told me you were coming to Pine Haven this year. How do you like it?"

"Um, good." Mary Claire glanced at Nicole, who was still talking to Alex and Jennifer. She chewed on the neckline of her T-shirt, seeming unsure whether she should go talk to Nicole or stay with me.

"What cabin are you in? Who's your counselor?" I asked.

"Junior Cabin Two." The neck of her T-shirt had a big wet spot where she'd been sucking on it. "My counselor . . . um." She closed her eyes for a second, then opened them and smiled at me bashfully. "I forgot her name already."

"Well, when you see her again, check her name tag, all right?" I advised. For the first week of camp, everyone wore name tags. We all had ours on now—they were little oblong slices of wood with a loop of lanyard string to go around our necks.

I glanced at Nicole, who seemed completely oblivious to the fact that her little sister was waiting to talk to her. Younger, I should say. For an eight-year-old, Mary Claire was a rather large girl. She came up to my nose, and by my guess she outweighed me by at least twenty pounds.

We walked over to the others. "This is Mary Claire. She's"—I started to say "Nicole's sister," but Nic stepped on my foot and pressed down with all her weight—"She's a Junior. This is her first year," I managed to say through the pain.

"Well, we should probably go," Nicole said to Jennifer and Alex. "It was great to see you!"

"Hi, Nicole," Mary Claire said as we walked toward Cabin 3.

"Hi," Nicole muttered back, and then as soon as we were far enough away, she snapped at Mary Claire, "Stop sucking on your shirt."

Instantly Mary Claire opened her mouth and released the edge of her shirt.

"You know your dad hates when you do that. We all hate when you do that. Why are you on Middler Line, anyway? You're supposed to stick with the Juniors."

Mary Claire didn't say anything. "I think she wanted to come see our cabin," I said lightly. "Maybe we'll come by and see yours tomorrow."

Nic threw me a dirty look and then turned her attention back to Mary Claire. "Look, you can come to our cabin for a few minutes, but then you have to go back to your cabin. You can't be coming over here all the time. You go to activities, evening programs, and assemblies with your age group. Got it?"

Mary Claire nodded.

"And remember what I told you. We kind of know each other, but that's it."

When we got to Cabin 3, Nicole blocked the doorway with her body and pushed open the screen door with one hand. "Darcy and I are on Side A." Nic pointed to the right side of the cabin. "I'm in that bed. Now go." Nic shooed her away like a puppy. "Make some friends. In *your* cabin."

"Okay. Bye, Nicole." Mary Claire walked away down Middler Line.

"I think she's a little homesick," I said. I looked around for Sarah, but she wasn't in the cabin. Maybe she'd left to find Whitney.

"She'll get over it. Let's go sit out on the hill till the bell rings for dinner."

The hill was like the center of camp. From there you could see the lake, the tennis courts, and the dining hall down below you. Also, the view of the mountains on the horizon was really beautiful.

We found a good spot to sit in the grass. The sun was just below the ridge of the mountains, and a soft, shadowy light hung over everything. Already the whole camp was much quieter with all the parents and cars gone. People were walking around and hanging out and enjoying the nice, cool evening.

"Nic, maybe we should look out for Mary Claire. Make sure she gets adjusted and everything."

"She needs to make her own friends. She can't hang around us all the time."

"Yeah, I know. What was that about you and Mary Claire kind of knowing each other, but that's it?"

Nicole hugged her knees. "I don't want anyone to know that her dad is married to my mom. That doesn't make us sisters, you know. She is *not* my sister."

"Well, why do you care if people know that or not?" I asked.

"I just don't want people to know, okay? I am so glad we have different last names. And we certainly don't look like we're related. No one will ever make the connection between us unless she goes blabbing it all over the place."

"Okay, fine. It's just that . . . remember how scared we were on our first day of camp? And we were ten; she's only eight. We can at least be nice to her when we see her."

Nicole snorted. "We'll be nice to her when we see her. But don't expect me to go looking for her. And don't you dare introduce her as my stepsister to anyone."

"I won't from now on. I didn't know you were disowning her for the summer."

Nic smiled at me. "Oh, not just for the summer. For always."

That seemed like a pretty extreme reaction—to hide the fact that they were related. Mary Claire was kind of a geeky younger kid, but she wasn't *that* bad. Lots of people have geeky little brothers or sisters. But I would keep my mouth shut. And I'd also keep an eye out for Mary Claire. Somebody should look out for her.

# CHAPTER 4

When we walked into Middler Lodge after dinner, I had a sudden rush of memories of all the funny skits, games, and contests we'd done in here during past summers. The lodge was a big open room with high rafters, lots of benches for sitting, and a stone fireplace. But tonight it was too warm for a fire, and all the benches had been pushed along the walls to leave an open space in the middle.

All the counselors were lined up in front of us, and they started off the evening program by having us sing some camp songs: "Pine Haven Forever," "Nothing Is Better Than This," and "The Middler Charge." The new campers all looked around and tried to mumble some of the words. I remembered what that was like—to have a bunch of people around me singing songs I didn't know the words to yet.

"Good evening, ladies!" said our counselor, Libby. "We have a lot of activities planned to help you get to know each other. So here's what we want you all to do." Libby explained that we were going to be grouped into categories based on different things about ourselves.

The first game was called "Where are you from?" and counselors scattered all over the lodge and held up signs from different states. We were supposed to get into the group with other people from our state, which meant Nicole and I had to split up.

Then they grouped us by zodiac signs. The groupings turned out to be a good way to get people to talk to each other. I found out that Ashlin, one of the new girls in our cabin, had a birthday two days after mine. The weirdest category was hair color. Nicole and I got to be together in the brunettes group, but it wasn't like having the same hair color gave the group a lot to talk about. The blondes kept yelling, "We're having more fun!" It was pretty lame.

Then the counselors told us to group ourselves by whether we were the oldest, youngest, or middle child in our family. There was also a group for only children. I automatically walked over to the "Oldest" group, but then I had to stop and think about it. I could've gone to the "Middle" group too. Paul has two sons, Jonathon and Anthony, but sometimes I forget that they're my step-brothers now. They almost feel more like cousins than brothers. They're both in college, and we hardly ever see them. Usually just at holidays. I wondered if eventually I would start thinking of Jonathon and Anthony as brothers.

I looked over and noticed that Nicole was in the "Only" group. I didn't give that a lot of thought until I remembered Mary Claire. If Nicole counted her as a little sister, then she could've moved to the "Oldest" too. At first I was a little annoyed that Nicole didn't remember Mary Claire. Or maybe she did and decided to ignore her existence. But then I reminded myself that I'd done the exact same thing—went to the group that matched my biological order instead of my step order. I couldn't really blame Nicole.

When the games were over, we had some time to just hang out. A group of us wandered out to the porch. It was already dark and it was nice and cool. The air smelled like pine trees, and frogs were croaking down by the lake.

Whitney had adopted Claudia, Natasha, and Ashlin, the new campers in 3B. She absolutely adored being a one-woman welcoming committee. "Oh, I'll help you learn all the songs. I have a songbook back in the cabin. Anyone who wants to can borrow it," she was telling them.

While Whitney chatted away, Sarah very quietly walked over to her. Ever so slowly, she held her hand up, opening and closing it like a yakking mouth beside Whitney's face. The newbies tried not to laugh while Whitney kept talking, totally oblivious.

"Oh, this is interesting—there's this one song called 'Camp Days.' My grandmother and some of her friends actually wrote that song. I always get so emotional whenever we sing it!" Whitney sighed while Sarah's hand made sock puppet expressions at her.

"I've been having some serious déjà vu," said Nicole, finding an empty spot on one of the benches.

"Really? Me too. Tell me about yours," I said, jumping up to sit on the handrail.

"Doesn't this remind you of our first summer, when we played that get-acquainted game?" asked Nicole.

"Oh my gosh. It totally does! We were in the same group. And we had to write down all the answers to those questions . . . hometown, birthday, favorite book, favorite food, favorite actor—there were lots of favorites on that list!"

The counselors had put us into small groups and gave us a sheet of questions to answer. Then, instead of reading off what we'd written down, we had to switch papers, and the other person "introduced" us to the rest of the group. Nicole and I happened to sit next to each other, so I introduced her and she introduced me.

"Yeah, and we figured out that both of us had parents who were divorced. You were a real mess that summer. I wasn't sure you were going to survive," said Nicole.

That summer, Mom and Daddy had only been divorced a few months. Everything in our lives was so strange. My parents fought every single time they laid eyes on each other. I would just lock myself in the bathroom and throw up; then I'd come out and try to act like everything was okay when it wasn't. I hated all the fighting and yelling. I like things to be peaceful and happy, like they are now with Mom and Paul. At the time I hated that my parents were getting a divorce. But if I had to choose between my parents living together and fighting all the time or living apart and being happy, I'd definitely choose them being happy.

"Coming to camp was the best thing that ever happened to me," I said. "It got me out of that crazy environment for a while." I slapped at a mosquito on my arm. I should've put bug spray on before we came to the lodge.

"Yeah, and then we met. On the very first night of camp. And we were instant best friends," Nicole added.

"I know! I was so glad I finally had someone to talk to about my family problems. You were a lifesaver."

Nicole laughed. "You were always asking me a million questions: 'Who do you spend the holidays with?' 'Do you have your stuff at both houses, or do you keep everything at your mom's and just take what you need to your dad's?' 'Have your parents started dating other people?' 'Who comes to the parent-teacher conferences?' Yak, yak, yak!"

I smiled at her. "Well, you were the expert. Your parents had been divorced since you were six." Nicole and I talked about everything that summer—all my worries and stresses and fears. All that private stuff about my parents I hadn't told anyone before. "I know this sounds weird, but what if we'd been in different groups for that get-acquainted game? Then we wouldn't have met each other."

"Impossible. It was destiny that we got in the same group. Anyway, let's say we didn't meet at evening program. We had a whole month together. We would've met at some point for sure," Nicole reasoned.

I laughed.

I'd like to think that Nicole and I were destined to

meet and become BFFs, but sometimes I wondered if it worked that way. Mom had picked out two camps for me to choose from—Pine Haven and Camp Willahalee. The main reason I picked Pine Haven was because of the name. It was easier to pronounce.

What if I'd picked Willahalee instead? Then Darcy Bridges and Nicole Grimsley never would have met each other. Was it destiny? When good things happen, it's nice to think that it's destiny, but when stuff goes wrong, you have to wonder why destiny is giving you such a rotten life.

The counselors called us inside for graham crackers and milk, and then we got into the good-night circle to sing "Taps."

> *Day is done, gone the sun,*
> *From the lake, from the hills, from the sky.*
> *All is well, safely rest,*
> *God is nigh.*

"This has been a great first day," Nicole said, as everyone crowded through the doors of the lodge and started up the stone steps toward the cabins. A lot of the old campers were rushing to get to Solitary first so they wouldn't have to wait for a stall.

"Yeah, it sure has. We're going to have an amazing summer," I said. I hadn't had that homesick feeling all evening. I was pretty sure it was gone for good. As much as I wanted this summer to be exactly like last year, or the year before, I knew it didn't really matter. Even though this new summer could never be exactly like the old ones, I was absolutely positive it would be an awesome one.

## Monday, June 16

"Anyone who's interested in taking riding lessons, you do need to sign up for those—and it's a good idea to do it as early as possible. I'm going to the stables this morning. Feel free to join me." Whitney was over on Side B getting her troops in order. Jamie loved the fact that Whitney had put herself in charge. The more Whitney took over, the less Jamie had to do.

"Are you going to sign up for riding lessons?" I asked Sarah.

"No. I'm allergic to those hairy beasts. Do you mind if I hang out with you and Nicole?" She glanced at Patty, who was looking for something in her trunk. "You should come with us," she told her. "Stick with the normal people and you'll be safe." She made a smirky face in Whitney's direction.

"If we're normal people, what does that make Whitney?" I wanted to know.

Sarah thought about it for a second. "Deranged. Oh, Whitney darling! I'll see you after your lesson!" she called over to Side B as we all left the cabin.

"Let's go to riflery. Jamie says she needs the company," Nicole suggested.

"I miss Whitney already." Sarah sighed. "Her little turned-up nose. Her dimpled, rosy cheeks. I wish she was right here with us this very moment."

"You two have the weirdest friendship I've ever seen in my life. You obviously like her, but you make fun of her constantly," I said. They were such completely different people, I wondered what had made them friends in the first place.

Sarah covered her mouth in shock. "I would never, ever make fun of Miss Whitney Louise Carrington, third-generation Pine Haven camper!" Nicole and I could not stop laughing. Poor Patty just walked along with us, not knowing what to think.

When we got to the riflery range, Jamie was thrilled to see so many of her Cabin 3 campers. Nicole and I took spots beside each other on the shooting platform, but Sarah and Patty ended up three spots down from us. Since it was the first day, Jamie had to explain to everyone what to do and tell us the rules.

There were bare mattresses lined up across the shooting platform. Prone was the first position in riflery—we had to lie flat on our stomachs and prop ourselves up on our elbows to shoot.

We all loaded our rifles and took aim at the paper targets tacked to the boards across the range from us. "Okay to fire," said Jamie, and then the pops of the rifles firing exploded all around us.

"Hey, I have a great idea," I told Nicole as I squinted through the sight and squeezed the trigger. "What if we ask our parents if you can come home with me on the last day of camp? You can stay for a week, and then we'll drive you home."

"Nope, I can't. My dad and Elizabeth are picking me up on Closing Day. They get me for a whole month after camp is over."

"Oh, yeah. I forgot you usually visit your dad at the end of the summer." Nicole's whole arrangement of splitting time between parents was different from mine. Blake and I spent every other weekend with our dad, but since Nicole's parents lived in different states, she had long visits with her dad during the summer and over the school breaks.

"It's the highlight of my year," Nicole said sarcastically. "Maybe this summer Elizabeth might even let me use a towel. Most of the time I just drip-dry because the towels on the towel racks aren't supposed to be touched by human hands. Their house looks like a model home. Their trash cans are so spotless, I'm always afraid to throw anything away."

Nicole's description of her stepmother always cracked me up. Since I was laughing so hard I could barely aim, Nicole kept going. "It's not that Elizabeth doesn't want me there. She just doesn't want me to eat, sleep, shower, or go to the bathroom. If I stand in the middle of the living room and don't touch anything, that's okay. Wait, that's not okay either! I'll leave dents in the carpet!"

When everyone had finished shooting, Jamie told us to put our weapons down and turn on the safeties before retrieving our targets.

When I saw my target, I burst out laughing. "I only hit the target three times!" I yelled. "That's your fault. You made me laugh too much."

Nicole's score was much better than mine. At least all of her shots had hit the target. We took down the used targets and tacked up fresh ones. Sarah explained to Patty how to score her target.

"You can laugh all you want about it, but everything I'm telling you is true. I hate going there. I feel like I waste the whole month."

"I know Elizabeth gets on your nerves, but at least you get to see your dad."

"I don't need a whole month to visit him. The first two or three days, he asks me all about school and friends and stuff. After that, we're caught up and I might as well go home. It's a waste! I hate it. I don't consider that my home, and I don't consider them my family. Yeah, he's my father, but so what? We're not close. At all." Nicole turned and walked abruptly back to the platform. From the way her shoulders were tensed, I could tell she was getting upset.

We both stretched out on the mattresses and waited for Jamie to give us the order to fire again. Once the rifles started popping, I felt like it was safe to talk without everyone else hearing us.

"But that could change. Maybe this trip, you could try to get closer to your dad."

Nicole kept her eye trained on the sight and didn't look at me. She kept aiming and firing till she'd shot all of her bullets.

"Think of things the two of you can do together— like maybe go out to breakfast. Or go for walks. You

♥ 44 ♥

could even get Elizabeth in on it. Tell her you need her help to get reacquainted with your dad, so she won't mind if the two of you do some stuff together." Nicole stared at her target, even though it was fifty feet away and it was impossible to tell where any of the bullets had landed.

"It's just a suggestion," I added. "I'm only trying to help."

"I don't need your help."

I sat up on the mattress and looked at her, but she was totally absorbed in putting the safety on. She wouldn't look in my direction.

"Don't be mad, Nic." Now I felt all tense. It was like we had a giant rubber band between us, and if she got wound up, it would wind me up too.

Nicole made a grunting noise. "I'm not *mad*. What a stupid thing to say."

"Okay to retrieve your targets," said Jamie, and Nicole jumped off the platform and had her target down before I even had a chance to stand up. I ran to catch up with her, but she was so busy staring at her target, she didn't even acknowledge my existence.

"Wow. Good score. You beat me again."

Nicole walked just enough ahead of me so that she wouldn't have to look at me.

"You know how sad it makes me to leave camp in July?" I said. "It's bad enough that we have to say good-bye to each other, but it's even worse when I think about you going to your dad's and being all depressed and lonely. I can't stand that."

Nicole spun around and glared at me. One eyebrow shot up. "I am not depressed and lonely. Stop feeling sorry for me. I *said* it was a waste of time. There's a big difference."

Nicole and I walked down the wooded path together, but I didn't bother to say anything. I was getting tired of having my head bitten off repeatedly. Nicole held her paper targets in front of her and studied them like a road map. When Sarah and Patty caught up with us, they immediately knew something was up.

"I sense . . ." Sarah started before I gave her a look. "I sense an attack of hay fever coming on! Hurry, Patty! Help me find some Kleenex before my sinuses explode!" She rushed Patty up the path ahead of us.

"I'm sorry," I said finally. I didn't know what else to say.

Nicole rolled her eyes in disgust. "If anyone should apologize, it should be me."

"You? Why you?" I asked.

"I'm sorry I don't have a perfect family who takes

walks together and goes out to breakfast and chats about how great our lives are." She swatted tree branches out of her way as she walked along the overgrown path.

It was such a ridiculous comment, all I could do was laugh. "Nic, you have to be kidding me. If you think *my* family is perfect after all that stuff I told you . . . remember, you know all my darkest secrets. You're the only one who knows that stuff."

"Just don't give me any advice on how to deal with my family, all right?"

"Fine." We didn't say anything for several long minutes. I'd always turned to Nic for advice about my family troubles. Why was it so wrong now that I was trying to help her?

"It's all your fault that the plan didn't work out," I blurted out suddenly.

Nicole turned around and stared at me. "What are you talking about?"

"The plan. If you'd followed the plan the way you were supposed to, we'd go home together at the end of camp. As sisters." I tried to look serious.

Nicole's mouth twisted into a smile when she realized what I was talking about. "My fault the plan didn't work? No way! *You* didn't get your mom to wear the right dress!"

"*You* were supposed to make sure your dad stopped in town to eat lunch at that little restaurant my mom liked so much. And you should've warned him not to wear white socks with sandals!" I burst out laughing, remembering the first time I'd met Nicole's dad.

Nicole covered her face with her hands. "Omigod. White socks with sandals. And he was wearing that stupid plaid shirt that looked like a picnic blanket." By now we were both cracking up.

"It was a total and complete failure. My mom was supposed to take one look at your dad when they came to pick us up from camp and fall for him like a rock. We blew it, Nic!"

"*The Plan*," said Nicole dramatically. "I wonder how many hours we spent that summer working on the plan?"

Sometime during our first summer together a bolt of lightning came out of the sky, and I had an absolutely astounding, brilliant idea. All Nic and I had to do was get our parents together and let them fall in love with each other so that we could become sisters. At that time her dad was still single, and even though Paul was one of Mom's many online "friends," I'd never even met him. It seemed like our parents really needed our help with their love lives. It was pretty ridiculous, but we were ten.

"I still have that notebook," I told Nicole. "With all our lists. Sylvia's likes. Dan's likes. Sylvia's dislikes. Dan's dislikes."

We got to the end of the path, and Nicole collapsed in laughter when we sat down in the field of grass by the edge of the road. "I put down 'tomatoes,' 'country music,' and 'reality TV shows' as my dad's dislikes! And you were so worried because your mom puts tomato sauce in everything!"

I smiled at the memory. "We were absolutely convinced they were a perfect match. Except for the tomato sauce."

"I can't believe your mom ruined everything and married Parrothead instead." Nicole stretched out in the grass and covered her face with her arms to keep the sun out of her eyes.

I was going to say something about her dad screwing things up too by marrying Elizabeth, but I stopped myself.

Parrothead. That was Paul's screen name when he and Mom were IMing each other. That name seemed so creepy to me. But his wasn't the only weird screen name. *Crazeecapricorn*. *Chicago_son*. *Sirluvalot*. Gross. Two years ago I thought my whole life depended on keeping Mom from chatting with all those online weirdos.

How could I have known that Paul would turn out to be such a nice, normal guy and that "Parrothead" just meant that he liked Jimmy Buffett's music? And then last summer he and Mom took Blake and me to a Buffett concert, and everyone was wearing grass skirts and funny hats and playing with beach balls; we all decided to be parrotheads after that.

"Why did it work in *The Parent Trap*, but it didn't work for us?" I wailed.

"Because that's Disney. And real life is nothing like Disney," said Nicole.

"Yeah, I know." I sighed, trying to act like I hadn't heard the bitter tone in her last remark. I was just glad that I'd been able to steer the conversation toward a happy memory for a while. I didn't want to bring up her father and Elizabeth again. It seemed like it was better to avoid that subject as much as possible.

What if life *was* like a Disney movie, though? Would it have been so unbelievable for Nicole's dad to marry my mom and for us to become stepsisters? It was just too perfect.

But things were pretty good now. I've always been glad that Mom picked Paul instead of Crazeecapricorn or any of the others. But what if she'd never even wanted to meet Paul? What if she'd met Sirluvalot instead and he ended up being my new stepfather?

"Our families sure are crazy. I'm glad we have each other," I told Nicole. "At least destiny worked for us, even if it totally bombed at bringing our parents together."

Nicole had a big smile on her face when she sat up. "I miss the plan. Maybe we should come up with another project for the summer."

"Like what?"

"Like figuring out how to get my dad to divorce Elizabeth! Just kidding. Let's go to canoeing and we'll think about it."

# CHAPTER 6

## Thursday, June 19

After lunch there was an enormous traffic jam on the dining hall porch as we all crowded around the rows of wooden cubbies to check our mail. Already I could see a few pieces of mail peeking out of my cubby.

I skimmed the printout of Mom and Paul's e-mail first, thinking there might be some big announcement. There wasn't. In a way, I wished I didn't know about the whole baby-planning thing. That way, if it never happened, I wouldn't be so disappointed.

"How many letters did you get today?" Nicole asked as we squeezed through the crowd and walked up the hill toward the cabin.

"Three. An e-mail from Mom and Paul, one from my dad, and a card from my friend Olivia."

"Lucky you," said Nicole, unfolding the printout of the e-mail she'd found in her box. I always got more mail than Nic did, and she always seemed bothered by that. I couldn't help it—either my family was really big on writing or hers wasn't.

"Hi, Nicole. Hi, Darcy," I heard someone say behind us.

It was Mary Claire. Another Junior girl was with her.

"Hi, Mary Claire. Who's your friend?" I asked.

"Alyssa. She's in my cabin. She's on the top bunk, and I'm on the bottom."

"That's cool. So how do you like camp?" I asked.

"Good," said Mary Claire. The neck of her T-shirt wasn't wet today, but it did look all stretched out and wrinkled. While Nicole read her e-mail, I made small talk as we walked up the hill together.

Alyssa was a lot smaller than Mary Claire. She had long hair that hung in her eyes, and enormous front teeth. It looked like she'd gotten her permanent teeth before her mouth was big enough for them.

"Mary Claire has been talking about being friends with Middlers, but I thought she was lying," said Alyssa.

"No, she really does know both of us," I told Alyssa.

"Huh. I'm surprised Spud has friends."

"Spud?" I asked.

Mary Claire smiled nervously. "That's my nickname. Alyssa gave it to me."

Alyssa laughed. "Yep. This girl loves her taters. You should've seen how many she ate the other night. Hardly left any for the rest of us. Right, Spud?" She poked Mary Claire's belly. Alyssa was undoubtedly the most annoying kid I'd ever met in my life.

We were at the top of the hill now, so I said goodbye to them, and Nicole and I headed toward Middler Line.

"Mary Claire has a new friend," I said, as if Nic had missed the whole conversation completely.

"Thank God." Nicole glanced up from her e-mail. "Mom writes such great letters. It's all about the fight she had with Richard over the credit card bills. He's using the wrong cards again, the ones with the really high interest rates." Nicole offered me the paper. "Want to read it? It's riveting."

"Uh, no thanks." My parents never wrote me about their credit card bills. Mom told me about cute things the dogs did, and Paul had written me a funny poem. Daddy's e-mail was a bit of a surprise. He said he'd bought a motorcycle! Good thing Mom wasn't still married to him. Actually, if they were still married, she probably wouldn't have allowed something like that.

"Don't worry. You're not missing anything," Nic assured me. As we walked into the cabin for rest hour, she crumpled the paper up and dropped it into the trash can by the door. I always thought it was weird that Nicole threw most of her mail away right after she read it, but now I could sort of see why.

I decided to go ahead and write Daddy and Mom and Paul back right away, since last summer I'd gotten lots of complaints from them about not writing often enough. Sarah had her bat mitzvah coming up in November, so she spent rest hour studying her Torah passage.

When rest hour ended, Nic and I met up with a group to go to Angelhair Falls. About six or seven of us showed up for the hike, along with Rachel, one of the hiking counselors. It was a fun tradition to go to the falls during the first week of camp, so I'd really been looking forward to this.

It was an absolutely beautiful hike through the woods. As we walked along, I felt like we were inside a green, leafy cavern. Sunshine came filtering through the branches overhead and made a pattern of dancing light on the leaf-covered ground. I loved being totally surrounded by trees like this. It always made me feel like I was a part of nature.

"I can't believe how beautiful everything is around here," said a newbie, coming up beside Nic and me. "It's nothing like living in the city."

"Just wait till you see the falls," I told her.

"Oooh! I can't wait. I'm Brittany, by the way." She was really bubbly and smiley.

"I'm Darcy, and this is Nicole. So how do you like Pine Haven so far?"

"Oh, I love it! Everyone's so friendly. How many years have you been coming here?"

"This is my third," I said.

"Hey, I have a question for you. Why do they call the bathrooms here Solitary?"

I laughed. "I honestly don't know. I wondered the same thing my first year too."

"Hmm. Interesting. I figured there was some story behind that name. Well, what about the CATs? Where'd they get that name?"

"Oh, I do know the answer to that one. It stands for Counselor Assistant in Training," I explained. The CATs were the oldest group of girls—the sixteen-year-olds who weren't old enough to be counselors yet.

"How much farther to the falls?" asked Erin Harmon, giving Rachel a wink.

"How much farther? How much farther?" Rachel teased. "Are you tired already?"

"No, we're not tired. Just eager to get there," said Brittany.

"I'll let the rest of you tell me when we're getting close to the falls," said Rachel. "Whoever's the first one to hear it will get a prize." She winked back at Erin.

We tried not to crunch through the leaves and underbrush too loudly, so that we'd be able to hear the sound of the falls.

"Pretty annoying, huh?" Nicole whispered to me as we walked along.

"What is?" I asked.

Nic jerked her head in Brittany's direction. Now she was just ahead of us, talking to a couple of other girls.

I shrugged. What was so annoying? "She's just being friendly," I whispered back. Actually, I'd been pretty impressed that one of the newbies was so outgoing. Usually they waited for us to talk to them.

"You call it friendly? I call it pushy," Nic murmured. "I hope she gets the prize."

We hiked for another half hour or so until one of the newbies near the front of the group stopped. "Wait. I think I can hear running water." We all paused and listened. The sound of a little babbling stream came through the trees.

"Kayla gets the prize, since she was the first one to hear it," announced Rachel. Erin dropped back so she could walk next to Nic and me. "Be ready for the signal," she told us. Nic and I nodded.

We cut through the trees until we came to the falls, which were tiny by most waterfall standards. The drop from the top of the rocks where the falls formed to the pool of water below was no more than ten or twelve feet.

"I was expecting something a little bigger," Brittany admitted.

"See why these are called Angelhair?" asked Rachel, pointing to the way the rocks made the water pour over the edge in threadlike streams.

"Okay. What's my prize?" Kayla wondered.

"We throw you in!" shouted Rachel, rushing at her. When she said that, Erin, Nic, and I rushed forward too, and we grabbed her by the arms and legs before she knew what was happening.

We carried her down to the edge and started swinging her back and forth over the water as she screamed her head off.

"One . . . two . . . ," yelled Rachel, and then on

three we laid her down gently in the damp moss by the stream. A newbie always got this joke played on her, because the rest of us knew to keep our mouths shut.

The newbies who were watching all cracked up over the sight. It took them a couple of seconds to figure out the inside joke. Kayla sat up and heaved a sigh. She still had a look of terror on her face. "Now I'm wet," she said, inspecting the moss underneath her.

"This is a great home for Nellie," said Rachel, slipping her backpack off her shoulders and unzipping it. She took out a glass jar with an orange newt inside. "I had to catch this little critter yesterday. Remember? It had a part in last night's skit for evening program." We all watched while she unscrewed the lid and shook it gently. The little salamander crawled out and paused on the carpet of moss before disappearing under a rock.

Everyone was peeling off shoes and socks to wade into the rushing stream. "Hey, Darcy, Nicole—come on in!" called Brittany. She stood in the stream with her arms stretched out, desperately trying to keep her balance on the slippery, moss-covered rocks.

"Sure!" I yelled. I couldn't wait to let the cold water cool off my sweaty feet.

The water was so numbingly cold that it made my legs ache all the way up to my knees. I could feel the pull of the current swirling past my ankles. We waded and splashed around till we were soaking wet. It was so much fun, but I looked around and realized that Nicole was still sitting alone on the bank. I didn't even notice that she hadn't followed me in.

"Aren't you getting in?" I called to her. But she just shook her head and didn't move.

I felt like I should get out and go sit with her, but this was what we came for. Yeah, the water was icy cold and the rocks were so mossy and slippery that it made wading pretty treacherous, but nobody really cared. I stayed in for a few more minutes, then got out and grabbed my shoes.

"It was great! Really refreshing," I said, sitting down on the bank by Nicole. I wiggled my wet feet into my dry, dusty socks.

She didn't say anything.

"What's wrong?"

"Nothing." She watched the water spilling over the rocks and wouldn't look at me.

"You sure?"

Nic nodded. She did that sometimes, got moody and quiet. I knew something was wrong, but I wasn't sure what. Did it annoy her that I'd spoken to Brittany? That seemed like such a trivial thing. Or was it that I'd gone in with everyone else instead of staying with her? Or something else completely, maybe even something that had nothing to do with me?

"I'm freezing! I'm soaked!" Brittany shrieked as she ran up to us and grabbed her shoes. "This is so much fun!"

I smiled and nodded, but I didn't talk to her this time. It made me feel silly, not talking to her in case that was what was making Nic mad. I didn't want to be rude.

Here we were on this beautiful, sunny day, surrounded by woods next to a scenic little waterfall. It was almost perfect.

Except for the dark little storm cloud beside me. I hoped that the weather would be nicer tomorrow.

# Saturday, June 21

On Saturday, Nicole and I skipped afternoon activities to make sure we each got a hot shower. Usually on the first Saturday night of every camp session, Pine Haven would have a dance with the boys from Camp Crockett. *Usually*, but not always. The counselors had an infuriating habit of not announcing dances till the last minute. They wanted us to go to activities instead of spending the whole afternoon getting ready.

Nic and I weren't willing to take a chance, and we weren't the only ones who assumed there was a dance with Camp Crockett tonight. Everyone was busy getting ready.

"Have you decided what you're going to wear?" I asked Nicole when we got back from the showers.

"Well, these jeans"—she pulled a pair of denim capris from her trunk—"and I was thinking this shirt." She opened my trunk and searched around until she found my pink-and-white American Eagle rugby. She laid the clothes out on her cot for my approval. "Cute, huh?"

"Oh, so you're assuming *I'm* not wearing that shirt tonight?" I teased her.

"I know you're not wearing it because you're wearing this instead." She took my flouncy khaki skirt out of my trunk and draped it across my bed. Then, from her trunk, she pulled out a violet tunic with a scoop neck and puckered sleeves. She knew that was my favorite shirt of hers. "There. Now we both know what we're wearing, and that's always the hardest part." Nicole had been in a good mood all day. Times like this reminded me of why she was my best friend.

"Are you going to wear my earrings?" I asked, since she still had my little hearts in, the same ones she'd been wearing since the first day.

"If you don't mind."

"Of course not. If you'll let me borrow your shell necklace. I just wish we lived close enough that we could swap clothes and jewelry like this all year long."

Whitney came in dressed in riding pants and boots and gave us a quick hello.

"Where's Sarah?"

"Still in the showers. How was your lesson?" I asked her.

"Fine, thanks. Caroline says my posture during jumps is exceptional." She pulled out her hair elastic and shook her head so her reddish blond hair fell across her shoulders.

Just then Sarah walked in the door dressed in her robe. "What did I miss? What's exceptional?"

"Nothing. Caroline just complimented me on how well I took my jumps today."

Sarah clapped her hands. "Did she also tell you your bowing was exceptional? And your handstands? And every single thing about you?" Whitney had always made sure we knew about her multiple extracurricular activities—violin, gymnastics, not to mention all of her riding accomplishments.

"As a matter of fact, she did," said Whitney, not even looking at Sarah. "I'm glad you're all here. I've been waiting for a chance for the old campers to be alone. We need to talk about the very serious problems occurring right now."

Sarah rubbed her wet hair with a towel. "You're right. But which problems are you referring to? Global warming? Or the lack of blueberry syrup at breakfast?"

I had to laugh, even though I tried hard not to. This morning Whitney had been very upset that only maple syrup was served to pour over the blueberry pancakes.

Whitney pointed at Sarah. "Global warming is everyone's problem, Sarah. We all live on this planet, but that's not what I want to talk about. It's Cabin Three and all our troubles."

"Oh, you mean the whole Jamie thing again?" I asked. Jamie, as a first-year counselor assistant, was turning out to be a major disappointment for Whitney. Jamie didn't stress over cleaning the cabin for inspection every morning or making sure no one was cabin-sitting instead of going to activities. Basically, Jamie didn't stress over anything. Why should she when she had Whitney around to do it for her?

"Well, yes. There's that. She has no respect for order and discipline. She doesn't even care if we talk during rest hour. And she offered us M&M's and Starbursts the other night when we all know candy's not allowed!"

Sarah gasped. "She should be fired! What was she thinking? Doesn't she know we're all in our cavity-prone years?"

Whitney ignored Sarah's remark and kept going. "And then there's Natasha and Ashlin. They've completely shunned Claudia."

"Whitney—that is *so* not true! Natasha and Ashlin are too nice to shun anyone," I assured her.

Whitney let out a long, frustrated sigh. "That's not all. Have you noticed how Claudia marks every day off the calendar? She's been counting down the days till camp is over since the first day! That girl is literally wishing her life away."

Sarah collapsed on her bottom bunk and draped her arm across her face. "You're right! The whole cabin is falling apart!"

"We are the leaders here," said Whitney, standing up to make her point. "The four of us, being old campers, need to take charge and address these problems. Are you with me?"

Sarah waved at her from her bunk. "We sure are. Thank you so much for bringing all this to our attention." She sniffed loudly. "Do I smell horse manure?"

"No, you don't. I always scrape my boots before I leave the stables. So, here's my plan. The four of us will—"

"Whitney, darling, did you see the line for the showers? If you get down there now, you'll only have an hour wait. Tell us your plan when you come back."

Nicole nodded. "Good idea. Darcy and I love plans. We're very good at them."

Whitney let out a little sigh. "Fine. It's just that the four of us need to be a united front. I hope we all agree about that."

"Absolutely," I assured her.

Whitney went over to Side B to get her towel, soap, and shampoo.

Once she was out the door, Sarah sat up on her bed and looked at us. "Is anyone else relieved she's gone?" she asked.

"Yes!" I shouted.

"Me too! Sarah, doesn't she drive you insane?" asked Nicole.

"You guys know I love her to death, but lately . . ." Sarah trailed off.

"She's just disappointed that she hasn't been able to turn the four newbies into Whitney clones," I said, laughing. As far as I could tell, all the new girls were getting along just fine. Natasha and Ashlin had become instant best friends, Claudia was busy with some swim class, and Patty spent all her time at canoeing. They didn't need Whitney directing their lives.

Nicole stood up and threw her shoulders back. "My posture is exceptional. And I placed second on vault and fourth on bars at regional this year."

Sarah ran her comb through her wet hair. "She's

always been a control freak. And she brags too much. None of this is new. But lately, she's really starting to get on my nerves. Do you see what I have to deal with?"

"Dump her," Nicole said. "I couldn't stand to spend two minutes with her."

"Yeah, hang with us instead." I picked up my pillow and hugged it. There was something so deliciously fun about gossiping. I felt so connected to Sarah and Nic at this moment. "Why are you even friends with her, Sarah? I've never been able to figure that out. You two are so different."

Sarah's forehead wrinkled while she thought about that. "I don't know. Because last summer our beds were right next to each other. And making fun of her is what gives my life meaning. But . . ." She shook her head. "Things are different this summer. I used to think she was funny. Now I just think she's annoying."

I supposed that made sense, that they got to be friends because Whitney was close by—literally. It was like me being friends with Emma Barrett in fifth grade because her desk was in front of mine. But last year we were in different classes, and we barely spoke to each other. It wasn't the same type of friendship that Nic and I had, where we both had so much in common.

"Seriously—Nic and I are here for you. I'm sure the

Crockett boys will be falling all over Whitney, so while she's busy being prom queen, you can chill with us tonight," I said.

"She is my best friend, but there are times when I want to . . ." Sarah picked up her pillow and crept toward Nicole, then sprung on her, trying to press the pillow over her face. Nic screamed, and I bopped Sarah with my pillow. We were all cracking up when Natasha and Ashlin walked in.

"Oh, hi! We're just gossiping," said Sarah. They smiled at us before going over to Side B as fast as they could. All the newbies seemed to think we were weird, for some strange reason.

Soon everyone showed up, and the cabin was a madhouse while we all got ready. I was looking forward to seeing Blake tonight. I'd written him two letters this week, and he'd sent me one postcard.

*Darcy,*
    *My counsillor is making us write letters to our family. C U at the dance. Bye.*

He hadn't even signed his name. I couldn't wait to hear how his first week of camp had gone so I could give Mom, Paul, and Daddy a full report.

Whitney came back from the showers and went straight to Side B to get dressed. Even though we'd made fun of her, I was still curious about what she wanted us to do to solve Cabin 3's "problems," so when the bell rang for dinner, we all walked to the dining hall together.

"Whitney, how about telling us your plan now?" said Nicole, her voice dripping with sarcasm.

Whitney looked at us. "I think the four of us should set an example. We should make a point of never talking about other people behind their backs." She looked directly at me in a way that made my blood turn to ice water. "I know I brought up the problems we're having, but I only want to make our cabin the best it can be. Maybe I don't always put things the right way, but I always try to be nice to everyone."

Sarah looked at me with this totally horrified expression.

Whitney kept going. "The other part of the plan is that we shouldn't make fun of people just because they happen to be talented. *I* would never laugh at Natasha if she told me she'd scored a bull's-eye in riflery. And I wouldn't say mean things about Patty if she mentioned that she was going on a river trip with the canoers." Whitney's voice cracked when she made that last comment, and I looked away. If she was going to break down, I didn't want to see it.

Sarah, Nic, and I didn't say a word. I could not believe what was happening. I felt like a cockroach. Why didn't Whitney just step on me and put me out of my misery?

"The other part of the plan is that we should be honest with each other. Sarah, if you were doing something that really bothered me, I would find a way to talk to you about it. But I would do everything I could not to hurt your feelings."

I looked up and saw that Whitney's chin was quivering. Sarah opened her mouth to say something but then closed it. She looked like she'd been struck by lightning.

Whitney let out a long, shuddering sigh. "So that's my plan."

There was the longest, most humongous silence I'd ever heard in my life. It pressed on us like it weighed five thousand pounds. It felt like a black, hairy, suffocating nightmare.

*Somebody say something!* I psychically shouted at Sarah and Nicole. But apparently they couldn't hear me.

We walked into the dining hall and took our seats around Cabin 3's table. Whitney calmly put her napkin in her lap without looking at any of us.

Libby poured bug juice into plastic cups and passed them around the table. "Why is everyone so quiet?"

Everyone else started talking, but Sarah, Nicole, and I kept our mouths shut. Too bad we'd learned that lesson a little too late.

## CHAPTER 8

When we walked into Camp Crockett's dining hall, I looked around for Blake. I saw him in the crowd of boys and motioned for him to come to me, but he looked away, pretending not to see me. So I marched across the big empty space between all the Crockett boys and the Pine Haven girls. He tried to duck out of my way, but I grabbed his shirttail.

"Come over here and say hi to me, you little creep."

"Whoever you are, you're not my type." He wriggled away from me, and all the boys around him started laughing.

"Blake, I'm warning you. Mom told me to check up on you."

"Is that your sister? I thought she was just some weird girl," said the boy next to Blake.

"Yeah, that's my sister. And she is a weird girl." Blake walked up and stood inches away from me with a really defiant look on his face. His hair looked like he hadn't shampooed it in three days, but he had a clean shirt on at least.

"How's it going? Are you having a good time? Have you made some friends?"

Blake crossed his arms and tried to stare me down. "Good. Yep. And yep."

"Okay, fine. Just thought I'd say hello." I walked away, but I could tell by the look on his face that he enjoyed this attention and didn't really want me to go. I'd come back and talk to him later when he wasn't being so obnoxious.

I found Sarah and Nicole in the clump of Pine Haven girls still huddled near the screen doors. I waved my hand in front of Sarah's face because she was staring, unblinking, at a spot on the floor.

"I should be boiled in hot oil. Thrown into shark-infested waters. Drawn and quartered." She looked up at Nicole and me with a hopeless expression. "What is drawn and quartered, anyway? I hope it's incredibly painful."

"I'm pretty sure it is. Where's Whitney?" I asked.

Sarah nodded toward the dance floor, and I saw that Whitney was already out there with a boy. "Can you believe how well she dances, considering she has a knife stuck in her back?" asked Sarah.

"Excuse me, but not one person has brought up the fact that Whitney was obviously eavesdropping on us," said Nicole. "She's not totally innocent in this whole thing."

"The only thing she's guilty of is wanting everyone in the cabin to get along and to love camp as much as she does," moaned Sarah.

It made me cringe to think of Whitney just outside the cabin door, listening to everything we said. Had she accidentally overheard us? Or did she stick around, waiting to see if we were going to talk about her after she left? Not that it mattered. What we did was brutal.

Sarah's eyes followed Whitney and her guy. "I can't believe I said those things. I crushed her spirit. Like a grape." Sarah stomped on the floor suddenly, apparently squishing the grape.

"Honestly, she doesn't look that crushed to me," said Nicole. "She'll be fine."

"Stop beating yourself up. We were just as bad as you were," I told Sarah. I thought about how much I'd enjoyed dissing Whitney. It had felt good, in a sick sort of way. It made me feel like I was part of something—a gossip club.

"The thing is, Whitney *is* annoying," Nicole hissed. "Everybody thinks so. Maybe it was good for her to hear us saying stuff that we could never say to her face."

"You're annoying!" Sarah's voice rose with emotion. "Darcy's annoying! I'm annoying! That guy over there in the black 'Rock Star' T-shirt is annoying!" Sarah pointed at the guy and yelled, "Hey, you! Yeah, I'm talking to you. Wipe that annoying look off your face before I do it for you!" When the poor guy realized Sarah was talking to him, his face turned seven different shades of red before he scooted behind a group of boys.

"Sarah, would you get a grip?" I told her, pulling her away. "Look, um . . . there's a way we can fix this. Let's go apologize to Whitney right now." I could do it if Sarah and Nic went with me. But I definitely didn't want to face her alone.

Sarah shook her head adamantly. "No. Absolutely not. I will never be able to face her again. I'm going to go live on the moon. That way I'll never accidentally run into her and have to look her in the eye. I deserve a cold, dark, deserted life."

"This makes no sense to me," Nicole argued. "I can

see why she'd be mad at Darcy and me, but you say mean things to Whitney *all the time*. To her face. She's probably not even mad at you."

"It's not the same! She expects me to mock her to her face. She doesn't expect me to go behind her back and tell other people that she's driving me crazy! Can't you see the difference?"

"Hi, Ugly." Blake had snuck up on us, since we were so totally focused on our girl crisis.

"Who is this hobbit?" Sarah snapped. "Shoo! Go find some dwarves to play with!"

"Sarah, this is my little brother, Blake. Have you danced yet, you little dweeb?"

Blake clutched his throat with his hands and made gagging noises. "You think I'd dance with any of you Pink Haven losers?"

"Hi, Blake. Wow, you sure have gotten cute." Nicole put her arm around Blake's waist. "I'll dance with you, Handsome."

Blake evaporated into thin air. The next time we saw him, he was on the other side of the dining hall, hiding behind a bunch of boys. He obviously knew them. I was glad to see he was making a few friends.

Now Whitney had stopped dancing, and she was standing with Jordan Abernathy and Molly Chapman.

She didn't seem to notice that the three of us were across the dining hall watching her.

"She's probably over there right now, telling them what happened," Nicole speculated. "I bet she'll try to turn the whole camp against us."

Sarah shook her head. "If you believe that, you don't know Whitney." She wrapped her arms around herself, like she was trying to ward off cold weather. She looked like she was on the verge of tears. "Even if I said I was sorry, I still hurt her . . . so *much* . . . I don't think she can ever forgive me. I can't forgive me," Sarah finished off, her voice just above a whisper.

She walked out the door to the porch, leaving Nicole and me standing there.

Nicole let out a long breath. "Wow. I can't believe the drama!"

"Well, we were hoping for a new project. Maybe this is it. Getting Sarah and Whitney back together again."

Nicole raised her eyebrow. "You think? I'd say Humpty Dumpty stands a better chance than those two."

## Monday, June 23

"Sarah, you have to come with us," I insisted.

"No, thanks. I'm not going to be good company today. I'll see you guys later."

"Look, Whitney's at her riding lesson, so you wouldn't be going to activities with her now anyway," I reasoned. "If you come with us, we can talk about this and try to come up with a plan." Plans. If we'd ever needed a good one, now was the time.

"Okay, fine." Sarah got up off her bunk and we left together.

"Let's go to Crafts Cabin," I said. "It'll be easy for us to talk there." Sarah didn't say anything, just walked along, staring at the ground. She was totally depressed, worse than I'd ever seen her. She wasn't even cracking jokes anymore.

"Oh no, here comes trouble," said Nicole. I followed her gaze. Mary Claire and her little friend Alyssa had spotted us and were heading in our direction.

"Hi, guys," I said, walking up to them. Nic had said we wouldn't go looking for Mary Claire, but when we saw her, we'd be nice to her. I was going to hold her to that. I introduced them to Sarah, being careful not to mention the word "stepsister."

"We're going to crafts. Where are you guys going?" I asked.

"Archery," said Mary Claire.

"*I'm* going to archery. Spud's just following me." Alyssa peeked out from under her bangs. "Hey, my shoe's untied." She stuck a grubby pink high-top sneaker out, and Mary Claire dropped to her knees to tie it for her.

"Double-knot it. Do the other one too while you're down there."

I glanced at Sarah and Nicole, but they didn't seem to notice what was going on.

If no one else was going to say anything, I would. "Wow, Alyssa. You mean you don't know how to tie your shoes yet? Most kids learn that when they're five." Maybe if I embarrassed her, she'd stop being so obnoxious.

"I know how. But Spud does it for me. She does all my chores."

"Fascinating. Well, see ya later," said Nicole.

I couldn't believe what I'd just heard. "What do you mean, she does all your chores?"

"This girl makes my bed. Does my chores every day. She's not bad to have around. If you can put up with her bad breath." Alyssa smiled, showing off her over-size teeth. It drove me insane the way she called Mary Claire "this girl," like she wasn't even there. That was even worse than "Spud."

I looked at Mary Claire. "You make Alyssa's bed for her? And do her chores for her?" Every morning we all had a chore to do to get the cabin ready for inspection—sweeping, emptying the trash, making sure all the wet towels and swimsuits were hung up. Every cabin had a job chart, and each camper's chore changed from day to day.

Mary Claire shrugged. "I don't mind." She reached for the neck of her T-shirt but then stopped herself.

"And your counselor is okay with that?" I was really fuming now. Sarah was in a trance, staring at the grass. Nicole just stood there with one eyebrow raised, like she couldn't wait to get away.

"She's always in the shower. Anyway, she wouldn't care," said Alyssa.

❤ 81 ❤

I stepped up really close to her, trying to intimidate her. "You might not know this, but it's a rule here at Pine Haven that every camper has to make her own bed and do her own chores. If your counselor did find out, she would not be happy. And if Eda, the camp director, finds out, you'll be in big trouble." I tried to sound like an authority figure.

"That's not true." Alyssa stood in front of me with her hands on her hips and shook her head.

"Yes, it is!" I looked at Mary Claire. "Mary Claire, you don't have to do her chores for her, okay? If *this girl* gives you any problems, come to us."

"Bossy Middlers," I heard Alyssa say as we walked off.

"Thanks for backing me up, guys. You were a huge help," I said to the two mutes beside me.

Sarah looked up. "Oh. Sorry. Who were those kids?"

Nicole shot me a quick glance. "The fat one lives in my neighborhood. She's always following me around."

"The fat one? You are so mean," I snapped. "You better not call her that to her face. You'll give her an eating disorder."

"What are you so mad about?" asked Nicole.

"Hello? Did your spaceship just land? Doesn't it make you mad to see your . . . *neighbor* bossed around like that?" I wasn't sure which made me madder—the way that brat had treated Mary Claire or the fact that Nicole didn't even care.

Nicole kept quiet, but I could tell she was offended by the way the corner of her mouth was bent down. Nobody said anything else.

By the time we got to Crafts Cabin, I'd calmed down a little. Gloria Mendoza, the crafts counselor, was busy putting out plastic trays full of fabric strips on all the wooden tables.

"We're making pot holders." Gloria seemed really sweet, with her soft voice and shy smile. She was new this year. New counselors usually got stuck with a boring activity like crafts because no one else wanted it.

"Thanks. We'll work outside," I told her. Crafts Cabin had a porch on the back that overlooked the lake. It was shady and cool out there; plus it would give us privacy while we talked. I carried one of the trays out with us and we sat down on the wooden benches.

"Why did I even come along?" moaned Sarah.

"Have you even tried to talk to Whitney?" I asked. I set the tray on the bench between Nic and me so we could both reach it. She still hadn't said anything.

Sarah shook her head. "I can't." She picked up one of the fabric strips and wrapped it around her thigh, then twisted it like a tourniquet.

I wove a red strip of fabric over and under a row of yellow and green pieces I'd laid out in a crisscross pattern. It was good to have something to do with my hands.

"You know, if Whitney hadn't overheard us, everything would've been fine. Yeah, she was getting on our nerves, but we all like her. And she's your best friend. As mean as it was to say stuff about her behind her back, we weren't trying to hurt her feelings. We were just venting."

Lots of times I'd vented to one friend about another one, and afterward I always felt better. In some ways I thought it was a good thing. Blowing off a little steam about a friend who was bugging me probably kept me from getting really mad at her.

"I know, but she did hear us. And yeah, she can be annoying at times"—Sarah's voice dropped to a whisper, as if Whitney might be lurking under the porch— "but she's such a good sport. She's always put up with me making fun of her. How many people would do that? And she's a sweet girl. If Whitney had been there when we were dissing someone else, I guarantee you she would've told us to stop it."

Nicole gave Sarah a skeptical look. "Wait a second. Whitney was criticizing all the new campers—listing all their problems and saying we needed to fix them."

Sarah let out a low growl and twisted the tourniquet tighter. "It's not the same. She wants everyone to get along. She wants peace, love, and harmony. She's such a good girl!" Sarah wailed. A couple of people sitting inside looked at us through the open door.

"I still say we just apologize to her. We all feel bad about it. We're really and truly sorry. I'm sure she'll forgive us." If Whitney was such a good girl, how could she turn down a sincere apology?

Sarah twisted a piece of fabric between her fingers. "Okay. I'm going to apologize to her. But I want to do it alone. If you guys want to talk to her after, fine. But I think I owe her a private apology first."

Nic and I agreed that that was probably a good idea. I wasn't really looking forward to facing her either, but it was something we needed to do.

"When are you going to do it?" asked Nicole.

"I'll go right now. I'll be waiting for her when she comes back from her riding lesson." She stood up and dropped the fabric pieces back into the tray.

"Good luck," I told her as she walked away.

Nicole waited till she was sure Sarah was gone. "I don't really get why Sarah's so upset. It doesn't even seem like she likes Whitney that much. I always thought she just liked having her around so she could make fun of her."

"Well, I guess that's not all there is to their friendship."

Nicole looked at me. "Are you mad? Because I didn't talk to Mary Claire?"

"No, I'm not *mad,* but I wish you'd stick up for her a little more."

Nic grinned. "Well, I would, but you're a better big sister than I am." She handed me her newly finished pot holder. "I made this for you. A token of our friendship."

I laughed. "How sweet! Guess what? I made you one too!"

# CHAPTER 10

## Wednesday, June 25

"I hope things go better today with Sarah and Whitney," I told Nicole as we left the cabin for morning activities.

"I'm sure everything will be fine. Sarah's making a bigger deal out of this than it needs to be," said Nic.

Monday after Sarah had left us at Crafts Cabin so determined to apologize to Whitney, I thought we would finally resolve the problem. But she totally chickened out. She told us she'd panicked, that she just couldn't bring herself to face Whitney. This morning Sarah said she was going to try apologizing again at tennis.

Nic and I were on our own for the time being, so we decided to go to the climbing tower.

The climbing tower was gigantic. At the bottom, humongous tree trunks were propped against each other and lashed together at the top with some rope, like a teepee without the skin. Above that were more logs and ropes and a wooden platform at the midway point. Higher up, there was some rope netting that looked like it should be hanging from the crow's nest of some pirate ship. At the very tip-top of the tower was the highest platform, with a roof over the top. I've always wanted a tree house, but our yard didn't have tall enough trees. Getting to the top would be like being in my very own tree house.

"Think I can make it to the top?" I asked Nicole, gazing up at the towering logs and ropes over our heads. So far we'd only made it to the midway point, but I'd always wanted to get to the highest platform, just to see if I could.

"I don't want to go to the top." Nicole frowned.

"You don't have to. You can belay me while I go. Then we'll switch places."

We had to wear safety harnesses when we climbed the tower, and every climber had to have someone on the ground belaying her. The belayer would hold the rope and keep enough slack in the line so the climber could climb easily, and if the climber happened to slip, the belayer would pull up the slack so the climber wouldn't fall very far.

"You look like you're ready for a challenge!" said Rachel, handing me a helmet and helping me step into the harness.

"Yeah, definitely!" I said, although my heart was already pounding like crazy and I hadn't even left the ground yet. "How high is it again to the very top?" I hoped my voice didn't sound as nervous as I felt.

"Fifty feet," Rachel told me, locking the carabiner on my harness to the climbing rope. "But you can practice your climbing skills without going all the way to the top."

Whew. *Fifty feet*. That was so high. I wanted to back out already! "I'm going to the top!" I blurted out. Saying it out loud committed me. Now I had to do it.

Jerry, the hiking guide, heard me say that and grinned. "Sounds good, but just do what you're comfortable with." He was helping Brittany, the chatty girl from the Angelhair Falls hike, into her harness. Erin Harmon was belaying her. Rachel and Jerry stood behind the belayers to facilitate.

"Climbing," I said to Nicole, to let her know I was ready.

"Climb on," she answered.

The climbing tower was similar to climbing walls in some ways. It had the same kinds of holds all up and down the logs.

I was moving along at a pretty good pace in the beginning; the holds were close together, so it was easy to find my handholds first, then my footholds. Little by little, I was working my way up. But it didn't take long until my arms got tired. I stopped to rest and catch my breath.

I made myself look up and plan out the best way to get to the midway platform. The calf muscles in my left leg started quivering from the exertion I was putting them through. I tried not to think about it. I had only a short way to climb until I was high enough to grab the edge of the platform and wriggle myself onto it.

"Great job, ladies!" Jerry shouted from below us.

It felt so incredibly comforting to have something solid underneath me. I sat perched on the platform and peered over the edge at Nicole and the other belayers on the ground. Looking down made my stomach do flip-flops, so instead I looked up at the maze of beams and ropes over my head.

The top was still at least twenty feet above me. I looked up at the highest platform and imagined myself already up there, looking out over the whole camp and the surrounding woods, feeling such a huge sense of accomplishment because I'd made it.

That was a trick Paul had taught Blake and me when

we shot hoops together. He'd tell us to picture the ball swooshing through the net before we made the shot. I wasn't sure if it worked, but it seemed like I'd gotten better lately.

Brittany's head appeared at the edge of the platform, then the rest of her. She pulled herself up so she was sitting beside me. "What a view!" she said when she'd caught her breath.

"I know. Just imagine what it'll be like at the top," I said.

"This is far enough for me. Are you gonna keep going?" she asked.

"I think so. Wish me luck." I looked down at Nicole. "Climbing!" I yelled.

"Climb on," she called back.

I'd never made it this far. I concentrated on finding my foot- and handholds and wouldn't let myself think about how high up I was.

"Up rope," I yelled down to Nicole because there was too much slack. I wanted to be sure that if I did slip, I wouldn't go very far. I felt her take up the slack from below. Then I let go of the pole so I could reach above me for the next handhold.

I'd made it all the way to the spider's web—the rope ladders that would take me up to the highest platform.

It looked like it would be easy to climb, but with every step, the rope webbing swayed, making me feel like I was going to fall right through it. I kept going.

I concentrated on picturing myself at the top, and before I knew it, I was almost there. I pulled myself up and onto the top platform, legs shaking. Far below me I heard everyone burst into cheers and applause. The view was so scary, I couldn't look down. In fact, I wanted to get down as fast as I could.

"Rappelling!" I yelled. Slowly they let out the slack and belayed me down to the bottom.

"You're the first Middler to make it all the way to the top this summer," Rachel announced. Everyone was patting me on the back and congratulating me. My legs wouldn't stop shaking, but other than that I felt great.

Brittany came up and gave me a high five. "Wow, I'm impressed! You got to the top of that thing in no time! Want to give me any pointers?"

I laughed. "Yeah. Rule number one—never look down! But the other thing that helped was staying positive. I kept visualizing myself at the top."

"I wonder if people who break their legs visualize themselves at the hospital," Nicole commented, which got her a few laughs. I knew she thought the whole "positive thinking" theory was ridiculous. Anytime I brought it up to her, she usually made fun of it.

I sat down in the grass next to the belay bench and tried to make my muscles relax. I looked up at Nicole. "Ready to try it? I'll belay you now," I offered.

"No, thanks. I'd never be able to follow in your footsteps," she said.

"Hey, that's not the point," said Jerry cheerfully. "You're supposed to challenge yourself, not try to compete with each other. Just go as far up as you're comfortable with."

But it was obvious that Nic didn't want a turn today. She was ready to leave.

"That was so much fun! I'm really glad we did this. Thanks for coming with me," I said as we walked back toward the cabin.

Nicole didn't say anything at first. Then, after a long pause, she said, "We'll have to do it again. Considering you're such an expert climber." Her voice had an edge to it. The way she said *expert* sounded more like an insult than a compliment.

"Oh, is that what you're mad about? So what? I got to the top before anyone else. It's not like I'm making a big deal out of it."

"You can be a little too competitive sometimes, Darcy. Ya know?"

"What? How am I competitive?" I honestly didn't think of myself as competitive at all. Not with other people, anyway. I only liked to challenge myself.

"Well, you're always saying that you can't believe I get mostly As when you're pretty much a straight-B student," Nic said, conveniently pointing out that she was a better student than I was.

*One time* I'd made a comment to Nic about how I couldn't believe she got such good grades. Now all of a sudden it was *always*? "Nicole, I *admire* the fact that you make mostly As. I thought A students were a myth that teachers made up to pressure the rest of us."

"Oh, thanks for admiring me."

"What is wrong with you? Are you mad at me about something?" Why did it seem like lately we were on the verge of fighting about really insignificant things?

Nicole snorted. "No! Why do you always think I'm mad?"

"Because you're always so moody. I'm really getting tired of it. What's your problem anyway?"

"Oh, shut up!"

"Fine. I will shut up," I snapped.

Now we were both in a vicious mood. Neither one of us said a word. I didn't even care that she was mad.

I was mad too. I was getting really sick of her constant attitude.

So I decided to pull out the big guns. I had never suggested that we do separate activities because I didn't want Nic to take it the wrong way. Now I was beyond worrying about hurting her feelings. I actually wanted to make her even madder.

"We don't have to spend every waking moment together, you know! It might be a good thing for us to take a break from each other for a while!"

Nicole spun around and glared at me. "That is the best plan you've had all week!"

CHAPTER 11

Neither one of us said another word on our way back to the cabin. We walked in to find Sarah sitting on her bottom bunk.

She took one look at us and asked, "What's wrong?"

"How'd it go with Whitney?" I totally avoided even looking at Nicole. I was still fuming.

"Forget that. What's up with the two of you? You both look like you're ready to scratch someone's eyes out." Sarah looked back and forth between Nic and me.

Nic made a snorting sound. "Nothing that major. We just need a break from each other. *Right?*" She glared at me.

Sarah jumped off her bed, her eyes wide. "Oh, no way! You two can't be fighting! We can only have one war going on in this cabin at a time. What happened?"

I refused to say anything. Let Nic tell her own version of the story. This should be pretty interesting.

But Nic kept quiet too. Finally I started off. "Okay. So we went to the climbing tower, I made it all the way to the top for the first time ever, and Nic got mad at me." I brushed past her and went to sit on my bed. "Sounds pretty ridiculous, doesn't it? You'll have to ask *her* what possible reason she could have for getting mad at me for a thing like that."

I yanked off my sneakers and sweaty socks and tried to toss them toward the spot where all the shoes were lined up on the bottom shelf, but they just banged against the wall and knocked everything out of order.

"Oh, yeah. That's exactly what happened! You totally left out the part where you said I was being mean and you didn't want to hang out with me anymore! Make it sound like it was all *my* fault! Turn Sarah against me too!" Nic was screaming now. I'd seen her mad before, but this was a surprise.

"I never said that!"

Nic growled in frustration. "But you said all that other stuff, didn't you? About how you don't want to be my friend anymore."

I hated that Nic and I were fighting like this, but I couldn't help it. I was still mad. I am not *competitive*. Nic was just jealous because I happened to be good at something she wasn't so great at. If the tables were turned, I knew for a fact that I would've told *her* what a great job she'd done. I was always happy for *her* whenever something good happened. Why couldn't she be the same way for me?

"Hey, stop it!" Sarah warned. "If you two don't stop yelling at each other, I'm gonna bang your heads together like coconuts."

I glanced up at her. "You'll do what?"

"That's what my mom's always threatening to do to my brother and me when we start yelling like this." Sarah came and sat on the end of my cot. "Okay, start at the beginning. Who said what and why?"

I closed my eyes. "Sarah, do you mind just staying out of this?"

"Hey, don't yell at Sarah!" snapped Nic.

"I am *not* yelling at Sarah," I corrected her. "I just don't want to talk about this. If you want to tell her your own fictional version of the story, fine by me." I plopped back on my cot and stared up at the wooden rafters overhead. On the beam right above me, someone had written GOPHER LOVES BEN with a thick black marker. I lay there thinking what a strange message that was.

"Fine. I will." Nic came and sat on her cot. For the

first time all summer, I regretted that our beds were three feet apart. "Here's what really happened, Sarah. We were on our way back from the climbing tower, and for no reason at all, Darcy made this comment about how I was acting totally mean."

She glanced at me and then looked back at Sarah. "Okay, maybe she never said 'mean,' but she implied it. And then she said, 'What's your problem? I think we've been spending way too much time together and we need to take a break from each other.' I mean, that really hurt my feelings!"

I sat up and looked at her. "Nic, I'm sorry. I'm not trying to hurt your feelings. It hurt *my* feelings that you got all mad at me for being good at something. And she called me competitive!" I told Sarah.

"But you know how sometimes you can be—," Nic started to protest.

"Wait a second!" Sarah yelled. "I think I see the problem here. Darcy, you apologize for saying you don't want to hang out with Nicole anymore. You didn't really mean that, did you?"

I sighed. "I said I was sorry five seconds ago, but obviously nobody heard that." I glanced at Nic. "And you know I didn't mean that. Of course I still want to hang out with you."

Nicole looked a little relieved, but then she started yelling again. "No, I didn't know that! How else was I supposed to take that comment? I figured—"

"Hold it!" Sarah raised her hands over her head. "Stop right there. Okay. Now, Nicole—you apologize to Darcy for calling her competitive."

Nicole frowned. "I will, but Darcy, you have to admit that you were making a big deal out of something that's not—"

"Nope! Don't say anything you'll regret. Just apologize," Sarah directed.

"Fine. I'm sorry I called you *competitive*," Nic said with just a slight touch of sarcasm in her voice. It wasn't the best apology I'd ever gotten in my life, but it was better than nothing. I guess.

"Okay. Now you two hug and be best friends again." Sarah stood up and brushed her hands together. "My work here is done."

Neither one of us moved. We just sat on our cots and looked at each other. "You know we never fight," I said finally.

"I know."

"Well, I *am* sorry," I said.

"Me too." This time she sounded like she meant it.

Fighting was weird. When you were in the middle

of it, you always felt like you'd rather swallow broken glass than apologize or admit you did anything wrong. You're always so sure it was the other person's fault. It's like running up against a wall, and you're not going to back down for anything. But then, little by little, the wall starts to crumble.

"See? Now that wasn't so bad, was it?" asked Sarah. She stood there smiling.

"So what happened between you and Whitney?" I asked. "Did you go to tennis together?"

Sarah's smile evaporated. "Uh . . ."

"Uh what? You were supposed to ask her to go play tennis and apologize to her then," I reminded her.

"Yeah, like that's a good idea!" Sarah threw up her hands. "How can you possibly carry on a meaningful conversation with someone when you're on opposite sides of a tennis court!"

"So I take it you didn't go to tennis. Did you at least talk to her?" I asked.

Sarah heaved an exhausted sigh. She refused to make eye contact.

"Okay, then. You settled mine and Nic's fight. Now let's finally take care of this Whitney situation."

Sarah took a couple of steps back. "Just . . . I want to do it my own way."

"Sarah! You're a total hypocrite! Nic and I had a fight that lasted all of ten minutes and you insisted that we make up. I'm gonna go find Whitney right now so we can settle this." I stood up and started to grab my shoes, but Sarah jumped in front of me to block my way.

"Darcy, don't! Please, please just let me handle this by myself." Nic kept quiet and watched us.

"Sarah, today's Wednesday. It's been *days* and you haven't handled it yet. Come on. I really think it'll be easier if Nic and I are with you when you talk to Whitney. You know, you're not the only guilty party here." I looked at Nic for support.

Nic finally spoke up. "If Sarah doesn't want to do it, we shouldn't force her."

I couldn't believe what I was hearing. Obviously, having a referee had really helped us, but now neither one of them was willing to let me do the same thing for Sarah and Whitney. I could totally understand why Sarah was nervous about talking to Whitney, but I thought Nic would back me up on this.

"I swear I'll talk to her soon. Just let me do it alone, okay?" Sarah pleaded.

I let out a sigh. "Well, okay. Anyway, thanks for being here for us."

"Yeah, thanks." Nic looked at me shyly. "You're not still mad, are you?"

"No, of course not. Are you?" We both felt better, but we were still a little shaken up over the fact that we'd had a fight to begin with. It was our first one.

"No. But for a second there, I did wonder if you were going to dump me."

I was shocked to hear her say that. I threw my arm around her shoulder. "Not a chance. BFFs, remember? The second F stands for *forever*."

"Hey, Nic. Are you asleep?" I whispered. In the dark I could see her outline in bed, but I couldn't see her face at all. Lights had been out for almost an hour by my guess, which meant it was probably around eleven o'clock.

"Not yet. What's up?" We had to be really quiet so Libby didn't shush us.

"I just wanted to say one more time that I'm sorry. It was a stupid argument."

I could see Nicole prop herself up on one elbow. "I know. I'm sorry too. But it's not your fault. You were pretty moody today."

We both chuckled softly. I was so glad we'd made up, because there was something I wanted to talk to Nic about.

"I'm worried. I'm having trouble sleeping," I whispered.

"What is it?"

"My dad. His letter about the road trip. Nic, I can't stop thinking about it. You know how he does risky things sometimes? I'm really afraid he's going to get into an accident." Daddy had e-mailed me that day to say he was taking his new Harley on a road trip for a week or so. For some reason, the second I read that, I totally panicked.

He didn't wear a helmet, for one thing. He said he loved the feeling of the wind on his face and in his hair. And he said he wanted to get the new motorcycle on the open road to see how it handled, which I took to mean he was going to see how fast it would go.

"I'm sure he'll be okay," Nic whispered. "You have to trust that he'll be responsible." She reached across the space between our cots and patted my arm.

"That's what I'm worried about. You know that problem he has sometimes." It was a problem my dad used to have, after the divorce. Nicole knew all about it.

"How's that been lately? I thought you said it was getting better."

"It has been. It's been a lot better lately. But I always have this fear it'll come back. You know?"

I heard Nicole sigh. "I know. But if it's been better lately, you have to remind yourself of that. You have to forgive him for past mistakes."

"But why do I feel so scared? When he first told me he'd gotten a motorcycle, I was fine. It surprised me, but I didn't think that much about it. But when I read his e-mail today, it was almost like . . ." I paused, trying to think of how to explain it. "I suddenly imagined him smashed against the asphalt. With his bike all mangled, and . . ." I stopped because my throat felt all constricted and I wasn't sure I could keep talking without sounding like I was going to cry.

Nic waited. When I didn't go on, she said, "You can't think thoughts like that. Whenever you feel that way, just push them out of your head."

"You know what I'm afraid of? I read his letter and I felt scared. What if he's destined to die in a motorcycle accident and I'm getting some psychic message about it? That stuff happens, you know."

"Have you ever known stuff was going to happen before it did?" whispered Nic.

"No. But there's always a first."

"Think positive thoughts. Visualize him being safe. Imagine him having a good time and getting home without even a scratch."

I had to smile over that. I thought it was so sweet that Nic would try to cheer me up with the "positive thoughts" philosophy.

"I know, but . . . I'm obsessing about him having an accident."

"Darcy, I'm not saying an accident couldn't happen—it's just not that likely. Millions of people drive motorcycles every day and don't get into accidents. And even if they do, they're sometimes just minor accidents. My teacher told us he drove a motorcycle from Maine to California when he was in college, and he crashed twice, but he was fine."

"Yeah, but was he wearing a helmet?" I whispered.

"Why don't you write him and tell him you really want him to wear a helmet, that you're worried about him, and that he should do it for you even if he won't do it for himself? Dads love that kind of stuff from daughters."

I thought about that for a second. "Well, I can. But there's no guarantee he'll do it."

I could see Nic sit up in her bed. "What about laws? Some states make you wear a helmet. You could remind him that he might be breaking the law if he goes through certain states."

"That's a great idea!" Immediately I felt a lot better.

I'd write my dad first thing in the morning so the letter could go out in tomorrow's snail mail. "Thanks," I whispered.

"Feel better now?"

"Yeah, tons. You always know how to cheer me up." Ever since our first summer, I'd talked to Nic about all my problems, and it never failed: She'd come up with an idea or say the right thing, and then I'd feel so much better.

A soft breeze came in through the window screens. I could hear crickets and frogs, and somewhere in the trees, a bird was making cooing sounds. I loved so many things about camp, but sleeping with the windows open was high up on the list. At home during the summer we always slept with the air conditioning on.

"What should we do tomorrow?" asked Nic softly. The cabin was so quiet, it sounded like everyone else was asleep.

"I don't care. You pick, since I picked for today."

"You sure we don't need a break from each other?" she whispered.

"I'm positive." Had she really thought I meant that comment seriously? I couldn't believe it when she said she was afraid I was going to dump her. She should know I'd never do that.

"Then let's go to free swim and lie in the inner tubes. And maybe crafts. I know the stuff we make there is lame, but it's fun to just sit on the porch and talk."

"Yeah," I agreed. I imagined what a great day we would have tomorrow, and then I was eager to go to sleep so I could wake up and enjoy it. I was so glad that we'd put that stupid argument behind us.

But there was something that still bothered me, just a tiny bit. Even though Nic had apologized for calling me competitive, she'd never congratulated me about getting to the top of the climbing tower. I was really proud of myself for that. And I couldn't stop thinking about how happy I would've been for her if she'd done something like that.

Oh, well. It didn't matter. We'd both apologized. I knew we couldn't stay mad at each other forever. Even if Sarah hadn't been there, we would've made up on our own eventually. Now all we had to do was make sure Sarah and Whitney worked things out. The one thing a person can't live without is her best friend.

# CHAPTER 13

## Thursday, June 26

"What would you be doing if you were in school right now?"

Nicole opened her eyes and squinted at me in the sunlight. We were both lounging in inner tubes, our arms and legs draped over the sides, our backs soaking in the cold lake water.

"Hmm, I'm not sure. What time is it?"

"A little after twelve, I think. Would you be at lunch?"

"No, last year we ate lunch at eleven twenty, so we'd be back in class by now. I'd be in social studies. Miss Johnson would be writing notes on the board about Mesopotamia or something. Maybe the Greek myths. We spent a long time on those."

I smiled while I listened to Nic talk. My tube floated gently sideways. The sun made the black rubber so warm that I had to keep splashing cold water on it to cool it off. "I'd be in science right now, probably doing a worksheet. Isn't this better than worksheets and Mesopotamia?"

Nicole closed her eyes and sighed. "You know it."

All of a sudden there was a huge splash that completely soaked us and sent both our inner tubes spinning in crazy circles. When I wiped the water out of my eyes, a wet head came bursting up from under the water and grinned at me. A head with gigantic front teeth.

"Bossy Middlers! Take that!" Alyssa was laughing her head off at the way she'd jumped in and caught us off guard. Squinting, I could see the silhouette of Mary Claire standing by the edge of the lake.

I closed my eyes and rested my head against the edge of the inner tube, like I didn't care. "Oh hi, Alyssa." I waited a few seconds. Then I leaned forward out of the inner tube and tapped her so that her head bobbed underwater.

As soon as Alyssa went under, she popped up again like a cork. "Hey. Cut that out!"

A short toot on a whistle made me look up. Claudia and her friend Shelby stood on the edge of the lake, keeping an eye on the swimmers. "Hey, Darcy. No dunking. I'm not going to make a big deal out of it, but . . . if I don't say something to you, I get yelled at." Claudia shrugged with the same bored expression she always had. She was taking some kind of lifeguarding class, and they had to hang out during free swim and help the swim staff watch over us. Libby stood a few feet away and nodded approvingly.

I smiled back at her. "Okay. Sorry."

Alyssa smacked the water with both hands so a spray of water splashed all over us.

This time Claudia blew her whistle with full force. "No splashing!" she yelled. "Or you'll spend ten minutes sitting out!" Then she gave Nic and me a little wink.

"She's not the boss of us," scoffed Alyssa.

"Oh, yes she is," said Nicole. "They're both training to be lifeguards."

"Huh," said Alyssa.

I looked up to watch Mary Claire still standing on the edge of the lake, delicately sticking her big toe in the water. Then she squatted down and examined the tadpoles swimming around in the shallows. She was wearing a flowered two-piece with a white ruffle across the top and bottom, and her belly was bright pink. I hoped she remembered her sunscreen.

"Aren't you getting in?" I called.

She looked at me and shook her head. "Too cold."

"Come sit in an inner tube. It's nice and warm in the sun," I told her.

"Huh. Spud in an inner tube? That girl will sink it for sure."

I decided my new strategy would be to ignore this little hamster as much as possible. I was glad to see Mary Claire walk over to the pile of inner tubes and grab one. She launched it into the water, hooking her arms around it as she left the lake edge. Her teeth clenched when she hit the cold water, but she kept kicking till she'd joined us in the middle of the shallow end of the lake.

"What's your problem, Spud? Go back and get me one."

Nicole sat up in her inner tube, propping her elbows on the side. "Don't do it, Mary Claire. Make her get her own."

Alyssa pushed wet strands of hair out of her eyes and curled her lip at us. "I'm not getting my own. I'm already in."

"Then I guess you won't have one, will you?" I said. I was so glad that Nic had finally said something to Alyssa. Maybe she was warming up to Mary Claire.

Mary Claire held on to her tube with one hand and

looked at Alyssa. I could tell she just wanted to give it to Alyssa and go get another one for herself.

"Sit it in like this," I told her. "It's more fun this way."

Mary Claire flopped around as she tried to get into her tube. She kept trying to lean back and sit on top of it, but every time she jumped up, she would force the tube away from her. Alyssa laughed hysterically through it all. Finally I held her tube still so she could sit down without it moving.

Alyssa ignored us and practiced handstands under the water. Her skinny little legs swayed back and forth as she tried to keep her balance. I was just glad her head was under water. I liked her much better that way.

"There's a wide-open lake here," Nicole pointed out to Mary Claire. "Feel free to float around wherever you want."

"Okay." Mary Claire continued to float beside us, apparently missing Nicole's hint. Nicole sighed impatiently, but she didn't say anything else. The three of us floated lazily around. Now Alyssa was busy trying to catch tadpoles in her cupped hands. When she didn't have any luck, she went back to practicing handstands.

"You should really put on sunscreen. You're starting to burn," Nic observed.

"Okay."

"Really—you need to remember to do that. It's bad for your skin. Plus it must be pretty painful," she said. "I have some in my cabin if you need to borrow it."

"Okay. Thanks, Nicole." Mary Claire grinned widely, looking absolutely thrilled about Nicole's offer. She kicked her legs playfully and splashed around. It was pretty major for Nicole to even acknowledge that she was alive, much less to be nice to her.

Alyssa's legs fell sideways under water and then she stood up, blowing water and sputtering. "I'm ready to get out. Get my towel for me, Spud."

Mary Claire started to extract herself from her inner tube.

"Don't do it, Mary Claire!" Nicole warned. "She can get her own towel."

Alyssa stood in the shallow water up to her waist, hugging herself. "I'm getting cold. You're almost all dry. Go get my towel!"

Mary Claire bit her lip and looked first at Nicole, then at me. "I think I might stay in for a while. Okay, Alyssa?" she said softly.

"Fine. Stay in here with these bossy Middlers. I don't care if you all freeze." Alyssa splashed Mary Claire just lightly enough that she wouldn't get the whistle blown at her again. Then she paddled to the edge of the lake and got out.

"Good for you. You can't let her boss you around like that," I said.

Mary Claire watched as Alyssa picked up her towel. "Maybe I'd better go. She'll be mad at me."

Nicole grabbed Mary Claire's inner tube and pulled her close. "You can go, but only if you really want to hang out with her. Don't do it just because you think she'll get mad."

"Yeah. If you guys have a good time together and you like being friends, that's great. But from what I've seen, she doesn't treat you very well," I added.

"But she's my best friend. She told me so."

Mary Claire wouldn't take her eyes off Alyssa. I looked over my shoulder and watched Alyssa dry off with her towel. Then she started to walk away, but she stopped when she saw that we were all watching her. Slowly she turned around and went back to the pile of towels lying around on the rocks by the lake edge. She picked up a pink-striped towel, bundled it up, and hurled it into the water, not once taking her eyes off us.

Mary Claire made a little squeak.

"Was that your towel?" I asked.

"That little creep! I'm gonna teach her a lesson!"

Nicole spilled out of her tube and lunged for the side of the lake. I was right behind her. Alyssa was about to walk away, looking extremely satisfied with herself. But lucky for her, Libby got to her before Nicole or I did.

Libby held Alyssa by the shoulder. "Excuse me. Can you tell me what just happened here?" she asked. Libby was amazing. She had a way of talking in this really sweet, calm voice. But behind the sweetness there was something else that let you know she meant business.

Nic and I stood beside them, dripping all over the place. Alyssa stared straight ahead, her eyes two little slants. "I was *trying* to throw my friend her towel. I guess I missed."

"She was mad because she tried to make Mary Claire get her towel for her, Libby," said Nicole. "When Mary Claire wouldn't do it, Alyssa threw her towel in."

Alyssa shook her head slowly, still staring straight ahead. "Not true. These Middlers are known liars."

I could see Libby suck on her lips to keep from smiling. "Well. This is a problem. You say it was an accident—that you were trying to do a nice gesture for a friend. And these *known liars* say you did it intentionally. I tell you what. I think you owe an apology to the girl whose towel got wet—whether it was intentional or not."

For a second it looked like Alyssa wasn't going to

budge. I could see her clamp her jaw shut, and she clutched her own semidry towel to her chest. But after a pause that stretched out for a full minute, she finally looked over her shoulder and bellowed, "Sorry!" at Mary Claire, still floating in the water.

"Okay. Thank you for apologizing. And from now on, remember that it's never a good idea to throw a towel to someone who's still in the water. Wait till she gets out and hand it to her." Libby released Alyssa, who strutted off in a barely contained cloud of rage.

"Can you known liars get that towel out of the lake for me, please?" Libby asked, pointing to the soggy mass floating on the surface.

"That kid's a known brat!" I said.

Libby smiled at us. "Let's just say Juniors have a lot of growing up to do. And you older girls can help them with that." She patted my back before she walked away.

Nicole looked at me and shook her head. "Do you realize Libby just saved that brat's life?"

I laughed. "Yeah, I do." I waded in and pulled out Mary Claire's towel, which now weighed approximately thirty pounds. Mary Claire was busy trying to wrangle all the inner tubes ashore.

"Alyssa's really going to be mad at me now," she said softly.

I wrung her sopping-wet towel out as best as I could. "Are you kidding me? Aren't you mad at her after what she did?"

"Yeah, but if I'd gotten her towel for her, she wouldn't have done that."

"Mary Claire! She treats you like her slave! You needed to stand up to her. Aren't there other girls in your cabin you like?" asked Nicole.

"Not as much as I like Alyssa."

Nicole and I exchanged looks. "Well, think about who else you might hang out with," I suggested. "Of all the Junior girls, I'm sure you'll be able to find a few new friends."

Nic tossed her towel (which was actually one of my towels that she had borrowed) to Mary Claire. "Here ya go. I'm practically dry now anyway."

"Thanks, Nicole! You sure are being nice to me."

Nic nodded knowingly at me. "You think so? Glad you noticed."

# CHAPTER 14

When we went back to the cabin to change clothes from free swim, hardly anyone was there. Just Natasha, Ashlin, and Whitney over on Side B. Whitney politely said hello to us, like she always did.

I'd been feeling pretty good about myself since we'd helped Mary Claire stand up for herself. And we'd done it without beating up her little tormentor. But as soon as I saw Whitney, it brought me down a couple of notches.

"We really need to say something to Whitney," I murmured to Nicole as we changed out of our wet swimsuits.

"No! Not without Sarah," Nic whispered back.

"I think we should," I insisted. "We've waited too long." Sarah hadn't talked to Whitney yesterday like she'd promised. Somebody needed to do something.

"Hey, Whitney? Could you come over here for a second?" I called.

Nicole gave me a look that said, *Are you out of your mind?* But I didn't care. Whitney came over to our side of the cabin and stood by Libby's bed, very straight and still, with her hands clasped in front of her. She looked like she was bracing herself for what was next. "Yes?"

"Uh," I began. How was I going to say this? A speeded-up version of our Whitney-dissing played through my head. *Control freak brags too much dump her.* "You remember the dance on Saturday?" I asked weakly.

Whitney remained perfectly still. "Yes."

"Uh. Well. When you walked out, Nic and Sarah and I said some stuff." That was as far as I could go. Nic obviously wasn't going to jump in and take over.

There was a long pause as Whitney waited for me to go on. "Some stuff?" she said finally.

"Yeah. Some really mean stuff. Whitney, we know you heard us. And we all feel really, really, *really* awful. We are so sorry—all of us."

"Do you feel awful because of what you said or awful because I happened to overhear you?" Whitney asked quietly.

Ouch. The truth was, if she hadn't *happened* to overhear us, then we would've dissed her, laughed about it, and then never given it a second thought.

"We feel awful because of what we said. But we were just being . . ." *cruel, heartless, vicious,* ". . . gossipy, and none of us meant any of it. You know how it is when a bunch of girls get together. One person says something about someone who isn't there and then everyone else starts talking and you're just saying stuff that you never expect will get back to the person, and . . ."

This was not going where I wanted it to go. I looked to Nicole for help, but she just raised her eyebrows at me. I knew what she was thinking—that incredibly annoying people were at constant risk of being ridiculed every time they left a room. She still thought Whitney had brought this all on herself by being so . . . Whitney-ish.

Whitney let out a little impatient sigh. "No, Darcy. I don't know how it is. I make it a practice never to say mean things about other people—ever."

I slumped over and held my head in my hands. "That's a really good practice. One I'm going to follow from now on. Whitney, we are really, really sorry. We said a lot of terrible things, but we didn't mean any of it. I guess we thought we were being funny, but we weren't. We were just being horrible."

Whitney nodded, like she was considering everything I'd said. "I'm curious about something. Today's Thursday. And this happened on Saturday. Why has it taken you *five* days to bring this up?" From the way she said "five," I could tell she'd been counting off every single day that went by without us apologizing to her.

"Well, Nicole can explain that," I said, spiking the ball to her when she totally wasn't ready for it. But why should I be the one doing all the talking? I wasn't the only one who was there.

My comment hit Nic right between the eyes and woke her up from a daydream. "Oh. Uh. We . . . kept wanting to, but we were pretty embarrassed about the whole thing. We didn't really know what to do."

I guessed that was an okay explanation. Not the way I would've put it, but at least I'd made her speak.

"Whitney, we are so sorry! Really, we are. Do you forgive us?"

Whitney pressed her lips together. She seemed to be giving it serious thought, like the decision was a tough one that could go either way.

"Yes, I accept your apologies. I still haven't heard from Sarah about this issue."

"Well, let me tell you—Sarah is absolutely devastated. She feels worse than Nic and me put together."

That didn't really come out sounding right. "She feels absolutely horrible, Whitney! And she's told us what a great friend you are, how sweet and kind you are, and how you'd never treat anyone this way. Which is why she can't even bear to face you. Trust me. This is breaking her heart."

"That's true. Devastated is a good word to describe Sarah right now," added Nicole. "Can't you tell?"

Whitney didn't say anything. We looked up when the screen door opened. Sarah was about to walk in when she saw the three of us inside talking. She did a quick U-turn and started out the door.

"Where do you think you're going? Come back here!" I shouted.

Sarah looked over her shoulder at me. "I'm going to the bathroom. Is that okay with you?"

"No, it's not. I want you to come inside so we can settle this."

Sarah let the door close behind her, and she stood in front of us. No one said a word. Sarah stared at the floor, Whitney looked expectantly at Sarah, and Nic had a strange look on her face—like she was about to burst out laughing.

"Sarah! Say something!" I urged.

Sarah wouldn't look up. "I don't know what to say."

"How can you not know what to say? Why don't you tell me you're sorry?" Whitney blurted out.

Sarah looked at her. "I *am* sorry! I've never been so sorry in my life. I'm the worst person in the world. You have every right to hate me and never speak to me again."

"I don't hate you! But why haven't you talked to me for *five* days?"

Sarah covered her face with her hands. "How could I?"

I looked at Nic and nodded toward the door. Nic followed me outside without a word. We were halfway down Middler Line when she finally spoke up. "What got into you?"

I looked at her. "I don't know. Think I should open my own practice?"

Nic burst out laughing.

"You had the weirdest look on your face—like you thought this whole situation was really funny," I said.

Nic shook her head. "I didn't think it was funny. I just thought it was going to be major drama. Why did you make us leave? I wanted to stay and watch the whole thing."

"I thought they needed to be alone. This is the first time they've spoken to each other in almost a week," I said.

We walked down to the dining hall to wait for lunch to begin.

Half an hour later Whitney and Sarah showed up at Cabin 3's table for lunch, along with the rest of us. They both had red eyes and blotchy faces. Whatever had happened between them, it must have been pretty intense.

After lunch ended, the two of them were walking together through the crowd of people leaving the dining hall. It didn't look like they were going to make a point of filling me in on everything, which I didn't think was very fair, considering I'd played a pretty big role in it all. So I rushed up to them.

"Okay, I hate to be rude, but can't you at least tell me what happened?" I asked.

Whitney smiled at me. "We're friends again!"

"Finally!" I turned to Nic, who'd walked up beside me. "They made up."

"Darcy, you were right. All along, if I had just talked to her, it never would've dragged out for so long. I can't believe I was so stupid," said Sarah.

"You're not stupid!" Whitney protested. "You were just embarrassed. And you avoided the problem instead of facing it and trying to solve it. It's okay, though. We've worked everything out."

Sarah held up her hand like she was taking an oath. "I promise to never, ever talk about people behind their backs, especially my best friend—Whitney Louise Carrington!" She threw her arms around Whitney, and they both got all teary again.

"And I'm going to Sarah's bat mitzvah in November," Whitney announced. "She'll read a whole portion of the Torah out loud. In Hebrew! Isn't that amazing?"

"I am so happy! It's about time you two worked everything out," I said. "I always knew one way or the other, you'd make up somehow."

Nic smiled at them. "I'm glad you guys are friends again. But now what will we do for drama? Maybe Natasha and Ashlin will have a big fight."

"That's a terrible thing to say!" I blurted out. "Do you like seeing people miserable?"

Nicole looked shocked. "It was a joke."

"Was it?" I asked. After all the fighting we'd had in our cabin, how could she possibly hope someone else would have some major friendship war? There was nothing I hated more than having people around me fighting with each other. I didn't get why she seemed to love drama so much.

Nicole rolled her eyes like she couldn't believe my reaction. "Of course. You know I didn't mean it. I'm glad everyone has made up now. Honestly."

I took a deep breath. I didn't want to make a big deal out of nothing. "Okay. No more fights—that's all I'm saying."

"I hear ya," said Sarah.

"Me too," Nicole said, giving me a playful bump with her hip. "We promise that from now on, everyone in Cabin Three will be one big, happy family."

I smiled back at her. "Sounds good to me!"

# CHAPTER 15

## Friday, June 27

We had just come back from a three-mile hike to Lookout Point. We were hot, exhausted, and dirty, but the hike had been worth it for the great views.

"Thanks for coming with me," I told Nicole. "I know hiking isn't really your absolute favorite activity."

"Well, maybe not my favorite, but it was fun," she said. Lately she'd been a really good sport about doing the stuff I wanted to do. Tomorrow I'd make sure we did something she liked.

We were walking down Middler Line when we saw Claudia heading our way. "Hey! I am so glad I found you. You have a visitor waiting in the cabin for you."

"A visitor?" I asked. "Who is it?"

"She says she's Nicole's neighbor. She's pretty upset

about something. I was just coming to look for you guys."

"Okay, thanks," I said.

Even before we walked in the door, we could hear the sobs through the window screens. We walked in to find Mary Claire all alone in our cabin, sitting on Nicole's bed and crying her eyes out.

"What's wrong?" I asked. Nic and I both sat across from her on my bed.

"Alyssa. She's being so mean to me," she managed to get out between sobs. From the looks of it, she'd been in here crying for a while.

"What's she doing to you now?" asked Nicole.

"Well, she . . . she threw my pillow on the roof of the cabin!" Mary Claire wailed. "And then she said *I* did it—that I was sleepwalking, and that *I* was the one who put it up there! But I know I didn't do it. I don't sleepwalk, do I?" she asked, like she needed Nicole's reassurance to convince herself.

"No, of course you don't sleepwalk. She's just a vicious little brat."

"What did your counselor say about this?" I asked.

"She helped me get my pillow off the roof. She knocked it down with the broom handle."

"Is that all?" I asked. So far I hadn't been too

impressed with the way this particular counselor super-vised her cabin. It seemed like a lot of stuff was going on that she either wasn't aware of or maybe she just didn't care about.

"She told us to be nice to each other and respect other people's property." In between talking to us, Mary Claire sniffled and chewed on the edge of her shirt. It was a weird habit, but it seemed to comfort her a little.

"Like that's going to help," scoffed Nicole. She looked directly at Mary Claire. "You want Darcy and me to take care of this problem for you?" I glanced at her, not sure exactly what she was volunteering me to do.

Mary Claire nodded. She reminded me of a puppy with an old sock in its mouth.

"Okay. We will." Nicole stood up. "Let's go find Alyssa. We'll straighten her out." Her eyes were flashing with anger, and her mouth was set in a thin line.

I didn't move from my spot. "Ah . . . how? What are we going to do?"

"We will teach her the meaning of the word 'respect,'" said Nic, half-jokingly, half-threateningly.

I shook my head. "That won't work. We can't threaten the kid." I thought about all my failed efforts to deal with Alyssa. And how stubborn she'd been with Libby. She wasn't easily ignored or intimidated. That strategy might work with some little kids, but not this one.

"Sure we can!" Nic rubbed her palms together eagerly. Mary Claire had stopped crying and now she sat and watched us, sniffling quietly.

"Look, I'm not saying I wouldn't enjoy throwing *her* on the cabin roof. I just don't think that threats are going to work. We have to think about this—figure out how to get her to be nice for a change."

Nicole rolled her eyes. "There's not an ounce of *nice* in that little monster. She wants to bully someone? Well, bring it on! We'll let her know that she'll get worse than she gives if she doesn't lay off Mary Claire."

"No, if we do that, she'll just . . . dump all of Mary Claire's clothes in the lake. Where's it going to end?" I looked at Mary Claire. "You can't do anything to get back at her. You need to take the high road."

Nicole snorted. "The high road? Where'd you hear that expression?"

I'd heard it from Paul. He used it a lot. Anytime someone honked at him, Blake begged him to give it right back. But Paul wouldn't. *Take the high road*, he'd tell us calmly.

"Everyone's heard that expression." I picked up my pillow and clutched it to my stomach. "If Mary Claire tries to get back at her, or if we do it for her, it'll just make Alyssa that much meaner."

Nic sat down on the bed beside me, obviously disgusted that we weren't going to go threaten a little eight-year-old girl. "We can't let her push Mary Claire around!"

"I know." I had to think about this. "Why were you friends with Alyssa anyway?" I asked.

"Because she's in my cabin. Her bed's above mine."

That whole "you're friends with whoever's nearby" thing again. "That can't be the only reason. Why Alyssa instead of the other girls in your cabin?"

Mary Claire gave this some thought. "Well, Alyssa started talking to me. She asked me what activities I was going to, and then we went together. That's why I liked her. And she liked me because I was nice to her."

Nicole raised her eyebrows. "No. She liked you because she could push you around."

"No, she didn't!" I said suddenly. "She liked *pushing you around*. She didn't like *you*. And she didn't like you because she didn't respect you." I pointed to Nicole. "You're right. Teach her the meaning of the word 'respect'!"

Nic looked at me like I was delirious. "What are you talking about?"

"Think about it! Sure, I would love it if someone jumped every time I snapped my fingers, but I wouldn't really like the person." I turned to Mary Claire. "You think you're being nice to Alyssa when you act like her servant, but then she has no respect for you. You can be nice to her, but don't let her push you around. That's how you'll earn her respect."

"Darcy, can I say something without hurting your feelings?" said Nic.

I looked at her cautiously. "I guess so."

"I know you mean well and everything, but you're not very good at giving people advice. That's really more my department."

"Oh, really?" I tried not to be offended, but that was a pretty blunt thing to say.

"Look, don't get mad. I'm trying to help Mary Claire," said Nicole calmly.

"Well, so am I! What do you think she should do?" I asked helplessly.

"I think *we* ought to let that little munchkin know that if she doesn't leave Mary Claire alone, she'll have to answer to us."

I clenched my teeth. "That won't work! Remember the lake? I think she threw the towel in mostly to get back at us instead of Mary Claire."

"Okay then." Nicole patted Mary Claire's hand. "You be nice to your little friend and all your wildest dreams will come true."

"I could give her my peach cobbler," said Mary Claire.

Nic and I looked at each other, confused by this totally random statement. "Um, okay," I said.

"One time I gave her my peach cobbler. I'm allergic to peaches, so I gave her mine. She was really happy. She didn't expect it."

I smiled. "So she didn't say, 'Hey, Spud. Give me your peach cobbler,' that time, huh?" We all had a laugh over that. "Good idea. Let's think of other things you can do to be nice to her."

"I didn't mind making her bed. I'm taller than she is. She can't reach the top bunk like I can. But then after I helped her, she told me to empty the trash too. That was her job that day. I didn't want to, but I wanted her to like me."

"See, that's the difference! It's okay to be nice to her, but don't let it cross over so that she's using you." I thought about it for a second. "Tomorrow morning, why don't you offer to make her bed? Tell her you want to help her out, since it's harder for her to do it than it is for you. But tell her you won't do any other chores for her. And if she starts being mean, the favors stop."

"Perfect! That'll solve everything," said Nic mockingly.

"Maybe you could pick her some wildflowers . . . or make her something in crafts," I went on, ignoring Nic's remark. I saw my pot holder lying on the shelf beside my bed. "Here. Give her this pot holder. Tell her you made it for her in Crafts Cabin and it's a token of your friendship." I tossed the pot holder to Mary Claire.

"Hey! *I* made that for *you* as a token of *our* friendship. And you just give it away like it means nothing to you." Nic turned her head away and tilted her nose up, trying to snub me, but I could see that she was trying not to laugh.

Mary Claire looked at us. "Okay. I think I remember what to do. One, I'll make her bed. Two, I'll give her my peach cobbler the next time we have it. And three, I'll give her this pot holder. Then she'll like me."

Nicole let out a sputtering laugh. "You do all those things and you'll be BFFs before you know it!" Then I started giggling too. I had to admit, it sounded pretty ridiculous.

"Darcy's Three-Step Guide to Turning All Your Enemies to Friends!" Nic laughed. We were really cracking up now. The sight of Mary Claire sitting there holding my pot holder and watching us just made us laugh even more.

"Should I give her my banana pudding too?" she finally asked. That question made us scream with laughter. I sat up and looked at her, trying to get a grip on myself. Nic was gasping for breath.

"This is what you need to remember. Tell her that you're going to be nice to her, so you expect her to be nice to you. Don't let her boss you around. If she's mean to you, don't do mean things back. And if all else fails, try the banana pudding!"

## Monday, June 30

The rising bell hadn't even rung when we heard the knock at the door. Then the screen door was pushed open and Madison Abernathy, one of the CATs, peeked around it. "Darcy Bridges?"

Even though I'd been half-asleep when I heard the knock, hearing my name made me sit bolt upright in bed. Why was Madison coming to our cabin so early, looking for me? "That's me," I managed to squeak.

"You have a phone call in the office." Then Madison closed the door softly, and we could hear her walking back down Middler Line.

My heart stopped beating. My lungs stopped working. I sat in the exact same position, staring at the screen door where Madison's face had been.

Eda, the camp director, told our parents to avoid calling unless there was an emergency. They could write or e-mail us every single day if they wanted to, but phone calls could supposedly make us homesick. In my three years at Pine Haven I'd never once gotten a phone call. Never. I could feel Nicole looking at me from her cot, but I couldn't move.

"Darcy? You'd better hurry, hon. Whoever it is must be waiting on the line." Libby got out of bed and reached for her robe hanging from a hook on the wall.

Sarah sat up and looked around groggily. "What time is it?"

"Seven thirty. You girls stay in bed till the bell rings." Libby came over to my bed. "Are you cold, sweetie? Get dressed and I'll go to the office with you."

I realized I was shaking like crazy. But it wasn't because I was cold. As soon as Madison had said my name, I knew what the phone call was about—my dad.

"Do you have a robe? Can I help you find some clothes?" Libby asked me.

I pulled myself out of bed, feeling wobbly and faint. I couldn't stop shaking. In a daze I managed to find some clothes and put them on. I was on total autopilot.

Everyone was being really quiet. Libby started

toward the door with me. "Can Nic come with me?" I croaked.

"Of course. That's a good idea."

It took Nic five seconds to put her clothes on. Then we were out the door, walking down Middler Line. In the early morning everything felt fresh and cool. Even though I'd grabbed Nic's gray hoodie to put on, I still couldn't stop shaking. Nic hadn't said a word. We just walked briskly along, completely in step. Watching our feet move gave me something to concentrate on.

"It's my dad. He's . . ." I couldn't finish the sentence. He'd never written me back about wearing a helmet. Maybe he didn't get my letter. Maybe I'd sent it too late.

"You don't know that! It could be anything," said Nicole. She put her arm around my shoulders. "Whatever happens, I'm right here."

Now we were walking through the dewy grass on our way to the office. Who would call to give me the news about Daddy? Would it be my mom? Or maybe Grandma? Or possibly even some doctor from a hospital?

Had they called Blake, too? Not yet. They'd call me first since I was the oldest. Then would I have to be the one to tell Blake? If Mom and Daddy were still married, she would be making all the phone calls. But maybe that was my job now.

I realized I was about to live through the worst day of my life. As bad as the divorce was, it was nothing compared to this. And I had one other horrible, selfish thought: If something bad had happened to Daddy, today was my last day of camp.

We walked up the wooden steps to the office. Campers hardly ever came here. It was Eda's territory. The downstairs was the camp office, and Eda's living quarters were above that on the second floor. I knocked on the screen door. Eda appeared instantly, like she was waiting for me.

"Come in. You have a phone call." She was completely calm about it. She didn't want to be the one to tell me.

Nic was about to follow me inside when Eda stopped her. "Why don't you wait out here for her? Give her a little privacy."

I looked at Nic. "Don't move, okay? I want you right here when I get off." I clutched her hand and gave it a tight squeeze.

She squeezed my hand back. "I'm not going anywhere."

Eda took me through the door and into another room. Wood paneling on the walls. Desk. Chairs. Filing cabinets.

"There's the phone, sweetheart. I'll let you talk in private." And then she disappeared.

The phone was an old-fashioned kind with push buttons on the base and a long, twisted cord. The receiver was lying on the desk, waiting for me. I sat down in the rolling chair and picked it up. I could hear my heartbeat pounding deep inside my head behind my eardrums. I propped my elbow on the desk to keep my hand from shaking.

"Hello?"

"Darcy?" Mom's voice said. "Hi, sweet girl!"

"Mom! What's wrong?" Tears were already rolling down my cheeks.

"I have some news for you!" she said in a singsongy voice. "Guess what? I'M PREGNANT!"

A weird, animal-sounding noise came out of my throat, and now I was bawling. "Mom! I thought something terrible had happened! You scared me to death!"

"I took the test this morning! And it came up positive! I ran straight to the computer to send you an e-mail, but then I thought, 'This is too good for an e-mail! This news deserves a phone call.'"

I couldn't stop sobbing. Tears gushed out of my eyes, and my nose was running like a faucet. I had been so terrified. And now I had a gigantic, humongous sense of relief. But it made me even weaker and wobblier than the terror had. I had to prop both elbows on the desk to keep from collapsing in a puddle on the floor.

"So what do you think, sweet girl? Are you excited?"

"Are you kidding? This is the best news I've ever had in my life! I thought someone was calling to tell me Daddy got killed in a motorcycle accident!"

"Oh, honey. A motorcycle accident?"

"Yeah, didn't you know he bought one?" Now that they were divorced, Mom hardly ever knew what Daddy was up to.

"He needs a motorcycle like he needs a hole in his head!" Mom laughed. "I'm sorry I scared you. But isn't it exciting?"

"Are you sure, Mom? The test couldn't be wrong, could it?" When news was too good to be true, it always made me worry a little.

"It was most definitely a plus sign on the tester. I saw it and Paul saw it. Of course I'll go to my doctor ASAP and confirm it. And I've already calculated my due date. It's March seventh."

"When can we find out if it's a girl or a boy?" I asked.

"Not for a while. Do we want to find out ahead of time? I didn't want to know for either you or Blake. I wanted it to be a surprise."

"Yes, we definitely do! Or . . . maybe it would be

fun to wait. Oh, gosh! I don't know! This is so exciting!" And this was just the beginning. I wanted to savor every single second. Years from now I'd be able to tell my little brother or sister about how I was away at camp when I got the great news.

"Mom, is everything going to be okay? I know you and Paul were kinda worried."

"Well, love, my mother and my Nonna both had babies in their forties. We just have to cross our fingers and say our prayers and trust that everything will turn out all right."

I let out a shuddering sob that had been trapped somewhere deep down inside. "Oh, I hope so! I'm going to be a big sister! Again!"

Mom giggled. I could tell by her voice that she was on top of the world. "You want to say hi to Paul?"

"Of course!"

Mom put Paul on. "Hey, Doodle-bug!" Paul always had weird pet names for everyone.

"Hi, Dad!" I shouted at him, and then I felt a little embarrassed. I never called him Dad, but I meant he was about to be a dad. Again. I figured it didn't matter what I called him, considering the circumstances. "Have you smoked any cigars yet?" I added to sort of explain the Dad remark.

"No, but I have been doing cartwheels. Just so you know, I'm pulling for a girl. We need another female in the house to balance things out more, don't you think?"

"Absolutely!" I was secretly pulling for a girl too.

"But don't mention that to Blake. He'll feel outnumbered when Jon and Tony aren't around. And even if it is a girl, remember: You're still my first daughter."

Now I was really sobbing. Before Mom and Paul got married, he'd taken me aside and said, "I don't know anything about raising girls, kiddo. You'll have to help me out." But he'd been a natural. He drove my friends and me to the mall without trying to butt into the conversation, complimented me on my clothes, and talked Mom into getting a cell phone plan that gave me unlimited texting.

Paul and I talked for a few more minutes before he put Mom back on the phone to say good-bye.

"I'm sorry I called so early, but I wanted to catch you before you got busy with your day."

"That's okay! I'm *so* glad you called!" And I was. It had been worth being scared to death. Now I couldn't get over how happy and excited I was. "Are you going to call Blake, too?"

"I'll probably just e-mail him. He's a boy, you know, so I don't think he's going to be nearly as excited as you are. This whole pregnancy thing will be something fun for you and me to share. How's everything else? Are you having a good time?"

"The best! As always! And now it's even better! Maybe this year I won't cry so hard on the last day. Because I'll have something exciting to come home to."

Mom just laughed. "Well, keep having a great time, and I'll keep you posted about all my news. I love you, sweet girl."

"I love you too, Mommy! Bye."

When I hung up the phone, my ear was hot and sore from the receiver pressing against it. My nose was still gushing like a fountain. I raced out of the room and banged open the screen door.

When Nicole saw me, she actually jumped a little. She had this terrified look on her face. "Oh my God, Darcy!" she gasped, seeing my teary face and runny nose.

"No! It's not what you think! That was Mom on the phone! She's pregnant!"

I grabbed Nicole and squeezed her, almost knocking both of us off balance.

Nicole looked completely stunned. "Oh. So it's good news then."

"Yes! She was going to e-mail, but she didn't want to wait. I am so happy!"

"Wow. That's a surprise," said Nic. She still looked kind of numb from the whole thing. She just kept staring at me with enormous eyes. "Why were you crying?"

"Oh, I just got so emotional. You know, one second I think I'm getting the worst news of my life, and then it turned out to be the happiest."

Nic nodded, but she kept quiet. Then we heard the big bell on the dining hall porch clanging, and we looked down to see Eda tugging the rope. That meant it was eight o'clock.

"Whew! I'm still shaking from the scare. Oh my God! I don't know what a heart attack feels like, but I think I had three of them this morning."

"Yeah," Nicole agreed as we walked up the hill toward the cabin.

"You should've heard my mom. She sounded so happy! And Paul said he was doing cartwheels. Her due date is March seventh. How am I ever going to wait nine months for this baby to be born? I'll have to put a new countdown clock on my blog."

Nicole was quiet for a minute. "Then you won't have a countdown clock for camp to start next year."

I laughed, because right now the last thing I was thinking about was camp starting *next* year. "The baby will be born before camp starts next year. First things first. You know what else I want to do? I want to get a notebook at the camp store and start recording every single thing that happens with this pregnancy, starting today."

When we walked into the cabin, everyone was in the middle of doing morning chores for inspection. All eyes turned to me, and everyone paused.

"My mom's having a baby!" I shouted, and then something really amazing happened. Everyone started whooping and shouting and applauding like crazy. They crowded around me and gave me hugs and pats on the back. I almost started crying again.

"Congratulations!" said Patty. "I love babies."

Libby gave me a big hug. "What wonderful news! Be sure to give your mother my best the next time you write to her."

I grinned. "I will. I'm going to write her later today."

"B'sha'ah tovah," said Sarah. "That's Hebrew for 'May the baby be born at a good time, and not in the backseat of the car on the way to the hospital.'"

My mouth fell open. "Really? That's what it means?"

She smiled at me slyly. "More or less."

"I have a nephew, Eli, who's five months old," said Jamie. "My sister sent me some pictures last week—I can't believe how much he's changed since I saw him."

"I wish I lived close to you," said Whitney. "I'd help you babysit."

"Is your mom having any morning sickness yet?" asked Ashlin.

"I don't think so! She just found out this morning."

"Be sure to send all of us announcements when the baby's born," said Natasha. "And pictures."

"I will!" I promised.

We were all chattering away about baby showers, names, and baby clothes. But something didn't seem quite right. Something was missing.

And then I realized what it was.

There was a big, empty, yawning space. Nicole had been really quiet ever since we got back to the cabin. While everyone else congratulated me, wished me happy thoughts, and talked about babies, my Best Friend Forever had not said one single, solitary word.

CHAPTER
17

"Do you see what I see?" asked Nic, nodding at the hand-ful of girls wandering around while we stood in line outside the camp store. "Over there. Mary Claire—in the pale blue T-shirt. She's all by herself."

Small groups of girls were scattered up and down the hill and along the road as they walked to the tennis courts or the lake or the cabins. But when I saw Mary Claire, she was alone. We were far enough away that she didn't notice us, and we couldn't go say hello to her without losing our place in line.

"I guess your advice didn't work. She looks pretty friendless," observed Nicole in a satisfied tone.

"Why are you happy about that?" I asked.

"What makes you think I'm happy about that? I feel

really sorry for her. I should've had a little talk with Alyssa. It was a big mistake to tell her to be friendly to the girl who's making her miserable." Nic followed Mary Claire's aimless walk with her eyes.

"Okay, fine. After we're done here, we'll go find Alyssa and stuff her in her trunk. That'll solve everything."

"There's no reason to get mad," said Nic calmly. "I know you meant well, but you gave her the wrong advice."

"So you've mentioned," I said, shifting my weight from one foot to the other. For some reason Nic had been moody all morning.

"Look," Nic said, "you've said yourself that I give great advice. I've always been able to help my friends with their problems. I practically saved your life our first summer together."

"You did," I admitted. It was something I'd always loved her for, but it was getting annoying to be reminded of it constantly. "I probably should've kept my mouth shut. After all, Mary Claire is *your* 'neighbor,' not mine."

Nicole ignored the neighbor comment. The line inched forward. The camp store was a tiny, one-room building, only big enough for a few people to be inside at one time, and since it was only open during a.m. free time, there was usually a line out the door.

A CAT named Lydia Duncan was behind the counter when Nic and I finally got inside. "Can I have one of those Mead composition notebooks? A yellow one."

Lydia turned to the shelves behind her, which were lined with bars of soap, bottles of shampoo, razors, toothpaste, and Camp Pine Haven T-shirts, sweatshirts, hats, and stationery. "Here you go. Darcy, right? What's your last name again?"

"Bridges—Middler Cabin Three." Lydia nodded and made a note in the ledger to deduct the cost from my account. We didn't have any real cash on us at camp—just an account that our parents had set up for us for little expenses.

"Need anything?" I asked Nic.

"No. I just came along because I didn't have anything better to do."

That comment struck me as slightly strange, but I ignored it. I tried not to stir up trouble by drawing attention to her little sarcastic remarks.

"Mind if we go to the cabin and drop this off?" I asked. "I don't want to have to hold on to it during lunch." I looked around for Mary Claire, but I didn't see her. I was hoping for an update on the Alyssa situation.

"Whatever," said Nic casually. We started up the hill

toward the cabin. "That notebook is just like the one we outlined 'The Plan' in, remember? Only that one was red. Red for romance."

I smiled. "Yeah, I remember." We'd written THE PLAN on one of the blank lines on the front cover.

I'd picked yellow for this one because it was a neutral color for either a boy or a girl. I couldn't wait to write the first entry. *June 30. Mom called me at summer camp this morning to tell me some great news. You are going to be born! We think your birthday will be sometime around March 7. We already love you and you aren't even born yet.*

"What should I write on this cover? I'd like to put 'My Little Sister' or 'My Little Brother,' but I don't know which. I guess I'll put 'Our New Baby.'"

Nic didn't say anything for a while. Then she asked softly, "You really think this is a good idea?"

"What do you mean?"

"You're going to write down everything about your mom's pregnancy, right? Darcy, don't take this the wrong way, but . . . what if something happens?"

I stopped walking and stared at her. "How can you even say that? Take that back right now!"

"Now see—you're getting all upset. I just don't want to see you getting so excited and then if something did go wrong . . ."

"Shut up! Shut up right now!" I screamed at her. I felt like hitting her with my notebook, covering her mouth with my hand, anything to keep her from even suggesting something so horrible.

Nicole sighed. "You are just so emotional about this."

"Of course I'm emotional! Don't you dare ever . . . EVER say anything like that again! I'm really superstitious about stuff like that!" Maybe it was the Italian in me. But I wasn't the only one. At breakfast this morning, when the talk turned to baby showers, Sarah had mentioned that some Jewish people didn't like to have them or to even set up the nursery before the baby was born because they thought it might be bad luck. I felt like Nicole had cursed my mom by even *thinking* those thoughts, much less saying them out loud.

Nic didn't say anything else. My heart was pounding from yelling at her. When we got to the cabin, I put my new notebook on the shelf by my bed. I had wanted to write the first entry right away, but now I didn't really feel like it. I figured I'd wait till rest hour to do it.

*Thanks for totally wrecking my mood*, I felt like saying. But I didn't. I would try to keep my mouth shut till her moodiness passed.

I just hoped I wouldn't have to wait too long.

## CHAPTER 18

## Thursday, July 3

I had to admit that the highlight of all my days now came right after lunch when we got our mail. Nic and I checked our cubbies on the way out of the dining hall. Today I had an e-mail from Mom and Paul, a postcard from Daddy, and a letter from Blake.

The postcard from Daddy was a huge relief. It was from North Carolina's Outer Banks, and he said he'd be home after the holiday weekend. And he added, *About the helmet—I got one because I got tired of picking bugs out of my teeth. JK, but when a cricket hits you in the face when you're going 65 mph, it hurts!*

Next I read Blake's letter. He wrote me about the hike he'd been on and how many times he'd done the zip line, and finally in the last sentence he said, *I told*

*Mom UR dying to have the new baby share UR room. Ha ha!* He's such a little goof.

Then I read Mom and Paul's e-mail, saving the best for last. Mom said she wasn't having any morning sickness, but she did eat a bowl of chocolate ice cream with crushed potato chips sprinkled on top, and she said the salty/chocolate combo was delicious. She also said Paul was burning a CD of all his favorite music so he could start playing it at her belly. And she'd scheduled her first doctor's appointment for next week.

"You're smiling," said Nic. "It must be more good news."

"No. It's just a funny story about something the dogs did," I said, folding up the piece of paper. It had become really clear in the past few days that Nicole was already bored with all my talk about the baby. So I figured the less I brought it up, the better.

"Oh, I thought maybe your family had won the lottery," she said sarcastically. "Something wonderful like that."

I had no idea how to answer that, so I decided to let it go. We walked along in silence. "You want to read the letter I got from my father today?" asked Nic.

"Only if you want me to," I said, feeling a little nervous. If Nic asked to read Mom's e-mail, she'd confront me about lying to her. Our first summer together, I was always asking her to read my parents' letters and e-mails to help me analyze all the things they were saying. Now we rarely did that.

"Go ahead. You'll see how great my life is." She pushed the letter toward me, so I took it and skimmed through it.

> Please try to be pleasant for this visit. You seem to enjoy causing conflict with Elizabeth. We will try to have some activities planned for you to do, but we can't spend all our time entertaining you. And no, I can't take time off work while you're here; it's just a matter of bad timing as I'm in the middle of a big project. So come with some books to read and a good attitude. We'd like to enjoy our time with you instead of being in a constant battle.

"Remember how you told me I should try to spend more time with my dad on this visit? Take walks with him and go out to breakfast? Well, I wrote him and asked if we could take a trip together—maybe go to the beach or something. There's my answer."

"Yikes. I'm really sorry. Maybe he was just in a bad mood when he wrote this. You know—all stressed out from work or something," I suggested, handing the letter back to her.

Nic's dad was really serious and spent all his time at work. I was secretly glad that he and Mom had never hit it off. I couldn't imagine having him for a father.

"No, that's how he always talks," Nic assured me.

She seemed almost glad about it. I knew her home life wasn't the happiest and that she especially hated going to visit her dad, but what I couldn't figure out was why she liked to point out to me how bad her life was and how great mine was. I knew exactly what her dad meant about how she seemed to enjoy causing conflict. I knew how she could be that way sometimes.

"Hey, what if you asked your dad if I could come home from camp with you? Maybe just for a few days." The minute I made the offer, I wished I could take it back. Ordinarily, I'd jump at the chance for Nic and me to be together as much as possible over the summer, but she'd been so moody lately. Plus it would mean I'd have to wait that much longer to see Mom after camp ended.

"You're just saying that because you feel sorry for me. I know you don't really want to visit me at Dad and Elizabeth's."

"That's not true! We could have a lot of fun. It would make your visit with them go by faster. You could at least ask," I said. I tried to act like I really wanted to go home with her. I just felt like I had to do something to cheer her up.

Nic shook her head. "I don't need to ask. I did already. Remember that time you asked if I could come home with you after camp? It gave me the idea, and I wrote my dad way back then and asked him. The answer was no." She looked so depressed it made me feel guilty that I hadn't really wanted to come home with her.

"Well, we'll just have to IM the whole time you're there."

Nicole walked along without looking at me. "So—you got a postcard from your dad, too. How is his road trip going?"

"It sounds like he's having a good time. He did get a helmet, by the way. I am so glad you thought of that. That was a really great idea you had. I would've been a wreck all week if you hadn't talked me through that crisis," I said.

Nic made a little laughing sound in her throat. "Oh, you don't need me anymore. Your life is perfect."

"How can you say that? I'll always need you.

Always! And my life is so *not* perfect. Yeah, we're really happy about the baby and everything, but it's still scary. I mean, Mom's forty-one. She's old to be having a baby. And Paul is forty-seven. Do you realize they'll be in their sixties when the kid graduates from high school?"

I couldn't believe what I was saying. I felt like I was having to look for problems so Nicole would feel better about her own life. And why should I cheer her up by hiding my own happiness?

"Look, you don't have to say those things," said Nic, practically reading my mind. "I can see how happy you are. I think it's great that your mom found someone and stopped chatting with all those sleazy guys on the Internet. At least I'm assuming she doesn't still chat with *Sirluvalot*." Nic glanced at me and snickered. "Remember that picture of him in the Speedo? How gross was that? You think your mom saved it somewhere on her computer?"

I felt suddenly nauseated, like my lunch was going to come up. "Why are you bringing that up now? That was two years ago. Of course she doesn't still chat with any of those guys. All that stopped when she started dating Paul."

One time when I'd snooped around on the computer,

I'd found a folder full of pictures of Mom's online "friends." *Sirluvalot* in a Speedo, lying on a lawn chair. Sickening. Nicole knew how much that bothered me.

"I think it's kind of funny that your mom found your new stepdad on the Internet."

"You swore you'd never tell anyone that," I reminded her, my face feeling hot.

"Don't worry. I never have. I've never told anyone about that or about your dad's drinking problem."

I wanted to grab her and scream in her face, *Are you trying to pick a fight?* But I reminded myself that she was upset about the letter she'd gotten. Maybe bringing up my old family problems would make her feel better about hers.

I took a deep breath. "It's been under control for over a year now. I told you that."

"Well, you mentioned you were worried about him drinking and riding his motorcycle."

I'd never said *drinking*. I always just called it his *problem*. Hearing Nicole say those words out loud—your dad's drinking problem—in broad daylight with other people around made me feel like I was walking through camp completely naked.

Natasha and Ashlin walked past us, laughing about something. "You know I don't like to talk about this with other people around," I reminded Nic.

"Don't worry. They can't hear us. Anyway, I'm happy for you. I'm glad everything in your life is going so well," said Nicole.

"Thanks," I said hoarsely. "And I hope you have a great time at your dad's."

I said it to get back at her for bringing up my family's dark secrets, but she didn't seem to notice. We were at the cabin now and it was time for rest hour, which was a good thing. I didn't want to continue this conversation. My face was still on fire. I knew no one had overheard us, but I couldn't get over hearing her say those things out loud.

I stretched out on my cot and reached for my notebook. Nicole glanced at me from her cot and gave me her annoyed look. I could tell she thought it was stupid that I was writing in this every day. But I didn't care what she thought right now. My pen scratched away on the paper while I wrote down Mom's weird craving for chocolate and salty things. I tried to put an excited look on my face because I knew that would annoy her even more. But I couldn't stop thinking about what she'd brought up.

When Mom and Daddy were going through their divorce, Daddy's drinking was just one more thing for me to stress about. We'd always go out to dinner when Blake and I were with him, and he always ordered a beer, and then another. Then we'd drive home, and I'd watch him carefully to make sure he was driving okay. When we got home, he'd sometimes have another beer while we watched TV.

He never acted drunk, but it worried me. Mom would've told him he didn't need another one, but she wasn't around him anymore. I wondered if that was my job now, but I was afraid to say anything. He only did that right after the divorce, and then I noticed he'd cut back to one beer at a time. Once I even asked him, "How come you never have two beers anymore?"

He'd just patted his belly. "Too many calories. Don't you think I'm getting a little chunky?"

Whatever it was, I was so glad he'd cut back. Nic knew all about this. We had talked about it a lot. She knew how much I worried about it, and how it embarrassed me.

I told myself to just let it go. I knew it had to be hard for her, seeing me so happy about the new baby, knowing that I actually liked my stepfather when she only tolerated Richard, Mary Claire's father, and despised Elizabeth, her dad's wife.

There was a time when we'd shared our family problems the same way we passed clothes back and forth.

Nic seemed to miss those times. In a weird way I did too—a little. It had brought us closer together.

I was glad I had a whole hour to cool off. I couldn't stay mad at her for the remarks she'd made. She needed me now.

## CHAPTER 19

# Friday, July 4

"They did that in my grandmother's day too. In fact, one year she was the riding counselor who woke everyone up yelling, 'The British are coming! The British are coming!'" said Whitney.

We were talking about one of Pine Haven's Fourth of July traditions. This morning, instead of waking us up with the usual rising bell, one of the riding counselors mounted a horse and raced all through camp doing the whole Paul Revere bit.

"Seriously?" asked Sarah. "That is so cool! Hey, everyone, a hundred years ago today, Whitney's grandmama played Paul Revere on the Fourth!" Sarah announced to everyone sitting nearby. "Only in her day, the rider was naked, right?"

Whitney smacked Sarah with her empty paper plate. "Paul Revere is never naked! That's Lady Godiva. And it was *not* a hundred years ago."

We were all cracking up over this conversation. It was great watching Sarah tease Whitney just like old times. The whole camp had just finished eating a buffet dinner out on the hill, and now we were waiting for it to get dark enough for the fireworks show over the lake to begin.

"My grandmother told me another story about how one year the whole camp was really excited because the new flag with forty-nine stars was coming out—for Alaska. And then the next year, it had fifty stars because Hawaii had just become a state. Do you know that she still has the little flag with forty-nine stars that they gave everyone on that Fourth of July?"

"Okay, now *that* really is cool," admitted Sarah. "A flag with forty-nine stars."

"I know! And just think—my grandmother sat on this very hill, just like we're doing right now, and waved that little flag. Isn't that amazing?"

"Yeah, that is pretty amazing," I agreed. I looked around at all the girls sitting nearby. The sun had already set, and everything was a soft gray. It was easy to let my eyelids droop a little so I wasn't seeing anything very focused. Then I could imagine we were back in time—thirty, forty, even fifty years ago.

How much had really changed at Pine Haven during all that time? We'd often seen old photo albums of girls at the lake or on the porch of Middler Lodge with the backgrounds looking exactly the same as they do now. Only their clothes and hairstyles let you know it was some other time. I looked at the mountains off in the distance and thought about how many hundreds, probably thousands, of girls had sat here on this hill with their friends and looked at the same view.

"Those little Junior girls are waving at us," said Whitney. We looked over and saw Mary Claire with two other girls, sitting nearby. I motioned for them to come to us, but Nicole grabbed my hand.

"Don't bring them over here," she said. "They'll hang out with us all night."

"Oh, is that your neighbor?" asked Sarah.

"Yeah," said Nicole, realizing she wasn't going to be able to ignore Mary Claire. "Darcy, come with me. I'll go say hi, and then she'll leave us alone."

Nic and I brushed the grass off the backs of our legs and went over to where they were sitting. "Hi, Mary Claire. How's it going?" I asked.

"Great! These are my friends—Gracie and Samantha.

They're both in my cabin." The little Junior girls looked up at us and waved. I didn't see Alyssa anywhere.

"Cool. You made some new friends. That's good. Well, we just came over to say hi," said Nicole, hoping we could leave now.

"Hey, guess what? Nobody in our cabin likes Alyssa anymore. She's too mean," said Mary Claire.

"Yeah. We were going to short-sheet her, but we don't know how," said Gracie, the tiny one with red hair and freckles. "Do you know how?" she asked hopefully.

"Well, sort of," I said. Last summer Reb Callison taught me how to short-sheet, but I'd never done it to anyone. It cracked me up to think of these little Junior girls trying to figure out how to do it.

"No, Gracie. If we short-sheet her, then she'll short-sheet us, and then she'll throw all our clothes in the lake and set our beds on fire. Right, Darcy?" Mary Claire looked up at me and smiled.

"She won't set our beds on fire. She doesn't have any matches!" said Samantha.

"Whatever," said Mary Claire. "We just ignore her when she says mean stuff to us. She told me my body odor smells like a goat that died."

"Tell her that a family of beavers wants to adopt her," suggested Nicole.

I poked her in the ribs and shook my head at her, but I had to admit it was a pretty good comeback. "Good plan to ignore her. Well, I think the fireworks are about to start, so we'd better sit down."

Nic and I found a spot in the grass. "Oh, I'm so glad!" I told her. "Mary Claire has Alyssa under control. And she has some new friends! Didn't she look happy?"

"Yeah, she did. You're a great big sister," she said.

"Thanks," I said. But then I looked at her. It was so dark now I couldn't see her expression. Was that a compliment? Or was she being sarcastic?

"So are you, you know. Mary Claire really looks up to you, in case you haven't noticed."

"No, she doesn't. She likes you better than she likes me. Not that I *care*."

*Well, maybe she'd like you if you said more than two words to her.* "I know you think she's annoying now, but when you're older, maybe you two will be closer."

"Don't count on it. Maybe by then Mom and Richard will be divorced, and he and Mary Claire will be out of my life completely. Nothing lasts forever, you know."

I wasn't sure how to respond to that, so I didn't.

"Well, it looks like your advice worked. *Take the high road.* You should think about starting your own column. You can name it Darcy's High Road."

"Look, they're starting!" I shouted. An explosion of silver sparks appeared over the lake, lighting up the water below. I was so glad to hear the popping sounds of the fireworks. It meant we could put an end to this conversation.

## Saturday, July 5

"Guess what? I actually got a semiwarm shower!" announced Sarah as she came in the door. We were all getting ready for the second dance with Camp Crockett.

"How long was your wait?" Patty asked her. "I was in line for twenty minutes."

"Lucky!" said Sarah. "My wait was more like forty-five."

"What are you looking for?" I asked Nicole. She was kneeling in front of her trunk, sorting through all her clothes. All day things had been pretty tense between us, but I was hoping that we could have fun together getting ready for the dance, like we did the last time.

"I can't find my red tank top," she said. "I want to wear it tonight."

As soon as she said that, my heart sank. "Uh, I was wearing it yesterday. Remember?" She knew I'd worn it yesterday—she'd seen me in it. This whole search through the trunk was just an act. It gave her one more reason to be mad at me about something.

Nicole stopped looking through her clothes and glared at me. "I don't remember you asking to borrow it."

I tried to think of the best response to that. *I didn't know the rules had changed. You didn't ask to borrow my white shorts, either. Why are you being so snappy about everything today?*

"I'm sorry. I didn't know you were going to wear it tonight," I said finally. It seemed safer than those other responses.

Nic slammed her trunk shut and went over to her laundry bag hanging on a nail by the wall. The red tank top was wadded up inside. "Great. This is just great. Now I won't be able to wear my own shirt." She pulled it out of the laundry bag and held it up for me to see, like I needed to look at the evidence of my crime. Patty and Sarah glanced at us and looked away.

"Borrow something of mine," I offered. I went to my trunk and opened it up. "Go ahead. Take anything you want."

"I don't want to wear any of your clothes. I want to wear my red tank top."

"I have a white tank top you can borrow," offered Patty.

"Or you can wear this," said Sarah, holding up a red T-shirt. "It might be a little big on you, but you can tuck it in."

"You're all missing the point," Nicole said, tossing the tank top toward the laundry bag. It missed and fell to the floor. "Darcy took my tank top out of my trunk without asking me if she could borrow it."

"I'm sorry. I could . . . wash it out if you want me to," I suggested, knowing that wouldn't be good enough either.

"It'll never dry in time!"

"Nic, please. Can't you find something of mine you'd like to wear?"

"No, I can't! I just wish you'd have a little more respect for my things." She turned her back on me and went back to searching through her trunk.

It would've been so easy to snap back at her, to list the dozens of shirts, shorts, and pieces of jewelry that she'd borrowed from me in the last month. Two days ago she'd worn my pink flip-flops because they matched the shirt she was wearing.

I walked over and picked up the tank top from the floor and dropped it into the laundry bag. "Why are you mad at me?" I asked softly.

"I am not mad!" she said through gritted teeth. "It just annoys me, that's all."

*Everything annoys you these days,* I wanted to say. But I kept quiet. We all did. Sarah went over to Side B so Whitney could French braid her hair. Natasha and Ashlin came in from the showers. I was glad that other people were around so I didn't have to be alone with Nic when she was in a mood like this.

In my head I did a quick inventory, trying to remember if I had any more of her clothes in my trunk. But if I took them out now and gave them to her, would it make things better or worse?

Nic had picked out a black tank top, and now she was standing in front of the little mirror on the wall, brushing her hair. Then she stopped and went back to her trunk for something.

"Here," she said, approaching me with her hand out. "These are yours. It was really rude of me to keep them for so long." In the palm of her hand were my little heart earrings.

"I don't want them! You keep them," I insisted.

"No, they're yours. I always meant to give them back

to you. I just . . . kept forgetting," she said, her tone not nearly as hostile as it had been five minutes ago.

"I'm giving them to you. As a token of our friendship," I said.

Nicole's hand dropped to her side. She still clutched the earrings in her palm. I watched her expression change a few times as she tried to make up her mind what to do.

"Thanks," she said finally. Then she took the earrings and put them back into the little jewelry box in her trunk.

"I'm really sorry about the tank top," I said.

Nic didn't say anything at first. "Just ask me the next time, okay?" she said finally.

After dinner we had to wait while the CATs and some of the counselors moved all the tables and chairs out of the way for dancing. Some people went back to the cabin for last-minute touch-ups on their hair or makeup. Nic and I waited out on the hill with Sarah and Whitney.

"Is everything all right?" Sarah whispered to me when she got the chance.

I nodded, afraid to say much of anything with Nic around. So I wasn't the only one who'd noticed Nic's snippy mood. I just hoped it would improve once the dance started.

When the counselors opened the dining hall doors, we knew we could go inside. Pretty soon the vans and buses from Camp Crockett were pulling in, and as groups of boys came through the doors, I kept a lookout for Blake. I was really eager to talk to him about Mom being pregnant. He'd barely even mentioned it in his letters, but they did tend to be only three or four sentences long.

"Let me know when you see Blake, okay?" I told Nicole.

"Okay." She seemed to be over the whole tank top incident, but she'd picked one of her own pairs of earrings to wear—some tiny silver loops. I wondered if that meant anything, but I was too busy looking for Blake to really care.

I scanned the crowd of boys pouring through the doors and standing in a clump across the dining hall from us. Not a sign of him.

"He might be hiding from me," I said. "He knows I'll be looking for him."

"I don't see him either," said Nicole.

"There's his counselor in the gray Abercrombie polo," I said, pointing to Brandon. "But where's Blake?"

My eyes kept searching the crowd, but I still couldn't find him.

"Let's go over there and look for him, okay?" I suggested, and Nic followed me across the dining hall. We weaved in and out of the groups of boys standing around, some of them snickering, like they didn't know why we were coming to them.

I was really starting to get frustrated now. I was about to start yelling, "Blake Bridges, where are you?" I was convinced he'd spotted me and was ducking behind his friends, trying to keep out of sight as long as he could.

"Where *is* he?" I asked Nicole. Through the window screens, I could see the trucks and vans parked outside. Nobody else was coming in now.

"I . . . don't see him," said Nic. "I don't think he's here."

"He's gotta be here! Where else would he be?"

"Do you see any of his friends?" Nic asked.

I searched through the crowd, trying to find a familiar-looking face. "I can't really remember what they look like. We barely talked to him at the last dance."

Now I was feeling panicked. It reminded me of the time we'd gone to the state fair a few years ago, and I'd lost him when he needed to go to the bathroom.

"He is *not* here," I told Nic, trying to keep my voice steady. "I have looked at every single boy's face in this room about twenty times. He's not here!"

"Calm down. You said you saw his counselor? Maybe we should ask him," Nic suggested.

I made my way over to where Brandon was standing with a couple of other counselors. Nic was right behind me.

"Hi, Brandon? I'm Blake Bridges's sister," I started off. I was about to go into a long explanation about how I'd been looking for him, but I didn't get very far.

"Oh, hey! Wow, that was quite an injury, huh? Poor kid. Don't worry, though. He'll be out of the hospital tomorrow morning. I'm sure they're giving him the star treatment."

"WHAT?" I yelled.

"Yeah, they'll take care of him. It's really just for observation. He would've been fine in our infirmary, but with a concussion, they always want to keep a close eye on you. I've had two myself—one from football and one from lacrosse."

"*Concussion*? Where's Blake?" I screamed.

Brandon looked surprised by my reaction. "Didn't anyone tell you about the accident?"

"What accident? What happened?"

Nic grabbed my arm and held on to it, maybe to calm me down, maybe to keep me from jumping down Brandon's throat to try to yank this story out of him.

Brandon let out a long, low whistle. "Wow. I figured someone would've contacted you or something. Blake was trying to do a backflip off the diving board this afternoon. He went up, flipped, came down, and smack!" Brandon smacked his hand against his forehead. "His head hit the board, he fell into the water, the lifeguard on duty was, like, *Whoa!* So he jumped in, pulled Blake out, there was blood everywhere— the kid had a gash across his eye a foot long. He passed out cold right there at the lake. It was a major scene." Brandon nodded like he couldn't believe what a great story it was.

Meanwhile I was doubled over, clutching my stomach. I couldn't talk because I couldn't get any air into my lungs. Nic was kind of holding me up so I didn't fall to the floor.

"So a couple of counselors drove him into town to urgent care. He got twelve stitches. By now he's conscious and everything, but his vision's a little blurry from the clonk on the head. So they admitted him to the hospital and they're gonna keep him overnight. They do that when you have a concussion. They have to keep waking you up every hour or so, to keep you from going into a coma."

A little groan came out of my mouth. I leaned against Nic, feeling woozy as an image of Blake covered in blood swam through my head.

A counselor standing next to Brandon smacked his shoulder. "Dude, shut the freak up. She's gonna pass out," I heard him whisper.

"Do my parents know?" I squeaked. Blake was only ten years old. He couldn't pass out, get stitches, and recover from a concussion without Mom there to hold his hand.

"Oh yeah, we called them right away. Don't worry. He's gonna be fine. He really is."

"Are you okay?" the other counselor asked me. "You want a drink of water or something?"

I shook my head. Nic still had me by the arm. "Let's go outside and get some air," she told me. We walked to the door, with me leaning against her.

"I think I'm going to faint," I moaned.

"Seriously?" asked Nic, sounding really concerned. "Want me to get someone?"

"Uh, no. Just let me sit down." We went to the end of the dining hall porch and sat on the steps. I leaned forward, resting my head on my knees.

"Take deep breaths," Nic advised. "Maybe you do need a drink of water."

"No. Ugh. It sounded so horrible—blood, stitches, concussion. And he's all by himself." Then I started to cry. "I wish I could see him!"

Nic patted my back. "Maybe you can. Maybe you could see him tomorrow."

I put my head down and sobbed. I felt so scared and lonely for him. Had he cried? I knew he'd wanted Mom, but all he had were counselors, all those older guys, and he wouldn't want to cry in front of them. And was he really going to be okay? Blurry vision? A foot-long gash across his eye?

"What if he can't see? What if this affects his sight?" I cried.

"It won't! I'm sure he'll be fine," Nic said, rubbing my back.

"I'm so glad you're here. I don't know what I'd do without you," I said.

"I'm right here. I'm not going anywhere," she said.

"Thanks," I whispered, but there was something so familiar about this whole scene that made me feel like I'd done this before, felt this before.

The phone call from my mom. With Nic so supportive and concerned. Until it turned out to be good news. And she'd been mad at me ever since. Mad that I was happy, mad that my life was *perfect*.

"You're a really good friend," I managed to say through my tears. *As long as there's a crisis.*

"Thanks." She patted my back. But now her pats annoyed me and I wanted to push her hand away. But I didn't. I just cried and cried and cried.

Mostly I cried for Blake. But there was another reason. I had a horrible, sick feeling that deep down in some secret part of herself that she would never admit to, Nicole was enjoying this.

## Sunday, July 6

That night I fell into a half sleep that lasted all night long. I drifted in and out of dreams, rolled over and over trying to find a comfortable spot, and dozed off only to jerk myself awake for no apparent reason.

Mostly I kept thinking about Blake, lying in a hospital bed, his head bandaged. But there was something else that kept swimming around inside my head every time I started to drift off to sleep.

*I'm right here. I'm not going anywhere.*

Nicole had been a great friend, my *best* friend, the one I could talk to about anything. The one who'd helped me live through my parents' divorce, the one who could always give me advice when I had a problem.

But this summer, we'd fought more than ever. Well,

not exactly fought. It was just that she'd often been annoyed about something or other. And this last week especially, I'd felt like I had to hide my happiness from her, that I couldn't talk to her about how excited I was about the new baby without her getting all quiet and moody. But the second there was a problem, she was right by my side.

I rolled over and looked at the dark outline of Nicole in her cot. She was asleep; everyone was asleep. It was probably about two or three o'clock in the morning.

Something was not right. What kind of friend gets mad at you when you're happy, and enjoys it when you're having a crisis?

It wasn't that she was cruel. She wasn't *glad* that Blake had gotten hurt. But she did seem to enjoy being the one to give everyone advice, to help people with their problems. She wanted to be the shoulder to lean on.

Which was fine, really. I really had needed her tonight. But if she wanted to help me through the bad times, why couldn't she be happy for me during the good times?

I looked at the dark lump in the cot next to me. I was tempted to wake her up right now and confront her. *What's wrong with you? Can you only be my friend when I'm unhappy?*

I decided I had better get some sleep.

Finally, sometime in the early morning hours, I did fall asleep. But when the rising bell rang, I could barely open my eyes. I stayed in bed, not moving, for as long as I could. I remembered it was Sunday, and that meant we didn't have to clean the cabin for inspection, and we could go to breakfast in pajamas. I rolled over and buried my face in my pillow while everyone else got out of bed. A hot feeling was burning deep inside my stomach.

I felt a hand patting my back. I opened one eye to see who it was. Nic, of course. My *best* friend. The feeling got hotter.

"Time to get up," she said softly. I could hear the screen door opening and closing as everyone else left the cabin. I sat up so Libby would know I was awake.

"You feel okay?" asked Nicole, looking concerned.

"No. I feel horrible," I told her.

"Well, don't worry. Maybe you can talk to Eda about what happened. Maybe they'll let you go see Blake today. I'll go with you. To talk to her, I mean. And to go see him too—that is, if you want me to."

I stood up and slipped my feet into my flip-flops. I was cold with just a cami and pajama pants on, but I didn't bother to put my robe on. Every muscle in my body felt tense and ready to snap. The cabin was almost empty, except for Claudia and Jamie still over on Side B. I waited till they had walked out the door before I looked at Nicole.

"You'd like that, wouldn't you?"

A look of surprise spread across her face. "Like what?"

"To go with me and see Blake all bandaged up. Whenever I have a problem, you're right by my side, aren't you?"

Nic stared at me, her mouth slightly open.

"But if it's good news, if I'm happy about something, you can't stand that, can you?" *I should stop*, I thought. *I should walk out the door now. Go to the bathroom, the dining hall. Go somewhere where I won't be able to say these things.*

Nic cleared her throat. "You're my best friend. Of course I want you to be happy." Her voice sounded raspy, like somebody else's.

"Do you? Do you really? Because it sure seems like anytime things are going good for me, you get mad about it. There's something really twisted about a friend who only likes you when you're having problems."

Nicole was absolutely still, absolutely quiet. "Twisted," she said finally. It felt like a Ping-Pong ball that I'd slammed across the table at her, and now she was tapping it back to me, waiting to see what I would do with it.

I should take it back. Cup it in my hand and never let her see it again. Tell her I didn't mean it that way. But I did mean it. It was true. I remembered the look on her face when I told her Mom was pregnant. And the look she got every time I mentioned the baby or reached for my journal.

I should say something else. Explain the horrible, overtired feeling that the sleepless night had left me with. Tell her that I *did* want her to always be the one standing outside the door waiting if there was ever a frightening phone call. But there was something else I wanted to say to her.

*Pretend you're happy for me! Even if you're so jealous of my life that you can't hide it.*

"I'm sorry," I finally said.

But it was too late. Nicole had already walked out the door.

# CHAPTER 22

"He looks fine. Way better than I was expecting," I
told Mom.

"What about the scar? How bad is that going to
look?" she asked.

"Well, it looks pretty bad now—like Frankenstein.
It's long. It's above his right eye. But if he lets his hair
grow, it'll cover it." The scar was maybe two inches
long, not a foot, like Brandon had said. But it did look
really big the way it cut across his forehead.

"Are you sure he's okay? Maybe we should come and
get him—bring him home early."

"Mom, honestly, I'd be the first to tell you if I thought
you should do that. But you should see him. He looks

like they pinned a medal on him or something. He's loving every minute of this."

Blake grinned at me when he heard that.

"Mom wants to say good-bye to you," I said, handing him the phone. He sat up in bed, taking the receiver from me.

"NO! Do not come and get me! I have a whole week left! I'd miss everything!" he screamed.

"Calm down. You'll bust a stitch," I whispered to him, patting his legs through the blanket.

"Okay. Love you, too. Bye." He hung up before I got a chance to talk to Mom about how she was feeling. He picked up the hand mirror lying beside him and looked into it for about the fortieth time since I'd walked in.

"It's so cool, isn't it? It looks like I was in a wicked fight," he said, examining the neat row of stitches across his forehead. He had a black eye, too, but the nurse said that was normal with a head injury.

"Yeah, it really does. Are you sure your head doesn't hurt?"

"A little, but the nurse gave me some Motrin about an hour ago. I hope I don't have to spend the night here," he said. When they'd released him from the hospital this morning, the counselors had brought him to the Camp

Crockett infirmary. His concussion was a mild one, but they still wanted to make sure he got plenty of rest.

"And no more blurry vision? How many fingers am I holding up?" I held up two fingers on one hand and three on the other.

"Thirty-seven. When Rob drove me back from the hospital this morning, we stopped at Sonic, and I got a corn dog, a large order of onion rings, and a chocolate shake. He paid for it with his own money, too."

"Oh, that explains your stinky breath! I'm glad they're taking good care of you."

The nurse came in and smiled at Blake. "Do you think you're up for a few more visitors?" she asked.

"Yeah! Definitely!" said Blake. Five boys came pouring into the room, and they were all giving him high fives and oohing and aahing over his stitches.

"Sick! You look so cool!"

"Dude—you got a black eye and everything!"

"Brandon said your brain was oozing out. Did they shove it back in or what?"

I have never seen Blake happier than when he had all his friends crowded around him, admiring his wounds. A couple of them had cameras so they could take his picture. Then he told them the story of how his head had hit the board, slapping his hands together to make the sound effects and snapping his head back to show the impact. The nurse only let them stay about fifteen minutes before she made them leave.

"I should probably go too," I told him. "Oh, by the way, Mom and Paul said they were going to GameStop for *something*, so you might ask them about that when they pick us up on Saturday." Saturday—it was hard to believe camp would be over in a week.

"Cool. Thanks for coming to see me." He let me hug him before I left. I was really glad I'd had the chance to see him with my own eyes, and to talk to Mom. I felt so much better now.

Libby was waiting outside on the infirmary porch, talking to the nurse. "How is he?" she asked.

"He's great. He's an instant celebrity now."

The nurse assured me she'd keep a close eye on him for the rest of the week, and then Libby and I left. On the drive back to Pine Haven, Libby asked me all about Mom and kept the conversation focused on the new baby, maybe to take my mind off Blake's injury. But all I could think about was what I was going to say to Nicole when I got back to camp. I never should've said those things this morning.

"Okay. It's ten after five. I'm going to rush off to the staff meeting, but I'll see you later at dinner, all right?" said Libby as we pulled into camp.

"Sure. Thanks so much for going with me to talk to Eda. And for taking me over there. If I hadn't had a chance to see him, I would've worried about him all week," I told Libby.

We said good-bye, and she went off to Senior Lodge to meet with the other counselors for the weekly staff meeting. Now was the perfect time to talk to Nicole; we had about an hour before dinner. Maybe we could go out on the hill so we'd have some privacy.

I knew exactly how I'd start the conversation off—by telling her that she was the best friend I'd ever had, that I never could've lived without her the past two years, and that I wanted to share everything with her— clothes, jewelry, good news . . . whatever. We only had a week of camp left, and I wanted it to be a good one.

As I got to the cabin, I could hear voices inside. Nic's voice. "I'm sick of this! *Oh, we're so worried about Darcy. I hope her brother's okay. I hope her mom has twins.* Well, I've got news for you. This morning, when I was trying to cheer her up about her brother, she called me *twisted.* And I'm supposed to be her best friend."

I stood paralyzed by the side of the cabin. Frozen. Not breathing. Not moving.

"Give her a break. She was upset." That was Sarah.

"Oh, so if she's upset, she can say whatever she wants

to me. Everyone thinks Darcy's this sweet little angel."
Nic's voice had that edge to it. I knew that tone. "If only
you guys knew how screwed up her life really is."

"You need to stop talking." That was Sarah again.

"I agree. It's completely . . ." something I couldn't
hear. Whitney's voice. So she was in there too.

"You want to talk about inappropriate? Her new
stepfather, the one her mom's having the baby with—
you want to know how they met? There were all these
random guys that her mom picked up off the Internet.
Darcy was so freaked out by it. Her mom would spend
hours and hours online, chatting with these guys. That's
why Darcy's dad divorced her."

That wasn't even true! This was not happening. I was
dreaming this.

There was a thump, like somebody threw something.
Maybe a pillow.

"Don't throw things at me, Sarah!" yelled Nicole.

"Then shut up, Nicole! We don't want to hear this!"

"Everyone needs to calm down." That sounded like
Claudia. *Was the whole cabin listening to all this?*

"You all have this image of who Darcy is, but you
don't know her the way I do. Her family has all kinds of
issues, even though she tries to hide it. Her father's an
alcoholic, but she won't admit to it."

Then I could move again. Instantly, I was inside the cabin somehow.

"She's lying." I looked straight at Nicole. "That's a lie. Tell them you're lying."

CHAPTER 23

The strange thing was how calm I felt. Sarah, Whitney, Claudia, and Patty were all inside, all with the exact same expression on their faces when the door opened. Shock.

Nicole was the only one who didn't look that surprised to see me. A little at first when I walked in the door. But she got over it pretty fast. She tensed her jaw and looked right at me. Sarah closed her eyes and covered her face with her hands. She didn't want any part of this.

"She's lying. My father's not an alcoholic."

Sarah shook her head. "Let's not even go there."

"Good idea," agreed Patty. It was the first time I'd heard her speak up.

Nicole's eyes bored into mine. She wasn't backing off at all. I knew she wouldn't.

"I heard it all. Or a lot of it." Still so calm. I hadn't even raised my voice. I'd never been this calm in my life.

"So you were eavesdropping," said Nic, nodding. Like she expected that, like it was no surprise that I'd stoop that low.

"No. Not at all. Step outside. You'd be surprised how well you can hear everything through those screens."

"I have an idea. Let's all forget this ever happened," Sarah suggested.

"You want me to forget this ever happened?" I asked Nicole. We were the only two people in the room now. Everyone else had faded away. I couldn't even see them or remember exactly who they were.

"It's not a lie, and you know it." Nic challenged me to deny it.

Parts of it were true. Mom chatting with strange men—true. Daddy divorcing her because of it—not true. Daddy drinking too much at times—true. Alcoholic—not true. Partly the truth, but twisted to make things sound a little bit worse than they were. *Twisted*.

"I know the truth, and you know the truth," I said to her. "As long as we're telling the truth, why don't you tell everyone about *your* family and all *your* issues." Now, for the first time, Nicole did look concerned. I'd struck gold.

"Why don't you tell them about how both your parents got restraining orders against each other during their divorce? And how many times the police were called to break up their fights and how you'd hide under your bed when that happened?"

Nicole swallowed once. Her eyes were locked on mine and she couldn't look away. Somebody said something, but I didn't hear it. I couldn't hear anything over the sound of my own voice.

"And your own father doesn't even remember your birthday. How last year you waited and waited for him to call you, but he never did, and then four days later when he finally did remember, he called and yelled at you. And he blamed you for not reminding him. And how your very own stepsister goes to this camp, but you pretend you don't even know her. Mary Claire Mitchell—that little Junior who's always hanging around. Your *sister*, not your neighbor. Your family's so screwed up, you act like they don't even exist."

Sarah was standing in between us. "Both of you need to stop talking." She held her hands up like she needed to hold us back from each other, in case things got physical.

But it wasn't like that at all. We just stared at each other, daring the other one to look away. Neither one of us would.

Whitney stepped in. "Okay, people say things when they're angry, but it doesn't . . . you should . . ." Things must be bad if even Whitney was at a loss for words.

Then Libby and Jamie walked in the door, and they both came to a dead stop when they saw the looks on everyone's faces.

"What's going on? What's wrong?" asked Libby.

I unlocked my eyes from Nicole's and turned toward Libby. "Nothing. We were just talking."

# CHAPTER 24

## Tuesday, July 8

I tapped softly on the screen door in case somebody was inside. When I didn't hear anything, I opened the door and stepped in. The cabin was empty. Everyone was at activities.

Strange. Everything looked so different. If I didn't know this was Cabin 4 from the number on the door, I would think I was in the wrong cabin. The first thing I noticed was that the two sets of bunk beds on Side B weren't there. Now there were two singles and one set of bunk beds. I stood still for a few minutes, looking around. Then I tiptoed over to Side B.

I wasn't sure why I was being so quiet. I didn't need to be. Maybe because I was trespassing, in a way. This wasn't my cabin anymore. If any of the Cabin 4 girls walked in, they'd be surprised to see me, just like I'd be surprised to come home and find one of my neighbors snooping around in my house.

One of the single cots was pushed up against the wall—that was the spot I wanted to look at. I stood in front of the bed, leaning over so I could look at the wall. I didn't want to sit on whoever's bed this was with the yellow sheets and the purple cotton blanket.

Where was it? It had to be here someplace. It should be right here. But I couldn't find it. Last year our bunk beds had been against this wall. I knew this had to be the right spot. I was about to go ahead and sit on the bed so I could see better, but then I looked a little higher, and there it was. It was higher up than I remembered it.

DARCY AND NICOLE, written with a red Sharpie. Then under it, BEST FRIENDS FOREVER!!! Nic had been the one to write three exclamation marks. And the date. JULY 5. One year and three days ago. But it seemed longer.

We'd sat on Nic's bottom bunk to write it—Nic's bed with the pink-and-red polka-dot sheets—the same sheets that were on her bed right now in Cabin 3. It was right after dinner and everyone was leaving for evening program. We were the only ones in the cabin, and we'd decided we'd better sign the wall while we had a chance. We didn't want to wait till the last day of camp, when we'd be all sad and depressed.

I reached out and touched the rough wood. I wondered if any of this year's Cabin 4 girls had read this. So far this year, I hadn't gotten around to writing my name anywhere. It had seemed like I had plenty of time to do it.

I stood there and looked at the wall for a long time. I kept thinking I should leave, in case anyone walked in. If anyone did, I could easily explain why I was here—I'd just come by to find where I'd signed my name last year. No big deal. They wouldn't care. Graffiti covered the walls of all the cabins. Everyone signed her name somewhere.

Eventually I went back to my own cabin—Cabin 3. It was empty too. All summer long I had barely had a single moment by myself. And I wouldn't be alone now if I'd gone to afternoon activities like I was supposed to.

I sat on Nic's cot instead of mine, for some reason. I didn't really know why. Her bed was neatly made, with her pink blanket folded down so you could see the polka-dot sheets.

*What if.* What if I'd come back one minute earlier or one minute later Sunday, and I hadn't overheard Nic talking? But if I was going to play that game, I could say what if I hadn't called Nic twisted, what if I'd slept better Saturday night, what if Blake had sprung up two inches higher and hadn't hit his head at all?

Would we still have had this fight?

Mom believes in destiny. She thinks everything happens for a reason. One time she told me that she really believed the only reason she had married Daddy was because Blake and I needed to be born, and that once that was taken care of, they were supposed to go their separate ways. At the time I didn't believe that; I was still hoping they'd work things out and stay together. But now I have to admit that everyone is a lot happier.

But why had destiny made our family happy when Nic's family still had problems? It was like they'd traded one set of problems for another. That didn't seem fair. I'm sure Nic wondered, *Why is Darcy's life turning out so great when mine is still a mess?* I couldn't blame her for thinking that. I would too, if I were in her shoes.

The screen door opened, and Sarah and Whitney came in.

"Hi," said Sarah. She glanced at my empty bed and then back at me sitting on Nicole's bed. "We've been looking for you."

"You found me."

Whitney came over and sat on my bed. Sarah took

a seat beside her. "Darcy, you've both had a chance to cool down a little. Now it's time for you to talk to each other," said Whitney.

I shook my head.

"Don't try to get out of it! We're staging an intervention," said Sarah.

It was so easy to tell everyone else what to do. *Go apologize. Just talk to her. Everything will work out.* I never once thought about how Sarah felt, or how Whitney felt. All the hurt feelings, the anger, the embarrassment. I didn't think about how that all got in the way and made everything so much harder.

I knew we should talk. I just didn't want to. And Nicole didn't either. It felt better to just avoid each other as much as possible.

"We've looked all over for Nicole, but we can't find her," said Whitney. "She'll have to show up for dinner, and before evening program tonight Sarah and I are going to sit the two of you down and make you talk about this. I know neither one of you really wanted this to happen."

That sounded odd. Of course we didn't want to have a big fight.

Or did we? It seemed like for days before it happened, Nic had been pushing me. Almost trying to make me mad. But why? Why was she mad at me? And I'd gotten fed up too. I was the one who started it by calling her twisted. Or did she start it with the argument over the tank top? But even before that, she'd said those things about maybe Mom having problems with her pregnancy. It was hard to trace back when exactly things started falling apart.

"Thanks, guys. I know you're trying to help. But I really don't want to talk to her. Yet. Maybe later."

"No, not later. Today. You have to," said Sarah. "We'll be there with you if you want us to. Or we'll leave you alone. Whatever. But you guys can't go another night without speaking to each other."

"Maybe," I said.

If Nic and I were forced to sit down and apologize, there was a chance everything could somehow be okay. The way I felt now, it didn't seem like it could work out, but it might. Maybe she'd be the old Nic, the one who wasn't always annoyed with me about something, the one who I could talk to in ways I couldn't talk to anyone else.

But when we all went to dinner, Nic wasn't there. I waited for Libby or Jamie to ask about her, but neither of them did. They started passing around plates and food dishes like nothing was out of the ordinary at all.

"Where's Nicole?" Sarah finally asked .

"Oh, she went to the infirmary," said Libby. "After rest hour she told me she wasn't feeling well. I guess she's come down with that virus that's been going around."

Sarah and Whitney looked at me. I could tell they were wondering what I was wondering—was Nicole really sick, or was she just avoiding me? She might really and truly be sick. Because I knew one thing—I'd never felt so bad in all my life.

CHAPTER 25

## Wednesday, July 9

Late in the afternoon, after activities were over, Nic came back. I looked up when she walked in the cabin door. Natasha and Ashlin were over on Side B, but everyone else was off someplace, doing other things.

"Hi," I said. It was the first word I'd said to her since Sunday evening.

"Hi," she answered. She dropped a plastic bag of clothes on her bed.

"How do you feel?" I asked.

"Better. My fever's gone, anyway."

"You had a fever?" I asked. I guess she really was sick. Or maybe she'd made it up to make it sound better.

"Yeah. Not a high one—100.2. Where's Sarah?"

"She's with Whitney. Whitney's practicing for the

talent show. She's going to play the violin. It's tomorrow night, you know."

"Oh, yeah." Nic smiled a little. "Well, with Whitney doing an act, Cabin Three is bound to win."

Nic looked at the bag of clothes on the bed. "Libby brought me some stuff—my toothbrush and some clothes. That's your Pine Haven T-shirt," she said, nodding to the green shirt that had spilled out of the plastic bag onto the bed. "I guess it was in my trunk. I wore it because that's the only shirt she brought me." She picked up the shirt and handed it to me.

"I'm glad you're feeling better."

Nic looked out the screen window. "I thought *maybe* you would've come to see me."

I'd thought about it. Part of me wanted to go to the infirmary and check on her. But part of me was glad we didn't have to face each other. And I was sort of afraid to go. I imagined going to the nurse and asking to see Nicole, only to hear her voice yelling from some far-off corner, *Tell her to go away! Tell her I never want to see her again!*

"I wasn't sure . . . if you could have visitors," I said finally.

"You went across town to see Blake," said Nic, still looking out the window. She was watching a red bird on a branch right by the windowsill.

"He's my brother," I said, and the second I said that, I knew it was the wrong thing to say. But I couldn't take it back. I'd never be able to make it sound right. "I missed you, though," I added.

"Did you?"

"Yeah. I really did." *I still do.*

Nic didn't say anything for a long time. "Well, that's something at least."

I sat cross-legged on my bed, my elbows propped on my knees, staring down at my green Pine Haven shirt in my lap. "I wish I could rewind everything and go back to . . ." To when? When would I like to turn things back to? To the last time we'd really had a good time together. Whenever that was. Was it the first dance when we picked out clothes together? It hadn't been *that* far back, had it? "I'm sorry I called you twisted. I didn't mean it. I was just so tired that morning. And worried about Blake."

Nic had a strange smile on her face. "You know what I find the most interesting about all this?" she asked, turning away from the red bird to look at me.

"What?" I felt a tightness in my stomach, like I needed to brace myself.

"You said every mean thing you could think of—that stuff about my birthday, the restraining orders, Mary

Claire. You sure didn't hold back." Nic turned back to the window, but the red bird was gone now. "So much for the high road."

I could solve lots of people's problems by sitting back and watching and saying, *This is what should happen*. That was the easy part. It ended up being a lot harder to take the high road than I thought it was.

"I know, I know. I wanted to get back at you. For telling everyone my father was an alcoholic. You know he's not."

"You've said yourself that you think he might have a drinking problem. That you always have to watch him and count how many beers he has and make sure he's okay to drive. I didn't make that stuff up!" said Nicole, her voice rising with emotion.

"I told you it was better! It hasn't been like that for almost two years!" Why were we arguing about this, anyway? This wasn't what the fight was about.

Ashlin and Natasha left the cabin. They were the only ones who'd missed the big scene on Sunday, but no doubt everyone else had filled them in about it.

"I'm sorry I said all those things," I told Nicole. "I wish I could take everything back. I just want things to be normal again."

Nicole kept quiet. "Yeah. Me too," she said at last.

What did that mean? That she was sorry too? That she was taking everything back too?

"I can't stand it when we're fighting. We never used to fight."

Nic nodded. "I know. This was my worst fear. I've always been afraid this would happen."

"What?" I asked. I had no idea what she was talking about.

"That one day you'd dump me," she said very quietly. She wouldn't look at me.

"How can you say that?" I practically shouted. "Remember all those times when we said we'd be counselors together, and then we'd be college roommates? We were even going to share an apartment together one day."

Finally, she looked up. "Okay. So are you saying we can still be friends after all those things we said?"

I couldn't answer her.

"See? You don't think we can."

I let out a deep breath. "Yes, I do. I'm sorry. Please try to forgive me for all the things I said. I'm not dumping you." I looked at her. "And I hope you don't dump me either."

Nicole smiled. I realized it had been a long time since I'd really seen her smile. "I'm sorry too."

# CHAPTER 26

## Friday, July 11

I barely remember Thursday. Nic and I wandered through the day next to each other, but we weren't together.

We talked. We didn't fight or say mean things. But it didn't matter. The damage had been done. It was like we were polite strangers.

And then it was Friday, the day before camp ended. Tomorrow we'd all be going home. Late in the afternoon, a bunch of us were in the cabin, packing up trunks and duffels. Packing to go home was always a sad process, but this year it was so much worse.

I left at one point to go to Solitary. I just needed to get out of the cabin for a while. There was a time when Nic and I went everywhere together, even the bathroom.

But not anymore. As I was walking away, I heard the screen door open behind me. I looked around to see Sarah following me.

"Is everything okay?" she asked.

"No, it's not."

"Well, you're talking to each other at least. Can't you work things out?"

"It's not that easy. She's miserable and I'm miserable," I said. We could say we were sorry. We could ask to take back the horrible things we'd said. But that didn't automatically erase all the hurt feelings.

"I just want you guys to move on and get over this," said Sarah.

"I don't think we can," I told her.

"Of course you can. Just . . . keep talking to each other. Keep hanging out and doing stuff. Eventually you'll both feel better."

I went to a faucet and splashed cold water on my face. So many memories. Everywhere I went in this camp, even the bathrooms, reminded me of something.

"Big excitement over Jamie and the other counselor assistants, huh?" asked Sarah. "I wonder what the whole story is."

The counselor assistants had been caught trying to play a prank on Camp Crockett, and now they were in big trouble with Eda. They weren't the only ones in trouble. Natasha, Ashlin, and Claudia left the cabin after lights out while Jamie was away, even though Whitney tried to stop them. Now there was a new drama for Cabin 3, but I wasn't at all interested in it. I was too wrapped up in my own problems.

"Well, even though camp's almost over, Eda still wants to keep things under control. I doubt she'll really punish the counselor assistants that much," I said.

"You want me to talk to Nicole for you? Is there anything I can tell her that you're having trouble saying to her?" Sarah offered.

I thought about that for a second. "Not really. We've both said we're sorry, but sometimes that's not enough, you know?"

"Yeah, I know what you mean," said Sarah, but I could tell she wondered why she and Whitney could make up and we couldn't.

When we went back to the cabin, there was a neat pile of folded clothes lying on my bed. "I found some more of your stuff," said Nic. "Do you have anything of mine?"

"I might," I said. I rummaged through my trunk and pulled out a few of Nic's shirts and a pair of her jeans. "If I find anything else, I can always send it to you later."

"Yeah, I know. But it's easier if we sort things out now."

I nodded and turned away, acting like I was busy folding my clothes. My nose was stinging, and I knew any second I might start to cry. I didn't want my clothes back. And I didn't want to give hers back either. It seemed so final.

Why weren't things okay? We'd said we were sorry. We'd made up—I thought. Why couldn't we go back to how things used to be?

We finished packing and then left for dinner. The mood all over camp was different. People were already talking about how they'd keep in touch—e-mails, phone calls, instant messages. At dinner Eda had a bunch of announcements about girls who'd be flying out tomorrow or taking the bus.

After dinner all the campers walked down to Lakeview Rock together for the last campfire of the summer. All the campers had to wear their white Pine Haven polos and white shorts, and all the counselors were dressed in green polos. Being in the camp uniform made everything seem more serious and formal.

Lakeview Rock was a giant outcropping of rock that towered about twenty feet high and overlooked the lake. The campfire was lit in the center of the rock, and lots of girls were already sitting in a circle around it.

Sarah sat down first, and then Whitney sat beside her. I sat next to Whitney.

Then it happened. Nicole walked past the three of us so that she could sit on the other side of Sarah.

I hardly noticed when Ashlin sat down next to me. Patty had ended up on Nicole's other side. So this was how camp was going to end? Nicole wouldn't even sit beside me now?

I stared at the grass in front of me and didn't move. I wasn't breathing. I could feel Whitney and Sarah glancing at me. They both knew what had just happened.

If I got up and moved now to sit next to Nicole, what would happen? Would Nic get up and move to get away from me?

I almost did it. I would show her. We were still friends. I wasn't going to dump *her*.

But I didn't. I stayed put and didn't move. I focused on the grass in front of me. I stared at that grass until I couldn't even see it anymore.

Friends always sat together at the Circle Fire because it always got so emotional. Especially tonight, everyone wanted to be sitting next to her best friend.

I just needed to hold it in for a few more minutes. As soon as the campfire really got started, people all around me would start to cry. Then I could let it out. I stared straight ahead. If I made eye contact with anyone, I knew I'd lose it.

When the first song started, I sang along with everyone else. I knew all the words to all these songs so well, I could sing them in my sleep.

Then one speaker stood up and talked, then another. Eda always asked a few people to prepare little speeches about what Pine Haven meant to them.

Then there were a few more songs, and then Eda starting singing one of my favorite songs, "Memories Gone By." We never sang this particular song until late in the session, usually sometime during the last week of camp. We'd only sung it a few times this summer. It was to the tune of "Scarborough Fair," which was such a beautiful, mournful song, it always brought everyone to tears.

> *We must hold on to memories gone by*
> *Good times, friends, forever are mine.*
> *The times we spend at camp will not die.*
> *Summer days suspended in time.*
>
> *When we leave here we won't say good-bye*
> *Good times, friends, forever are mine.*

*We'll always have Pine Haven close by.*
*Summer days suspended in time.*

*In the winter, I'll think of you then*
*Good times, friends, forever are mine.*
*Soon I know we will meet again.*
*Summer days suspended in time.*

Now I could let it out. I didn't have to hold back anymore. Whitney patted my back while I sobbed. It wasn't embarrassing to cry so hard; almost everyone was crying now. The light from the campfire lit up everyone's faces, and I glanced over at Nic sitting beside Sarah. They were both crying too. For a second Nic's eyes met mine, and then she looked away, teary-eyed, and stared into the fire.

My heart felt like it was breaking. It was a real, physical, aching pain that I felt in my chest. It was over. Really and truly over. I knew that things with Nic and me would never be the same. Why? Sarah and Whitney could fight and get over it. Why couldn't we? Neither one of us wanted this. Did we?

It was time for the candle lighting. The counselors opened cardboard boxes and passed around white candles, each of us taking one. Eda spoke about how girls had been coming to Pine Haven since 1921. She lit her candle and then passed the flame to the counselor next to her, who passed it on to the girl beside her. One by one, the flame was passed from one candle to the next until each person in the circle was holding her lit candle in front of her.

Libby and Caroline Heyward picked up shovels and doused the flames of the campfire with dirt. Now we all sat quietly, holding our candles and looking at the little dancing flames that lit up the faces of everyone in the circle.

"Tonight on our last night at camp, I'd like you to think about what each of your flames has added to the fire at Pine Haven. And also think about what the fire at Pine Haven has added to each of your flames," said Eda.

I let the hot wax drip down my candle onto my hand. It burned a little, but not enough to really hurt. There had been happy times this summer. Lots of happy times. I'd have to remember those. I stared at my flame, wanting to burn the happy memories into my heart. My tears made the flame look blurry. I wiped my wet face with my left hand, carefully holding the candle steady in my right while I stared into the flame. I kept telling myself that looking at the dancing yellow flame would make some of the pain go away. I let out a long, shuddering sigh and the flame fluttered a little from my breath.

When camp had first started, I'd wanted everything to be exactly like it'd been in past summers. But then I would've missed out on making pot holders. Talking after lights out. Floating in the inner tubes. In lots of ways Nic and I still had a great summer together. And I didn't want to give that up.

I wouldn't have to. I would save this stub of candle in the box where I kept all my other Pine Haven mementos. The box was on a shelf in my bedroom closet at home. Inside it were lanyards I'd made at crafts, my old name tags, photos, the red notebook with THE PLAN written on the front. This year, just like every summer, I would go home and put all the things in my camp box that I wanted to keep forever.

# CHAPTER 27

## Saturday, July 12

For the past two years on Closing Day, I'd woken up really sad and tearful, but this morning the thought of seeing Mom and going home to all the baby preparations made me feel excited. It must have been noticeable, because Sarah took one look at me and said, "You're in a good mood."

I shrugged. "Well, I'll be seeing my mom soon—you know."

Nicole turned away while she got dressed. Her dad was picking her up today for her monthlong visit. I knew she wasn't looking forward to it, but she kept quiet. If only I could hug her and promise her that I'd text her every day. I wished I could say something to make her feel better. She probably hated me now more than ever, since I was happy to be going home and she wasn't.

After breakfast there wasn't much to do except stand around and wait for friends to leave one by one. A bunch of Camp Crockett counselors showed up to help carry luggage and trunks. I looked for Blake's counselors, but I didn't see them. I wondered if Mom and Paul would pick me up before or after they got Blake. All they'd said in their last e-mail was to look for them around eleven or twelve o'clock. That was hours away.

Whitney was the first girl in our cabin to leave. She and Sarah cried and cried as they said good-bye. "I'll see you in November," Sarah said, obviously embarrassed to be getting so emotional.

"I know, but that's a long way away," sobbed Whitney. "Who's going to make fun of me till then?"

Whitney hugged me before she got into her parents' car. "Thanks, Darcy. If it hadn't been for your intervention, we probably never would've made up. I hope you and Nicole stay in touch."

"Thanks," I told her, but I doubted that we would.

Then Ashlin left, and then Claudia. A group of us were standing around saying good-bye to Patty when I felt a hand on my shoulder. I turned around to see Nic.

"My dad's here."

I was surprised that she was even going to say good-bye to me. But I was happy, too. It would have broken my heart if she'd left without even speaking to me.

"Really? Already?" I asked. Down by the road I saw Nic's father and stepmother standing by their car, loading Nic's stuff into the trunk.

"Yeah. I have to go." Nic's face was tense. She'd cried last night at the Circle Fire, but now she was holding back the tears. I didn't want to say anything that might make her break down. I knew she just wanted to get into the car and leave.

"I hope you have an okay time at your dad's. Go ahead and use the towels, and don't worry what Elizabeth says," I said. I wanted to ask, *So, are we friends again or not?* Instead I just said, "I'll be thinking about you."

"Yeah, me too. Keep me posted on all the baby news, okay?"

"I will," I said.

She stepped forward and gave me a quick hug. I was glad she'd hugged me, because I wasn't sure whether or not I should hug her.

And that was it. She said good-bye to a few other people on her way to the car, and then she got inside and they pulled away.

I wiped tears away, but I didn't really cry too much.

Sarah was standing nearby. "You should IM each other when you get back," she suggested. "It's a lot easier talking to people that way than it is face-to-face. I'll bet by next summer, you'll be even better friends than ever."

"Maybe," I said. But I knew the truth.

Now the bus was loading, and since Natasha was leaving on it, Sarah and I went to say good-bye to her. In the group of girls standing around waiting to get on, I saw Mary Claire. She had a unicorn backpack on her shoulders, and she was carrying her pillow. When she saw me, she ran up and gave me a hug.

"Bye, Darcy!"

"Bye. I hope you had a good time at camp," I told her.

"I had a great time! Gracie and Samantha are my best friends now. I wish Nicole was riding the bus with me, but she's going to her dad's. Anyway, on the trip here, she wouldn't let me sit by her."

While Mary Claire was talking, I'd noticed something. "Cute earrings," I said, my pulse pounding a little. They were little hearts.

Mary Claire touched her earlobe. "I know. Nicole gave them to me before she left with her dad. You know what else? She said I can tell everyone that she's my stepsister now. She can be really nice sometimes."

"I know she can. If you ever have a problem, talk to

her about it. She's really good at giving advice," I said, my voice choking a little.

Eda was motioning everyone onto the bus, so Mary Claire got in line. Sarah and I stood and waved with the crowd as the bus pulled away.

And then I looked up and saw our minivan driving up the road with Paul at the wheel. "My parents are here!" I yelled to Sarah.

I raced over and opened the passenger-side door almost before the van came to a complete stop. Mom stepped out and I grabbed her, giving her a giant hug.

"You look beautiful! How do you feel?" I patted her belly, which wasn't any bigger, but I couldn't wait till it really started growing.

"Lousy. These mountain roads don't mix well with morning sickness," she said.

Blake slid the side door open and jumped out. I tried to hug him, but he ducked out of the way. He still had his stitches in, of course, but now his black eye was a yellowish green. Paul came around the van and lifted me off my feet when he hugged me. "We had to stop a couple of times so your mom could hurl," he whispered.

We all walked up the hill together to get my trunk and the rest of my stuff from the cabin. Sarah stayed down by the road, in case her parents showed up.

"We were expecting you to be crying your eyes out," said Paul. "Remember last year how we had to peel you off Nicole? I've never seen such waterworks."

"Well, Nicole got picked up early," I said, leaving it at that.

We walked into the cabin to get my stuff, but there was something lying on the top of my trunk that made me stop. It was my pot holder—the one I'd made and had given to Nicole when she gave me the one she'd made.

"What's that?" asked Mom.

"A pot holder," I said, holding it up for her to see. "We made it in crafts. I guess I forgot to pack it." I unzipped my duffel enough to stuff it inside.

Blake and Paul both grabbed an end of my trunk while Mom carried my sleeping bag and pillow. I slung my duffel over my shoulder, and we walked out together, leaving empty Cabin 3 behind.

I thought about the pot holder as we walked down the hill. A token of our friendship. Was Nicole giving it back? Or was she giving me a new token since I'd given hers to Mary Claire? I didn't know how she meant it. I could take it either way.

Maybe it was just something for me to remember her by. I decided to put it in my camp box along with the Circle Fire candle stub and this year's name tag.

Sarah's parents had just pulled up when we were loading the van, so I was glad she wouldn't be stuck here all alone.

"Thanks for everything," she said, giving me a big hug. "I'll see you next year, right?"

"I guess so," I said. "Probably." But I wasn't so sure. Maybe Mom would need my help next summer.

Libby and Jamie were the last ones I said good-bye to, and then we closed all the doors and slowly pulled away. It was sad to leave, but I felt better than I'd expected. At least I had a baby brother or sister to look forward to.

Despite everything, it had still been a good summer. And nothing could erase all the happy memories I had.

"As soon as those stitches come out, I'll start rubbing Vitamin E on the scar so it won't be so noticeable," Mom was telling Blake.

"No! I want it to look cool. I like having a scar."

"Well, it'll always be there—to remind you of your first summer at camp. At least Darcy managed to get through the summer scar free," said Mom, sighing.

I sat on the back bench so I could look out the rear window as we drove out of Pine Haven. I had so many great things to look forward to later. For now, I wanted to remember what I was leaving behind.

# Real life. Real you.

Don't miss any of these terrific Aladdin Mix books.

The Secret Identity
of Devon Delaney

Me, In Between

Total Knockout

Portia's Exclusive and
Confidential Rules
on True Friendship

Class Favorite

Chasing Blue

Four Truths and a Lie

The School for Cool

Portia's Ultra Mysterious
Double Life

Hershey Herself

# DON'T MISS ANY OF THESE
# TERRIFIC *Alice* BOOKS—
# NOW IN ALADDIN MIX!

# Do you love the color pink?
## All things sparkly? Mani/pedis?

# These books are for you!

From Aladdin
Published by Simon & Schuster

Sometimes a girl just needs a good book.

Lauren Barnholdt understands.

**FIVE GIRLS. ONE ACADEMY. AND SOME SERIOUS ATTITUDE.**

# CANTERWOOD CREST

*by Jessica Burkhart*

**TAKE THE REINS**

**CHASING BLUE**

**BEHIND THE BIT**

**TRIPLE FAULT**

Don't forget to check out the website for downloadables, quizzes, author vlogs, and more!

## www.canterwoodcrest.com

**FROM ALADDIN M!X    PUBLISHED BY SIMON & SCHUSTER**

# DORK
## diaries

She's a self-proclaimed dork. She has the coolest pen ever. She keeps a top-secret diary.
Read it if you dare.

## By Rachel Renee Russell

From Aladdin
Published by Simon & Schuster